DUST ON THE KING'S HIGHWAY

DUST ON THE KING'S HIGHWAY

A Novel

Helen C. White

CLUNY

Providence, Rhode Island

CLUNY EDITION, 2024

This Cluny edition is an unabridged republication of the
1947 Macmillan edition of *Dust on the King's Highway*.

For information regarding this title
or any other Cluny Media publication,
please write to info@clunymedia.com, or to
Cluny Media, P.O. Box 1664, Providence, RI 02901

WWW.CLUNYMEDIA.COM

Cluny edition copyright © 2024 Cluny Media LLC

ISBN: 978-1685953447

CONTENTS

To Olive

✳ ✳ ✳

✳ I ✳

A BELL ON A HEIGHT

I

Destiny comes to the doors of men usually in disguise, and of all her disguises the most frequent is the commonplace. So that morning of the first of August, 1771, it came to the door of Fray Francisco Garcés. It was certainly not the first time that Father Garcés had closed the Mass book on the last Gospel and turned to find strangers in the back of his church. But these were the strangest of all strangers, Indians of an appearance quite different from any he had ever seen before.

There were a good many things which the Franciscan missionary had not done in the three years that he had been at Bac. He had done almost nothing to beautify the bare stone and plaster church in which he had just finished saying the morning Mass for the children and the women and the old men of his mission. And he had done very little to improve the buildings of the mission, least of all his own house. The Indian village was a little better, but the missionary knew that was not much to say. The fields were in fair shape, and the stock, but Garcés had no illusions.

There was one point of his missionary charge, however, on which Francisco Garcés had nothing to fear. He had made some sort of contact with every Indian ranchería for miles around, so that hardly a week went by without strangers coming into the dusty little frontier outpost to see the "Old Man," as the stalwart young Franciscan was known from one end of Pimería Alta to the other.

But now as the friar turned again to kneel down for the closing prayers at the foot of the altar, he knew that the four Indians standing like giants behind his kneeling congregation were not the usual run of Pápagos and Pimas who came into Bac. They were taller and finer-looking, too, than

either of the Indian peoples he knew best. In a flash Garcés saw that they
wore no clothes but the deerskin sandals that indicated they had come on a
long journey, and that above the red and black paint on their faces the hair
was bound in a heavy crown about each erect head. All this could mean but
one thing—they were Indians from the north, from the lands along the
great rivers.

As he left the sanctuary, he caught another glimpse of his visitors standing immovable like bronze columns with the women and children gazing
half in terror and half in admiration as they sidled cautiously around their
motionless figures. When Garcés, having taken off his vestments, came back
to make his thanksgiving, they were still there, with the broad doorway behind them crammed with women's heads and children's open mouths and
scrambling arms.

They made no move to attract his attention, and the priest knelt down.
They might even be Yumas, those people up at the junction of the rivers of
whom he had so often heard, and then he remembered that if he were going
to the great rivers of the north, there might be weeks when he could not say
Mass.

As he expected, they allowed him to finish his prayer without making
any effort to claim his notice. Only when he left the sanctuary and came
up to them, did one of them speak, a single word. It was the Pima word for
"old man," but this was clearly an accent quite different from the one Garcés
knew so well, and the voice was softer and deeper. The Franciscan smiled and
stretched out his hands in welcome. And in turn each of the four strangers
gravely embraced him. Then he took the crucifix from his breast, kissed it,
and offered it to the first of his guests. The Indian took it reverently and held
it to his face as if he would breathe from the ivory and wood some invisible
exhalation. Garcés heard the excited whisper of Ignacio, his acolyte, in the
doorway, "They are Christians. They have kissed the crucifix," and the hiss of
a woman's hush.

But the visitors said nothing as they followed the missionary into his little house. And they waited in complete silence while Ignacio brought them
bowls of atole from the cooking shed and scampered off to the storeroom
for some jerked beef. While they scooped up the porridge in their fingers,
Garcés took down the tobacco box from the shelf above his bed and broke off
a handful of leaves from the end of the roll. Then he waited patiently while
his guests filled the thick reeds which always to the Spaniard, mindful of his

limited supply of the precious weed, seemed so cavernous. Only when they had begun to puff at the tubes of smoking tobacco, did the Indian who had already spoken, and was clearly the interpreter for the party, begin to speak very slowly and deliberately in halting but quite understandable Pima.

They had come a long way, he explained, hardly to the surprise of the missionary, who had not missed the dust caked on the brown bodies, or the ravenous fashion in which they had gobbled up the porridge and torn the strips of meat. The speaker went on to tell how many days' journey they had come, and their host's heart leaped. For at an Indian's speed they could well have come from the Gila and even the Colorado. They had come through the land of their enemies, and that the Franciscan had known, too, from the elaborately-feathered arrows and the long bows which they carried.

They were men of the Yuma nation, living near the junction of the rivers, the interpreter went on slowly, apparently oblivious of the effect of his words on his host. They had heard from the Pápagos, men of no account, whom better men tolerated simply for their ridiculous dancing and juggling, that the Old Man had visited them and had told them many things. They were good things the Old Man had told them, and he had given them good gifts, and he had promised more good things to them. These things the Old Man had done to the Pápagos whom no man could take seriously. But the Yumas were good men, upon whose friendship men could rely, and who were worthwhile allies in time of trouble, and they wanted to see the Old Man, and to hear his words.

As the leader went on, saying the same thing over and over again as if the repetition would give conviction, it flashed across the mind of Garcés that doubtless strange things had happened to what he had said to the Pápagos when they boasted of them to the Yumas. He had been careful on the promises, too; at least, he hoped he had. Three years at San Xavier del Bac had chastened his rhetoric, if not his hopes. The religious virtue of prudence was not, he realized, one that instinctively appealed to his nature, but he was coming to value it out of necessity. He wondered how much he had said to the Pápagos, on that last trip, when they had come in such a throng, and he had remembered suddenly that it was the eve of the feast of Pentecost. It had been the most inspiring moment of his life when he looked down into the pool of dark faces there in the firelight, and for an instant he thought he knew how the Disciples must have felt when the tongues fell upon them. The next day he had tried to recall just what he had said. At the time it had seemed a little flat for so high an occasion. Now he wondered if it had been flat enough for safe repetition.

But the Indian was going on. They wanted the Old Man to come at once to the people at the junction of the rivers. They wanted him to come before the people would be scattered for the fall planting and harvest. They would take him to their land, and the Yumas would make him welcome, and they would listen to the good things he had to say to them.

Father Garcés affected to consider for a few minutes, though he wondered if the Indians sitting so quietly there in the little adobe house could not hear his blood racing wildly in his veins: "Going therefore, teach ye all nations"—it was the vocation which he had been called to, which he had answered. But the Franciscan knew there was no use trying to deceive himself or his Master. He remembered irrelevantly a passage from the sermon which the old missionary who had come to his convent at Calatayud back in Aragon to recruit volunteers had preached to the whole seminary the day after he and a friend had volunteered for the missions of Sonora. It had been about the labors and the anguish of the missionary life, and the heroic sacrifice that these volunteers had made. Franciso Garcés had often thought of that passage since then with varying feelings of wonder and incredulity and even shame. And now he wondered, not for the first time, if a man who so much enjoyed the excitements of his vocation were worthy of it.

But as he was apt to do when he let himself think of his own feelings, he had lost the thread of the moment. He had waited a little too long to make the expected reply, for a note of pleading had come into the Indian's voice.

"They are like the sands of the desert, the people along the rivers," he said earnestly. "And the people to the south and the north have said that they will come to see the Old Man, too, but they are not men to be trusted."

And Garcés' heart leaped. For suddenly he had remembered that expedition which his friend, Captain Anza at Tubac, was always talking about. If only he could get the viceroy's backing, Anza was always saying, he would open a way from the old missions of Alta Pimería to the new ones of Upper California. Perhaps—but Garcés knew it was no use deceiving himself. It was not Anza's dream which made his heart beat fast. It was simply the old lure of the road, the prospect of a new people to come to know, to bring within hearing of the tidings he carried. So he answered with a quietness that surprised himself that he was honored by the Yumas' invitation and he would come.

The Indians had all sat very stiffly throughout their leader's harangue, but now that they knew their mission was accomplished, they settled back more comfortably upon their haunches, and their host went to the shelf for fresh tobacco. As he did so, his mind was already busy with plans. He knew he must be back in time for the harvest at Bac and the storing and making fast against the coming winter. The journey to the Yumas would take the best part of a month. There was very little time to spare; yet there were certain things he must tend to before he could go. When he turned to his guests, he found that one who had said nothing but who had seemed more intent even than the rest on everything that had been said, had fallen asleep where he sat in the corner. Two had vanished, he was sure, to prowl around the mission and the guardhouse and the huts of the Indians. But the interpreter still sat there, erect with patient dignity. To him the friar handed the fresh tobacco.

"Seven days from today when I have said Mass," he pointed to the church, "I will go with you."

The Indian sat back quietly against the wall. Garcés put the tobacco back on the shelf, and from another box took out a quill and began slowly to sharpen the point for writing. There was an extra priest visiting just now at Tumacácori, Fray Pedro Font; he could come over to take charge of San Xavier. He must send a note to Captain Anza at Tubac, too. The captain had been dreaming so long of that expedition to the river tribes. Here, at least, was a chance to scout out the ground.

But he had hardly finished the note to the father minister at Tumacácori when the voice of the captain of the guard of San Xavier del Bac rang outside the door, "What is this I hear about you gadding off again?"

Garcés smiled and pointed to the sleeping Indians.

The commander threw up his hands. "Aren't there enough heathen in this village without you going out looking for more?" he spluttered.

"It won't be over a month," and the friar spread his hands deprecatingly.

The indignant officer spat on the earth floor in contempt of the appeasement.

"A month! Two months, three months! All the saints know whether you'll come back at all. Haven't you heard some of those Pápago devils are on the warpath already? Two of my men are just back this morning with a story of some Pápagos they ran into, and they're getting set for a nice raid." In his indignation he choked.

The friar laughed. "Come, captain, you know how soldiers love to tell tales when they come in from a bit of hunting. A pint of aguardiente, and they have seen the whole forest turning into arrows and war feathers. All your men saw were the Pápago guides who brought in my visitors this morning."

The captain paused, and for a moment Garcés thought he was going to laugh. But something held him back, and in another moment he was snorting, "Aguardiente! Do you know that last weekend was the first one that all my rascals came back, and came back sober? Not a complaint from the Indian women. Not even a fight over cards. As quiet as a convent of Carmelite nuns!"

For a moment the friar stared. He remembered well enough how hot the little box in the church had been last Saturday afternoon, and the dreary round of confessions, so monotonously alike. Saturday night had seemed to the depressed confessor noisy enough, and Sunday—those were not hymns that the company had been singing in the guard canteen. But the captain seemed to have mistaken his hesitation for modesty, "The first chaplain I've had who knew how to handle men, and you go off gallivanting after those sons of Beelzebub up the river there, who were born to burn, and leave me alone with Christians who might be saved if you stayed on the job!"

"But," protested the friar, "it is my duty—"

"Duty!" The Commander of Bac threw his hands up in disgust. "To get yourself scalped by those sons of Lucifer! Look here, father, what good will it do anybody to get your name in the martyrology when alive you can do so much? Let that lady's chaplain over at Tumacácori take the place in the martyrology. He'd look very pretty in the stained glass windows, and you stay here!" Garcés could control his laughter no longer. But in a moment he felt conscience-stricken as the captain strode out with the lofty air of a man who has done his duty and been laughed at for his pains. The friar started after him, but he got no farther than the doorway.

For the little open space in front of his house was half full of men, women, and children, and they cried out when they caught sight of him. For a moment he was irritated. They should have been in the fields, and at catechism, and grinding at the metate. It was nice of them to be so anxious, but he knew, too, how easily the routine of the mission blew up at the slightest excuse. They were begging him not to leave them, and some of the women were actually crying. He felt ashamed of his annoyance, and then he remembered the strangers who had stolen out to see the sights of the village.

Undoubtedly, they had done a bit of swaggering about the success of their errand.

Quietly, he raised his hands, and began to explain. He was going away for just a few weeks, not more than a month at most. He would be back, and he would be very angry—he thought he saw one of the women smile, and he tried to harden his voice. He would be very angry if they had not done their duty just as carefully when he was away as if he were there. Now they must go back to their work. Tomorrow after Mass he would tell them what he was doing and why. Now they must not let this good day go by in the fields and at home. For a moment he stayed in the doorway and watched them go off, and a great affection welled within him, and, for the first time, a sense of guilt.

There were two who did not go. He invited them both in, and he put his hand on the shoulder of the boy. How he was shooting up these days, this little Ignacio! No wonder he nibbled whenever he had a chance. Garcés remembered the heaving paunch of the captain, and he smiled at the boy.

"May I come, father?" The large intelligent eyes gleamed, and the missionary was tempted. But he thought of the First Communion toward which they had been working, and the hope of a really good catechist which the clever little Pima had lately raised in his thoughts. He shook his head.

"No, Ignacio. You are getting on too well with your Latin. You must stay here with Father Font, and help him say Mass, and study your Latin, and your catechism. And if he gives me a good report of you, you shall have your First Communion like any Spaniard in the Indies, when I come back."

The eyes had clouded in the hard little brown face, and the boy stared at his master as if to make sure of the promise. But Garcés knew that Font would bring on the budding scholar twice as fast as he could; so he confirmed the promise with a nod, and the boy went off.

But the man stayed, and as he turned to face him, the missionary of Bac knew himself for the vagabond and the runaway he was. For Miguel Dominguez was the majordomo of the mission, who set out the tasks of the common labor and held each to his share, and not least his impulsive and unsystematic master. Now that master could scarcely look him in the face. It was a perfectly respectful and patient face, but the missionary saw that the premature lines of worry deepened in the sallow countenance of the mestizo soldier even as he spoke. But there was not a flicker of complaint in his voice as he asked his Reverence if he did not think they should begin to clear the field by the graveyard for the sowing of the winter wheat. He did not in any way suggest that if the missionary were there to lend a hand, the work would be done in half the time. And when he went on in that slightly querulous and toneless voice to ask if he should give the new wool to the women to spin, he did not remind him that when the father came in to the workroom, to teach the women hymns to sing as they worked, three times the thread was spun, and there were no quarrels. But his errant pastor thought of these things which Miguel Dominguez did not say, and for not the first time in his ministry Francisco Garcés wondered what had ever made him dare to preach to anybody else.

2

IN prospect this trip to the rivers in the north had seemed the most exciting opportunity for exploration that had yet come to Francisco Garcés. In reality the week that followed his departure from Bac proved easily one of the most disappointing he had ever known.

To begin with, it was an unusually dry and hot summer, and for the first time in his experience, the summer heat bore heavily upon the usually comfort-scorning friar. And then there was the problem of the horses. If he could have had even mules for the whole party, it would all have been much simpler. But the mission horse herd was in a bad way just then; so the messengers whom he had despatched with his letters had taken the last of his horses that were in any decent shape to travel. Captain Sotélo had readily enough found a couple of horses for the missionary's own use, but he had flatly refused to furnish any horses for the Indians, who, he swore, would never think of returning them.

So the company had started out, Garcés riding with his saddlebags, the two Pápago guides taking turns riding the spare horse, and the Yumas walking. The guard horses were not in good shape after the summer's work; so the Indians afoot had little trouble keeping the riders in sight. But it was a bad arrangement for any conversation with the Yumas, whom he had naturally hoped to come to know on the journey.

And the very circumstances of the first days on the road made intercourse still more difficult. For this was a well-traveled way, and they kept running into parties of Indians who hailed the friar with delight and trailed along with him so that he had very little chance to talk with the Yumas.

Garcés was relieved, therefore, when at the end of a week they left behind the last of the Pápago rancherías where he was known and struck out for Sonóita with only their own company. Though they were tired now, Garcés promised himself that on the morrow he would make up for lost time.

But here again he was doomed to disappointment, for on the morrow he woke to find only arrows where the four Yumas had been lying the night before. He tried to get some indication of what had happened from the two Pápagos, but all he could get was the older man's, "Everybody knows the Yumas are haughty men who respect nobody but themselves." They did not seem at all surprised, Garcés noticed, nor anxious. But after the Franciscan had trampled out the last embers of the morning campfire with the thick soles of his sandals, he noticed that the arrows had disappeared, and when he lingered to look around for any possible indication as to why his guides had left him, he found that for the first time the Pápagos were restless and impatient to be on the way.

At first Fray Garcés tried to follow the trail with a map in his mind's eye, but at the best of times he was not good at finding his way in a world of bewildering and fascinating detail, and this was far from the best of times. So now he found himself slogging along blindly through white sandy earth and hediondilla and mesquite and creosote and all the nameless underbrush of the desert, until the sun was high overhead.

Not since the calabash had smashed on the rocks in the morning and reddened the futile sand to mud with his day's supply of water had he drunk, and now his mouth was feeling as if it were full of wool. He screwed his eyes over the shimmering plain, and just on the edge of the rocks that bound in the oven of their world to the left he caught the motion that marked the progress of the forward guide on the other horse. The motion was broken now, for the invisible trail went over the rocks, but when the watching white man caught the flash of the bronze back in the sun, he marveled afresh at the slow steadiness of the Indian's progress. He had never given any sign of hurry, and yet all day he had kept well over a mile ahead of the Spaniard.

For a moment the Indian and his horse came up on a sudden rise of ground, and Garcés saw the slim, lithe figure shoot up like an arrow into the light blue sky.

"No fat on him!" And the friar added ruefully to himself, "As natural man he is a better man than those fat neophytes of mine, lazing in the mission fields." But the words stuck in his muffled throat, and suddenly he knew his thirst was past endurance. He looked ahead. The Indian was turning round from a further peak of shallow rock, and Garcés saw that in his abstraction he had gained on him. But he saw, too, that this spurt of energy was almost exhausted. He signaled the guide to wait, and he was relieved to see him slide from his horse and sit down where he was.

By the time Garcés came up with the squatting figure, his own tongue was hanging out. The Indian was chewing what seemed to be the pith of a stalk of cactus. Without a word he passed it to the friar.

It was brackish and weedy, but there was moisture within the pith, and presently Garcés found he could speak. He pointed to the sun, and he looked around where the rocks piled up with a thin overhang of shadow. But the Indian shook his head, and gestured to what seemed another unbroken shimmer of sagebrush-bristled sand just over the brim of the rocks. On the far horizon—Garcés could not be sure.

"Water before sunset," the Indian said briefly, and he started to his feet.

Garcés looked ahead. If that little smudge on the heat-blurred horizon were a pile of rocks steep enough to hold the rain water, it would certainly take till sundown to reach it, and perhaps more. Again, he looked at the Indian.

"A little sleep here," he spoke slowly, pointing to the thin shade; "we'll go faster afterwards."

But the Indian looked at Garcés for a long minute, and then he said one word, "Enemies," and swept the horizon with his outstretched arm.

Now Garcés began to understand about the arrows.

But how had they known? What had he missed?

Involuntarily, he tightened his cord about his habit, and then he looked behind. The other guide was at least a half mile behind, seeming to creep across the desert floor. He looked back at his companion.

The Indian shrugged his shoulders, "He is old, that one." And he mounted his horse and started on. Garcés wanted to look back again; he even thought of waiting, but he reminded himself that once having taken the trail, it is the Indian's way to keep on without any more words about it.

The Indian in front was already yards ahead of him. Garcés mounted his horse again and followed. The sun beat down without mercy, and the friar reached for the beads hanging from his rope girdle, but as he took them the medal whipped against his hand, and the hot metal burned the skin. He dropped it, and then more cautiously took hold of one of the wooden beads and trying to keep from moving his stiff throat, he began the first of the sorrowful mysteries.

He seemed to be moving in a coma now. And then he felt the tug of one of the saddlebags that had come loose. There was little in it but parched corn and Venice beads and the tobacco for the Indians, and his breviary. He had said only half of the day's office this morning, and now he should not be able to finish it. If only he had not slept so long! He thought of Saint Francis and how he would look upon his lazy son. Again he tried to begin the familiar words, "Mea culpa," but as he struck his breast, his breath came with a whistle.

He looked ahead. The Indian was like a brown stick standing up from his horse, now more than a mile away. All the plain between was dappled with shadow in and out among the tufts of sagebrush. And the smudge on the horizon was a heap of reddish-gold, even at this distance to be distinguished as stone piled on stone. For a moment he measured it with his eye, yes, high enough to catch and to hold the rain. From the look of the sky and the ground, they were more than halfway to sundown.

And then he remembered the Indian behind. But even as he turned hastily, he knew that he did not need to worry any longer about disturbing him. For though he was still a considerable distance away, in the clearer air of the afternoon the missionary could see that he was plunging along, head down, seeing nothing. And even as the friar watched in astonishment and growing bewilderment, the uncertain figure plunged to the earth and lay still. For several minutes Garcés waited, unconsciously measuring the distance between himself and that prone figure, feeling by anticipation the drag back and the slow haul forward. But the fallen figure did not move.

Garcés looked ahead. The forward Indian had reached the first swell of the hills from the desert, and though he was smaller now, he stood up more sharply out of the shadow-riddled plain. It was too far to halloo, even if the parched throat could have opened. Garcés watched the figure until it stood on the first of a heap of crags, and then suddenly it turned. Although it was much too far to see the face, there was no mistaking the fact that horse and rider had turned. Garcés raised his right arm and swung it round in a great arc until it pointed back. This he did several times so that there might be no mistake. When he had finished, the figure still stood there, as if watching. Then it seemed to the straining eyes of the friar that the Indian shrugged his shoulders and went on.

In a burst of wrath or anguish, he could not have told which, Garcés found the voice for a bellow. To his astonished ears it seemed as if the whole valley were ringing with that roar. But the figure in front of him went on, even as he stood watching. His throat was raw, but Garcés turned back. And now all his fatigue had fallen away, and one purpose had taken possession of him, to get back to the fallen man as soon as possible.

Sober second thought had reasserted itself, too. The Indian in front knew he was within reach of the indispensable water. Probably it was so high up that his only chance of getting there was to push on before the quick-falling desert night swallowed it up. Garcés turned and steered his way straight over the still blazing sand to that darker heap in the fast-shadowing plain.

The man had picked himself up now and was sitting in a huddle. Fray Garcés knelt down beside him and lifted his head. The face was dirty and torn from the dry brush into which he had fallen, and there was a foolish vacancy in the steady stare of the eyes.

The Franciscan asked him how he felt, but he seemed not to understand. Then the friar helped him to his feet. Once on his feet the Indian stood steadily enough, but he made no move to go forward, only gazing around vacantly. His tongue was hanging out, and he was panting lightly like a dog breathing. Garcés took his hand and dragged him to the horse. He came without any resistance, and somehow the friar managed to get him on the horse's back, and tie him to the saddle with his own rope cord. But even then, the Indian kept slipping in his bonds so that it was necessary for Garcés to hold him up as the horse started forward.

When his arm ached, Garcés stopped, and the Indian sat there for a moment, swaying a little, and then he toppled over. There was nothing to do but unknot the cord, and catch his weight as he fell. For a few minutes the friar let him lie in the sand there while he considered. They had covered perhaps half the distance back to where Garcés had been standing when he saw him fall. The shadows were heavier now, and the air was very still. The rocks ahead were a rosy color, and the sky had taken on a softness and a depth that could not be mistaken. There was no sign of the other Indian.

But worst of all the horse was starting ahead without his load. His rider, however, made no effort to catch him. For the animal was obviously played out as it was. To put the Indian on his back again would mean simply that in a little while Garcés would have to carry the saddlebags as well. He looked down at the man at his feet. He seemed to have fallen asleep. From the way the sinews stood out from the uncertain muscles, the friar saw that the Indian was older than he had thought. He was tall, but very thin—Garcés felt sure that he was still a good deal under his own weight.

Again it was a struggle, but he managed to hoist the still sleeping Indian to his shoulder, and sling him across his back like a sprawling sack. With one hand he steadied his load, with the other he clutched his staff. He thought of Saint Christopher and staggered forward.

Presently, he had struck his pace, heavy, deliberate. His parched throat was burning now, and his lungs pulled greedily on the heavy air. Bent under the weight of the Indian, he could not look up to the horizon. He could only follow the very light tracks in the sands and the dust-bruised sagebrush. When he stopped to reconnoiter, the rocks were perceptibly nearer, but they were much redder, and much higher than he had thought, with deep fissures of shadow through the pile. His second thought had been the juster. The Indian ahead would just reach the water before the dark, and he would not. He wondered if the man now lying beside him would last the night. He seemed to be awake now, but completely limp from exhaustion.

The man was muttering a little. But all Garcés could make out was the Pima word for "magic," mumbled over and over again. Magic—he had often wondered what his preaching became in the minds of those who heard it for the first time, and in the minds of those who heard it only indirectly.

Then for the first time he noticed that it had become cooler. The wind that blows in the desert night had come softly through the air. He hoisted the Indian to his shoulders, and again he strode on. In the cool he was walking faster now. When he looked at the rocks, they were aglow with the fantastic tenderness of color that succeeds the fierce glare of the desert day. If only he could outwalk the night!

The color had almost faded from the rocks when finally he reached them, brownish-yellow slabs and rubble, and before him what at first seemed an unbroken wall of folded and fissured sandstone. Garcés looked around. The light was going fast, and he knew that once it had gone, there would be no finding a hidden path. He was relieved to see that there was only the one opening in sight, a scrabbled fissure of rock fragments and pebbles and gravel between high walls. As he relaxed, his head swam, and he set his burden down once again.

The night came as quickly as he had feared, distorting everything his aching eyes looked upon. He was standing face to face with a seemingly unbroken pile of rocks, like great blocks set edgewise on each other, when the light went. The horse had completely vanished, and he knew there was no possibility of carrying his burden any farther. The Indian was still now, but his hands clung so tightly to Garcés' shoulders that for a moment he thought he could not loosen them. He spoke softly to the man, but the clutch did not relax. He wondered if perhaps he were already dead, but when he took hold of one of the hands, it was burning hot.

Garcés took off his habit and wrapped it around the sick man. He felt cool standing there in his shirt and drawers, but the coolness brought him a sudden sense of freedom and lightness of limb. He was starting off when he suddenly remembered that without his broad-brimmed felt hat, he would have nothing to carry water. He put it on his head, and with a sudden accession of amusement he thought of what a figure he would make there for the blessed saints, in his underclothes and his hat. And then he started up the rocks.

How far he had to go, he had no idea; and presently he lost all notion of time. For his breath was coming fast, and even to think of another stretch and climb was agony. Presently, he gave up. There is always strength enough for one step, he reminded himself, and gave all his attention to the rock above. And then when he had reached the top of that, he groped for the next. Once, finding a broad stretch, he lay down.

He must have fallen asleep, from sheer exhaustion, for the moon had risen when he next came to himself, and he was feeling chill and stiff. But as he rose to his feet, he was feeling curiously light, too. He started again.

And then he heard the sound for which he had been listening, it seemed to him for hours, a low, hollow, slapping sound, as if some creature were drinking from a pool. He waited. Presently, he heard a falling of stone off to one side, and then he went on. He could see his way now, where the moon whitened the stone-dark path. But even so he was surprised when his groping fingers touched the first spatter of mud. He moved over to one side and cautiously hitched his way up the broken stone.

And then he caught what seemed at first a dazzling light, waist-high across a gulf of darkness. He stood transfixed, and the light settled into the sheen of moonlight on a level pool. He thought of Father Kino's "Moonlight Water," doubtless some rock well seen like this, and he plunged forward, to lie flat over the blessed water and scoop up its brimming light into his parched lips. He drank until his head reeled, and the whole moonlight world with it. And then he remembered the fever-stricken man below.

Whether it was the water, or the moonlight, or the victory, or something of all three, Garcés plunged down the rocks like a man drunk on new wine. More than once, he missed his footing and poised perilously on the empty darkness, but each time he recovered his balance. The precious water slopped from the broad-brimmed hat, but he kept his grip on it. And when at last a low cry out of the darkness at his feet brought him to the Indian, there was still enough in it to give the man a drink, and to bathe his face and neck.

Only when that was done, did he realize that the Indian was pawing in the dark at his face and hands, and asking questions, as Garcés listened, apparently the same question over and over. At first he could not make out the key word, but there was no mistaking the strange mixture of awe and wonder and fearful curiosity in the question. And then he made out the word, a word which his Pimas used, but he could never quite be sure whether it meant "ghost" or "god." And then he realized that the Indian had seen his white body in the white shirt and drawers in the moonlight, seemingly above any contact with the earth, and Garcés was convulsed with laughter—a drunken friar for a god!

But the absurdity stirred his compassion, and he put out his hand into the dark to reassure the poor victim of his own folly. His hand hit the bare rock. He knelt down and carefully felt in the darkness at his side. But only the rough wool of his habit met his hand, and tangled in it, and then he reached with both hands. But the Indian was gone. He had fled from the terror of that spirit gone suddenly mad with laughter.

When he realized what had happened, the Franciscan flung himself on the rock, praying to every saint in his order who would listen to a blasphemous fool to have a care of the poor, frightened, fever-stricken creature whom his folly had driven into the night. He continued praying until at last he fell into the sleep of sheer and complete exhaustion.

3

ONCE Garcés roused when the darkness broke into sudden light and shouting. He made out the smoky flare of a torch and shadowy figures crowding around where the flame licked at the blackness, and then he looked up into the impassive face of the Indian guide who had gone ahead over the rocks.

He had not really doubted that he would come back. And then something less reassuring awoke like a prickle of pain on the edge of consciousness, and the worn-out mind shied away from the call to thought.

Again, his face was wet, and he thought the day had come, but it was too far to reach to the lighted surface of his restless dreaming, and he gave up the struggle. In the end it was a little thing that roused him, a soft rustle over his head, like a breeze in the dry corn stubble. It was quite dark around him except for a spilling of light overhead where the sound came from. It came again. And then he knew he was lying in a hut of twigs and sticks, with a loose splinter flapping from the flimsily bound walls. He sat up quickly, and for a moment his head reeled. For the dank rotting atmosphere of the Indian hut choked him.

He found the bark mat at the door and pushed out into the freshening air. A woman looked up at him from a metate and stared at him with her polished mano poised in mid-air. The sight of the gray meal on the stone slab reminded him that he was sickeningly hungry.

As he ate, the women of the village began to gather around the friar, their short bark skirts rustling as they crowded against each other. They kept a little away from him, gazing at him curiously, and presently the children began to peer out from between the skirts and gaze at him with solemn eyes.

He asked for water, and one of the women handed him a gourd, and they all watched as he drank. Then he remembered his breviary. He went back into the house, and there he found his staff and his saddlebags on an earthen shelf behind the heap of ashes on which he had been lying.

When he came out again, the men were pouring in among the huts. Foremost among them was the young Indian who had come from Bac, and then Garcés caught sight of the old Indian hanging back a little and gazing at the friar in bewilderment.

Garcés went over to him and asked him how he was. The man shrank back a little but said nothing. His eyes were still bright with fever, but he was obviously little the worse for his experience. The friar held out his hand, and the Indian touched it lightly, and then he began to examine the bare arm in the loose sleeve of the Franciscan habit. The friar stood very still, and the old man seemed at once to be more confident and yet more puzzled.

Now the other Indians gathered around, and began to examine his habit, and the knotted cord of his girdle, and his sandals, and the rosary. But the friar noticed that though they spared no part of his dress or person, no one made any move to touch the crucifix at his breast. He took the cord over his head, and holding the crucifix up so that all could see it, he kissed it. Then he held it out to the Indian nearest to him. Again, he saw that the man held it to his face as if breathing from it, and then he passed it on to the old man beside him. The old man did the same, and then he held it for a moment as if studying the look of it. Then he, too, passed it on, and so it went from one man to the next. The watching friar saw that only one man refused to take it into his hands. And, looking closer, he saw that he held a medicine man's little bag in his hand. There was the enemy, he said to himself.

But the old man whom Garcés had carried to the rocks came up and caught at his sleeve.

He was asking a question with great eagerness, saying something over and over, but Garcés could make out only a word here and there. It was something about cloth. The friar had often thought of taking cloth for presents, but he had never done so, for there had been so many things needed for the mission when he sent in the yearly list of goods to be bought by his stipend that he had never been able to manage more than the beads and the tobacco from what was left. Slowly he told the old man that he was sorry but he had no cloth. He spoke very deliberately, but he saw from the old man's face that he had not grasped the full meaning of the question.

The younger of his two guides saw the friar's bewilderment and came up to him.

"What is the old man," Garcés hesitated for the right word, "the old man who came with me, saying?"

"He is asking for the piece of cloth," the young Indian explained without looking at his fellow guide.

Garcés repeated the phrase.

The old man caught the volunteer interpreter by the arm and explained something eagerly. The young man shrugged his shoulders and turned to the friar. "He wants to see the piece of cloth with the woman who was killed and lives again," he spoke very slowly and patiently as if he were talking to a not very bright child.

For a moment Garcés was amused at the tangle of rumor and report in the wilderness, and then as he saw the light in the old man's eyes, he realized that this might be more serious than he liked to contemplate. For the brightly painted linen banner which he had had made with the picture of the Virgin and Child on one side and the picture of a lost soul on the other had been an object of great curiosity wherever he had gone, and until now he had thought it the readiest way to introduce his message to the primitive mind. But the rumors that had spread through the wilderness had jumbled together all his teachings into arrow-shafts of confusion that had flown far over the sands and rocks.

"Tell him," said Garcés anxiously, "that coming over the sands, I could not carry the banner. It is with your friends there," he pointed again in what he thought from the failing sunlight must be the direction of Bac. "Tell him when I come again, I will bring it."

He saw the old man's disappointment in his face. And then he was talking very fast.

"He says he is very old, and he may die before you come, and then who shall teach his grandson the magic, for his sons are dead?" Something of the old man's anxiety had come into the young man's voice as he spoke, and he looked at the friar, half in disclaimer and half in pleading.

"Tell him if he is dead, I will teach his grandson—" Garcés groped for the Pima word for "truth" and came up again at the blank wall of the language that so far he had mastered only in the words of everyday intercourse.

But he had heard too much in the last days of the word "magic" to risk any misunderstanding he could help; so he revised his sentence, "Tell him that I shall teach him the things that are good for him to know."

He watched the old man as the young Indian translated. He was not yet satisfied, for he was talking very fast now, pointing to Garcés as he spoke. Anxious as he was, the friar yet wondered at the change in the old man's manner. The traditional slowness and impassivity of the Indian had vanished, and he was talking very fast, the torrent of the words seeming to galvanize the slow-moving gestures of his body. The restlessly milling crowd of women and children, silent now, was listening intently, and the men stood looking with what seemed to the friar ominous gravity at the object of the old man's harangue.

The young man looked doubtfully at the old man and then no less doubtfully at the friar. "He says that last night he was nearly dead, and you went away, and you came back a ghost, and you brought him back to life, and here he is as all men may see."

"Oh, that," protested Garcés, and he felt his lips quiver. But the look on the young man's face stopped him. And then the memory of the night before came back, and he wondered if the warriors pressing around him now could see the blood he felt so hot in his cheeks.

"He says that he sat up and he looked for you, and a clown was laughing at his side, and he was afraid, and he fled. And yet when the others came, you were there sleeping so hard that one could not wake you," the interpreter concluded helplessly.

The Indians were talking to each other now and shifting restlessly in the gathering shadows between the huts. Garcés turned to the man whom he took to be the village headman.

"When you have built your campfire tonight, I will tell you what I have to say to you," he said, and the interpreter nodded.

Instantly, the crowd broke up, and presently over countless little fires women could be seen stirring pots of atole and calling to their children.

When the camp fire was blazing comfortably in the cool of the night, Garcés took his place in the squatting circle of warriors on the fringe of its heat. For a few minutes after he had sat down on the warm sand, no one spoke. Presently, the headman handed him a little of the tobacco he had given him, now pounded into paste in a corn husk. Garcés took a pinch and put it on his tongue. As he expected, it had been pounded with a bit of limestone to assuage weariness.

Then one of the old men was speaking, "The peoples beyond the mountains have a dance. The god comes and he dances in a mask, and the clown mocks at him."

"But he has no mask," said another.

A figure lying beyond the headman, with his feet to the fire, lifted head and shoulders, and the old man spoke, "I saw him, and he looked white like one who came from the ashes of the funeral pyre."

"Nonsense," said the Indian whom earlier Garcés had judged to be a medicine man, "you had a fever, and you did not know what you saw."

But before the friar could come to the rescue of the old Indian, another voice came from the darkness beyond the firs, "The men from the coast tell of a god who died and who came to life again." The friar turned eagerly to the voice in the dark—"the men from the coast!" So that was the way the shells came. He held his tongue, however, for the minds around him were opening their gates.

Then the old Indian lying by the fire spoke again, "Many villages tell that the Old Man visited them. He said he would make them live forever."

"He is a god who can do that," said another.

Garcés cleared his throat, and lifted his hand, "O men of the Pápagos, I am a man like you." He waited for the rustle of questioning to arise, and for the young man who had played the interpreter before to repeat what he said in words of a little different order and accent with now and then one he did not understand. But the paraphrase was faithful. "I am a man," he repeated, "but I bring you word of a god, of the one God." Slowly he went on in simple, arrow-straight sentences to tell of the one God who made the world, and who judged the deeds of men and yet who loved them so much that He came into men's world that he might take them to his heaven. He found that the young man had trouble with the last word. And he tried to think of a simpler way of saying it—"Heaven is where the good men go when they die."

The medicine man laughed scornfully, and the sharply hissed answer hardly needed an interpreter, "That is no news. We are not such fools but we know that the good men go there," he pointed upward, "and the bad men stay there," and he pointed to the earth. There was a little murmur of assent, the first response from the crowd sitting around the fire, and kneeling behind in the shadows.

"Who are the good?" asked Garcés quietly.

The laugh was more general as the medicine man answered, "Any woman-child knows that. The good are the Pápagos and Pimas, and the Pimas of the Gila, and some of the Yumas."

There was silence, as if the inclusion of the last name were not so certain.

"And the bad?" said Garcés. He did not recognize all the names which the medicine man hissed forth, but there was no mistaking the main fact that this was the roster of their enemies, and he noted that it was much longer than the list of their friends.

Then Garcés lifted his voice so that it would carry to the edge of the now half-hidden crowd, and slowly and patiently began to explain that the God whom he was bringing to them loved all men regardless of their tribes, so long as they were good men. And that God wanted all men to love each other and to be brothers. And he wanted to bring them all into his heaven, and not leave one man lying with the bad in the ground. To know God was to live forever no matter what happened to the body of a man in this world. Filled with his theme, the friar spoke at greater length than he had intended, but not a sound broke into his speech. Then he waited anxiously for the interpreter to repeat what he had said.

He found now that he could allow for the difference of accent and follow more easily the young man's words. He spoke with mounting enthusiasm. The first part went very well. The God who loved all good men and wanted to save them proved easier to manage than Garcés had feared. But now the interpreter was beginning to repeat with elaborations. The god of the Old Man loved all good men like the Pápagos and the Pimas and the Pimas of the Gila and the Yumas who were friendly. The god of the Old Man wanted the Pápagos and the Pimas and the good Yumas who would be true friends of the Pápagos—and the interpreter repeated this last obviously controversial element again—he wanted all these good people to be happy with them in his heaven. And the bad people—and here he repeated the litany of the enemies with tremendous gusto—he would leave them lying in the ground where they belonged. And if they would listen to the Old Man, his god would do these things for them.

Garcés groaned in his horror at what had become of his sermon, but no one seemed to hear him in the universal murmur of approval that followed the completion of the interpreter's paraphrase. Before the friar could protest, the leader of the Indians was speaking, slowly and deliberately as befitted the man who must deliver the verdict of the village.

"The Old Man is a man," he said firmly. "He is a good man, and he tells us good things. He will stay with us, and he will tell us more good things, and we will listen to him." And again the low murmur of approval swelled.

That night Garcés lay out under the stars. He was very tired, but though he took off his habit and shook it out as vigorously as he could without waking the other figures sleeping around the fading embers of the campfire, there was still one flea that he missed. The third time he took off his habit, one of the figures stirred, and the friar pulled on the garment and lay down again. It was probably the poor fellow who had given the fleas to him the night before.

For a few minutes lying there looking up at the stars, the Franciscan tried to think of the proper saint to invoke for patience under such a ludicrous affliction. Saint Martin had shared his cloak but had very wisely given rather than lent. But Garcés had caused enough trouble last night capering around in his tunic. Saint Francis had been very patient with his weak brethren, but the simply foolish? And that young interpreter! When the tale of that sermon went abroad in the land, the preacher would find a very different welcome in some villages.

The moon had come up now and the sleeping figures lay dark around the graying ashes. A great tenderness came into the troubled heart of Father Garcés. Poor children of an unknown father, so eager for the magic, for the word that would break the prison of their fearful days! And for not the first time since he had come to Pimería Alta Francisco Garcés wished that a better man could reach their groping minds. And even as he wished it, it came to him that he had scant reason to be so condescending to any man's mind, and on that thought, having found as it were his level, he slept.

4

But Garcés was soon to lose that tenderness for the ranchería of Sonóita. For it took him more than two precious weeks to persuade the leading men of the village to help him go on to the Yumas. It was not unfriendliness on their part. Quite the contrary. They listened to him with deep attention whenever he spoke; they watched fascinated as he turned the pages of his breviary; they gathered around as he said his prayers, and they repeated over and over again the names of Jesus and Maria and the simple Christian greetings he taught them. A couple of the boys even learned to sing a stanza of the hymn, the *Alabado,* which he sang in the morning and at night. This last cheered him a good deal, though he had to admit that the effect of their unusually solemn rendering of the familiar notes was dismal enough. But to all his requests for guides to the Yumas he received the same answer, "Do not go to the Yumas. They are proud men. They will do the Old Man no good. Stay here with the Pápagos, who are good men."

In the end he stole off by himself early one morning. But though he did after several days of rather anxious wandering reach what he judged to be the Gila River, it was a lonely and uninhabited stretch. The cottonwoods along the bank that almost concealed the river were a welcome sight after the arid stretches to the south, but he was too uncertain of the course of the river to trust it. So in the deepest despondency he had ever known he went back to Sonóita.

The enthusiastic welcome he received did little to cheer him, but the next morning half a dozen of the Pápagos came and offered to take him to the Yumas. Foremost among them was the old man who had already caused him so much trouble. "The headman," said the Indian, "sees that the Old Man will not be content to stay with the Pápagos until he has seen the Yumas. When he has seen the Yumas, he will know he had better come back to the Pápagos."

Garcés wondered if he were not obtaining his guides on false pretenses, but he was too tired to do any more explaining. He tried feebly to dissuade the old Indian from further travel, but that stout soul professed himself fully recovered. So there was nothing to do but commend him to Saint Francis and hope for better luck.

That better luck held for three hot September days, until it was clear from the look of the land that they must be coming into the neighborhood of the river again. Garcés began to think that perhaps after all he would reach the junction of the rivers where the Yumas were to be found. But on the fourth day the curious perversity of fortune that had seemed so far to govern this journey, reasserted itself.

They had gone much less than a morning's journey when the friar saw one of the Indians pick up a feather from the scarcely visible track they were following. Nothing was said, but presently the scouts ahead left the path and plunged into the stretch of tall grass which they had been skirting. Without a word the whole file followed after them, swishing quietly through the dry grasses.

The sun was fast moving to the zenith, and tine increasing heat and the steady jogging of the file of Indians were beginning to make the friar sleepy. Once he blinked a little, and then he opened his eyes wide, and determinedly scanned the horizon of low-lying greenish-brown hills. Idly he watched a thin wraith of smoke curl into the colorless light of the open sky. Then he opened his eyes wide. Only two of the Indians were to be seen ahead.

He looked behind. The old man alone remained, and now he came quickly until he was within speaking distance.

"Enemies," he said.

Garcés stood still. "They will not harm you when you bring me to them," he said quietly.

Then he looked ahead. The Indian nearest him was waiting.

He pointed off to the left. "We will go there," he said briefly.

"Is the river there?"

The Indian laughed at the stranger's mistake, and he pointed ahead.

"Then I will go there," said the friar, "for I have promised."

The two Indians looked at each other. The old man grabbed the sleeve of the friar's habit. "They are bad men, and they will do bad things to the Old Man."

But Garcés smiled. "They are friends," he said.

He watched the Indians start again. They were near a little clump of trees in a fold of the level country now, and the friar wondered if they would go past it. Apparently, while they had been talking, one of the Indians ahead had vanished. Now the second went steadily into the little wood. One moment the watching friar could see the brown figure between the tree trunks, the next he had lost him. He turned to look behind. There was no one in sight.

He was completely alone now in a great stillness of earth and sky. There was no more smoke to be seen on the hills to the right, and the only sound on the earth was the swish of his own passing and the sleepy hum of an occasional bee or insect. The sense of absolute solitude came to him like an unexpected release. And insensibly he relaxed. This was the most precious of the gifts of a missionary's life, he thought, this freedom of perfect alone-ness. "Our Lady of Solitude," he thought, of all the names of Our Lady her loveliest.

Now he realized how hungry he had been for this freedom and stillness, this fullness of self-possession. He was walking slowly, for a little breeze had sprung up from nowhere, and the smell of the sun-steeped grass was sweet, and he was content.

He had come to a low slab of rock that lay straight across his path. He could not be far from the river now, for the mesquites and live oaks of the place where the last of the Indians had vanished had given way to what looked like cottonwoods in the little clump ahead. He laid his staff across the rock as across a table, and he took out his breviary from the bundle at the end. He knelt down, and opening the book on the rock, he tried to remember the day. It was already more than a month since he had left Bac. He found what he calculated must be the place, and began to read the familiar words.

The voice of Garcés rose with sheer delight in the majesty of the noble Latin periods. Presently, he began to chant the lines as if he were back in his college chapel at Querétaro, and he knelt very erect at his improvised prie-dieu.

He must have been half through the day's office when he became aware of a little movement behind him. He did not stop. In the community recita-tion of the office at Querétaro he had learned not to yield to the inevitable petty distractions of group prayer, the wheezings of the aged, the fidgeting of the young body with difficulty held to the same position, the coughing of the wandering, the tension of the fervent. So he kept on, his voice rising a little in its firmness.

A moment later, another rustle, now in front of him, broke into his attention, and with a sickening shock he remembered that he was not in the chapel at Querétaro but out in a field somewhere, miles from any human habitation. Without moving his head he looked up, and just on the fringe of vision he caught a movement of brown legs. Had—but he knew the Pápagos had not come back. Even if they should grow ashamed of their desertion, they would not come back. They would wait for him farther along the way and bring food to his campfire.

Some instinct made him keep on with his chanting. And then behind the shield of the familiar words he began to think, and the little worm of fright in the pit of his stomach grew still. If they were any of the tribes whom he had visited, they would wait until he had finished his prayers before giving him a friendly greeting. If they were some of the river folk whom he had not yet visited, they would have heard of the Old Man from their neighbors, and they would be curious. And if they were neither, his heart stood still for a moment, but his voice went on, now curiously remote as if from a long way off—well, there would be nothing better that a friar could be doing when his Master sent for him than saying the day's office.

So Garcés completed the office, rounding out the last blessing as slowly and as resonantly as if he had been praying in the chapel at Querétaro. Then he looked around.

He was completely surrounded by, it seemed, a score of Indians, naked but for their red and black paint. They held their bows in their hands, and each man had drawn the long shaft of an arrow, and held it, so the frightened priest felt sure, pointing straight at him.

They could not be Yumas, for they were shorter and darker—then he caught sight of the sandals of woven reed. They were the dreaded Cajuenches from across the river. Stretching out his hands in greeting, Garcés went up to the nearest of the Indians and embraced him. And he felt rather than heard the indrawn breaths around him, and the rustle of the hands falling with the taut bows.

As he stepped back to survey the company, the man whom he had embraced, slowly took the arrow he held into both his hands and broke it, and laid the pieces at the friar's feet. And then one of the Indians who had stood just behind the rock at which he had been praying stepped forward and spoke to him. It was not a language he knew; so there was nothing to do but resort to the sign language. He went back to the rock and took from the handkerchief bundle at the end of his staff the roll of tobacco and broke off a piece.

Gravely, the chief accepted the present, and all the Indians sat down on the grass around him. Then for the first time he noticed behind the circle of men, one little figure still standing, a small girl, perhaps ten years old, staring at him with large and frightened eyes. He beckoned to her to come near, but she shrank back, and he saw that her face was swollen as if she had been weeping.

Now the whole group was watching him as if it were his turn to speak. So he looked around the circle, and he asked quietly, in Pima, "Does no man understand the speech of the Pimas?"

There was silence, but he felt the hostile stiffening of the figures about him at the sound of the Pima tongue. And for the hundredth time Garcés resolved that he would pay more attention to the speech of the tribes he visited.

Then a young man on the other side of the stone answered, first in the unknown tongue, and then a little stiffly in Pima: "They are bad men, the Pimas, and good men do not have them for friends."

It was hardly the place or the time to argue the point. So the friar politely recalled the fact that last winter he had met some of the Cajuenches on a trip to the Gila River, and they had been good men who had not stopped him.

As he had hoped, that, translated by the young warrior, produced a general relaxation in the circle around him. For, as the young man went on to explain, they had heard of the meeting with the Old Man, and they had heard good things of him. And the friendly interest and curiosity with which this gambit was received emboldened the friar to tell his new acquaintances that he was making a journey to the west, to the Colorado River. He hoped, as he said this cautiously, that he had remembered the home location of the Cajuenches correctly.

And to his relief it turned out that he had. He felt a little ashamed of not being quite straightforward. He had planned to go and see some of those people one day on his way to or from the Yumas; but he seemed to remember some disparaging remarks about the Cajuenches from his recent Yuma visitors. So he judged it wiser to conceal the main point of his journey.

If hardly heroic, that decision proved wise, for there was an unmistakable movement of concern in the squatting group around him. This the inter-preter hastened to give voice to, "Does the Old Man know that to reach the Cajuenches one must pass through some of the Yuma lands?"

There was no need of his saying more. The very intonation with which he pronounced the word, "Yuma," was eloquent enough.

And now the Franciscan noticed that the little girl standing on the edge of the circle seemed to shrink back into her small self, and she began to cry noiselessly. Garcés looked at her, but he thought it best to go cautiously. So he suggested tentatively that since he went only to bring good news and to help men to make peace, the Yumas would hardly do him any harm.

There was a common movement of protest at this. Surely the Old Man must have heard that the Yumas were thieves and murderers. The little girl seemed to double up in her noiseless crying, and Garcés wrestled with the impulse to call her to him.

He was glad he did, for in a moment the chief was leaning forward talking very fast, and the interpreter was repeating his words with much excitement. The Yumas were bad men. They themselves had just been to one of their villages, and they had burned their houses.

The friar caught the spark of excitement in the group. They had burned their houses and set fire to their corn. They had run like women, the Yumas. Only an old woman and a girl had stayed. Garcés looked at the little girl for a moment, and then he turned to the interpreter, "What good are women to warriors?"

The old woman they had left for dead at the edge of the village. But the girl—what are girls good for? Four or five summers from now they would give her to one of their warriors, and when she had a son, she would lead them to her village, and they would slay them all. Garcés saw the little girl raise her head with one horror-stricken look. He considered. Then he spoke very slowly and tentatively that they might not take offense. That would be many moons yet, he suggested. Would it not be better to let him have the girl for a guide, and then the Yumas would see him safely to the Cajuenches, and he could come back to his friends the Cajuenches and tell them good things.

There was silence at this. Then one of the warriors asked if it would not be better for him to come with the Cajuenches now and leave the Yumas alone in their wickedness. But Garcés answered firmly that he had promised to go on to the river people. And as he saw the man who had asked the ques-tion shrug his shoulders at the inevitable, he gave thanks that to an Indian a promise was something that must be kept.

For some minutes they sat in silence. Then one of the Indians said it was a poor thing to come in from a raid with empty hands.

"But is it nothing to a Cajuenche to have burned his enemy's village?" asked the friar, and the grunt of satisfaction proved that the compliment had been accepted.

"A girl is only a burden to a party of warriors," went on the friar pensively.

Gloomy silence gave assent to that. Then Garcés opened the handkerchief at the end of his staff and took out his little store of tobacco and of brightly colored beads. He felt the eyes of all the company on him. Carefully he divided the tobacco into two portions, and put half of it on the rock, and then he took two of the four strings of beads and put them with it. The rest he tied up firmly in the handkerchief.

Then he offered the tobacco and the beads to the chief of the company. The latter looked at the friar, and then he took up one of the strings of beads and measured it to his forearm. Satisfied, he put it around his neck. Then he called to one of the men, who took the little girl by the arm and pulled her to the rock. Now the child was making no effort to restrain her tears.

The leader took the other string of beads, gave them to the Indian holding the child, and as the latter relinquished his grip on her arm, he pushed her to Garcés, and all the company rose at once. The chief turned to the friar and bade him go fast to the river and come back soon to the Cajuenches. Garcés had hardly made the promise when the Indians had gathered up their bows and arrows and were filing quietly through the grass in the opposite direction from the river.

For several minutes the friar stood there with the little girl, watching them go off. Not a one turned to look behind; none spoke. And then Garcés noticed that the cold little hand in his was no longer shaking. He looked at the child.

He pointed at her; he made the sign of a tent over his head with his forefingers, and he pointed to the right. The child gazed at him with solemn eyes, now no longer frightened. Then a look of intelligence came into them, and she shook her head, and pointed to the river. Garcés gave her a little push in that direction, and the child stared at him with bewilderment slowly giving way to incredulous relief. Suddenly she smiled and, turning, ran through the grass so fast that the friar was put it to it to keep up with her. And as she ran and danced along, the little brown heels kicking up the hanging bark strips of her brief petticoat, she seemed the epitome of childish carefreeness, and the Franciscan blessed the spirit that could run so gayly back to a burned village.

5

As the sun set, Garcés called the little girl to him, put one of his two remaining strings of beads about her slim neck and signed to her that she was free to go where she wished. For it had occurred to him that the people of the burned village would hardly spend the night in its ashes, and she might want to scout out familiar haunts before the night settled too heavily. He was feeling tired and hungry, now, and he suspected she could find food at some campfire where she might hesitate to bring a stranger. For himself, it was not the first night he had spent in the open without supper.

But having sent his small guide off, he found that he was still far from ready to make his night camp. It was fairly open country in which he was now traveling, with little groves of cottonwoods in the hollows, and he felt sure that he must be fairly close to the river. So he kept on as the long shadows fell through the tall grass, and a thousand sounds, muffled in the day's heat, waked around him. And not for the first time he mused on the blindness and deafness of man that moves unseeing and unhearing through so eloquent a world of living and moving things.

It was quite dark now, but still he kept on. The long grass had thinned around him, and the ground was growing rougher. He must be coming close to the river. Once he thought he saw a light flash ahead of him, but it did not come again, and he feared that his senses through fatigue had begun to deceive him. He was feeling giddy with hunger, and moving ahead seemingly without effort. Again, a light flashed, and then another. There was an encampment between him and the river. It was getting cold now, and suddenly he remembered the key to the flashing lights. The men were warming themselves in the Yuma fashion, waving firebrands about their naked bodies as they moved between the trees.

He had come over a little rise of ground when he first saw the campfire perhaps half a mile away. Then from the neighboring trees he heard an owl hoot, and then another. Unconsciously he had been walking very quietly, watching for the strange lights. Now he strode along as noisily as possible. Presently, shadows rose and moved between him and the glow of light as he reached the level of the fire, and he could hear a considerable moving of bodies. Suddenly a cluster of torches detached themselves from the glow.

But, as he had half expected, the first of the Indians to reach him had hardly lifted his torch to scrutinize the stranger before a little figure with a rustle of bark strips and a necklace swinging into the light had hurtled into his path.

The friar stood still while a dozen torches crowded around him. The little Indian girl slipped a moist hand into his, saying over and over again a single strange word as if repetition would pierce his dim understanding. But though the Indians pressed curiously around him, they made no inquiry as they led him to the campfire. And he gave thanks for the hospitality that took him into friendly warmth and produced parched corn and some nameless roast meat with a charred gaminess to its flavor, before anyone asked him any questions.

He was sleepy now, and with his grace he added a prayer for a clear head in the interrogation that he knew must ensue. But to his surprise a number of the men about the fire now arose and reached into the fire for long brands, which they half quenched in the ashes. He watched them until he was aware that somebody was talking to him in Pima. He thought he recognized that voice and looked more closely. It was the leader of the Yumas who had come to Bac. By the time a dozen men had drawn out their brands, he had mastered the gist of the speech. They were only camping here for the night. Farther down the river there were more of their people, and they were having a dance, and they would make the Old Man welcome.

Garcés started to ask how far it was, and then he remembered the Indian dislike of irrelevant questioning. It was not so easy to walk now, for his head was heavy with sleep, but he fell into the line, hoping that the rhythm of the group would carry him along if he fell asleep.

So they plodded along, it seemed to him, for hours. His head fell forward on his breast, but still his feet went on. As the fuddled mind struggled slowly to the surface of consciousness, he wondered if they would ever stop. They must be tired, too, having their village burned behind them this morning, or was it yesterday morning? It seemed as if he had always been going along half-asleep in this flickering line of dark backs and tufted heads wavering from light into darkness with the moving of the firebrands over shivering breasts and thighs.

He felt rather than heard the pulsing of the drum, and the sound of singing like the wash of the outgoing tide licking at the shores of the night stillness. And then the whole night spilled over with the sound of the drum and the voices, and rounding a clump of cottonwood and willow, they saw the stretch of river margin lighted by a great fire, with rosy figures dancing into the light and out, and all around in the half-light rank upon rank of hushed faces and shining eyes.

Presently, the priest was alone on a low hillock from which he looked out upon the campfire as upon a stage. It must be long after midnight; yet the drum throbbed and the gourds rattled, and the voices rose above the beat in a curiously flowing, almost monotonous, yet vibrant chant. And the dancers ducked into the light and swung back as if some mighty hand had been pulling invisible wires through the darkness. It was the organic quality of the scene before him that held him spellbound. For the drum and the voices, and the swaying bodies of the dancers, and the dark ranks with the shining eyes and the clapping hands beating the time were like the breathing of one great body.

And he wondered about the thoughts and the purposes that thus beat against the night. Through what strange gods did these men reach to the one God? "When I was a child, I spoke as a child, I understood as a child, I thought as a child," the familiar words of Scripture ran through the beating of the drum.

Then he was aware that in the darkness beside him someone had come up, and again he heard the voice of the man who had come to Bac. Garcés' head had cleared now, and he no longer felt anything of the evening's weariness, but the words blurred to the singing; so he leaned toward the dark voice.

"Palma, the great chief, is here," those words he finally made out, and he guessed from the way the man stood there waiting in the darkness that he had been ordered to conduct the visitor into the chief's presence. The friar was quite awake now. For he felt sure that this Palma was the chief who had sent the deputation to Bac.

Palma sat apart from the circle about the fire with a firebrand stuck in the sand beside him so that his head stood out quite clearly in the smoky light. It was a dark, proud head with something tense and watchful in its poise and yet something very serene and aloof in the repose of the clear-cut features. It was quite the most arresting face which the Franciscan had yet encountered among the Indians, indeed, one of the most striking faces he had ever seen anywhere. And the impression was deepened when with, it seemed, a single and unbroken line of movement, the Yuma sprang to his feet. He was no longer young, but he stood there slim and tall in his complete nakedness. He did not speak for a full minute but stood there, with a dignity of mien that held the eye and made all the noise of the night fall away from his quiet presence.

"I have heard many things of you, Old Man, and they are good things," he began with great dignity.

"And I," said the priest gravely, as one potentate to another, "have heard many good things of the great captain of the Yumas."

And now the friar saw that a number of men had come up with fire-brands in hand, and stood there, moving them slowly through the still air. There was enough light now for him to see quite clearly the dark face of the Yuma chief, serene and proud, and yet with something tight-clenched in the lean contours, and something sharp and hungry in the bright eyes.

As the Indian Palma looked at him, the friar yearned to tell him that he knew where to point him for the food for that hunger, for it was not in him. But already the Yuma was holding out to him a reed tube and a handful of tobacco. And as the friar began slowly to puff at the tube, he saw the impatience blaze out of the quiet face. It was gone in a moment, but it deepened the sense of inadequacy in Garcés.

As he watched his host stuff a tube with tobacco, he said slowly, "Many guests have come to do honor to the great chief's dancing."

He felt rather than saw the pleasure at the friendly compliment in the men around him, but Palma was not thinking of that. For he said curtly enough, "It is strong magic this," and then he waved his hands in a quick, light motion. And the men who had gathered around vanished. But not before Garcés had had a chance to perceive that of all the tall, slim Yumas Palma was the tallest and the straightest. He thought of the old figure as arrow-straight, but there was a strength beyond that in the man before him. A spear, perhaps, and then as the wind blew the smouldering flame of the torch into a clean yellow flame that made the brown face shine, he thought rather that this man was like the torch stuck in the ground at his back.

When they were alone, the Indian came closer to the friar, and he spoke quickly in his rough Pima, "It is strong magic, but the Old Man has a stronger magic."

Garcés considered. That word "magic" frightened him, and yet obviously that was the gate through which he could reach this hungry mind.

"The only magic I—" he was going to say "have," but the word was not true; so he hastily substituted a safer word, "the only magic that I know is the power of the things that are true."

He had put it badly, and he saw that he had not touched the mind of the man who was waiting so eagerly. "There is no good thing in me," he thought with a sudden chill of discouragement, and then the challenge made him try again.

"The power is not in me," he said slowly, suiting the gesture to the word, and trying to hold the keen glance of the Indian. "It is in Him who sent me to you." He pointed to the sky. And as he did so, he saw that high against the now graying night lights were moving. No, they were not falling stars, for they moved slowly on one plane. And then he remembered that the Indians had said that there were high bluffs below where the great rivers met. He must be there now, and the thought of the end of his quest gave him new courage to try again.

But the Indian was speaking as if in rebuke of his distraction. "All men know that there is no power in them like the power of a god." It was said with an indescribable blending of contempt and of wistfulness.

"Man is man, and God is God," answered the Franciscan carefully, "but Christ is both God and man, and it is of him that I bring you news."

"A man who became a god?" asked the Indian eagerly.

"No," said the friar, "God who became man."

The firebrand was guttering now, and the friar could not see his companion's face, but he could hear the snort of his disappointment.

"He became man to bring man to God," he went on.

The Indian repeated it slowly after him. Then he said, "That is better." But something of the first disappointment still lingered in his voice.

And suddenly the friar was overcome by the day's weariness in a great dark wave. And for the first time he noticed that the singing had died down, and the great glow of the campfire. Overhead where the lights had moved, the sky was whitening.

"It is nearly dawn," he said to the Indian, "and I have come a long way." And even as he spoke, he lay down on the bare ground where he stood. He tried to pray, but the tired mind unravelled too fast.

The sun was high when he awoke, and the heat of noonday seemed to be baking the night's stiffness out of his body. As Garcés sat up and looked around, he nearly cried aloud in his astonishment. For he seemed to be entirely alone in the middle of a meadow by the river. Above, he could see the great height of the bluff hanging over the river with some low shrubs projecting into the clear sky.

He stood up. Now he could see where the campfire had been, a patch of gray ashes, half trampled into the reddish-brown earth. And he could see where the dancers had moved in the trampled grass that surrounded the patch.

But he was astonished to see how little evidence of the throng that had filled the night remained there. Then he became aware that he was not alone. He caught a flicker of slim brown legs around a bush just above the water, and he saw that someone was sitting on the bank.

But before he could call, there was a flash and a twist of a small net, and a fish was thrashing in the grass. The fisherman pulled up his legs and turned to the friar.

"Your slave will roast it for you," he said in slow but still perfectly intelligible Pima.

"My slave," repeated the friar, wondering what new formula of hospitality was this.

And then the little girl with the beads about her neck came up and grasped the fish in her hands.

"She is free," he said, opening his hands wide. The little girl stood still, looking at him, as if she thought he was jesting.

"Free?" repeated the old man. He shook his head. "You will never get rich that way, giving away what you have bought."

The friar smiled. "Send her to her father."

The old man peered up at him curiously. "Her father is dead, and her mother. I am her grandfather."

"Then you take her home with you."

The old man gazed thoughtfully at the little girl. "She will be marriageable in four or five summers more. Then you shall have her."

The priest laughed. That margin was safe enough. And the little girl stood twisting the beads until her grandfather pointed to the fish.

While the fish roasted on the sand below the bank, the priest asked what had happened to all the company of the night before. The dance was over, the old man answered briefly, and they had gone back to their villages to prepare for the fall planting. They were full of the power of the dancing, he added, and from it they might hope for many good things.

"And Captain Palma has gone back, too?"

The old man nodded, and then he added as an afterthought.

"He bade me stay to show you the way to his village."

"He is a great chief," said the friar politely.

The old man said nothing while the little girl came up the bank with the fish in a handful of grass. Then as the friar began to eat, he observed to no one in particular, "He has too many dreams, that Palma. He does not know when he is well-off."

6

BUT as it turned out, the friar did not go to Palma's village that day. Some business detained the Yuma chief on the way, and he sent a messenger back to tell the fisherman that he would make his camp that night on the top of the bluff across the river. So the friar and the fisherman and the little girl went for a stroll down the river, walking along the stretch of river bottom under the lee of the high bank until they reached a more level region.

It was slow progress that they made. Partly it was due to the fact that it was the heat of the day, and neither of the Indians was disposed to hurry in that heavy air, and partly it was that all along the way they kept running into people. Now it was an old man binding together bundles of heavy marsh reeds to make a narrow raft, or a man planting ears of corn, or a woman picking up ironwood nuts that had fallen from the high bank above, or a boy with a small net dabbling at the river's edge. All of them responded to the friar's friendly greeting, and, as he stopped to watch their work, by sign and by a brief word or two which the old man absent-mindedly translated, they asked him about his habit, his cord, where he was going, whether he was man or woman, and so on.

They were friendly, too, a woman giving him a piece of melon she had dug out of the sand, a man carrying two rabbits offering him one, which the little girl promptly undertook to carry for him. And always the little girl proudly exhibited her beads, glancing back shyly at their donor, and making some explanation which the old man did not bother to translate for the friar.

They all spoke briefly of the dance. Some of the women said their husbands were still sleeping, and more than once the travelers came across children asleep between the cornstalks or tangled up among the pumpkin vines, little brown creatures hardly to be distinguished from the reddish-brown earth on which they sprawled so companionably. Several of the men said they knew the Old Man brought them good things to tell, but they seemed in no hurry to hear them. And, knowing that the evening campfire would provide a wider audience, the friar was content to go on, insensibly relaxing in the warm, moist river air. In this sunny, lush world by the broad river water it was easy to sink into a vegetable mood, to let the lazy moment suffice, and to watch the slow scroll of the low-lying river scene unfurl as they moved.

Nothing could be in sharper contrast to the world of last night than this, and yet he had a feeling that at bottom they were one and the same. Last night it had been tight-clenched, fiercely articulated, pounding its blind passion against the darkness. Today it lay sprawled out, relaxed, disintegrated. And yet in it all he felt a potency that made him yearn to set the cross on the high bluff above their heads, to give all this lush generosity a new focus, a fresh integration.

But now they had come to the narrow gorge below the height. The sudden quickening of the current filled all the air with the dazzling brilliance of the sun-struck waters. The old man pointed to the heavy gray wool habit of the friar, and with shame the latter explained that he could not swim. There had been a good many times these last three years when the loyal son of the College of Querétaro had had occasion to reflect that the course for the preparation of missionaries could be profitably expanded to include several subjects not usually treated in novitiates. There had been a time when a course in the cultivation of corn had been his prime suggestion. There had been another when the knowledge of which cactus stalk could be counted on to yield moisture to the lips of the guide-deserted traveler in the desert seemed the most pressing need. Now it would be swimming—Garcés smiled at the thought of Reverend Father Novice Master leading the novitiate to the river bank.

Then he remembered how concerned the good father had been that his pupils should understand ahead of time the temptations to pride in their lives among primitive people. Now as the friar saw the Indian turn to look at his tall frame appraisingly, he wondered if the old missionary had forgotten the many times when the superior man of civilization suddenly finds himself helpless before the demands of a situation which he has never met before in his world. But the Indian was working now at something that looked like a forkful of hay down on the river bank. Coming nearer, the friar saw that it was a bundle of tules like that at which he had first found his guide working. As he came up, the old man finished tying the shapeless bundle and pushed it out into the water; then he signed to the friar to embark.

Cautiously, Garcés pushed one foot out to the floating straw. The old man laughed and signed to him to lie down flat. The little girl was laughing now, the first time he had seen her laugh, the precious beads jangling as the slim body convulsed. For a moment Garcés measured the bundle of reeds with his eye. It seemed hardly adequate, but he reflected that though he was of larger build than most of the Yumas, he was probably no heavier than some of those well-muscled warriors. So he stretched out on the half-submerged bundle, clutching the slippery sides of the matted tules.

The old man and the little girl plunged into the stream without any hesitation, and, swimming easily, began to push the little raft on either side. And to his surprise, though the current thrashed the bundles of reeds with a good deal of force, the water kept well below the level of the friar's head. Presently, he relaxed a little and began to look around. And then half-blinded by the light of the early afternoon sun on the swiftly-running water, he looked up to the great crag. They were opposite the crest of the bluff now, and for a moment it rose sheer against the sky like a great wave of earth about to break upon them. And, as he looked, the friar saw in his mind's eye the cross of the mission and then, behind it, the bell tower of the church. It would be the most magnificent site in the Indies, and the sound of the bell at morning and night would drift up and down the great rivers for miles. And men would come there for the precious gift—he tried to remind himself of the vanity of the imagination which presents to the mind's eye the sweetness of things done without the labor, but his heart swelled within him.

Nor was he in any degree disappointed when a little before sunset, after many a twisting and turning and sliding back on the narrow paths, they arrived at the top of the bluff. For to his astonishment he found a broad, almost level tableland stretching back from the precipitous river front. Here could be built not only a church, but a substantial array of mission buildings as well.

As he looked out over that vast panorama of river and shore and meadow and tangled marsh and high bank and wood, miles and miles spread out before him as if the whole natural world were lying there at his feet, he could not tether his thoughts to the particular patch of mud and sand and reed and grassland where the individual he hoped to redeem was even then squatting to the unending food-getting of primitive man. And yet as he saw those little

dark figures bobbing up and down on the edge of the river and in the yellow-
ing of the cornfields and threading invisible trails through the deep-grassed
meadows, he was filled with a yearning for the winning of each one of these
souls walking so darkly in all the brightness of the river light. They looked
so gentle, so settled there in the peaceful labors of the earth, that it seemed
as if half the labor of the missionary in the Indies, the labor of gathering up
and rooting to a settled spot the wandering children of desert and mountain,
were already done for him.

The brilliance of the midday had already yielded to the softening of the
afternoon. From this high point one could see how swiftly the day was sinking to its dusk, and how all the colors of the earth were softening in the
tenderness of the coming evening. It was not so rosily opalescent as the late
afternoon of the desert, and yet there was an even tenderer freshness and
delicacy of color in this imperceptibly mist-touched river world. Nowhere
since he had come north from Sonora into this world of Pimería Alta had he
had such a sense of assured peace.

He felt rather than heard a light breathing behind him, only a little more
focused than the diffused breathing of the wind in this high place. He waited
for a minute until the new arrival should have had time to recollect himself
after the strain of reaching the top, and then he slowly turned.

As he had expected, it was Palma. He was quite alone, and he was standing within arm's length of the friar, gazing over the scene below, seemingly
unaware of his companion. The latter looked away, and stood silent, too. He
had often wondered just what the feelings of the Indian were in the presence
of the often dramatic scenes in which his daily life moved. Was he stirred to
delight by the wide and fruitful spread of valley and field seen thus unrolled
with something of an anticipation of the serene and blessed vision of the
saints? The Indian as Garcés had known him did not easily find words for
these things. And yet the friar had always felt sure that those who do not easily find words for the feelings of things may yet experience brooding depths
of contemplation unknown to their more articulate brethren. And as the love
of God may well out of silence beyond the reach of words, why not, too, the
appreciation of the beauty of His creation?

It was Garcés who at length broke the silence, spreading out his hands
over the air before him as if he would bless all this waiting world, and then
lifting his eyes to heaven and looking at the Indian ruler. The latter looked at
him so long that the friar wondered if he had understood at all. But suddenly

the Indian smiled and embraced him, and sweeping his arm around half the horizon, he ended by pointing to the friar.

Then he began to talk slowly and carefully in a very rough and labored Pima which Garcés had to follow with close attention, for every so often the not too familiar word blurred, and he groped vainly for identification. Yet the main meaning was clear.

"It looks peaceful," said the Indian chief, "but the river is red with the blood of endless wars."

That seemed hard to believe, with it all lying there so still before him, and yet the reports of the tribes whom Garcés had met to the east and the south bore out the rueful verdict of the Yuma chieftain.

"But you who hold this height have a good chance to keep the peace on the rivers," suggested the friar hopefully.

He was not sure that Palma could follow his by no means fluent Pima. But he must have understood, for he shook his head sadly, as he answered, "There are a dozen peoples in the valley and on the heights of the great rivers. And they grind each other like the mano on the metate."

"The King of Spain would have all the peoples at peace with the Spaniards and with each other. He would have them all at peace so that the missionaries who bring the news of the world's great King may help all the peoples of the rivers to know Him," he spoke very slowly, using every gesture he could think of to express the meaning of the abstract words. Again, that hungry look came into the keen brown face beside him. Seen now in the daylight, the features of the face seemed even sharper and more tense than they had appeared at night, and Garcés was troubled by the incongruity between the tension of the look and the spacious peace before which they stood.

"These are many things that you say," said the Indian with a sudden gust of caution, or so it seemed to his companion, "and I want to hear more."

"I shall be very glad to tell you more," said the priest hopefully. "It is to tell you these things that I have come to see you and the peoples of the river."

Palma looked at him sharply. "They say, the men of the tribes whom you visit, that you come and you tell them good things, but you do not stay."

"I, too, have a captain," replied the friar, "and I am told where I shall make my camp. But I shall ask my captain to let me come and make my camp here with you."

The Indian's face lighted with a somber radiance. "When will you do that?"

The friar knew that this was no child's question, to be answered the readiest way possible. "Listen to me, O great captain," he said solemnly, "I cannot come to live with you until you have made peace with your neighbors. For I cannot join in your fighting. My Master bids me love all men. When you have made peace, I shall come and teach you."

"But those others who make war on us?" Suddenly something very practical had come into the voice of Palma, and something hard into his face.

The Franciscan looked down the river. Mile on mile, it stretched out before him, seeming all to be waiting there before his very eyes.

"I will tell them, too, that they must make peace and keep the peace."

The dark eyes gleamed. "When?"

It seemed to Garcés that he had never before encountered an Indian to whom time seemed so urgent a matter.

"As soon as we have finished our talking together, great chief," he said.

The Indian seemed to consider. "Tomorrow," he said regretfully, "I must go down to the village that was burned."

"Then," said the friar, "tomorrow I will start down the river."

"You have not been down the river?" asked the Indian.

"No. Will you give me a guide?"

The Indian nodded. "I will give you a horse."

And then Garcés knew that Palma was, indeed, in earnest, for he was giving of his most precious possessions.

In words adequate to the occasion he expressed thanks to the chief. The latter was watching his guest intently now. Presently, he broke the silence again, "You ride far, you Spaniards."

"Our king has sent us to make peace and to carry the good things we have to tell the people whom he loves and wants as friends."

The Indian nodded, but he said nothing.

And in that silence looking out over the world before him, Francisco Garcés seemed to hear the Angelus swinging out on the evening breeze. And he thought of Saint Francis on the island in Lake Trasimene, and of the words he had found for that spot, "This is a holy place." And the words so spoken of that little place in the old world so long ago seemed to him the fittest blessing for this vast place in the new. And he lifted the crucifix from his neck, and, holding it aloft, he blessed the world of the rivers, while the Indian looked on with inscrutable eyes.

Only when the friar had completed the blessing, did the chief break the silence, "And when you have made peace among the nations, you will come and make your camp here?"

The friar nodded and gave his hand to the Indian. And in that moment he knew that he had come into the fullness of his calling. For that high place was like a bridge over which men might pass from one end of the Indies to another, from the old world of Alta Pimería to the new world of Upper California. There the thrusts and darts of the ragged frontier of Spain might be firmly knit up in the king's great peace. And in that peace all the wandering children of the forests and the desert and the mountains and the shore might be gathered into one fold and made free of their heritage of immortal life. It was for this that he had come to the Indies. It was rash, he knew, for a man of thirty-two to feel so sure that he had his life's work in his hands. But in that moment and in that place he knew he had, if only he could find the grace to rise to the height of that great task.

$*$ II $*$

THE TWO KINGS

I

THE light of that vision stayed with Francisco Garcés through all the laborious weeks that followed down to the very tidewater of the Colorado, and then back up the great river to its meeting with the Gila, and across the sands to Bac. But the actual realization of that dream seemed a very remote possibility, as he took up again the routine of his life at the mission of San Xavier. Indeed, the day after his return when he had seen his long-suffering substitute off on the way to his own post, he made up his mind that that vision must be put away as a dangerous distraction from the plain obligations of the work already in hand.

But whether it was chance or his own good nature, or some mysterious conspiracy between the two, this regretful good resolution of Father Garcés was not destined to last very long. For early the next morning he awoke to hear that some Spaniards had been discovered camping just beyond the hill to the east of the settlement. And when he came out of the church after Mass, he met the party riding into the plaza in front of him.

The man spurring his horse ahead of the rest was a complete stranger to Garcés, and for a moment he wondered. But something in the keen look of the rider thrust forward on his horse's neck stirred the friar, for all his good resolves of the night before, and a wild hope shot up through all the illusions of reformation.

"Father Garcés?" asked the rider, lifting his plumed hat, and the friar knew it was Captain Anza.

It was three years ago that the famous frontiersman and soldier had first sent word to Garcés that any information he could gather in his missionary journeys would be warmly welcome for the explorations which Anza hoped himself to make some day. It was with a good deal of diffidence that the friar had sent his first brief, ill-scrawled report to the captain at his frontier presidio of Tubac, but he had received so warm and understanding an answer, that ever since he had sent Anza notes on all of his trips. Indeed, one of the consolations which the by no means literary-minded friar had found in the making of the inevitable reports on his travels for his superiors at Querétaro had been the supplementary reports which he always sent to the captain, for in his letters to Anza, Garcés could retail the moments that make the excitement of the explorer's life at more leisure, certain that he would not have to explain or rationalize the irrelevancies of curiosity.

Now the captain was hardly off his horse before he was asking about his friend's trip to the rivers.

He let the friar tell his story in his own way and in his own time. And as he sat there serenely puffing away at cigarette after cigarette, with the steady bright eyes leaning out of his long, keen face, the friar lived again every step of the journey. And as he did so, his enthusiasm kindled, and he told Anza what he would not have dreamed of telling Font, of the great, invisible network of trade and visit and foray and hunt that bound together the world of the Indians, and how that network might be used to bring them the good tidings of the Gospel that would make civilized men of these loved savages.

Garcés knew well that no man's mind quite keeps step with another's, because each is moving in a world of memory and perception and yearning and purpose very different from any other's. So now he was quite aware as he talked that what he saw as a Franciscan friar, Captain Anza saw as a soldier and a servant of the king. And yet he knew that in the soldier burned a flame of enthusiasm and high purpose akin to his own, and in that realization his own enthusiasm expanded.

It was well into the afternoon before the friar had completed the recital of the journey which he had covered very well in an evening's talk with Font. He apologized to his guest for having given no thought to his refreshment in his absorption in the telling of his own story. But Anza brushed aside his apology with the reminder that he was an old campaigner, quite content to forget his stomach for a day when the campaign was going so well. Even when the friar went to the door to call the boy dozing in the cooking shed, he began to ask questions on the journey.

Anza wanted to know about possible day's marches, water supply, chances for forage for horses, and many other matters that the friar travelling alone or with an Indian or two had never even noticed. But the whole journey was so vividly in his mind's eye that he found, often to his surprise, that with a little concentration on the neglected area he could fish up the detail which the captain wanted. And gradually the friar became aware that the captain had a very serious and immediate motive for his inquiries. Presently he admitted as much.

"Have you ever heard of my father?" he began.

The Franciscan hesitated. Like so many men with an eye for the dramatic whole or the clue to the whole, he had no gift for the isolated detail. What did not find meaning in the already existent context of his speculation or his inquiry, found no ready place in his memory. One thing he did remember, however. Captain Anza was a native of this frontier world of war and exploration and precarious settlement. His father had been a soldier here before him, and he had lost his life in the struggle with the Indians.

He looked at the captain with compassion, but the latter smiled.

"It's a long time ago, and he died as a soldier would like to die," he said. "But there was one thing he always wanted to do, that I have often thought I should like to do for him. It is the kind of thing that if a man could not do it himself, he would like to think of his son doing after him."

He paused with a sudden access of delicacy that made the friar smile in his turn, and he nodded his reassurance.

"What I mean," said Anza, watching the smoke curl up from his pipe, "is that he felt sure that it would be possible to go from these northern presidios to California. The Jesuits had something of the same idea, you know, but what my father wanted to do was to open up a permanent trail that could be widened and secured and held. He had even begun to make plans for it when that extraordinary silver discovery was made at Arizonac in his territory, and then he had his hands full with white devils of all sorts. And then when that was in hand, those red devils of Apaches took to the warpath, and you know the rest. That is the trouble with being the commander of one of these presidios. You just get things in hand and think you are really going to get at something that will be of some permanent good, and everything blows up under you."

He sighed and turned his attention to rolling another cigarette.

"I fancy that is true of most men's lives," said the friar gently.

But Anza was clearly looking at something else. "I want to do what my father wanted to do, and I think I have a better chance to do it than he had."

"Things seem fairly quiet," said the friar encouragingly.

"Not that," Anza shook his head. "You never can tell. But I think there is a chance now that I might be commissioned to get an expedition together. Bucareli is a very different sort from his predecessors. An idea for him is something to do something about, not just talk. He isn't the first viceroy to think about the problem of holding on to California, with English adventurers and Russian fur-traders and the rest in the offing. But he's the first man to do something about it. But then you know all about it with those friars of yours there."

Garcés had not thought of it from that angle before. So he said slowly, "I have heard that it is difficult to get word there, let alone supplies. You never know whether the ships will get through, and even if one does, half the grain in the hold may have sprouted when they are able to land. And many of the friars who would like to go cannot face the thought of the voyage."

Anza's face lighted. "Then you think your superiors at Querétaro would let you go with me as a guide?"

It was characteristic of Francisco Garcés that he hesitated to answer that question, and characteristic of Juan Bautista de Anza that he slapped his modest friend's back and swore that he would go with him himself to Querétaro.

As it turned out, Anza's confidence in the force of this joint appeal was more than justified. For Captain Anza was a man to give authority confidence. He was at once modest and confident in his bearing; though still well under forty, he already had, even the absent-minded friar knew, a legend behind him. Had he not slain the great leader of the rebellious Pimas and Seris in single hand-to-hand combat? He was known, too, as a firm disciplinarian in the rough-and-tumble life of the frontier, and he was lay brother of their own college here at Querétaro. It was, the friars felt, a sound, manly piety which he showed as he knelt in their chapel long after Mass was finished. And this they felt, too, as he expounded his plan in the chapter room.

His large dark eyes flashed as he talked. "Once we have this way from Pimería Alta to Upper California, it will be like a bridge between Sonora and the Californian frontier. Then you can get men and goods at will from the old and established settlements to the new frontier. It will be new lands for his Majesty, and it will be new chances to sustain the missions, and new souls to convert." His appeal to the enthusiasm of the missionary was so frank and so ingenuous that Garcés could not help smiling. It was a golden vista he opened before them, and Garcés saw something of his enthusiasm kindle in the younger faces around him. But in some of the older faces he perceived, or fancied he did, a half-regretful, half-cautious reserve, the mark of the older man's suspension of judgment.

It was not long before Garcés began to guess a little of what was in their thoughts.

It was Father Procurator who gave him the first clue.

"But how are you going to hold this bridge of yours when you have once won it?" he asked with his familiar air of "show me the precise figures for what you are talking about."

Garcés saw Anza hesitate for a moment as if he were trying to guess the personality of the speaker before weighing his question. Obviously, something had made the soldier cautious. In the frontier world of Tubac the captain was the supreme civil authority, but here, doubtless, like a friar he had his superiors, and promises which could soon be reported to those superiors had best be given carefully. Even as he tried to probe his friend's hesitation, Garcés saw the answer very clearly.

"It is the Yumas who will keep that bridge for us," he put the flash of vision into words.

"The Yumas!" The scorn of Father Procurator rang through the recreation room. One or two of the younger brethren tittered.

"How many of them are Christians now?" asked one of the older brethren, as if trying to come halfway between the fantasy of the young man and the contempt of the old.

Garcés hesitated, and he felt the blood warm under his tanned skin. It was an old trick of his, this leaping from the hope of the present into the dream of the accomplished future, and he was shocked to catch himself at it again.

It was Anza's turn now to come to the help of his friend. He looked confidently at the friar, "That great captain of theirs, Palma, certainly sounded as if he would be glad to have instruction, didn't he?"

But honesty made the friar cautious. "He looks to me like a man who might be won. And," the memory of his river trip freshening in his mind, he added, "they are a friendly people, those Indians of the river."

There was no mistaking the dry snort from the front row where some of the older brethren sat leaning on their sticks, "Friendly!"

"All men, even Indians, are friendly to Fray Francisco Garcés," said the captain with a half-bantering, half-admiring look at his friend. There was a little flutter of friendly applause at this, and then Father Procurator was back at his statistics.

"But it will take missions, a chain of them," he plunged with a sharpening of growing outrage in his dry voice, "to hold this bridge, as you call it."

But the memory of the river was too strong now for Garcés, who again saw himself on the height below the meeting of the rivers looking out over all that shining river world. "One mission on the height there at Concepción—it is a great height just below where the rivers meet—would draw the Indians from all the river region." And then, as he faced the uncompromising scorn of the older man's experience, he added conciliatingly, "At least one would do for a beginning."

"A beginning! That is what they all say, and then there will be more. Where shall we find the men? We have trouble enough as it is. And then every one of these missions must be stocked. When I was in Mexico City last month, I talked with the bursar of the San Fernando friars. A pretty time they are having with those new California missions of theirs, and Serra is expected this month asking for more!"

But here Anza was on safe ground. "But don't you see, reverend father, the land route to California will save at least half that? That is what makes it all so expensive now."

"You may save it in California, young man, but you will spend it on the Colorado."

"I am sure the king will be gracious," said Anza with vague significance.

There was a sudden silence, of awe on the young faces, it seemed to Garcés, of something cooler, more reserved on the older. Before anybody could speak, the father guardian rose and looked around the room.

"I am sure," he began quietly, "we are all grateful to Captain Anza for so graciously sharing his plans with us for this"—he swallowed deliberately—"this very interesting project." All the gray figures that had risen to their feet when he began to speak waited expectantly, but he said no more. After a few low words to Anza, naming an hour in the morning in his cell, he retired, and the company broke up.

✳ Only Fray Francisco Garcés did not move from where he stood.

2

ONE of his friends of the novitiate came up and began to chaff him, "So, Fray Francisco, you will have your mission on the height above the river, and then you will stop all your gadding about the desert."

Garcés shook his head. "Father Procurator will not let me go—"

For a moment his friend stared at him. Then he shook his head, "You are stupider than I thought, Fray Francisco. Father Procurator will count his pesos. But do you think the council will forget for a moment that the most famous captain of the frontier has come to ask for you as the chaplain of his expedition? The captain is a cautious man, but he is an honorable man. That mission of yours will not be dependent on your savage friends' good humor. It will be as nice as a grant from the viceroy himself."

"You think they will let me try to win the Yumas?"

His friend slapped him on the back. "This is one time, my friend, when the followers of the two Kings see heaven down the same arroyo. It doesn't happen often, but this is it."

As it turned out, Fray Hilario proved right. Half an hour after the interview with Anza the father guardian summoned Garcés.

With overflowing heart Garcés faced his superior. The latter nodded to him curtly, and then he looked him up and down as if appraising his large, lean frame. Presently, he shook his head.

"He says he wants you for a chaplain, and that I can understand, for even if you are an enthusiast, you are no fool. But he says he wants you for a guide. Now I've not forgotten that when you were here, the only penance you ever did was when you got lost in those dirty little streets of the Indian quarter. And while I would be the last to deny that those trips of yours are a great credit to the college, I have always suspected that the truth of them was that you got lost and thought you were coming home when you were pushing out into space."

His eyes twinkled as he grumbled, and when the young man sank to his knees, he gave him his blessing with hearty good will.

"You as good as have your mission on the height," said Captain Anza, when Garcés emerged from the father guardian's cell. "Now for the viceroy!"

But it was not to prove so simple. That night brought a messenger from Tubac. The Apaches were on the warpath again. So far it had been only the horses of a few isolated rancherías that had fallen victims to their passion for fresh mounts and fresh meat, but there was no telling how far they might go if some effective measures were not taken promptly. The most effective the harassed frontier officials could think of was the report that Captain Anza was coming.

Anza looked his disappointment, but he had spent his life answering such calls as these. So he hesitated only for a moment, his strongly-beaked face hardening and his eyes for a moment dark with suppressed anger. Then he turned to the friar.

If it had been the Apaches that had fallen to his share, Garcés would not have hesitated for a moment. For he had yet to meet the Indian whom he could not sit down and talk with. But the viceroy and still more the viceroy's court was another matter. He tried to persuade the captain to let him go up and get acquainted with the Apaches on his own. Anza laughed in his face. And then the friar remembered how Anza's father had met his death. In that moment's hesitation Captain Anza took advantage of his friend to appeal to the father guardian.

So it was that Garcés found himself quite alone when he faced the viceroy in Mexico City. Although he had often at Bucareli's invitation sent him labored copies of the journal of his travels, the friar had never seen the man who held the supreme command in New Spain. So now he looked in surprise at the thin figure bent over his papers at the other side of a vast table covered with a magnificent rug. For some moments, the viceroy seemed unaware of his visitor. Then he lifted suddenly an odd, long face, and with a piercing look he nodded to the waiting friar.

"I am Fray Francisco Garcés from Bac," Garcés began awkwardly.

The effect was electric. Bucareli was on his feet and at his guest's side in a moment.

"Father Garcés! Why didn't you tell the secretary who you were?"

The odd face had lighted with a kind of dry enthusiasm that at first confused the friar. But so warm was the clasp of the thin hand and the crooked smile of the great man that Garcés found courage to murmur, "Your Excellency has so many."

The viceroy laughed, "Who month after month and year after year push out the boundaries of the Indies and send me the most enlightening accounts of the natives? And never ask a peso of me or, so far as I can make out, anybody else?"

The honest friar lifted up a hand in protest, "Your Excellency must not forget that I am a friar, and it is my calling."

The smile faded from the long face, and suddenly it looked very weary. Bucareli settled in his chair, and then he laughed a short, dry laugh, "Do you think there are so many in this house that labor in their calling without any thought of reward as that?"

Again, the old question came to the friar's mind. What credit could he claim for this thirst that sent him out, this curious magnetism of the road that pulled him on? It was nothing to take up the viceroy's time with, this muddy uncertainty within, nor could he have found words for it even if he had wanted to. So he took refuge in the conventionality: "Your Excellency must not give me credit I do not deserve. I serve both Kings as a good Christian should, but it is to the other King I look for my reward," he said as lightly as he could.

Bucareli smiled with a touch of whimsicality lifting the downdrawn corners of his mouth, "No man who has seen as much of courts as I will deny that that is wise of you. And as one who here at least for a little while is at the giving end, and that for a king who, though glorious, is not possessed of the means of a universe, I could wish all Christians were of your mind."

"It is easier for a friar," said the other tolerantly. He was surprised at the slight flush on the yellow cheeks of the viceroy. For a moment the veil in the shrewd eyes seemed to be drawn aside, and then Bucareli remembered the business in hand.

"This Captain Anza," he said, sitting back in his chair and putting his hands judiciously on the broad oak arms, "do you think he is the man to carry through this expedition of his?"

But before the friar could reply, he nodded, "I do, too. That is why I sent for him, and for you, too. For you have done a good deal of this already yourself."

Again, the friar hastened to correct too optimistic a report,

"No, your Excellency, I have not been able to go all the way, but I have seen the way men could go, and I am sure from the things that I have seen in the desert and have heard from the Indian tribes along the river, that men do go that way all the time."

The viceroy smiled at the sober denial. "You have done the hardest part of the job. And you have done it all alone. That is the worst."

But on this point the Franciscan was quite clear, and he had no difficulty finding his words now, for in some obscure way he knew that this was crucial. "Oh, no, your Excellency. It is always easier for one man to go alone. For there is no planning as there must be for a company, and one is not burdened with the anxiety for another."

Again, the viceroy yielded to an impulse of rueful amusement, "It is all right for a religious to be so reckless of himself, but I must think of ordinary sinners who have no reason to be in any such hurry to meet their Maker. I am a practical man, my Franciscan friend, and I must think of the safest way."

In his complete surprise the friar forgot the rank of the man he was talking to, "But it is always the safest way to go alone."

The long face sharpened. "Safe!"

"Safe!" Even to the speaker's ear it sounded like a resolute echo. And then the yearning to reach the mind before him, to penetrate into its veiled fastnesses, seized him. "Don't you see, your Excellency. When you go alone, without any arms or any way of doing them harm, then even the remotest and the most savage of tribes are perfectly secure. There is nothing to disturb them, and they can look you over without any alarm, and presently you can tell them why it is you have come."

The viceroy laughed. "I can see that they feel safe, but I don't see why you feel safe."

"But don't you see? Men are dangerous only when they are frightened. If you don't frighten them, they will not hurt you."

The viceroy had sobered. For several seconds he sat there perfectly still, his eyes fixed in fascination on his visitor's face. Then the corners of his mouth relaxed a little, and he looked up quizzically at his visitor. "I take it that what you would like to do is to go look for that way all alone."

For a moment Garcés' heart leaped, and then he saw the face of Anza when he received the message calling him back to the border.

"No," he said firmly, "it is the captain's project. It is the thing he wants to do for his Majesty the King. It is a way to do service to both Kings."

"And yet if you could choose?" teased the viceroy.

"I have a double duty," said Garcés thoughtfully, "and so has the captain."

"Does he think of that?" probed the viceroy, curiously.

Garcés was puzzled as to what the other man was driving at. He felt the presence of a line of thought beyond his own range, and yet he could not chart it.

"How will Captain Anza think of the Indians? Does he share your confidence?"

Garcés smiled in his relief at having at last come near his companion's thought. "He knows that his first responsibility to the Indians is to do all he can for their conversion. He will not only help our brethren in their work, but he will do everything in his power to see that his men do not in any way obstruct it."

Again, that curious look, half of cynicism, half of wistfulness came to the thin lips and the slightly narrowed eyes. "Ah, my missionary friend, that is the hardest of all, isn't it? To make Christians behave like Christians, that is something harder than making heathen into Christians, isn't it?"

The hungry and inscrutable face of the Yuma chief came to Garcés' mind, and the old wonder as to just how he should reach the mind behind that face. He looked doubtfully at the viceroy, wondering how he should begin to explain that unknown land behind the eyes of a man whose language one cannot yet understand, whose life one has only caught glimpses of in the torch-lit gleams of a sleepy night.

The viceroy laughed. "Go ahead then, and win your river people, and your desert people, and make that frontier fast. And then come back here to Mexico City, and I'll give you some real heathens and some real savages to convert." And he rose from his seat.

3

IT was a couple of weeks before the friar was able to overtake the busy captain at Altar. Several times he had thought of entrusting the precious viceregal commission to a messenger, but he remembered Anza's fear of the intrigues of some of the other frontier officials; so he kept on, sometimes finding a mount in a party of soldiers or traders going from one frontier post to another, sometimes picking up a horse or a mule for a solitary ride of his own, sometimes in a village from which all the good horses had been taken by the raiding Apaches or the king's service, setting out on his own sandaled feet.

But when at last he saw the face of Anza, he forgot his own fatigue. For the captain's large eyes had the wooden, fixed look of weeks of overstrain, and his usually fine beard looked as draggled and unkempt as his long dark hair. Indeed, for the first time Garcés was aware of a little dusting of white at the temples. But when Anza caught sight of the friar in the doorway, he seemed to leap into fresh life, and he embraced him and led him up to the wide fireplace, in which a fine blaze of hard-grained mesquite roots seemed to leap out at the frozen traveler.

The cavern of the fireplace was crowded with half a dozen men, three or four soldiers and a couple of Indians. Without a word they all moved away as Anza thrust out his arms in a command for room. But when he caught sight of the seal on the letter which the friar now handed to him, the captain waved it around his head and called to the whole company to come near. Then slowly he read the long-hoped-for decree for his expedition. When he had finished, there was a cheer from the company, but the captain soberly turned to the friar, "It is your doing, my friend. I do not know how I shall thank you."

Grave as Anza looked at this fulfilment of his old dream, his fatigue seemed completely to have fallen away from him, and his eyes were shining in the firelight.

With his usual high spirits he settled his guest by the fire and produced a bottle of raw country brandy. Then he called the friar's attention to the Indians over by the door, so completely pushed into the shadows that it was impossible to tell whether they were asleep or awake, "One of those is a run-away from the new missions in Upper California."

"Are you sure?"

Something of his usual easy confidence had returned to Anza's face as he reassured the friar, "There's no doubt of that. Palma had satisfied himself before he brought him in."

"Palma? Is he?" Garcés looked over at the two Indians.

"No, I tried to get him to wait to see you, but he said he was needed back on his river." A grim smile played for a moment on Anza's red lips. "I suppose those Indians cofots, or whatever they call them, have their nuisances behind their backs like the rest of us."

"What did you think of Palma?"

For a moment Anza hesitated. Then he lowered his voice, "I am not entirely sure. I think," with emphasis on the last word, "I think," he repeated, "that he is all right. But you know as well as I do how hard it is to be sure with these people. At first, it seemed quite simple. He brought the runaway in to curry a little cheap favor with us. But when a couple of days had gone by, it was not so easy to tell. It seemed as if he were looking us over. And I couldn't be sure what he thought of us. Then he pulled out." A little apologetically, he added, "I wanted you to talk to him, but I didn't think it would do to use any force."

"Quite right. I doubt if it would have done any good with him. He's the man on the hill I told you about."

Anza whistled softly. "That one. He might be pretty important."

Garcés agreed a little dryly. But he did not find himself any farther along in his wrestling with the wonder of that encounter. And now the fugitive!

"How did the runaway get here? Will he tell?"

Anza s face lighted, and then it sobered. "I think he's telling all he knows, but it is not so much as you'd think. And some of it sounds—well, not encouraging."

"But he's here," said the friar stoutly.

"Yes, but you see there were three of them started out, his wife and some relative of his, and he's the only one of them to get through. They got lost in the sand dunes between California and us."

"It was not the worst season of the year, either," said Garcés thoughtfully.

But Anza shook his head. "Palma is satisfied that he is telling the truth, and if Palma is to be trusted, that is better than we could do for ourselves."

"How much does he know about the way he's come?"

"That's the trouble," the captain sighed. "Apparently, he didn't take any of those trails that you think the Indians use for trade. He says he doesn't know anything about them, and that seems likely. He told the Yumas that the fathers had brought him from his country up to the mission between the mountains and the sea."

"That's possible. Serra said they did take a few natives from Lower California to help them get a start with the Upper California tribes. The latter are pretty primitive, they all say, much behind the people of the rivers."

Anza smiled. "Wait till you see them. You'll probably have some wonderful tales of their potentialities."

Garcés laughed, for by now he was quite used to the teasing to which his enthusiasm for the Indians had exposed him in camp and convent alike. "Still he would have tried to inquire his way."

"You forget he left in a hurry, probably pretty upset at that."

"What's his story there?"

Anza shrugged his shoulders. "What you would expect. In fact, he has two stories. You can take your pick. He told Palma, I gather, that the Spanish soldiers had been abusing the native women. Apparently, he had made some sort of protest, or perhaps more. For he told me that he was afraid the missionaries would order him to be beaten."

"Perhaps both are true," suggested Garcés. "We don't know what measures he took, and I understand from some things I heard in Mexico City that there have been difficulties between missionary and military authority. Under those circumstances I can see where in a muddled case the missionary might have consented to making an example of an acknowledged troublemaker, perhaps, alas, without looking into it fully enough, perhaps after looking into it."

"I am glad you acknowledge that possibility," said the soldier dryly. "At any rate, you can talk to him in the morning and see for yourself. He must be either a very rash or a very proud man who would risk that desert rather than a beating. I couldn't decide which, myself. But that isn't what I'm really interested in. What I want to know is whether we can count on him as a guide beyond where you have been."

But when he talked to the Indian himself in the morning, Garcés was not any surer than Anza. There was no question of the hardships which the man had been through. The evidences of them were apparent still in spite of the good food which the Yumas had given him. And, in what was normally an impassive face, there was a tension of anxiety for all the superficial confidence. The Franciscan became aware of it when in one of his questions he flicked what was obviously a raw spot. They had reached the end of Sebastián's Spanish, and the Yuma who had been left with the captive by Palma had translated the friar's question. The question itself had been harmless enough. Garcés had asked him if he was quite willing to go back to the California missions with Captain Anza. He was puzzled that the Indian had not understood the question in Spanish, for it seemed to him to involve no obscure words or involved turns of expression. But he was too familiar himself with the difficulties of communication in any imperfectly mastered language not to realize that it is often the simplest question that is hardest to follow.

When the question was finally made clear to Sebastián, he said that he was quite content to go with Captain Anza. The captain had promised that he would be free to come back with him if he chose, when he reached California, and Salvador Palma, for so he had christened the man who, he said, had saved his life, had asked him to guide the Spaniards of Captain Anza wherever he wished. Although the friar was curious as to the relative responsibility of Anza and Palma for the Indian's willingness, he judged it wise to push that line of inquiry no farther. Rather, he asked the California Indian if he were not afraid of the way on which he had so nearly lost his life. Again, that look of vigilance came over the man's dark face, but he answered soberly that with the captain and his company he did not think he had anything to fear. Quite clearly, Sebastián had no adequate notion of the problems of moving a company of men over dangerous country.

Then the friar took up the immediate business in hand, the road to the coast. He was encouraged to find that the fugitive had a very good notion of the way over the mountains of which the friar had already heard on his Colorado trip. But when Garcés mentioned the intervening desert, the Indian became vague and, again, the watchful friar was conscious of a tightening of tension in the gaunt face before him.

"I should like to know what that man dreams of at night," said Garcés to himself. But though he approached the matter from several angles, he could get nothing definite out of the Indian. There were many things Garcés was curious about, but they would have to wait. All that could be done by direct questioning had for the present at least been done.

Anza seemed relieved when the friar reported that in his judgment the Indian fugitive could be trusted to take care of everything but the desert.

But when Garcés suggested that it was consideration of the Yuma chief, Palma, that gave them their surest ground for relying on the fidelity of the fugitive, Anza smiled. "You have that Indian on the brain, I see. Well, I shall try to keep an open mind till I see him again."

4

THE care and extent of the captain's preparations for the expedition were a source of amazement to the casual-minded friar. And yet all his meticulous planning proved inadequate in the face of the event. For just a fortnight before the time set for their departure, the Apaches without warning struck at Anza's own presidio of Tubac, where the main herd of horses for the expedition had been assembled, and drove off practically the entire lot. The soldiers who had charge of the horses reported the disaster with becoming concern for the captain's loss, but they added piously what a mercy of God it was that the Apaches had not murdered them all, as they had been known to do in former raids. The captain was a humane man, but he could hardly be blamed if for the moment he wondered at the dispositions of Providence which saved such a worthless lot of incompetents at the expense of the best mounts which he had been able to squeeze out of the by no means well-stocked frontier.

There was nothing to be done, therefore, but make the round of at least some of the frontier garrisons, picking the most promising mounts out of the half-starved herds of these desert posts. The best prospects were in the Altar Valley to the southwest. There was nothing for it, then, but to give up any hope of dodging the desert by a northern route and take the Altar Valley. Under the circumstances they would save time, and the earlier the start the better the chance of getting across the desert before the summer heat dried up every pothole of water and turned the sands to blazing coals.

All this Anza patiently explained to Garcés when the latter joined him at Tubac. And disappointed as the friar was at giving up the northern route, he saw how much harder the blow was to the preparations of the hard-working commander of the expedition. And so he sympathetically settled himself to listen to the captain's weary calculations of possible replacements.

Perhaps, he suggested, moved by the hollow look in the captain's eyes, the frontier commanders had not sent all their best horses at the first call. But Anza rejected that comfort as a reflection on his own discipline. He had asked for their best, and he felt sure that he had got their best.

However, both the captain and the friar forgot their misgivings when the expedition at last clattered out of the mean outskirts of Tubac and took the highway to the frontier. It was a brilliant winter morning that January day, with a light breeze at their backs, and the winter sun warm and friendly on their faces. The men sang lustily as they rode, and unconsciously, as they drank in the warm, brisk air, they leaned forward on their horses, and the whole company started off at a gallop. It took some minutes of shouting for the corporals to slow the company down to a pace that could be maintained for the day.

Even as he scolded, the captain smiled in his beard. Men and horses were in better fettle than he could have hoped for, and the adventure was off to as good a start as any man could ask.

"This is as much fun as an Apache raid without the danger," exclaimed one of the young men, as the friar rode for a moment by his side.

"I should not be too sure of that, my son," said one of the older men, shaking his head at such youthful exuberance.

The pack train was not so cheerful. Some of the mules had apparently been loaded pretty heavily. When the friar asked if they had not perhaps been overloaded, the head muleteer, Christóval Galindo, spat his disgust. "This would be nothing for a really first-class mule to carry, but look at the slats on that one there!"

The men in charge of the cattle were uneasy, too. Perhaps they would be able to feed them up a bit on some good grass ahead, but if these were to give any steaks to the missions in California, then his Reverence had better start saying some prayers. For the men in charge of the cattle were morally sure that their colleagues in the other garrisons had kept their best. As for the ranches which had been asked to make their contribution to the public interest, well, his Reverence knew what thieves they were to begin with.

Soon the road was beginning to twist and climb as it prepared to swing around the Tumacácori Range, and spontaneously the whole cavalcade slowed. With relief the priest slackened the rein on his horse's neck. He had worked late the night before hearing the confessions of the soldiers, and he had been up early to make the last preparations for the High Mass. Now he was tired and quite content to ride along in the warm sun, drowsing a little with the steady rhythm of his horse's motion.

And he was grateful when, having come out on the river between the Tumacácori Range, and the Santa Rita Mountains, the captain decided not to try to stretch the short day any farther but to make camp there on the other side of the ford. As the winter sun dropped behind the snow-capped mountains, the men set cheerfully about preparing their first camp supper, and the friar joined the captain to walk through the camp and see how the careful preparations had worked out. For there was still time to pick up anything needful from the mission and garrison towns along the well-travelled highway of the next ten days' journey to Caborca. When they had completed that inspection without finding any serious omissions, the captain piously thanked God and went into his tent, inviting the friar to come in with him for some warm porridge, for the night was likely to prove cold.

After the rush of the last few days, the next days seemed to Garcés almost a holiday. For once Mass had been said in the morning and the sacred vessels cleaned and put back into his saddlebags, there were only the small emergencies of the well-travelled way to claim his attention. It was colder now, and the men were little disposed to talk as they rode along, their shoulders pulled up into their broad-brimmed felt hats, their horses jogging along steadily in the hardened ruts of the roads. For the first time now, the friar had time to think of his companion.

It had been his idea that he should have a companion, someone to keep the records of the expedition properly, for Garcés hated the labors of composition, and he was quite aware that his small cramped handwriting made abominable reading for anybody else. Fray Juan Díaz he remembered from the chapter room and the recreation room of Querétaro as an active, intelligent man with a gift for putting things well in words, and so he had asked for his company. He was, Garcés knew, only a couple of years older than himself, but Díaz's rather severe, thoughtful face made him seem much older. Of his personal interests Garcés had little notion. Now he rode beside him to begin to find out what manner of man he had for companion.

Garcés had vaguely thought of Díaz as a scholar, but he was astonished to find what a thorough knowledge his companion had of the history of the country through which they were riding. This road from Tubac to Caborca was an old story. The earlier portion of it he had himself been over on his way to the Colorado, and so had several other members of the party on various errands of the frontier. He knew pretty nearly every Spanish settlement and ranch and Indian village on the way, and he had a fair notion of the movement of the seasons in the tall grasses along the streams, and the shrubs and bushes by the road, but for him the present preoccupations and the occasional dreams of the future had been enough. True, he had heard stories along the road and in camp and canteen at the end of the day's travel, but to his simple though lively imagination, there was little difference between near and far.

Not so, he soon found, to Fray Juan Díaz. He was modest enough about his researches, but to a sympathetic listener he soon revealed that he knew the history of the whole region with the same lively detail and interest with which Garcés himself knew the present Indian population. He had read all the standard accounts of the explorations of Father Kino and the other Jesuits who had begun the missionary enterprise in this land, and he had read each of them not as Garcés had, as a guidebook to an adventure of his own, but as a whole and complete experience in itself.

It astonished Garcés, this preoccupation with the past, almost as if the past were as vivid as the present and yet infinitely more appealing. And he who had always been fascinated by the way in which the shifting lights of the day and the seasons changed the aspect of the most familiar landscape listened entranced to the stories of his companion.

Here in the beautiful Arivaca valley the Pimas had run wild, burning the settlements and killing every living thing, human or animal. And here, too, the Spanish had come back, and had killed the Pimas by their tens and their hundreds. When the rain on the rising mountain slopes held them marooned for hours about their campfires of pinon wood and mesquite, he told the story of the discovery of the great silver nuggets to the east at Arizonac, which had sent the name of that remote spot over the world and had caused so much trouble to Captain Anza's father. And when the weather cleared, and they were able at last to make their way down the Altar valley, he had another endless round of stories to tell of Father Kino and his Jesuit colleagues.

Yet much as Garcés enjoyed all these stories of the past, the real delight of this first part of the journey, as they made their way southwest, from frontier garrison to mission post, was the coming into the little mission villages and finding standing in the open doorway of the church, ready to bless the travelers, old friends of the novitiate and the recreation room of the house at Querétaro. For, when the blessing had been given and the *Te Deum* sung before the high altar, the Franciscan brother would remove his vestments and take the captain and the two friars into his little house to sit down at a rough board table, and there over a festive cup of sour country wine the host would ask hungrily for news. At this point, Captain Anza, who had courteously accepted the first cup of wine, would excuse himself on the plea of some business at the guardhouse. And the three Franciscans would settle themselves comfortably to the gossip of a large and scattered family.

And then when the news had been duly chewed over and laughed over, the host would usually hear a knock at the door and open it to find that some of the good women of the village had been busy. It would be a chicken or some fresh beef or a baked fish and some newly-made tortillas on a straw tray with a gourd half full of chili. And presently the captain of the guard would send up a little present of aguardiente to help shut out the cold; so over the biggest feast which the missionary had seen in many a long day, he would regale his guests with all the trivia of his job. For this chance of counsel and, above all, sympathetic listening was one he would not have again for a long time.

So they came through the beautiful Altar Valley to Caborca. Hardly had they caught sight of the white walls of the town with the church and its twin towers rising above, before the whole settlement was streaming out to meet them. For this was the mission post of Fray Juan Díaz, and the entire town and the surrounding countryside had been waiting and watching. It was a very proud home-coming for Father Díaz, and he lost no time in taking up his role as host.

But the home-coming feast had hardly been eaten and the two guests settled to the pleasant rite of complimenting their host on his model mission, when a soldier arrived post-haste from Captain Anza at the guardhouse asking Father Garcés to be so good as to come as soon as possible.

The friar knew at once that something was wrong, for Anza who had excused himself from Díaz's hospitable board a scant half hour ago could hardly have tasted the local commander's aguardiente. But Garcés had not long to wonder, for the captain himself was standing outside the guardhouse, staring fixedly at a seeming stampede of mules and horsemen and muleteers.

When he caught sight of the friar, he flung his arms above his head and charged through the mêlée to grab the sleeve of the Franciscan's habit.

"Tell me," he cried hoarsely, waving his free arm, "did you ever see such a crawling bone-heap in your life? And this is what is supposed to take us to California!"

The Franciscan looked, and the words of encouragement faded on his lips. The desperate captain was right. There was in all the milling throng hardly a decent mount with a handbreadth of good flesh to spare on his ribs. As for the crossing of the desert—the friar stared at the captain in consternation.

"Yes," exploded Anza, "all the way it has been the same story: 'These are the best we have, but when you get to Caborca, you will be able to get better mounts and sturdier mules, for they have had rain at Caborca, and the grass is better there.' And here we are at Caborca, and this is what we get!"

The holiday was over. The hope that had kept Captain Anza from communicating his anxieties about his equipage to his company had gone, and he faced the beginning of the test of his journey.

Díaz, suspecting some difficulty, had followed Garcés at a tactful distance. Now he came up to the distracted captain and warmly invited him to make himself at home at the mission until he could send out into the neighboring ranches and haciendas for horses that, if no better-looking, would at least be hardier.

"How long would it take?" asked the captain with what for him was an unusual curtness.

The missionary thought. "In two weeks I could have enough to make the start sure."

The captain shook his head. "In two weeks we shall have lost any hope of either weather or water to get us through the desert."

As Díaz looked slightly incredulous, Anza appealed to Garcés, "You know the desert as well as any man. What do you say?"

He started to say, "I have been in the desert later," and then he remembered the shallow water holes, and the dried-up arroyos, and the thin grass turning gray in the dust. For a company of men and their beasts—sadly he shook his head.

"We start day after tomorrow," said the captain. And then he turned to the guard and the village officers, "Our souls be on your heads if you cannot find me better than these."

And with that he strode back into the guardhouse. There a few minutes later Garcés found him sitting with his half pint of aguardiente before him, still untouched.

5

TRUE to his resolution, Anza started off again two days later. Fray Juan Díaz sang a High Mass in the church of Caborca, and, as usual, the whole pueblo streamed out in fiesta spirit far beyond the white walls of the little town to see the party on its way into the great plain ahead. But once the last stragglers had been left behind, it was apparent that the holiday was over. The captain rode, grim and silent, at the head of the procession, and gradually his silence spread like a cloud over the rest of the company.

And as they grew quiet and stared ahead over the winter-gray road, the most careless faces sobered. For every man knew that this was the last of any civilized Spanish settlement he was going to see for many a long day. Immediately ahead lay the vast desolation of the Papaguería, and beyond—but there was no need of going further to look for trouble, for enough of that land was known to make even the most light-hearted think twice.

As Garcés pointed out to the morose and discouraged-looking leader, there was no uncertainty of the road to vex them here. The Pápagos had, for centuries perhaps, worn their light trail through its wastes, and Kino and Mange and the rest had long ago found their way from the pleasant valley of the Altar to the wild land of the Yumas. Not so long before Garcés himself had been over the trail, and only yesterday in the vast stretches of this ancient land, Palma had brought the Indian Sebastián to Anza at Altar. Clearly, that was not the cause of the captain's worry.

During the next couple of days Garcés was to discover with dramatic certainty the reason for the captain's anxiety. With complete confidence the friar had told Anza the day before they had planned to leave Caborca that it would be quite possible for them by starting early and riding a little past sunset to reach Arivaipa, where at this time of year there was bound to be plenty of water in the stream bed of El Coyote. The grim look on the captain's uncharacteristically stony features had not relaxed at this suggestion, and the friar had given up trying to cheer him, thinking that it was better to let his mood wear itself out. But they did not start at all the next day, for Christóval, the head muleteer, who had gone off to a neighboring camp for some shoes for the mules, had delayed his return. And the next day, what with the mules and one thing and another, they made a very late start.

Yet Garcés did not worry. The air was cool and brisk, and the warmth of the sun seemed to send fresh life coursing through the line of march. The sun was well on its way to the horizon when the friar first became aware of the fact that they had covered much less than half of the way to the river. At first he thought he must have forgotten the route; so he scanned the horizon all around for remembered landmarks. But the more he looked the surer he became of his first impression. Leaving Díaz, he took his way to the scouts at the head of the march.

"We'll be lucky if we reach the Arroyo El Coyote tomorrow," said the Pima interpreter, who had often been over the road. Garcés looked ahead to the captain. Even as the friar looked, the captain turned and rode back to him.

"We shall have to make camp where we can on the road tonight," he said briefly, as if now that he had faced the inevitable, he had found it not so strange.

The friar rode a little ahead to spy out the road. For half an hour he tried to remember where it was he had spent the night on his first return from the wilderness to Caborca. Then he recalled the little ravine to the left where he had found some springs running out over the rocks into a green stretch of deep grass. He waited until he had made sure of a little clump of hills to the west with some giant saguaros at the foot, and then he rode back to the captain.

But there was no relief in Anza's face when the friar made his suggestion.

Rather it was a smile of pity that for a moment broke the grimness of his face. "San Ildefonso? I remember it, when I was hunting through here once." The smile faded, but the captain made no move to urge the company toward this haven. It was getting colder now, and the short winter day was nearly over.

Vaguely uneasy, the friar rode back. He wondered if the captain were ill. And then just as the sun hung poised over the tops of the low hills to the west, Garcés caught sight of the almost invisible trail that turned aside from the main road into the ravine.

He was soon at the brink of the little ravine with just enough light from the setting sun falling into its depths to catch the sparkle of the springs. His horse, sniffing the water, neighed with delight, and behind him in the thickening shadows he heard another horse catch up the cry of anticipation. Then he plunged down the rocky slope, the stones rattling ahead of him to the bottom.

There were the remembered springs. As he knelt down to catch the cool gush at its source, he heard his horse gulping noisily below where the water spilled out on the sandy ground. It was a moment of pure content, the delight of the drink reenforced by the animal's noisy satisfaction. Suddenly, another horse neighed and another, and, behind, a mule's hoarse voice was suddenly raised.

Even as the friar sprang to his feet to run and point the way, a terrible thought came to him. As Anza had said in the beginning, he had always done his path-finding for one man or at most two or three. But now—he saw that his horse had left off drinking and was quickly cropping his way down the bottom of the ravine. For a moment he stood frozen in horror. For fast as the shadows were darkening, he could still make out enough to see how shallow was the pool where the spring ran out on the sand and how fast it washed away into the deep grass.

As he stood there, he heard a step behind him, and he knew without turning who it was.

"What did I tell you?" growled the deep voice of the captain. "How many horses do you think can drink there before they begin to pile up in the stampede?"

And then before the horror-stricken friar could begin to stammer out his apologies, the captain had turned his horse, and shouting, "See if you can find out how far this grass goes," he rode back to the main trail.

In a moment Garcés had caught and mounted his horse and was cantering briskly along the bottom of the ravine. There was an abundance of grass at least, but conscience-smitten as he was over his failure to grasp the captain's problem, he carefully measured with his horse's pace the extent of the pasturage.

When he returned to the main road, he found the captain, his old brisk self quite restored, shouting to the soldiers to keep their horses going down the road away from the teasing smell of the water.

"When you have tethered your horses safely, then come back here. Every man can go down to the spring once, and that must do for today." And then the captain rode along to ask the muleteers to hold their charges back until the men should have had their drink, and the weary horses could be turned to graze.

After supper on some roast meat fortunately brought from Caborca so that little salt would be needed to stir half-satiated thirst, a number of the soldiers went back to help the muleteers bring up the mules and the cattle by lantern light to nibble the already trampled grass. In the process a couple of the mules broke loose and rushed with loud roars to the water. When they had been recaptured, the friar held up the lantern to see what had become of the springs. They had completely vanished in a puddle of mud.

Even in the morning when the friar looked again, there was but a brackish trickle. Carefully, he swept out as much of the mud as he could in the little time he had while the mules were being loaded, in the hope that they might be flowing again when the next traveler should come by. The captain found him there and jeered good-naturedly at the seemingly futile labor. He himself had not lain down for sleep until all the animals had been taken care of, and that was long past midnight. But the early-morning rising found him miraculously fresh, and full of his wonted serenity and confidence.

Even when at noon the first scouts who had gone ahead returned to report that the Arroyo El Coyote at Arivaipa was quite empty of water, he only shrugged his shoulders. "That often happens at this time of year," he said and pushed west along the river.

Not until the sun was already getting perilously close to the mountain tops to the west did the scouts whom he had sent down the river to test the sand with sticks report that water was flowing into the holes. Then he set every man not needed to take care of the cattle to digging the little wells in the dry river bottom that were their one chance of water for that night. When finally there were enough wells flowing, he ordered that the thirst-maddened mules should be released to drink, while their keepers went out to look for grass.

So the battle went. Some days there was water and no pasturage; some days there was pasturage, thin and dry and ill-tasting, but still food for the packhorses and the herd, but no water. Sometimes there was water for neither man nor beast, and then the cattle were restless and the horses sluggish, and the brown faces of the men sharpened, and they said little or nothing through their cracked lips. On such occasions, Commander Anza rode at the head of the straggling line, his head held high in the blazing sun and his hand on the bridle, while the brown hide of his horse shone with sweat through the gray dust of the road.

And then there were the blessed oases in that long march of endurance, moments of cool green arrival and refreshment to be dreamed of in the long hot noons and the chill, weary nights. There were the springs of running water at Quitobac, fresh and abundant and seemingly endless in their bright rills. And there was the marsh at Sonoita with water for all and grass for all the herd as well as the horses on its green edges, cradled in the dark hills about it. Even the terrible story of the tortured missionary that haunted the ruined pile of the ancient mission church could not shadow that delightful memory of abundance of refreshment for man and beast.

But the most wonderful of all these oases came when they reached the rock tanks in the mountains beyond El Carrizal. The way to them had been hard enough. For what had at a distance appeared a fairly level plain between the mountains was presently discovered to be furrowed and ruddled with deep gashes of dry river beds and stony ravines. Down the sides of these the horses slipped and struggled, the falling pebbles often gashing their legs and flanks, and the riders bracing and tugging and perspiring under the blazing sun. And then as the hours passed, and in the softening light of the afternoon, the first shimmer of white rose ahead in the softening blue of the sky, the friar remembered that it would be well into the next day before even the best of their horses could reach the point where the dark rock of the mountain turns suddenly light, and the canyon opens to lead to the water.

That night the men had only the flat, brackish contents of their water bottles to drink with the inevitable beans, and little of that, for most of the available water had gone into the boiling of the beans. For the horses, there was neither water nor grass, only the cool of the evening turning the mountains white about them, and then mercifully washing out the hot dusty day in sleep. The next day the road grew steadily rockier and sandier until the dark rock ended, and the lighter rock of the Sierra Pinta came into sight. Then Captain Anza put spur to his horse, and with the two Indians and Garcés at his back, he hurried along to find the mouth of the canyon, through which, high up on the mountainside, he hoped to reach water.

Again the tired friar tried to remember the tank in the rocks. "The Aguaje de la Luna," Kino had called it, turning the labors of the night into poetry. To Garcés, coming hot and parched over the sand and the rocks, it had seemed a vast pool of endless coolness that autumn night now more than two years behind him. But for all these men and horses, and still more for the slow-moving cattle train coming up behind them now for two days at least without water—the captain had tethered his horse to a pinon tree and now he was scrambling up the rocks with the two Indians bounding lightly and sure-footedly at his side, their bare brown flanks gleaming wetly in the rosy sunlight. Presently, the captain and the friar were crawling up on hands as well as knees, clutching at the rocks above their heads to pull themselves up the steep slopes. When Garcés at last reached the deep cool darkness of the water, now reddening a little in the light of the setting sun, Anza was there ahead of him, holding on to the rim of the rock, and noisily catching his breath.

When he saw the friar, he shook his head. "There will be barely enough for the pack mules and the cattle train. The horses will have to go on." It was brutal to send them on again with the smell of the water in their nostrils, but this time tomorrow, if not later, the cattle would be coming up more dead than alive.

In a few minutes the captain had scrambled back to his horse and ridden out to the mouth of the canyon. And in a few minutes more he had sent the now wildly pawing horses on for a couple of miles to where they would be spared at least the teasing awareness of the nearness of the forbidden water. Presently, he was leading a company of volunteers armed with crowbars and picks up the rocks to work on the path for the watering of the cattle tomorrow. Then he hurried back to overtake the jaded company of horsemen, grimly forcing their restive animals away from the long-anticipated refreshment.

It was a weary and a dispirited company that gathered about its campfires that night. There was little water even for the porridge, and some of the hungriest slaked their hunger with parched corn. But most of the party lay there listening to the restless stamping and neighing of the horses until the fires died down, and they rolled into their blankets.

It was still a jaded company that started to work the next morning with the sunrise. Both men and animals were slow and cross, and the captain sent the Indians ahead to report on the state of the famous tanks beyond El Carrizal. The friar wondered why the captain should worry about these tanks, which were known never to run dry, especially so early in the season as this. But when later in the morning, the Indian guides came back to report that the tanks were so full that water was running steadily down from the higher rocks into the lower, the electric effect on the plodding company vindicated the captain's foresight. The whole expedition quickened and urged the horses forward until the latter caught the smell of the water, and then the only care of the horsemen was to hold the frenzied animals from stampeding.

There was water and to spare for many times the horses that crowded round the lowest of the rock tanks, pushing and scrambling over the heaps of horns and bones that marked the place where the Indians had so often lain in wait to kill the deer and the big-horned sheep that came to drink at the tanks. The men climbed higher to the second and third tanks and gazed blissfully up to the shining ribbon of water spilling down from the tanks above with a soft rustle like the wind through leaves.

But even as some of the men began to strip off their leather jackets to bathe in the miraculous flood, the captain was calling for volunteers to go back and help the pack train get its exhausted creatures to this haven. The worst, he said, was now over. They would get to the Colorado without any real difficulty. And with the cool sound of the falling water in his ears, the friar sat down in the shade of the overhanging rocks to begin to catch up on the neglected breviary. While the soldiers shouted and splashed water on each other, and the horses whinnied their pleasure, he repeated Isaiah's words, "In the wilderness shall waters break out, and streams in the desert."

6

So absorbed had the commander of the expedition and his Franciscan advisers become in the struggle with nature that they had no time to worry about anything but the day's quest for water and grass. True, one or two of the men whose only field experience had been the campaigns against the treacherous and resourceful Apaches had asked Father Garcés if they should not watch out for trouble from the Indians. But he had lost no time in reassuring them. After all, they were on a familiar trail, and this was the Papaguería. Everybody knew how gentle and harmless the Pápagos were.

But now they had come into the mountains beyond which flowed the Gila River. Indeed, as they paused before plunging into the pass that would take them through the Gila Range, they could see to the north the line of willows and cottonwoods that marked the course of the great river, for this region second only to the Colorado. As they started through an easy gap in the mountains, the captain sought out the two friars.

"We are leaving the Papaguería now," he said. "I think we should warn the men to be a little more on the look-out. Presently, we shall be in the land of the Yumas, and they are a very different race."

Garcés was prompt in his protest. "They are taller and more manly-looking, but I have found them friendly enough for anyone."

The captain smiled, "I think that will be true enough when you have your mission, Father Garcés, but you will admit at least that as yet we know very little about them. You know that I am not a man to take stranger and enemy for one, but when you do not know, it does no harm to be cautious."

As if in answer to the captain's warning, the sentries dragged a strange Indian into camp that night. Anza looked the man over, and with a curt nod sent his zealous soldiers back to their post. Then he gestured to the Indian to come up to the fire, for the night cold had settled heavily into their rock-rimmed world. The man squatted down and held his hands to the fire. A coyote howled off in the darkness of the mountainside, and a couple of the mules brayed in sudden fright. But the Indian warmed himself at leisure.

"Now," said the captain quietly, "what do you want?"

"Luís," replied the stranger, with a gesture to indicate that it was his name. At that, Garcés who had been saying his beads quietly to himself in the shelter of a small mesquite tree jumped up and came into the light of the fire. Seeing him, the Indian, also, sprang to his feet and ran up to seize the cord of the Franciscan's habit. He pointed to the medal at his own neck, saying over and over, "Jesús-Maria," and then he began to talk to the friar in his own tongue.

His Pápago was enough like San Xavier's Pima for Garcés to make out the gist of the Indian's explanation that he was Luís the Pápago, a Christian and a good friend of the Spaniards and of the Old Man. At the last, the missionary smiled and put his arm around the Indian's shoulder. "Captain, this is a friend of mine, one of the Indians of Sonóita, who has just come from the junction of the rivers."

"Good," said Anza, "ask him—" But the Indian was talking easily now and gesturing with mounting excitement. The friar's face sobered, as he listened, and the captain watched the un-understandable conversation with growing impatience. For the friar was looking clearly puzzled.

"He says," he held up his hand to stop for a moment the flow of Pápago—"that he has come to warn us. He says that we must go carefully. Palma and most of the other chiefs are friendly, but some of the Yumas living in villages down the river are planning to ambush the party and kill the men and take the horses and the pack train. He says a very powerful wizard, who is called Captain Feo, Chief Ugly-Face, is the leader."

Anza drew his knees up under his chin and looked over them at the friar as if trying to weigh what he had just heard.

"Ask him where that precious Palma is in all this," he said at last, and the rapid flow of Pápago started again.

Even before Garcés answered, the captain could see the relief on the friar's lean face. "He says Palma is all right. He has told them they are great fools, that surely the Spaniards will come and kill them all and burn their villages if they do this thing."

"Quite right," said the captain grimly. "That will be enough for tonight. Here," he kicked gently one of the soldiers, stretched out with his boots to the fire, "take this man and get him some food and keep an eye on him."

He waited till the Indian had gone to the other side of the fire where the bean pot still hung. Then, speaking in a low voice, he turned to his friend, "Well?"

"He can be trusted all right, but you know how gentle and quiet folk often are. They relish stories of plots and of violence they would never think of attempting themselves. He wouldn't have spoiled the story, certainly. But then, you notice, he says Palma is opposed."

"He'd better be. The Yumas may be tall for Indians, but these muskets of ours will give Captain Ugly-Face his answer."

The friar was worried. "We had better leave that end of it to Palma; he can take care of it better than we can."

"He had better for his own good," said the captain, calmly lying down to sleep. But though he affected to make light of the warning of Luís the Pápago, he lost no time the next morning in sending for the Indian and despatching him back to Palma.

"Tell him," said Anza slowly to the friar, "that the great king's captain bids him come out on the trail to meet him. If he wants to be counted a friend of the Spaniards, he will come at once. Tell him he can have a horse to go after Palma, and tell him that when he brings Palma back, he will have a reward more valuable than the horse. Have you that straight?"

There was much speculation among the men as to whether Luís the Pápago would take the heaven-sent chance of a good horse to strike out for himself. Garcés, on the strength of his general knowledge of the Pápagos, insisted he would not. Captain Anza was equally sure that he would not because of his knowledge of Palma. And for the first time he told his Franciscan friend that he had improved the occasion of Palma's bringing Sebastián to Altar to let him talk to some veterans of his Apache campaign. Those men could be depended on to give the visitor an adequate account of the vengeance which Spanish arms were capable of taking on the enemies of the king.

Whatever the reasons, both friends proved right. The next morning before the chill of dawn had yet worn off, the Indian Luís was seen riding up the trail with a party behind him. As they drew near, one of the party rode forward beside Luís, brandishing a smoldering firebrand. There was a startled shout from some of the advance guard of soldiers. "What does he plan to burn?" asked one of Anza's seasoned campaigners.

"The man is simply warming himself," explained the friar hastily.

The veteran spat in disgust, "He certainly needs to," for as he came near, it was seen that Luís' companion was stark naked on his saddleless mare.

There was a roar of laughter, and the captain hissed savagely for silence. But it was soon quite apparent that the leader was not Palma.

"Ask him what happened to his promise to bring Palma?" the captain sternly commanded Garcés.

The latter translated the question into more courteous terms, and Luís presented his companion, explaining that he was one of the Yuma headmen come to welcome them in the name of Palma. And then as the Yuma headman drew himself up in obvious readiness for a formal address, the friar signaled to Luís to translate.

This he did so slowly and deliberately that Garcés was able to convey the main sense of the address to the captain and the soldiers standing around, even as the man talked. There were a good many repetitions, some circumlocutions, some figures of speech of rather opaque significance, but the main drift was clear and heartening. Palma was away from home. Having been left in charge of the village by the cofot or chief, he, the headman, had sent messengers for him, and had come himself to welcome the Spaniards. He then proceeded to do so with certain general observations that brought a smile to Anza's lips—Palma was a good man, all the Yumas were good men, the Spaniards were good men, all good men should be friends. So the Yumas wanted the Spaniards to be their friends.

"Tell him," said the cautious commander, "that rumors of treachery have come to us."

This Luís the Pápago repeated, and the headman shook his head in vigorous denial. True, he admitted, there had been some bad men, who lived far away and who did not know the Spaniards, who had talked foolish things, but the great chief Palma had sent messengers to them, and now they would know they were very foolish. There was nothing to fear, he hastened to assure the Spaniards.

And none too soon, for at that moment, there came a cloud of gray dust around the bend of the road down which the Yumas had just come, and out of it tumbled and dashed a mob of naked Indians, yelling and cheering and scooping up handfuls of the dust of the trail and tossing it into the air. Garcés hastily shouted to his companions that this was an entirely friendly gesture of welcome.

It was impossible to mistake the attitude of these scores of laughing, completely naked men. For not one was anything like properly armed, all the bows and arrows in the company being carried loosely in the hand, obviously for appearance rather than any thought of use. And the way they began to embrace the Spaniards, and to feel their clothes, and to touch their carbines, and to rub their hands and their faces, testified to the prevailing mood of friendly curiosity. Indeed, it was with difficulty that the Spaniards, so encumbered by these demonstrative hosts, managed to push the remaining miles to the Gila River.

The day was passing, and Anza was wondering whether he should not broach the subject of their crossing the river to the Yuma headman and his companion when a fresh mob appeared, seeming to come from both sides of their company, this time not only men, but, also, women and children. It was quite clear that this was as far as the expedition could get for this day. So the captain directed his men to make their camp here.

But though they set to work unsaddling the pack mules and turning the cattle loose to graze, it was soon clear that little could be done, for the friendly savages in an exuberant holiday mood were everywhere and into everything, touching, poking, rubbing, laughing and commenting like a nursery of children suddenly released upon some promised presents. The captain had finally sought out the friar to see if he could make any suggestions for dealing with this friendly pest, when there suddenly fell a silence upon the whole scene.

Startled, Anza looked up to see still another body of Indians approaching, this time a small group of braves, all but one of whom fell back as they neared Anza. That one came forward with impressive assurance.

It was Palma himself. There was nothing in his dress or lack of dress to mark him off from his fellows, but there was no mistaking the serene confidence with which he carried himself nor the air of complete and majestic authority with which he gazed around on the throng of his followers. At his look, the Yumas, if anything, fell more silent, every eye hanging on his figure.

It was Anza himself who broke the spell, coming forward and taking Palma by the hand and formally greeting him as a welcome equal. He made the Yuma sit down beside him on his own blanket, and he bade one of his officers bring some of the jerked beef and the parched corn which they had carried in their saddlebags. These he offered to the Indian with all possible ceremony, and then he produced some of his best tobacco.

When justice had been done to these refreshments to the obvious satisfaction of the onlookers, the Indian arose and began an even more formal speech of welcome than his lieutenant had given earlier in the day. With a dignity of mien which the viceroy, receiving the grandees of the Indies, might have envied, he expressed his regret that he had been absent when the news of the arrival of the Spaniards came, but, as they saw, as soon as the messengers from his village had reached him, he had hurried back to welcome them. As they could see, too, he had brought his people with him to welcome the great captain, as he had promised to do when he had seen him at Altar. For the Yumas were men of good hearts who kept their word.

He had heard that rumors had come to the Spaniards of bad men who had wanted to make trouble for them on their journey. He wanted the Spaniards to know that they were not any people of his who had such bad thoughts, but people who lived down the river in other villages. Now even those men had other thoughts, for he had persuaded them that what men said they were thinking was very foolish, and they had told him they were not thinking any such thoughts. So there was nothing to worry about. And all he and his people wanted was to have the Spaniards for their good friends, as they would be good friends to the Spaniards.

The friars had listened to many a speech from ecclesiastical authority in the chapter-house, and the soldier had listened to many a speech in the field and in the council chamber. Alike they agreed that they had never heard better, so far as pithiness and dignity of delivery were concerned. And Indians and Spaniards alike listened with deep attention.

Finally, the Indian orator concluded with a very dignified appeal for understanding of his people. Most of them, he explained, had never seen the Spaniards before; so they were very curious about everything concerning them, their dress, their arms, their persons. He, therefore, asked their guests to be patient while they satisfied this curiosity. And then, noticing that the Spanish soldiers still stood with their arms ready for action, he told them that they might relax. They had no need of those arms; they were among friends.

Hastily, Anza rose to explain that the warlike posture of the Spanish troops was a matter of military discipline and not of suspicion. And he gave orders to his men to be patient with the pestering of their guests and to take every pains to give no offence.

While he was speaking, the astonished Díaz could no longer conceal his admiration from his colleague. "To think that a naked savage should have such parts!" he exclaimed.

But Garcés shook his head, "I have sat in many an Indian circle around the fire, and I have heard many 'a naked savage,' as you call him, speak with a justness of sense and an eloquence that would put many a councilor and doctor to shame. It is the gift of God after all," he added gently, looking at Anza to see how he would make reply to this remarkable address.

But this was the sort of occasion for which the Spanish captain had his own particular genius. For he summoned one of his subalterns and whispered instructions to him. Then as the young man disappeared inside the commander's tent, the only one which the distracted soldiers had as yet succeeded in pitching, he directed the Yuma interpreter and the Indian Sebastián to gather all the tribe in front of the tent.

Then, when he had them all more or less assembled with the old men and the chief warriors standing on either side of Palma, and the women in the back of the crowd, obviously trying to keep the children from slipping through the ranks to stare wide-eyed at the Spanish leader, Anza raised his hand for silence. The noisy and restless crowd subsided, as the captain turned back to the tent and took something from his aid's hands. Then he faced the Indians again and asked them if they recognized Palma as their great chief and their ruler. The heartiness of the response left no doubt in Anza's mind. So lifting up for them all to see what Garcés now recognized was an old campaign medal of Anza's bearing the likeness of his Majesty King Carlos III upon its face, the captain explained that he was confirming the position of Palma that all might know that Spaniards as well as Indians recognized his authority. This medal he was giving to Palma in token of the obedience which he owed to the great king of the Spanish by whose authority he now ruled. The medal was hanging on a red ribbon, and this he slipped around the proud Indian's neck.

And then while Palma held the medal in his hand to make out the likeness on it, Anza made his speech. Anza could not compete with the Yuma orator in either majesty of bearing or eloquence of speech, but he made up for both in the loftiness of the concepts which he now laid before the assembled multitude. To the sympathetic amusement of the friars the soldier began in the way of most lay preachers with an appeal to basic principles. God, the one true God, made the world and everything in it, the moon, the sun, and the stars. And he made the men in the world, all the men in the world, Indians and Spaniards alike. God meant that all these men should live in peace together. And that was why the great king of Spain was the lord and ruler of so many lands, that they might have peace and serve their God. And the king of Spain loved them and desired nothing but their happiness in this world and the next. And what he desired for the Spaniards, he desired for the Indians, too.

And all he asked in return was their love and their obedience. That was why the Spaniards had come so far through the desert to see the Yumas. They wanted all the peoples of the rivers to live in brotherhood and peace with each other even as the Spaniards lived.

As Anza spoke, it all seemed so clear and simple that Garcés listened fascinated, as he had so often when in the refectory, some of the younger brethren had read the short instructions in the little stories of Saint Francis. And then, when the captain had finished, Palma arose again to say that this was good talk, and talk that the Yumas would carry away in their hearts, and no man would take it from them. And then Palma proceeded to launch upon a great oration that lasted for an hour. His people listened in admiration, and the Spanish soldiers, still holding their arms in their hands, under Anza's cold look kept as quiet as their tired muscles would allow. But when Palma had finished, Díaz turned to his colleague in astonishment and exclaimed, "Why, that man is half converted already."

7

To the relief of the leaders of the expedition most of the Indians went home during the night. So when Father Garcés began Mass the next morning, it was only the members of the expedition who gathered around the improvised altar in the mists of the river morning. But as the Mass progressed, the mist began to rise, and the first rays of the sunlight came through. It was in one of these spasmodic clearings that the celebrant, turning to bless the kneeling congregation, caught sight of a tall, brown figure on the outskirts of the crowd.

He felt sure of the identity of that still figure, although it was not yet clear enough to make out the expression on the man's features. The next time he turned, to hold up the Host before the kneeling throng, he saw the face of Palma, the dark eyes very tense and alert in the quiet face. Then he took the chalice, and, as he pronounced the familiar words, for a second he looked at the Indian. He had not moved, but it seemed as if his eyes were boring into the friar's face, and when the friar had finished the Mass, and was washing his hands, the Indian came up to him.

"What do you think of the Spaniards' worship, Palma?" he asked with a smile of welcome.

But there was no smile on the grave face of the Indian. "It is good magic," he said, gravely.

Before Garcés could begin to correct the dangerous impression, the captain was at his side. For a moment Anza stopped for a formal greeting of his Indian host, and then he addressed the friar, "Yesterday was all very nice, but we are cutting it pretty fine on the summer heat, as it is. So I think we had better get started on the crossing of the rivers before the Indians arrive for another fiesta."

Garcés laughed. "In their present mood they are ready for a week of rejoicing over their new friends."

The captain looked speculatively at the Indian. "Ask him where there is a ford for the horses and the cattle. I take it that it is nowhere shallow enough for wading over. Indeed, I'm afraid we'll have to make rafts for the saddlebags and the packs. It looks pretty deep to me."

The friar with appropriate gestures translated the captain's questionings into Pima. The Yuma was puzzled at the words, but he clearly understood the gestures, and with signs of which the friar was not entirely certain he made a reply that seemed to suggest that he would have the baggage of the expedition carried over the river on the heads of his tallest braves.

When the interpreter arrived with Sebastián, both Indians confirmed Garcés' translation.

"That is better than I hoped for," said the captain with relief. "Tell him that the great king of Spain shall hear of this brotherly deed of the Yumas for his Spanish children."

That message the experienced friar translated into still more formal terms worthy of the generous offer of the Yuma chieftain, while Anza went to get the packing up of the camp under way. Then Palma vanished, too.

"Do you think he knows what he has undertaken?" asked Díaz.

"Do you think there is anything in this camp that Palma has not seen?" responded his brother Franciscan.

"There is nothing," said one of the muleteers, who happened to be passing and overheard the friar's question, "that those red devils haven't had their fingers into. I caught some of them trying to butcher a cow, and the captain's servant says that he found some of them tasting the captain's aguardiente. Luckily for us, they didn't seem to know what to make of the taste yet. They'll learn fast enough."

"I guess we are not moving on any too soon," said Díaz thoughtfully.

But Garcés shook his head, "These are the problems we cannot run away from, for long."

But he soon forgot his anxiety, for hardly had the expedition stuffed its bags and corded its boxes, and brought up the horses and mules, when Palma reappeared, accompanied by, it seemed, half his tribe, men and women both. The holiday mood of yesterday seemed to have revived with the morning, for they came racing and tumbling and laughing in the highest of spirits. And soon there was a very lively contest for the honor of carrying the captain's boxes and bags.

But an appeal from Garcés soon brought Palma into action. Like a general he marshalled his turbulent horde, and started them down the river, each man and woman with a single box or bag or pack settled firmly on his head. Indeed, Palma, with his right hand clutching the medal of the king, strode down the line, making a little oration of which the interpreter repeated enough to reassure the captain as to the seriousness with which the Indian leader, at least, took the service of the king, his master.

And though it was obviously impossible for the grave chief to sober his company, it was equally clear that he had impressed upon them the importance of care, for they carried their heavy burdens with easy steadiness in single file down the river bank.

And when they reached the ford, each readjusted his burden before stepping into the swiftly running waters of the Gila. Then, when all the portable luggage had gone over, they swam back across the river and, still smiling, came up to lead the horses and their riders and, last of all, the cattle across.

It was still only mid-afternoon when the crossing of the Gila was completed without the loss of a single cow or a single bag. Obviously, such a feat deserved some recognition. When the friar suggested to the captain that this was perhaps the moment to strike, while the iron was hot, the latter looked across to the still wider Colorado, which must be crossed on the morrow, and agreed.

So he sent a couple of soldiers into his tent to open his store of beads and tobacco, and he sent the friar to invite Palma to marshal his tribe for the reward which he wished to give them in the name of the great king, beads for the women and tobacco for the men.

It was growing late when the last of the speeches and the last of the presentations had been completed, and the whole company was tired and hungry. So the friar suggested to Palma that they had all done all that even the great king could ask that day, and that it was time that they all rested so that they might be ready for the king's service tomorrow. This Palma conveyed to his people with enthusiasm, but even though he was able to drive away the great mass of them toward their encampment, it was growing dark before the last of the Indian stragglers had gone off into the shadows.

"Do we have to go through all that again tomorrow?" asked the captain wearily, as he joined the two friars in front of his tent. Garcés hastened to assure him that he had already found a ford across the Colorado which could be crossed without too much difficulty on horseback.

It was characteristic of Anza that at once he realized that the implied grumble of his weary question might seem like ingratitude.

"Your Palma has, indeed, stood me in good stead today," he smiled at the friar.

But it was Garcés' turn now to be circumspect.

"I don't think I can take much credit for Palma—as yet," he added, wistfully.

"Ah, I shall not forget that mission of yours," said Anza penitently. "I have been thinking so much of my own particular job that I am afraid I have not shown much thought of our common job today. That mission is just as important to my work as it is to yours. Crossing these rivers with enemies up on those heights would be a very different matter."

The friar tried to remind himself that the captain was very tired, and busy enough with the morrow's plans, but his heart was beating too high within his breast not to take this chance.

"You remember that site for a mission that I told you about?"

"Yes, that height that would hold the river both above and below."

"It was a church that I saw there," protested the friar. His companion laughed in the growing darkness.

"And being a soldier, I saw a fortress, of course. But come, my friend, I am too much indebted to your methods tonight to argue with you as to which is the better. Indeed, I will grant you that if you can do it your way, it is the better. Anybody would," he added sadly.

"You have done a great thing, today," said the friar, gladly taking the chance to put into words the admiration that had been in his thoughts all day.

It was a very humble man at his side who responded, "That was the one thing on the whole journey that I could do nothing about. Thank God that He has given it to us. I promise you, my friend, I shall not forget it. We must not throw away the chance which He has given us to hold this bridge, as you call it."

The friar held his breath. Again, the captain pressed his friend's arm, "Tomorrow when we have crossed the river, we will go up and look at that height of yours, and you shall pick out the place for your mission."

The captain was as good as his word. On the morrow he broke camp, and his men packed all the camp gear on the backs of the long-suffering mules. And they carried their packs across the narrow ford which Palma had pointed out to Anza on the previous day. The soldiers rode across on their horses, and then followed the cattle, driven by the muleteers. And in the water and out, a seemingly endless company of Palma's people danced and ran and jostled and swam and dived, and by turns got in the way and helped. If anything, it was an even more festive scene than that of the day before, for the pack animals did the actual work, and more of the jubilant Indians were free to enjoy the occasion to the utmost.

When the crossing had been accomplished, Anza told the assembled Indians and Spaniards that this was the first time that his Majesty's arms had crossed the great river, and they must make some observance of so notable an occasion. Thereupon, he commanded the soldiers to draw up their ranks and to make ready to fire a salute with their muskets. In breathless silence the Indians watched all these preparations. Then Anza gave the command, and the salute rang out sharp and clear in the sunny air. At the first sound the Indians flung themselves to the ground in terror. But when they heard the cheer of the soldiers, and then their laughing, they arose to shout with excitement and to laugh in admiration.

And when Garcés looked at the tall figure of Palma, who alone had not fallen, and asked him how he liked it, he needed no translator to understand the Indian's now familiar words, "That is very good magic." And again Garcés was troubled as to the meaning which all these things might have in the mind of the man beside him. But he soon forgot his anxiety.

For now Anza turned to the two friars, "My work is done for this day; let us give a little thought to yours." And he took the lead in starting the ascent of the great crag through which the Colorado cut its channel two or three miles below its junction with the Gila. The western bank of the channel was even steeper than the eastern, towering like a great fortress above the river. They went slowly, stopping now and then to rest and look back over the fringe of willows and cottonwoods that gave so freshly green a look to the course of the river in this dry season.

At first, the three men talked of the day's triumph, of the new advance of the king's vast realm that had been made that day. Then as they came higher on the great height, and more of the world of the rivers opened up before them when they stopped to rest, they fell silent.

When they reached the top, it seemed to Garcés that even his memory of the wonderful panorama had been surpassed. For to the north they could see the range of mountains through which the Colorado flowed, and to the east of that the range through which the Gila cut its way. The bare rocks were reddened now with the glow from the sunset so that the whole scene seemed illuminated as at the opera. And below them the two rivers flowed in one broad stream with its green fringe waving a little now between the high banks. For the night wind had risen after the day's heat, and the glare of the river bottom faded imperceptibly into an opalescent softness of light, even as the jagged brightness of the high saffron-colored bluffs sank slowly into the blue of the distant plains.

"Again the devil took him up into a very high mountain, and showed him all the kingdoms of the world," said Anza softly. And then as the astonished friars said nothing, he hastened to explain, "I was thinking of myself and not of you, my friends."

And understanding the mind of the captain, Garcés smiled, "I suppose a church on a height is a bit of a yielding to temptation for a Franciscan." And then he added gently, "I thought mainly of the bell so that they would hear it up and down the rivers. But, of course, we'll have a little adobe church here. It won't have to be big to be seen quite a distance."

"And," said the captain gazing around him with approval, "there'll be room for a guardhouse, too. This will hold the bridge for us all right."

"Yes," said Garcés gently, "the Yumas will hold it for us."

And as they walked slowly down the craggy slope in the fading light of the sunset, it seemed to Garcés that he could almost hear the bell swinging in the light breeze over his head.

In the anxious days that followed, Garcés often had occasion to give thanks for that vision of the heights. For as it turned out, the great triumph of the Yuma meeting was followed by the severest test of the whole journey.

To the difficulties of the country itself was now added the problem of finding the road. The first days down the river were deceptive and did much to confirm the mood of triumph in which the company had left the land about the confluence of the Gila and the Colorado. The river bottom proved to be almost lushly green, indeed, in places such a thick tangle of undergrowth that the Spaniards would have been put to it to find their way if it had not been for their Indian guides.

But not all the way was jungle by any means. Much of the time they went through the spacious and fertile fields which Garcés had so much admired on his earlier visit. It was still relatively early in February; so there was only the stubble and the winter-blackened vines to show where the corn and the melons and the beans had grown, but the wheat was green and high.

And a shadow fell over Garcés' sunlit thoughts when he heard one soldier say to another, "This would not be a bad place to collect the king's pension when we have a good strong garrison up on the hill back there."

But he soon forgot his uneasiness, for the captain was at his side, looking so worried that the friar promptly forgot his own anxieties. The Yuma guides seemed all to be turning back. At first, Anza admitted, he had been pleased to see the end of the mob that had cluttered their progress for the last three days. But, apparently, it had never occurred to him that the two or three whom Palma had recommended as special guides would turn back, too. He tried every inducement from tobacco to the promises of horses when they should have crossed the desert safely, but in vain. All but two flatly declared that the people ahead were not good, and they would not meddle with them.

But that day the friar was able to relieve the captain's worries by promise of fresh guides from some of the people lower down the river. And that promise was redeemed even sooner than he thought possible, for that evening as they came into the village of the Cajuenches, several Indians detached themselves from the watching crowd and rushed forward to claim the Old Man as a friend. And the next morning they took the road in high spirits to show the way ahead.

But again there came a moment when the Indians would not even cross the arroyo along which they had been traveling, for to do so was to ask for trouble. In vain the friar appealed to their charity, and the captain to their love of horses. In vain both assured them that they had nothing to fear from any man when they went forward under the protection of Spanish muskets. Some of the soldiers standing by suggested that perhaps the muskets might be better used at the backs of the Indians. But Anza curtly reminded them that his orders had been final—he would stand for no force or abuse where the Indians were concerned, and the friar assured the crestfallen advisers that force would have won them nothing. The Indians would have escaped or misled them.

Then Garcés tried again, promising the Cajuenches that they would be honorably returned to their villages and that he himself would come to see them and visit them. But the most he could win even on the grounds of acknowledged friendship was that they would point out the way ahead. They showed Garcés a high peak which he had remembered from his former journey. Near that, they said, was fresh water. Beyond, the way would be easy. But it was a hard day's march to reach it. They would have to start early in the day to reach it before nightfall wiped out all signs of the trail.

There was nothing to do for it but to make camp there where more shallow wells could be dug in the river bed, and where there was thin grass for the animals. While the rest of the company took the packs from the mules and tethered the horses to a rare mesquite tree and worked on the wells, Garcés rode up to the rim of the arroyo to reconnoiter. Before him stretched a sea of sand, blanched almost white in the blazing sun of midday. As his eyes became a little accustomed to the shimmer of the heat waves, he could for a moment catch the endless roll of the sand dunes, shafted with prickly spikes of sagebrush and cactus. And then his head swam, and his eyes darkened, and when he looked again, the whole world was reeling in that dervish-dance of sand and heat.

He felt, even before he heard, the light rustle behind him, and he held his horse steady. Then he turned around to look. It was, as he thought, the fugitive Sebastián. Often during the last days he had found the Indian watching him, but always there had been other people whose demands for attention had been more immediately pressing. Now he greeted Sebastián briefly, and still gazing out over the sand dunes, he waited for him to speak.

"Captain Anza is a good man," the Indian began, halfway between a question and a statement.

The friar did not turn. "He is a very good man," he answered solemnly, thinking how amused the subject of this conversation would be to hear it.

"When he makes a promise, he will keep it." Again, the curiously suspended intonation.

"You may be sure that what he has promised he will do."

The Indian seemed to be satisfied. For several minutes the two gazed out over the almost blinding scene in complete silence. Then the Indian raised his arm and pointed to the distance. "Do you see those mountains over there?"

"Yes."

"Do you see the tall peak?"

"Yes, the one the Cajuenches pointed out?"

"Yes. And do you see the dark line that runs down it over toward the setting sun?" There was something like excitement in the voice of the Indian now, for all the tense composure of his face.

"Yes, I think I do."

Again, the Indian pointed, placing the shadow on the distant mountain wall by means of intervening landmarks and peaks to the east and the west. When he was satisfied that the friar saw what he saw, he went on, "There is a pass in the mountains there. One may go through to the coast."

The friar again tried to place the pass in the pattern of the mountains and the sand dunes. It fitted very well with his memory.

"But do you know the way from here to there?" he asked presently. It did not look so far away for all the warning of the Cajuenches. Sebastián seemed to shrink a little. "A man may die before he finds the water," he said briefly, and baking as was the heat where they stood, the friar could have sworn the Indian shivered. He seemed about to speak again, but at that moment one of the soldiers came up to say that the captain was looking for the friar, for he needed his counsel.

Garcés reported the Indian's conversation to Anza. The latter was delighted, for he had felt for some time that Sebastián was not telling all he knew about the way ahead. But when Anza sent for the Indian, he would not admit any more than he had told the friar. He was sure of the pass through the mountains, but as for the sand dunes between, he had lost his way. Once as the captain tried to press him a little, he looked toward the friar, and it seemed to the latter that it was a glance full of suspicion.

Yet the two friends reassured each other. After all, they had horses, and they could be across the desert in a fraction of the time it would take a man on foot, even an Indian. And the friar, recalling his earlier view of the scene, agreed that the captain was justified in his confidence. By evening both were sure, for the captain had ridden up to the edge of the rim, and there over in the direction of the peak which the Indians had pointed out, he had descried a faint column of smoke rising from the ground.

It was with confidence, therefore, that they made their start just after dawn the next day that they might have plenty of time for the long day's march. The heavy shadows of early morning lay still on the dunes and gave them a cool, gray look. But the horses' hoofs sank in the sand, and their progress was slower than they had expected. Still they felt optimistic. And this optimism turned to exultation when only a few miles on their way the advance guard came on a pool of water, shining in the now oblique rays of the mounting sun.

All hearts leaped at this unexpected piece of good fortune, but the rejoicing was brief, for the first taste revealed the water to be too salty for anything but rousing the still-slaked thirst of the journey's beginning. Another couple of miles, and they were among the dunes, the light trail taking them toiling up the slippery rise of the sand, only to have the horses' feet jabbed by the prickly edges of the half-hidden cactus and sagebrush as they plunged down the trough of the dune. The sun was high over their heads now, turning all the sand about them to burning coals. The mules were already picking their way as if their feet were sore, and the cattle were lagging.

Again came the cry of a well, but though every mouth was now dry, there was no answering shout of enthusiasm. Everyone was waiting for the first taste of the water. This well was deep; so it took several minutes to raise the first bucket. Even then it was only half full. However, the first taste was good, and the men flocked round. But the second try brought no more than the half bucket, and Anza gave up any thought of watering the animals.

Even so, when the bucket came to the friar, who stood back, it was a third full of sand, and he drank little. They christened it then and there "The Deep Well of Little Water."

It was high noon now, and the whole world seemed to have turned into blazing flints that burned the eyes and parched the lips. A light breeze blew up, and the sand whipped the bare face and hands with an infinitude of tiny knives. Worse still it blew the sand across the lightly-trodden trail until it was covered completely. They were struggling up another dune now, trying to keep between a thin fringe of half-buried sagebrush and creosote, for they still cherished the illusion that this marked the trail, but when they reached the top of the dune, the little clumps of gray-green scattered aimlessly and still more sparsely over the surface of the sand, and nothing was to be seen but the swell of other dunes, seemingly in an endless tumbling of dancing heat across to the far-off mountains.

The friar and the captain who were riding at the head of the company did not look at each other, but plunged down the slope of the dune into the trough. The wind was blowing harder now, and it seemed to their dazzled eyes that the mountains of sand among which they found themselves were beginning to move dangerously. At that moment Christóval, the head-muleteer, rode up to warn Anza that the mules were already floundering under the heavy packs.

It had always been the captain's way to ask the suggestions of his men. He did so now, and the bluff Christóval gave his opinion at once and firmly. There was no hope of getting all this baggage to the mountains. So he recommended that they send half the men and half of their equipment back to the Colorado. Seeing that the captain looked anxious, he added that they might send one of the friars back, too, to keep all in order.

There was no denying the impossibility of getting the mules with their present packs across the desert. Indeed, at that moment none of the three men talking in the wind there in the trough of the sand waves felt any confidence that even the horses would last the crossing. So they rode up the next dune and looked across at the mountains. In the thickening air they looked too very remote and even sinister. The dark shadow of Sebastián's pass was not to be seen, but the mountain peak which the Cajuenches had pointed out was still visible, though seemingly even farther away than it had been yesterday.

For almost the first time in all his travels the friar hesitated.

"No," he said finally, "we do not yet know what we shall find when we come into the mountains. We may need every man for the safety of the party."

At first Anza tried to tease his friend. What was this about his always going anywhere alone? Did he think this company of thirty-four men together had less courage than he?

But Garcés retorted that Anza himself had always said that a party was a different matter from one man. Look at their muskets. Did he think that a company of armed men had anything like the chance of a single unarmed man to be taken as a friend in the Indian world? Anza's face sobered. He hesitated, looking anxiously at the friar. Presently, he proposed a compromise, that half the packs he left under guard at the Deep Well of Little Water to be sent for when they reached the peak near which the Indians had promised water. Garcés agreed with alacrity. It would hold them up, but the lateness of the season would no longer worry them once they had passed the desert.

So they went back to the well, and, sweating in the now intense heat, they lightened the packs of the mules, tightened the girths so that the tired creatures might not be galled any more, and started off again. But the wind was blowing more sharply, and the horses sank deeper into the sand. As they looked ahead from the trough of the dunes, the sand towered threateningly above their heads, and when with seemingly endless pushing and pulling, they had attained the crest, the peak toward which they were straining seemed to have withdrawn even farther into the remote distance. Their eyes burned, and they were beginning to talk thickly through parched throats.

Even the meager refreshment of the Deep Well of Little Water began to assume mirage-like proportions.

Garcés scanned the burning horizon. The peak was still visible, and for once about the same distance it had seemed that morning. But even he knew that there was now no chance of reaching it that day. So slowly and deliberately he scanned the horizon to see if there were any other landmark he could recall. The first shadows of afternoon were beginning to slant across the desert, and in the distance, some differences of texture and color were beginning to appear in the hitherto white haze of sunbaked space. Off to the south was something that gave his heart a sudden joyous start. That bare peak he remembered from three years back, sharp and black against the evening sky, the Cerro Prieto. It was bare volcanic rock, but there was an Indian village there, of Cajuenches, called San Jacome, and there was water and heavy green grass, he remembered, for his horse. But it was the Indian village with its friendly welcome that came most hearteningly to his mind now.

In a few words he told the captain of his discovery. If they turned south to that peak, they would not only find immediate help, but they would circumvent the dunes. It would be a little longer, but with water and pasturage—

Things where they stood were so threatening that it was not difficult to persuade the captain. So they turned in the direction of the volcanic peak, encouraged by the relative nearness of an objective little more than ten miles away. And as the sun went lower in the sky, and the first foretaste of the evening's coolness blew upon them, they urged their stumbling mounts forward. But the nearer they came to the peak, the clearer it became that there was no sign of life about it.

For the first time a look of doubt came into the captain's face when he asked Garcés if he were quite sure. But the friar was confident. True, he admitted at once, he might be mistaken as to the angle from which he had approached the volcanic peak. He never denied that he had no sense of direction. But for the look of a place when he had once been there, he was not apt to be mistaken. So the captain, his face clearing, sent two parties, one to each side to find the village.

The sun had gone down, and the night had settled in, grim and black, when they returned without any news. Then Garcés asked to be allowed to look. Anza agreed but insisted that he must take two of the soldiers with him. So escorted, the friar went out and searched the lower slopes and the deep ravines at the base of the mountain, but no sign of life could be found. Then he thought he heard a distant halloo, and he remembered that the waiting party would not have made camp yet. With a great effort he tore himself from the search and rode back to the fire which Anza had already started against the night cold.

Half the party were asleep around the fire when, after midnight, he reached them. The captain took one look at his face in the firelight and kicked the sleeping man at his feet, and bade him wake the rest and set about making camp for the night.

So on the morrow, without food or drink for man or beast, for the men were too parched to think of food, they made their toilsome retreat. It was afternoon before they reached the Deep Well of Little Water, completely worn out. So sick at heart was the friar at the disaster that his puzzling mistake had caused that he made no effort to join the crowd around the well but went off with Anza to take stock of the condition of the animals. Christóval reported that five of the beeves had already died. The rest were sick from the scant herbage they had eaten on the way, and they were slobbering foully. The mules were worn out, and half of the horses were sick. The men were sitting in the sand, too dejected, half of them, to open their packs and find food. At last the captain and the friar looked at each other.

"There is nothing else to do. We will go back to the river, and when we have rested up, we'll start again."

And the friar in all his shame and his weariness was cheered, for the captain had said not a word of giving up their undertaking. And then Garcés realized that in all his anxiety Anza had not let a word of blame escape his lips for his friend's bungling.

8

ONE fear at least was taken from the burdened mind of the captain by this delay, and that was the fear of loss of time. For too many precious days had been lost in the futile going-out into the desert and turning-back when ten days later the company reached the river again at the place which they had already christened Santa Olaya. It was now the twenty-third of February, and any hope of circumventing the heat of the desert was gone. They must be prepared to face the worst.

So while the cattle were turned out to graze and the saddle animals were left to drink their fill from the river, and the men, overjoyed at reaching the green world of the Colorado again, plunged and swam in the cool bright waters, and dozed on the sandy margin under the shade of the willows, Anza took counsel with the friars and with the head muleteer.

"You cannot get the herd across the desert at this time of year," said Christóval, with finality. His dark face shone with perspiration, but it was lined with the worry of the last weeks. Horses, mules, and cattle had fallen by the way, and there had been no time or means to save even the flesh for food. The buzzards had swooped down to the feast, and the sole effort of the muleteers had been to save the living cattle from their greedy beaks.

"But surely," protested the captain, "the loads must be lighter if for nothing but the food we have already eaten."

"And the mules are weaker." And then the long pent-up wrath of the honest servant exploded, "A mule is a mule. He isn't a devil from hell, doing what no proper Christian could do!"

Díaz's thin face was pale with shock, but the captain laughed and slapped the broad back of Christóval with sympathy. And then as Garcés joined in the laugh, the rest of the company relaxed.

But the muleteer's wrath had at last spent itself, "I meant no offense, your Reverence," he mumbled. "It's just the creatures—"

"I know, my friend."

But before the friar could say more, the man in charge of the cattle had broken in indignantly, "Well, if you think that of tough creatures like mules, how about my cows?"

The acting cowherd was a thin, lanky man, and the spectacle of his somewhat whining complaint trying to match the robust indignation of the red-faced muleteer filled the onlookers with delight.

Politely, Díaz deplored the insubordination, but Anza shrugged his shoulders, "They are quite right. Both are good men and know their business." Then he turned to Garcés, who had been looking very thoughtful but saying nothing, "They will appreciate any of those cattle that we don't use at Monterey, even if their other supplies come through. They can get grain by sea, but any reinforcements for their herd will be doubly welcome."

But here Garcés felt no hesitation. "It is the opening of the way that is important. You can send back for the herd later. Once you have found a sure way, you can do anything."

The captain laughed, "I knew that would be your answer, my friend." The friar hesitated, for it was an old jest of the soldier's that the Franciscan could never grasp the importance of systematic supply. But now the added confidence which the friar had given the captain was unmistakable. "That settles it. We leave the cattle and all in the packs that we can spare behind, but where?"

Again, the friar was quite clear. "Palma."

He heard the snorts of some of the bystanders. Anza was amused. "It is always Palma, isn't it? I am beginning to suspect that you have enrolled him among the patrons of your order, my friend."

Christóval was still lingering on the outskirts of the little group. At the sound of Palma, he darted forward, "Leave my mules to those thieving savages! I'd as soon risk the buzzards." Obviously, spirits had risen from the water and the green ease of the river bank.

Garcés had been given the moment he needed to bring up his reserves. "Palma is ready to be friends. Give him something to do, show that you trust him, and you will have him for the ally you want." And he added with a slight sharpening of his voice, "Who else is there?"

"Well—" began the muleteer.

But Anza lifted his hand for silence. "Father Garcés is right. Palma is our nearest help. We'll send for him."

And the friar soon saw that the thing that had made him hesitate in his proposal, the time it would take to send up the river and bring the Yuma chief down, only commended the scheme the more to the men, who were tired and glad of the rest for the animals and themselves. He was still sick at the thought of his failure to guide the expedition to safety and still completely baffled as to what had gone wrong. Suddenly he saw in the necessary delay at the river a second chance.

While they waited for Palma, he would go down the river to visit some of the villages he had visited the year before and see if he could not find out something more about the way to the mountains. The captain listened soberly to the friar's plans. Then he teased him with his inability to stay put in any one place. But when he saw from the rueful face of the friar that his shaft had gone home, he sobered and agreed at once that the effort was worthwhile. Only he made the friar promise he would not do any other scouting of his own. There was no time for him to get lost, and they must have his help for the crossing of the desert. Four or five days at most!

It proved a pleasant enough trip down the river, with a warm welcome for the friar at encampment after encampment and village after village. But he soon had to admit that the Indians could tell him little that he did not already know, that the way to circumvent the sand dunes was to swing as far to the south as possible, and then work one's way to the peak in the mountain chain. There was little to encourage the prospective guide in the results of the expedition.

So when he rode into the camp at Santa Olaya on the promised day, he was much cheered to find Palma standing tall and immeasurably dignified by the chest which Anza was using for a table. Gravely he returned the friar's greeting and then turned again to the captain. The latter hastened to lay his plans before the friar for his approval. They were going to leave all the cattle and most of the mules with Palma. Christóval was going to stay with them. The captain raised his brows a little as he said this, and the friar explained to Palma that the muleteer was very much attached to his animals. But there was no need of worrying about Palma's sensitiveness here. He had understood readily enough that a man with such valuable property in his charge from the king would not want to let it out of his sight.

For the expedition itself they would keep the bulk of the men, leaving only a few trusty soldiers and muleteers to take care of the cattle, the worn-out saddle animals, and the gear, As for the packs, they would take only the food needed for a month on the strongest of the mules. And so with the horses.

"We shall all be Franciscan enough, I assure you," said the captain, and then with pardonable pride, he told the friar that he had that morning talked to his men, and they had sworn to keep on to California if they had to walk the rest of the way. No wonder he was in such high spirits for his second try at the desert. And still not a word of blame or reproach for the lost village that had crowned their disaster.

It was still a very chastened friar who said Mass for the success of the expedition, and as he knelt down to make a brief thanksgiving in front of his improvised altar, he solemnly resolved that if only the disaster of the delay could be repaired, never again would he be so careless.

On the second day out Garcés had reason to think his prayer had been heard. For just as they had just reached a point that he judged must be half-way between the river and the volcanic height of Cerro Prieto, they ran into some of the Indians whom he had traveled with on his earlier journey down the river. Now, as they crowded around him, he asked them the whereabouts of the village which they had visited together. They seemed surprised that he should ask, pointing with confidence in the direction of the volcanic peak, and explaining that it was only five or six miles away. Then, as if in an after-thought, they added that the water had failed, and the Indians who had lived there had moved on up into the mountains. But at the sight of the relief and the satisfaction which the friar could not conceal, they looked puzzled.

Triumphant, with some of the Indians whom he had persuaded to come along as guides, Garcés rode back into camp with his news. Anza smiled at the story of the village that had been moved, and then perceiving how serious the friar was in his relief, he said gravely, "I should trust you for a guide any day, Father Garcés, for this world or the next." And his smile deepened at the embarrassment of the friar.

And then as the happy friar fell silent, he asked with mock severity, "And have you brought me no news of water? Or are you turned historian with Father Díaz, thinking more of the bygone stories of the past than the thirsty present?"

But he was grave enough at the friar's report, and he went out at once to give orders that camp should be made for the night, and all should sleep early against the morrow's effort. For now they would try the desert again, and this time they must not turn back. But the soldiers laughed at his anxiety.

"Without that blasphemer of a Christóval and his mules we shall make it this time, captain," they jested. "It was his curses that for very shame turned back all Father Garcés' modest Franciscan saints."

"For my part," confessed another of the laughing soldiers. "I did not mind the curses. It was the whining of that cowherd about his infernal cows that made me sick." The captain laughed, too, and went back, reassured, to talk with Garcés and his Indian friends about possible distances and what they might look for on the morrow.

At the break of day they started out, making a cheerful clatter on the edge of the desert. Seen in the dark shadows of the early morning, the prospect was grim enough. True, there was a warm rose light on the distant mountains, especially on that mountain to which they had now turned their horses' heads, and which the men had already christened the Cerro del Imposible. But, nearer to, the earth was hard and dark-looking, with strange fantasies of cactus rising larger than life in every direction. Sometimes they rose like green bayonets stuck in low tufts of grass. Again, they stood like soldiers on guard with one sworded arm out-thrust for the attack. And yet again, they seemed to writhe and twist like huge serpents, enveloping some shadowy Laocoön. It was a nightmare world through which the party marched that first hour, and the songs which they had tried to raise at the start, died away.

But when the light flooded the plain, it turned all these fantasies of line and mass to a soft green, like a slightly faded version of the green on old bronze. And although the heat of the day was settling like a blanket on the stifling plain, they could see their way, and the terror of the sand dunes swaying above their heads was mercifully absent.

But for all their renewed hopefulness, the day proved hard enough, and the horses with their tongues hanging out, and the men with their parched lips were glad enough when the peak began unmistakably to draw nearer and nearer. The shadows of night were slanting across the rising mountains, and the first breeze of the evening was bringing a welcome coolness over the purpling plain at their back when the scouts who had ridden ahead reported a low opening into the mountains at their left. Presently, Garcés recognized the gap as the way to a lake of which the Indians had told him on his former visit.

They found the lake, but there was cracked laughter from swollen throats when the water proved salt. And again the friar's heart sank. But the Indians soon found a well of sweet water in the midst of the marsh by the salt lake, and there on a spit of dry sand, with the coarse marsh grass waving greenly about them, they made their camp. After the day, it looked and felt like an oasis. And even when the sweet water ran out before half the horses had been watered, the men refused to be discouraged, for was not the wind coming out of the mountains now with a cool sweetness of pine and cedar and the sure promise of water on the morrow?

That night Anza and Garcés smiled at each other over their campfire of shriveled mesquite roots. There was trouble enough ahead in the canyons and the ravines and on the rocky slopes of the mountains, but there was water there and food. The terror of the desert was conquered. But when the friar woke once in the night at the howling of a coyote in the mountains above them, he found the Indian Sebastián at his feet where he had been sleeping ever since they came near the sand dunes. The Indian was awake, and it seemed to the friar that in the cold moonlight he was shivering. So Garcés arose and threw fresh wood on the fire. And as he looked to the high wall of the mountains above their heads, and thought of all the wilderness ahead, he wondered if they would find there any mystery so difficult of penetration as the mind of the man lying down quietly again at his feet.

✳ **III** ✳

SAN GABRIEL ARCANGEL

I

IT was late afternoon, nearly three weeks after that triumph over the desert, that Garcés who had been riding ahead into the sunset, caught the sound of a bell. At first, he thought it must be the same trick of fancy that had taken possession of him on the height of Concepción. But the look of incredulous joy on the face of the captain, who now galloped up to his side, told him that this time his ears had not deceived him.

Presently, through the trunks of the live oaks and the sycamores that were so characteristic of this land, he caught sight of a brown stockade. And then there was a yell, and it seemed to the travelers that the whole of the pleasant valley had come alive with brown bodies rushing upon them. The bells were ringing furiously now, and the sound of musketry could be heard, and soon soldiers in their own uniforms were rushing toward them, shouting and cheering as they ran. The men at their backs were breaking their horses into a run now. So the captain and the friar rode on ahead through the mêlée up to the gate of the mission where Fray Antonio Paterna, the superior of San Gabriel, was waiting in shining vestments to greet them.

Paterna lifted his censer to bless them, but his hand shook so that he could scarcely control it, and his voice quavered as he repeated the words of the Latin blessing. Then, abandoning all pretense at the proprieties, he handed the censer to the Indian acolyte at his side, and, bursting into tears, flung his arms around the kneeling captain and the friars.

Then he held them off at arm's length as if to test the reliability of his sight. "Have you really come from Sonora?" he asked incredulously.

"Yes, thank God," replied Anza, and he wiped his eyes and embraced Father Paterna afresh.

Then they turned to face the oncoming rout in a scene of indescribable confusion. The soldiers of the mission had taken the muskets of Anza's company, and with musket in one hand and the free arm around a guest's neck, they were asking over and over, the superior's question, "Are you really from Sonora?" And over and over again, the guests would answer triumphantly, "It's only five hundred miles away!" And desert-brown faces that had seemed as incapable of emotion as the leather jackets of their owners, vanished in a tempest of joyous weeping.

The friar could hear the happy mob beating at the stillness of the dark little timber-and-reed chapel while he knelt before the altar to other thanksgiving for their happy arrival. Presently, it sank into the background of his consciousness like the sound of the surf beating on a rocky shore. He tried to thank the patrons of the expedition, the Blessed Trinity and Holy Mary, for their help. But his happy mind seemed to dissolve as he tried to lift his imagination to that height. So he begged the little man in his own gray habit to find the adequate words for the triumph of the moment.

Then he caught the sound of feet moving around him, and he looked up to see that the captain had vanished, and he was alone with the two San Gabriel Franciscans, the superior, Fray Antonio Paterna, and a very eager young brother, who had just finished lighting the candles on the altar, and whom Paterna called over to present to their guest, Fray Antonio Cruzado.

Of course, they wanted to show him the little chapel. The whitewash was still fresh on the mud walls, and the rafters in the ceiling had the raw look of freshly-hewn wood, and the tules of the roof stuck out here and there through the cracks. There was the fresh smell of newly-cut timber, too, everywhere in the little room. And it was all spotlessly clean, with fresh linen on the wooden altar, and some wild flowers set in gourds. The unexpected brightness of their hue reminded the Castilian friar of the wild flowers he had plucked as a boy to put on Our Lady's altar in the old church back at Morata del Conde. But here everything was new except for the crucifix over the altar, painted with soft colors and gilded around the edges. It was a very sad and moving Christ who gazed out of the old crucifix upon the freshly limed walls and the gray floor of neatly packed earth.

"The viceroy gave us that crucifix," said Father Paterna with great pride.

"But we planned the chapel ourselves," said young Cruzado, with even greater pride.

"You have done wonderfully in so short a time," said the guest with heart-felt admiration, and the face of the younger brother flushed with pleasure.

But the superior shook his head. "It is slow work with such primitive minds."

However, Cruzado had pulled his sleeve, "Father, I am sure they are hungry."

With hasty apologies, the superior went up to the altar and carefully extinguished the candles. Then he sought out the captain, now directing the unloading of the mules in an open space behind the mission building, and invited him to come with the friar into his house.

This, too, was a single room, opening off the church, quite as new and bare as the church but not so white or so tidy. Here Father Paterna offered the captain the only chair which the house afforded, a rough-hewn oaken chair with a rawhide seat. And to the friars he offered a couple of three-legged stools.

The young brother had disappeared, and now through the open door came a welcome smell of corn parching. But it was some time before the friar reappeared with an Indian bringing a steaming bowl of beans and a bowl of parched corn. These they set carefully on the table, and the hungry visitor saw the eyes of the superior open at sight of these delicacies. Then they all fell to.

When the two bowls were empty and the earthen plates were clean, again the Indian appeared, this time with a plate of greens with a little oil glistening on the top, and a small iron pot from which the sweet steam of chocolate was rising. The friar was still hungry, but he noticed that Anza was looking curiously at the greens; so he exclaimed upon their attractive appear-ance, and passed his plate.

The superior had not missed Anza's hesitation. "We live like the desert fathers here, I am afraid, and the herbs of the field are our meat."

"Of course," said the captain courteously, and he passed his plate, too.

Then came the chocolate, steaming still, but disappointingly thin and bitter in small clay bowls. The friar saw a very thoughtful look come into Anza's lean, worn face, and for the first time he realized what it was that had baffled him on seeing Father Paterna again. He had remembered him from a meeting in Mexico City as sleek and handsome. Now the man's face was haggard it was so thin, and the arm protruding from his worn habit was little more than bone. And the young friar was quite as thin, though there was a flush of youth still in the drawn face.

When the meal was finished, the two hosts settled themselves to ask questions about the trip, but Anza interrupted to ask if he might not get some tobacco. He still had some left from the supply he had brought for the journey. And Garcés rose to say that he would just take a look at the company to make sure that he was not needed.

He overtook the captain in the open square in front of the mission where a great fire had been built, and where the men had just settled themselves comfortably on the ground. All around, the Indians seemed to fill the space clear to the stockade walls of the mission.

The captain went on, but the friar lingered for a moment, sitting down inconspicuously behind a large storage basket. Then the conversation which the arrival of the captain had obviously interrupted lifted up its head again. And soon the whole campfire circle was listening to a debate between one of the soldiers of the mission who was maintaining that the sufferings of the journey by sea were beyond anything that the soldiers who had come over land could imagine, and one of Anza's company who was maintaining with friendly rivalry that no one who had not come across that desert could know what hardship was.

"But, man, the seasickness," cried the mission soldier. "The waves rise like mountains above the ship."

"You should see those sand dunes above your head ready to fall down and swallow you up," retorted the desert veteran.

"But in the desert, at least the ground is firm under your feet." There was an air of unanswerable triumph in this last that roused the friar's curiosity as to what answer the desert champion could make.

"Not when the wind comes and begins to hurl it in your face until you don't know whether it is the sand or your own teeth that you are spitting out."

"But on the ship, the whole world slides from under you, and your very stomach turns over, and your head swims, and you don't know which is the groaning of the ship and which your own. And everybody else is sick, rolling and retching in the dark belly of the ship, and the waves toss the ship like a walnut shell, and you roll into your sea chest, and you do not know which is blood and which is vomit. Then, my friend, you think your end has come, and you see St. Peter at his gate, but the priest, poor wretch, is as sick as you are."

At that juncture, the friar rose quietly to his feet and stole back to the little house where Anza and the friars were talking quietly of the journey. Now they were discussing the Yumas and the prospects of their conversion.

Father Paterna sighed. "Some of our boys are making real progress with Spanish, and one is learning a little Latin. But we are not attempting anything beyond the doctrine so far. They say it glibly enough, and they are learning some of the hymns. But as to what they make of it, I am not so sure."

"Father Serra, they said in Mexico City, thought they were beginning to understand a good deal," said Garcés gently.

"Father Serra—" began Father Paterna, and then he seemed to change his mind. "He is a saint, and he cannot believe that the sight of the holy mysteries of the faith will not carry their own conviction."

But Father Paterna must suddenly have noticed how weary his guests were, for he leaped to his feet. "Forgive me for so churlishly talking of our troubles when we should be celebrating your victory. And now you must get to bed if you are to celebrate it properly tomorrow."

And so he led them to another little room, of whitewashed mud with bare timbers for the roof and packed earth floor. Only this room had no furniture but three low bedsteads made of rawhide stretched on wooden frames with short legs dug into the earthen floor for firmness. And on each bed was a blanket rolled up against the wall.

"But where will you sleep?" asked the captain.

"In the best place of all, the church," said the father superior, "for there there is plenty of room to stretch."

Before the captain could protest, Paterna had opened the door of the room and was bidding them good night. Even as he was speaking, there came a sound like a low moan out of the dark. All in the little room stiffened. Now the moan rose a little, and then, as the wind veered, it grew louder and sharpened into a sound like keening. The guests looked at each other in the thin candlelight. But the father superior shook his head, "It is the Indian village outside the mission wall. They are wailing for someone dead."

He looked puzzled, and he turned to the younger friar, "Have you—" and then he seemed to recall something. "Didn't you tell me that the Indian Sebastián is with you? His wife's family are in this village, and you said she died in the dunes?"

"But—" began Fray Díaz.

The father superior sighed. "Yes, it is pagan, but there is nothing we can do tonight. Tomorrow I will tell Sebastián that we will say a Mass for the repose of her soul, but tonight, I hope it does not keep you from getting to sleep."

But they were too tired to do more than make the door fast as their host directed, and stretch out on their taut cots. As they turned and twisted, the rawhide creaked, and the new wood whispered, and overhead the wind rustled through the tules over the rafters. And then all was still except for the distant wailing, thin and ghostlike on the edge of the dark and the cold. Once late in the night Garcés awoke and listened, and still the sound came, thinner but if anything more eerie, as if grief itself had found a voice and were going down the night wind looking for that one poor lost soul bleaching out somewhere in those vast sand dunes.

The rejoicing of the victory lasted through the High Mass which Garcés celebrated the next morning in the little church of San Gabriel Arcangel, with the door thrown open so that the soldiers and the Indians kneeling on the ground outside might look in and listen to the singing. Fray Antonio Cruzado's Indian choir furnished the music, strong on the rhythm of the music, weak on the enunciation of the Latin words, Díaz observed, but unmistakably a great addition to the splendor of the rite. And the soldiers of the expedition discharged their muskets when the celebrant held up the Host, with such effect that half of the Indians flung themselves on their faces. The bell did its share, sweet and clear, and that of all the trappings of the occasion gave the most pleasure to Garcés. That and the sight of all the solemn dark faces in the bright spring sunshine outside the door. It was a glorious moment.

But it was not Anza's way to rest long in contemplation of the success won. There were problems still to be solved. And the first of these problems faced him at the conclusion of the Mass when Father Paterna invited the two priests and the commander of the expedition into his house for breakfast. For all that appeared on the table was a little heap of tortillas and a bowl of chocolate, quite as bitter and as thin as the night before.

As his guests fell hungrily upon the tortillas, the father superior, who was still playing with his first one, apologized for the smallness of the heap on the plate.

"You see," his embarrassment giving way to frankness at the friendly concern of his guests, "the supply ship has not come yet. And it is still a couple of months to our own harvest."

The commander's face grew grave. "It is I who should apologize to you, for we have an abundance of cattle and corn in our bags at the Colorado. But we had to leave them all except what we could carry on ten mules packed lightly. It was just enough to get here. We shall need help to get to Monterey."

So candid was the commander on the theme of his misfortune and his disappointment at not being able to bring the needed relief, that Father Paterna proceeded to confess his troubles. He and the soldiers of the guard were down to a ration of three tortillas a day with whatever supplement they could gather out of the fields themselves.

"As for us, our Indian boys bring us what they can, but we have been so busy teaching them to be neat and helpful about the church that we have not had time yet to teach them any cooking," and Father Paterna smiled at his young colleague. "I am afraid we are both of us better at the building than we are at housekeeping."

Díaz, whom his colleague had caught the night before using a leaf of the salad to brush some dirt off his plate, had the grace to blush, and Garcés, who had become accustomed to shutting his eyes and holding his breath at many a doubtful mess in his travels among the Indian villages, hastened to assure his host that he was doing very well.

Father Paterna smiled at the kindness, but he shook his head. "No, there is so much to do that we cannot do it all, and I am afraid our guests pay the price."

"But we are not the important thing for your work," said the captain with a smile. "It is your Indians. They are coming on very well with their singing."

"Ah," said Father Paterna, putting his hand on the shoulder of his younger brother, "it is Fray Antonio Cruzado who trains the choir. I think he has a real talent for teaching these savages music."

The younger friar's thin face lighted with frank pleasure, "That is the easiest thing to teach them. If I could keep them at it properly, we could do something with them, I am sure. But you see, we have had to let them go to their relatives in the mountains these last weeks, and they forget what they have learned."

"But I thought," said the captain, "that you kept them in the mission once they came so that they would not return to their pagan ways."

Cruzado looked embarrassed as if perhaps he had said something he had not meant to, but Paterna shook his head sadly, "That is the trouble with this delay of the ship. You see, we cannot give the Indians their rations of beans and maize here in the mission; so we have to let them go to their relatives up in the mountains."

For a minute they all sat silent in the little room. Then Father Paterna smiled ruefully, "This is a poor way to celebrate your coming with this tale of our troubles. And the more because now with your way open, we shall be able to get supplies so much faster. Let us rather see what we can do for your plans."

So saying, he rose and invited the captain and the friars to come out to the mission storehouse and see what help they could give them. But although the stores of the expedition had been put into the little building for safekeeping, it was clear that if Anza took everything in sight, he would not have enough to take even part of his company to Monterey.

"When do you think that ship of yours will get into San Diego?" asked the captain finally.

The superior of San Gabriel smiled grimly, "It is a month overdue now. And do not forget that the ship may be lost. That has happened before, you know."

"Then if I take your corn, and the ship does not come, what will you do?" asked the captain.

Suddenly the worried look vanished from Father Paterna's face. "God will provide, as He has before," he said simply.

Garcés caught the look of admiration on the captain's face, and he marvelled that he should not have at once understood the Franciscan's reasoning. It was his duty to plan and calculate and take pains so long as there was anything he could do about it, but when that point was passed, then God had taken it out of his hands. It seemed so obvious to Garcés that he was embarrassed even to begin to try to explain it to his friend.

But as it turned out, he did not need to, for there came a sudden rush of flying feet and of shouting to the door of the storehouse. A dozen Indians were trying to burst in with two Indian leaders who were shoving them back with their elbows while they tried to collect their breath.

"The ship!" cried the foremost at last, and the joyous cry was taken up by the wildly thrashing figures standing in the doorway.

An incredulous look broke on the lean face of Father Paterna as he went to the door, and, thrusting aside the Indians, he looked out as if he might see the ship in the little mission yard. Two of the soldiers, less fleet than the Indians, craned their necks over the whirling crowd in the doorway.

"It's true, father. Father Lasuén has brought the news. He's down the road coming up." And in a moment two Indians wearing traveling sandals came up, escorted by half a dozen more of the Indians of San Gabriel.

And then all eyes turned to the man now swinging through the gate of the mission. He was a little, compact figure of a man with a great dignity of presence, and a smiling, open face that seemed entirely at ease with the world. And what made this sunny composure the more remarkable was that this was no youth but a man in the prime of life. Moreover, his smiling face was as thin as the faces of his Indians, and the habit in which he strode forward so confidently was in rags, thick with the mud of the road.

When they had embraced each other, and the superior had offered him the one remaining tortilla on the table, he laughed a low, musical laugh, and in a soft yet warm voice, asked, "Are you sure it is not the last in the house, father? Somebody hungrier may come, you know. And I've looked at the ship at least."

"I can let you have that one," said the superior smiling. "And I'll have the chocolate pot put on, while we go into the church. We have cause of thanksgiving, with the captain here, and now the ship."

"Captain Anza," said the ragged friar with as courtly a bow as if he had been a grandee in the viceroy's presence, "you see how much I admire what I have heard of you. For I left the ship to come and look at you."

"But how did the news come so fast? Isn't—" the captain hesitated, for he had not yet learned the stations of the friars in California.

"I was at San Diego, I confess, to see if I could do some begging—you see it is the same story everywhere. Some of the Indians came back from the mountains with a tale of creatures seen in the passes that from the descriptions sounded like centaurs. Father Serra had sent us word of your coming; so we decided it must be your party."

"But weren't you tempted by the ship?" asked Garcés.

"Of course, but I had begun to suspect that I had stayed away from home as long as I should. So when I heard all this, I was sure. Now I want to know all about how you did it, and what we can do." Garcés saw the captain's eyes flash. Clearly, this stranger was a man after his own heart. Thin, travel-stained, one bony shoulder thrusting through the rags of his habit, he was yet all ready for the golden future.

When they had finished their thanksgiving and returned to the little house of the missionaries, Father Paterna turned to Garcés, "You were asking about the Indians. Here is the man who can tell you more of the Indians than anybody else, for not even Father Serra himself has more of their confidence."

Father Lasuén lifted up his ragged sleeves, and holding them aloft, he laughed, "I believe it is because in my nakedness I am getting more like them every day that they trust me. Indeed, good Fray Vicente Fuster at San Diego was for keeping me off the road because of the scandal I might cause." And even as he sat down on the bench by the table, the rent at the shoulder pulled, and the worn cloth split further down the thin brown arm. But the friar only laughed, and the company with him.

"I can see that you and our Father Garcés are kindred souls," said the captain.

"But I have two habits," protested Garcés, "both new," and then as Díaz began to laugh and wink at Anza, he amended hastily, "Well, almost new. And one you shall have," he added, turning to Sebastián.

Lasuén's face sobered, and a look of warm gratitude came into it, "This is charity, indeed, brother. I don't mind the rags, but I was sorry when I didn't dare wash it for fear it would fall quite apart."

"I have an extra hood," said Díaz. "It will help to redeem Father Garcés' habit."

The bright laughter came back to the face of Lasuén, and he asked his host for water to bathe and permission to go into his cell and tidy up for the wonderful new garments. In a surprisingly short time Lasuén reappeared, standing majestically in the doorway, scrubbed and shining in his new garments. "I could preach decorum to a mother superior now," he cried gayly. "The holy habit is a beautiful thing," and he stroked the coarse folds of the gray wool with delight. But suddenly a finger caught in a little tear. He looked apologetically to Garcés, who jumped to his feet. There was a roar of laughter from Anza, and a more restrained jeer from Díaz.

Lasuén put his arm around Garcés' shoulder, "Never mind, you have saved my decency, and that is more than any of them can do for all their jesting."

And then, sobering in a flash, he sat down at the table, and turned to Anza, "You are going to Monterey?"

And all the laughter died out of the suddenly grave eyes of the captain. "That is my order from the viceroy. But—" he spread his hands helplessly—"if I took all the supplies in Father Paterna's storehouse which he has so generously offered to me, with what I have, I could not get half way to Monterey." And than he went on to explain about the supplies left at the Colorado, and then under the sympathetic questioning of Father Lasuén he went back to the Apache raid and the lost horses.

"It is so with any enterprise," said Lasuén thoughtfully. "One thinks to go straight to the goal, and he must wander in a thousand bypaths, and his best purpose is at the mercy of endless irrelevancies. Only Father Serra," and here his face lighted, "keeps the end m view always, and never in all the distractions for a moment loses sight of it. And I should have told you at the beginning that that blessed boat has brought Father Serra back to us."

The effect of that announcement on the California missionaries was electric.

"Have you seen him?" they asked in one voice.

"Yes, he came ashore in the first boat that came for water this morning."

With great dignity, Lasuén turned to Anza, "You must not judge us, sir, until you have seen Father Serra. We are the stumbling blocks in God's way, I am afraid. Father Serra is what I am sure He meant this missionary enterprise of Upper California to be, straight as an arrow to its mark."

3

FIVE days later Garcés set out with Lasuén for San Diego. He had been very anxious to visit the first of the Upper California missions; so he was delighted to be commissioned by Anza to see what he could obtain there in the way of supplies for the expedition to Monterey. The journey had to be made on foot, for there were no mounts to spare at San Gabriel, and Anza's horses must be rested for the important work ahead. But it was hoped that Father Garcés could ride back with the train that brought the hoped-for supplies.

So the two friars set out briskly with a couple of Indian companions racing back and forth, now ahead, now behind them. It was a delightfully cool and sunny spring day in the green environs of San Gabriel, with a sweetness of flowers in the air, that brought sharply home to Garcés the memory of spring in Castile. And there were trees, too, that had not grown in Castile, and yet they had a brooding air of antiquity in their gray-green, as if they had been there long before any men had disturbed their silence.

Fermin Lasuén named them all with a certain warm enthusiasm as if he had in the few years of his stay made them his own. And he knew, too, their affinities to other varieties of their genus which he had seen in Mexico or Castile. And as he talked, the flowers and the trees seemed to bridge the gap between the familiar and the new so that something of Mexico and Castile bloomed again in San Gabriel, and San Gabriel reached out and pulled into the moment something of that far-off past in Castile.

It was not Francisco Garcés' way to spend much time thinking of the past, and Lasuén was talking now of the splendors of the new land, "It is a desert still, but where a little water runs or spills, then it flowers almost fantastically. You should see the valleys to the north at this time of year. They are a carpet from Persia, the red-gold earth aflame with every hue, miles and miles."

Now they had left the green environs of San Gabriel, and Garcés was relieved to feel the ache of that past to which he had bidden farewell with his missionary vows melt away in a landscape that was entirely of the new world. For the road had unfurled now in a bare golden-brown expanse, with the familiar gray-green swords of the yuccas giving a solemn life to a shining white arroyo where the waters must have come full-flood only a little while ago.

"Everything but man grows lavishly in this amazing world," said Lasuén sadly.

"I have noticed that. The Indians at San Gabriel are not so miserable-looking as the people we saw in the mountains, but they are nothing like the people of the rivers. Of course, they are short of food just now," the visitor added compassionately.

The Californian friar hesitated. "I hope you will not think I am trying to excuse our failures, but I doubt if they are much worse off than they usually are. You know enough of the Indian way of life to know that the battle for food is a never-ending one. You don't find many fat Indians in the state of nature."

"Nor fat friars," smiled Garcés.

His companion laughed, "This is a very congenial world for our Lady Poverty. Only I wish we could have steady crops. So long as we can feed our neophytes, we can keep them with us for instruction. But when everything goes wrong, as it did this spring, then we have to let them go. Indeed, at San Diego they have never been able to provide food for the neophytes, and that is why it is so slow. But already San Gabriel shows what can be done. Another year, please God, and we ought to be on a pretty firm foundation with our own corn."

"The San Diego Indians are sturdier?"

"San Diego?" Lasuén turned in surprise, and then he looked ahead to where their two Indian companions were racing along gayly in the sun, their brown bodies shining in the sun. "Oh, they are from our old missions in Lower California. We've had them a good part of their lives now, and those that have not been killed off in the various sicknesses show it. The men about San Diego are shorter and more miserable-looking than any you have seen. When we first saw them, they were stark naked and half-starved, and so simple they thought our mules were some kind of men and used to talk to them, as they coaxed them along."

Garcés' eyes widened. "I suppose in some ways the mules are nearly as clever as they are."

A thoughtful look had come into the face of Lasuén, "I have often wondered about that. Certainly, in everything that pertains to physical things, clothing and food, and houses, they are very backward. But I am not sure how gravely we Franciscans should blame them for that. They are able to endure great hardships and great privation so they are not wholly destitute of the graces of poverty."

"All Indians might give us lessons there," said his companion thoughtfully.

"Yes, they are free of many of the greeds and lusts that vex more civilized people. And I suspect that in their world, with the things they know, they have their own intelligence. I have been trying to learn their tongue, and they have been telling me some of their stories. I may be wrong, but I think they have powers of fancy and of reflection that do not appear in their dealings with material things."

"All Indians have, I think," said Garcés, "if only we could understand."

Garcés thought of that conversation when three days later the friars arrived at the water front, and there busy with the unloading of the vessel, they found the president of all the Upper California missions. A little lame man, with incredibly quick and energetic movements, hobbling about on a stick—it was easy to tell at a glance that he was the centre of the life of the bustling scene. At the moment when the two Franciscans came down to the water's edge, he was engaged in a very lively altercation with a red-faced corporal, who was obviously blustering to conceal his being worsted.

"Stealing is stealing, and a hanging business in this world, and a burning in the next," he said with a combination of personal pique and righteous indignation that would have been amusing if it had not been for an obviously terrified Indian boy at his feet who was slowly rolling out of his reach, looking from the angry corporal to the indignant friar.

"Of course, stealing is stealing," said the latter, "and I hope your men will not forget it." That shaft obviously went home, to judge from the black look the corporal threw the friar. "But there are other ways of getting a thing into a man's head besides beating out his brains. I've told you that before."

Then he turned to another Indian at his elbow, differing in appearance from the Indian in the sand only in that he was neatly clothed in a loin cloth. To him Serra spoke crisply, "Agustín, give this man something to eat, and then tell him that if he will help with the unloading and steal nothing, and obey you in all things, he shall share in the pozole for dinner." But even as he spoke, he bent down and patted gently what the two friars could see was a bruised shoulder. Then he turned to face his guests.

Lasuén sank to his knees for his blessing, but before he could touch the sand, Serra had flung his arms about him. And then with a quick, impulsive courtesy, he embraced the Franciscan from Querétaro.

"I was coming up to see that wonderful captain of yours, and now we can go together. I want to know all about that miraculous journey. God has been so good to us." He spoke quickly but with a tender warmth that knit up the flashes of his speech into a surprising intimacy. And then before the friar could murmur more than the initial commonplaces of meeting, he was asking about their resources for the rest of the journey to Monterey. So friendly and direct was the father general that Garcés found himself telling without embarrassment of the gravity of their predicament.

But suddenly Garcés remembered Anza's careful questioning of Lasuén as to the extent of their cargo. "But, Father Serra, we do understand how you have waited for this ship, and how you count on it. So—"

"It is all the same work, isn't it? Do you think there is anything that ship can do for Monterey as important as getting you there? That will be worth whatever your men eat on the way many times over to all of us. So now, tell me, how many men have you?"

But when the dynamic little friar bustled up to the corporal with his request for the rations and the supplies for Anza's men, the latter exploded afresh in a kind of humorous desperation, "But, I tell you, reverend father, the governor has told me that I am to see that there is enough put into the storehouses so that there will be no more times like this. The soldiers have been starving, and soldiers don't get credit for starving like friars."

"Who spoke of credit? And credit with whom? Doesn't a soldier have a soul to save as well as a friar? Are only the clergy supposed to be Christians?" Again, the corporal was overwhelmed, and, again, a look half of bafflement and half of obstinacy came into his face, as the little friar wrote down his orders in his book for him.

"What will the governor say?" he cried at last in sheer bewilderment.

"I'll take care of the governor. My son, you don't mean to say that his Excellency does not want the king's highway to be laid from Sonora to Monterey? That highway means just as much to the governor as it means to the missions."

As he spoke, the sea wind blew his thin gray hair about his lean face, and his bright eyes flashed. For a moment, Garcés half expected to see him fling his arms wide and begin to preach to the waves, but the amazing little man patted the corporal's arm in a friendly fashion that left the astonished soldier gasping, and wheeled round and hobbled up the shingle to the two friars. "Come, my brothers, and let us give thanks to God who has brought you safely to us."

From the little church Serra led his guests to the mission house to share a more abundant corn and bean supper than San Gabriel's but no more elaborately served. And then with flashing eyes and a face that lighted like a lantern when the candle has been set within, he began to talk of the great chain of missions that would win the beautiful land of California for God and king. Sometimes Garcés found it difficult to determine which of the missions he spoke of so affectionately and so vividly were in existence and which still had being only in his glowing imagination. But always, whether it was of difficulty surmounted or plan in prospect, he shed over everything he touched the same bright enthusiasm.

For all the excitement of the day's labors on the shore, Father Serra was still talking when Garcés began to fall asleep on the rough pine supper table that night. And the next day when the younger friar came to full consciousness, he heard Father Serra's voice outside the little house, and he soon realized with mortification that the president of the missions had already said Mass and was on his way to the harbor.

When they came back that afternoon from the port to the mission, the little friar was quieter, but he set forth at a pace that for all his hobble forced his taller companion to lengthen his stride. And yet, presently, he made Garcés stop and watch the sea, incredibly blue and lovely, rolling in at the foot of the rampart of ground on which they stood. The wind had risen, too, and was turning to silver the coarse grass on the edge of the land, now feathering delicately the brilliant blue of the sky.

"God has been so good to us," he said presently, with great gentleness softening his usually brisk speech. "Our history since we came into this land has been one miracle after another. Your safe arrival is only the latest in a long series. I sometimes tell my young brethren that this is a land of miracles."

And he proceeded to tell the story which Garcés had already heard from other lips of the expedition to San Diego and of all the things that followed thereafter. But this telling was unlike any other Garcés had ever heard, for every disaster and every hardship that made up that heroic tale was remembered by its main protagonist simply in terms of the miracle of its relief and its deliverance. The endless mercy and love of God, who would not let his work be lost for the weakness of his servants, blotted out in its splendor all remembrance of pain and suffering. Indeed, that history, so nearly disastrous in the main, so full of privation and disappointment in the detail, became on the lips of Serra a litany of praise and wonder and thanksgiving for the never-failing goodness of God.

But he had not forgotten the preoccupations of his companion, for at the end of his story, he turned to him and said with the same glowing enthusiasm, "And now tell me all about your plans for Monterey. You know the corporal has promised to send all you need tomorrow at the latest."

The corporal kept his promise and despatched the supplies. But Serra was delayed by the seemingly unending problems of San Diego, and Garcés lingered to return with him. The result was that it was several days after the arrival of the supplies before the two friars reached San Gabriel.

The interval had served to cool a little but not to quench Anza's indignation at the condition in which the supplies had arrived. To the captain's astonishment, Serra replied that though they were in far from perfect condition, they were certainly no worse than usual. Then he went on to explain that ever since they had come into Upper California, he had been protesting the state in which supplies arrived, but it did not seem possible to do anything about it. He supposed that the ship's captains were hardly to be blamed if in their frequent anxiety to preserve their ship and their crew, they did not always take sufficient care of their cargoes. But, he added, he had never been satisfied that the men who purchased the government stores were sufficiently careful in their inspection of the commodities offered.

"Such carelessness is an outrage," grumbled the captain, who prided himself on his measures to make sure that full value was received for his Majesty's gold and silver.

But for once Serra was disposed to be more patient. "It takes constant vigilance in a religious order to make sure that the common goods are not wasted. In his Majesty's service where men have hardly renounced their own private interest, it is even more difficult."

If Serra in his more driving moments was an irresistible force, it was still harder to resist him in his gentler moments, when the charm of the man's unaffected charity cast its mollifying influence over all who came near him. So when Anza went on to ask how the San Diego authorities thought he was going to get some thirty men to Monterey on eight bushels of half-spoiled maize and beans, with a little flour and meat in not much better condition, Serra was so instantly sympathetic that the captain repented of his complaint. And when Serra looked at the horses and mules which had come up from San Diego and pronounced them the best which the settlement afforded, the captain made no complaint of their obviously inferior quality. Now it was Serra's turn to apologize, and this he did heartily.

"I think it is the judgment of God on our sins," he said ruefully, "that no matter how much I have protested by letter and in person to the viceroy, and no matter how much he has promised to our father guardian in Mexico and to me, the supplies that do reach us are far from good, and they cost so sadly much. I am afraid Father Lasuén is right that we shall never be quit of anxiety and annoyance here until we have cleared our own fields and planted our own orchards and bred our own flocks."

"If you had more settlers here to do those things for you, then you would be free to do your own work, wouldn't you?" suggested the captain.

But the friar shook his head. "Settlers are more trouble than you would think. They are quite ready to use the Indian to feed themselves. They are not much interested in doing anything to feed the Indian."

Anza sighed. "Well, we'll face that later when the time comes. Now the question is what to do for Monterey."

"Do you need all your men to go to Monterey?" asked the little superior-general who had been the length and breadth of the mission land with not much more than an Indian lad for escort.

"I suppose not," the captain agreed, "But those who are sent back will be disappointed. And then there is the question of discipline. We can't have anything go wrong when they get back to the Colorado."

Hot as it was in the little room where they were talking, Garcés felt cold for a moment. But he had long ago learned that disappointment had better be gulped down in one immediate swallow, if it is to lose its bitterness. So he hastened to volunteer his services to the returning group. And they were as promptly accepted.

And then Anza relented, and apologized to his colleague that he should not see the end of the journey he had done so much to make possible. "But it isn't just the business of getting the men back to the Colorado; I don't want anything to go wrong with our Indian friends when they get back there. And you can take care of that end as no one else can," he added a little coaxingly. But there was no need, for much as the friar ached to see what was at the end of the road, he knew clearly where his job lay.

"I wish all commanders were as wise," said Serra wistfully.

4

It was, then, that Garcés for the first time became aware of Sebastián standing in the doorway, his face quite as impassive as usual, but with an agony of interest in his dark eyes. Garcés had been much preoccupied with other matters since his arrival at San Gabriel, but now he recalled that several times he had looked up from the business in hand to find the Indian looking at him in the same intense way. Each time he had wondered what was going on behind that inscrutable face, and each time something had come up to claim his attention. Now in a sudden flash of inspiration he turned to the Indian, "Sebastián, will you come back with me, and help me get the party safely to the river?"

The brown lineaments did not change, but there was no mistaking the lightening in the dark eyes. "Yes, master, if you wish."

The friar smiled, "I am no master, Sebastián, but a poor friar. If the captain will let me have you for guide—"

That night at supper Garcés presented his request, and the captain immediately granted it.

But Father Paterna protested, "I am not sure that you should trust that man too much."

"What man?" asked Father Serra.

"The Indian Sebastián—you remember the boy we brought up from

Lower California."

"The one who was so quick and learned Spanish so fast?"

"Yes, that one. I am afraid we let him get above himself here. He struck one of the soldiers on some fancied wrong, and the man complained to the corporal. Other soldiers had had words from Sebastián, too, and he had apparently boasted that the friars would not let him be touched. The corporal was afraid of more trouble if we did not do something about it."

"Didn't you say something about a wife?" Serra asked Garcés.

But before he could speak, Father Paterna answered, "Yes, one of the neophyte women of our people here. I asked the corporal about her, and he said that she was pretty for these women, and that she liked to talk to the soldiers."

"Sebastián was not the man to be patient with a light wife," said Serra compassionately.

"But I spoke to her mother, or, rather, I had the majordomo's wife speak for me. The woman was sullen, and apparently all she said was that she had never thought any good would come of these new gods and the white men. You see, she has never come to the instruction, but has stuck to the village down near the river with other members of the tribe who have dodged us."

"Was it after that that Sebastián struck the soldier?"

"Yes, and the captain of the soldiers was so alarmed that he said that if I would not let him give Sebastián a few strokes of warning, he would not be responsible for his men not doing worse. So to save Sebastián, I gave permission." The kind face of Father Paterna looked perplexed, and Serra's grave, but the latter hastened to reassure his colleague, "After the trouble you have already had, I do not see what else you could do."

"I sent for Sebastián to tell him why I had consented, but he was not in the mission. That night the soldiers went down to his wife's mother's hut in the village, but they said they knew nothing of him. And next morning we found that his wife was gone, too. That is all we knew until about a week before you came. Then some of our Indians reported here that there was a rumor in the village that Sebastián had come back. Apparently, nothing was known at first about the wife and her cousin, but you heard the wailing the other night."

For several moments the little company sat silent. Then Father Serra sighed, "I thought very well of Sebastián; he was proud but he was not obstinate."

But Captain Anza shook his head. "I can guess what Father Garcés is thinking, at least, and that is that if you friars did not have to bother with us soldiers, it would all be much simpler."

Father Serra protested with his most winning smile, "There is one soldier we are all of us glad to see here, and we could wish he were staying, and that is your honored self, captain."

Garcés rose to excuse himself, "The Indians in the village were making a big campfire as I came by earlier this evening. So I think I will go down there for a little while to sit with them."

Father Paterna seemed anxious, and Serra turned to look curiously at Garcés.

But the captain only smiled, "Don't worry about Father Garcés. He is as at home in the circle around an Indian campfire as in his convent."

"I have a little present of tobacco for them," said Garcés gently. "I shall not stay long, I assure you."

But it was not so simple as that. For once outside the door, he almost stumbled over a figure seated on the ground with his back to the wall of the little house. The figure sprang up. "Old Man?"

It was the voice of Sebastián, no longer brusque and inscrutable but warm with emotion, almost fear, it seemed to the alert friar. The Indian took hold of the sleeve of the friar's gown and tugged it until they were out of possible hearing of the door.

"Do you know a magic that will make the unburied dead sleep quietly without any dreams?" he asked sharply.

"Have you not been baptized, Sebastián? And have you not been taught that it makes no difference what happens to the body if the soul is truly sorry for its sins?"

"Sorry for its sins," repeated the Indian thoughtfully, and then he caught his breath.

A sudden impulse made the friar risk his next question of the man so suddenly naked there beside him in the dark, "Sebastián, why did you strike that soldier?"

Apparently, some other overmastering emotion had blotted out the old anxiety and the old reticence, "He took my wife—" he said it calmly as if he were no longer interested in that old fear.

"So that is why you ran away?"

"No, the father said they might beat me." Now the Indian was on the alert, holding his breath as he waited.

"Why didn't you tell the father? If he had known, he would have had the soldier beaten."

"What good would that have done? He would have been still alive to talk to my wife."

"Is that why you took her away?"

The Indian had ceased to breathe so hard; indeed, he seemed to have relaxed. "Master, you have no wife."

"True," said the friar gravely. "So you had forgiven her?"

"Forgiven?" The Indian seemed puzzled.

Suddenly, he clutched at Garcés' arm, "She was dead, quite dead, master, when I went back."

The friar put his hand slightly on the Indian's arm, and then as he felt it stiffen, he dropped it.

"Did you see her first?"

"Yes. I looked back, and I could see him and not her. I tried to shout to him, but I couldn't—it was like that day when we turned back. But he saw me pointing, and he stood there until I came up, and then he followed me back." Again, the Indian was breathing hard.

"She was quite dead then?"

"Yes," and then it broke from him in a short, hard cry, "he said I had killed her."

"Did you strike him?" asked the friar.

A note of pleading came into the terror of the man's voice now.

"No. I wanted to, but he looked at me, and he ran."

"And then?" And as the Indian did not answer, the friar asked, "Did you run?"

"No, I sat down beside her." And he paused as if all words had failed.

"And then?"

"I do not know, master. But some time later, I do not know how long, Palma's hunters found me and brought me into his camp. That is all I know."

For a moment the friar said nothing. There was no need to ask Sebastián if he were telling the truth. For his answers had carried their own conviction to the man who had watched his silence for so long.

Then Garcés asked very quietly, "Why should the dead come back then, Sebastián, since you have done no wrong to the dead?"

"Her mother says she has seen her daughter all gray because I did nothing to save her, but left her to die there in the great sands."

Again the terror had come into the Indian's voice, "She is telling all the village."

"Does anyone down at the campfire," and the friar pointed to the little glow now visible through the tree, "speak Spanish?"

"One of the fathers' servants is there, but he will leave when he sees you."

"Then do you go down and bid him stay, for I will not tell that he was there."

Sebastián vanished, and when a few minutes later the friar came into the light of the fire and greeted the old man who seemed to hold the principal place in the campfire circle, he was reassured to hear a guttural voice on the other side of the fire speak out of the darkness.

Then he came and stood in front of the chief where all the eyes glittering in the light that, roving on the night breeze, picked them out of the darkness, might see him. And, after a pause, he knelt down and put his tobacco in a little heap in a piece of bark in front of the chief.

Suddenly, but very quietly, the old man at his side spoke. And then out of the darkness came the Spanish, a little slurred and halting but unmistakable, "Sebastián says the Old Man from beyond the great river is a good man."

"Sebastián says the men of San Gabriel are good men," answered the friar as if in an antiphonal response.

Again the silence settled heavily on the light breeze. It was the friar who broke it next, a little tentatively, "Sebastián is a good man."

The voice out of the darkness spoke again, Garcés fancied more sharply this time. At any rate he had hardly finished when a woman's voice screamed a few words in the tongue which the friar had never heard before. But he called sharply to the voice in the darkness, "Tell me what she said."

The voice was low and frightened now, but unmistakable, "She says Sebastián is a murderer."

"O men of San Gabriel, will you let me tell you a story?"

There was a grunt when the voice had translated the request, and slowly the friar began to tell the story which he had gathered from the frightened lips of Sebastián. After every second sentence he paused to make sure that the translator had understood. Sometimes he had to try again, using a more concrete word, but the voice did not fail out on the edge of the darkness.

He spoke very slowly and deliberately, taking care never to use the name of Sebastián. When he had concluded the story, he said simply, "He was no murderer, that man. He was much to be pitied."

He thought it was a murmur of agreement that arose after that conclusion, but he could not be sure. Only after some moments, a man's voice spoke from where the woman had screamed. And now, for the first time, the interpreter hesitated.

"What did he say?" asked the friar anxiously.

The voice hesitated for a moment, and then it seemed to take courage, "He asked, how shall one make sure the unburied dead do not walk again?"

"Tell him that tomorrow when the great bell rings, I shall sing the Requiem Mass for the repose of the dead."

He was not sure whether the interpreter understood that; so he waited anxiously. There were a few words out of the dark, and again the voice hesitated. Then when the friar urged, he said hesitantly, "That will be a good magic, he says."

With that he had to be content for that night. But the next morning when he opened the door to go to the church, he found Sebastián standing as if on guard, and beyond him, the whole mission yard, full of the dirty and all but naked Indians of the village.

"It is the biggest Mass we have had yet," said Father Paterna in astonishment as he came into the tiny sacristy to help Garcés vest himself. "What did you say to them last night to bring them all here?"

"I told them a story," said Garcés, reaching for the basin to wash his hands. "And now, please God, I am going to lay a ghost."

5

EARLY that afternoon Garcés assembled his party for the return to the river. He was conscious at once of a certain lack of exhilaration in the little company that now drew up in front of the mission gate. For everybody knew that Anza had taken the four strongest and most dependable of his men with him, and the best of the horses and mules.

One thing in their departure cheered Garcés, and that was the appearance of a little group of the Indians of the village who came out when the party neared the river, and marched along for a while beside Sebastián's horse as if it were a member of their own village whom they were escorting on an expedition for the common good. But presently, they drifted off, and Garcés was free at last to give his attention to his companions. One especially had roused his anxiety, a rather frail-looking lad whom he had already spent a good deal of time encouraging on the journey to California, and who was now lagging along sullenly at the very end of their train.

Juan Miguel's first response to the friar's attentions was not encouraging. He complained bitterly of being left behind with the old men while the others went on to Monterey. The boy's contempt for his hardy comrades amused the friar, who hastened to remind him that one could hardly dismiss so lightly any man who had won a place in this expedition. But it soon became clear that Juan Miguel really had no interest in his companions. It was of a certain very intelligent-looking but rather driving young woman whom the friar had noticed several times in Juan Miguel's company in Tubac that he was thinking. He dreaded Rosalía's tongue when she should hear that he had not gone to Monterey.

The friar laughed and assured the lover that Rosalía would be so glad to have him back safe that she would not complain. But he soon saw that there was more to it than that. For apparently Rosalía had decided that the captain's trip to Monterey was the prelude to a settlement there, and she had agreed to marry Juan Miguel if he would enlist for the settlement. The friar whistled at that shrewd conclusion and involuntarily exclaimed that Rosalía must be a very remarkable young woman. This tribute elicited a flood of enthusiastic agreement from the lover, and on that congenial theme the young man forgot some of his discouragement, and presently he had brightened enough so that the friar could turn his attention to the rest of the party.

He soon found that there was no real cause for worry in them. They were thoroughly healthy men, for whom the day as it came was sufficient, and now that the disappointment of Monterey had been assimilated, they were disposed to spend little drought on anything but the road ahead, and the ever-present problem of food and water. They had profited, too, even from the lean days of rest at San Gabriel, and the wine of success was in their veins. They knew from experience that whatever hardships the desert held in store for them, they would soon be over. The whole company, therefore, addressed itself to the task of getting through the blazing sands with something approaching zest.

Another aid, the friar received, and that of the most unexpected kind. Ever since the Indians of San Gabriel turned back, Sebastián had kept his horse slightly ahead of the friar, as if ready to shield his new-found master from danger. At first, he had ridden along in silence, and then he had begun to talk of the road. The friar, preoccupied with his own wistful meditations on the possibility of a northern way, at first paid no attention. But, presently, he woke up to the fact that the seemingly disjointed and aimless comments of the Indian were really very shrewd observations of the movement of the hills and canyons about them, with often a quiet suggestion as to where from the look of the country water might be hoped for.

At first, he wondered if now that time and the happenings at San Gabriel had effaced some of the horror of the flight across the sands, Sebastián was perhaps remembering more of the details of the route. But when he questioned the Indian as to the course he had taken across the desert, the latter professed still to remember nothing of the crucial part of his journey. And Garcés found no reason to doubt his word. Rather, he decided, the torpor which had apparently seized upon the Indian's mind when they approached the sands on the former journey had lifted, and his intelligence was now functioning with something like its normal acuteness in this world in which, once again, it found itself at home.

At any rate, Sebastián entered with immediate and constant attention into the friar's effort to find a shorter way than the one which they had taken earlier. Garcés himself, from the very circumstances of the traveling he had done already in such country, had something like the Indian's sensitiveness to the landscape, and something of his imagination in interpreting its signs, but, as he was the first to acknowledge, he had nothing of the Indian's instinct for direction. Now he had, it appeared, found the ideal complement to his own gifts, for Sebastián seemed always to have a firm grasp on the relations of what they were looking at now to what they had just left, and the probable lines of the country into which they were presently coming.

As a result, between the two of them, the Indian and the friar, they did find their way to the east of the black mountain. And it was a much more direct and easy way that, Garcés soon saw, would bring them to the Colorado much farther up its course and nearer to the junction with the Gila. This was, also, a much clearer route, with distinct and easily recognizable landmarks to set down on the rough map which one of the soldiers, was making under the friar's direction. And, not least important when the problem of equipping parties for this trip was considered, it cut a good many miles off the stretch of desert to be covered. It was altogether a very pretty little triumph of path-finding.

Garcés was modestly rejoicing in the goodness of Providence when the first cloud rose on the smiling horizon of his success. In the beginning it was a very simply thing. Two Indians were espied at some distance, shuffling along the edge of a small precipice on a mountain side to the northeast, so high above the road which the party was following that there was no necessity for them to flee, as otherwise they most certainly would have done at sight of so numerous a company of strangers. Sebastián looked at the friar, and the latter nodded. So the Indian rode off alone to the foot of the mountain.

A turn in the road soon hid him from view, and it was some time before the party caught sight of him again on a lower spur of the height, absorbed in conversation with the two strangers. The latter seemed to be talking with great vigor and with many gestures about something exciting. And the friar smiled at the sight, partly from relief, and partly from the amusing thought that if this had been in some less familiar spot, he would have been anxious to know the cause of the excitement. But here, where they were so close to their destination, he had ceased to feel any anxiety.

So he shouted to Sebastián to bring his new friends down. But they seemed quite unwilling to come. Again he shouted, bidding Sebastián promise them some tobacco, but they seemed still too shy. So the two other Indians who rode with the Spanish party then started for the crag above the road, but at sight of them the strangers turned and fled, scrambling up the crag out of sight.

"What happened?" asked the friar as Sebastián returned to his side.

For a moment the Indian was silent. The other two Indians murmured a few words to each other, but they were still some distance away. Then Sebastián spoke, very slowly and deliberately, "I do not think they are good men." And more he would not say, although some of the men who had ridden up to ask about the strangers laughed at him and tried to tease him into saying more.

The company soon forgot the incident when they sighted a rabbit which one of the Indians rode off to chase. But Garcés, covertly watching the tense face beside him, found himself growing uneasy. Nothing more happened however, till the next morning.

Again, they met a couple of Indians, coming from the direction of the river. But this time, Garcés and Sebastián had ridden out alone to look over the road while the rest of the company were packing up from the last night's encampment. So it was that this time the two Indians did not flee, but waited until Garcés had come up and exchanged greetings. They spoke in the Cajuenche language, and this time Sebastián was able to talk to them with ease, while the friar could pick up a word here and there. He was, therefore, quite able to guess that the first question which Sebastián asked with every appearance of concern involved in some way the party of Spaniards who had gone to Monterey.

He saw the Indians glance at him, and then they answered Sebastián's question, speaking so rapidly that he could make no guess as to the meaning of what they said. Garcés urged Sebastián to detain the strangers, but they hurried away. And Sebastián remained there looking after them until the friar joined him. Then he raised very grave eyes to meet his master's look ol inquiry.

In the warm sunlight Garcés felt suddenly cold, and then he took a firmer grip on himself. Surely, he of all men should know that all kinds of rumors flew up and down the faint sand trails of the Indian world.

"What has happened, Sebastián?"

The Indian lifted a clearly puzzled and uncertain face to his. "I do not know, master. These are not bad men, but they do not say good things."

"What do they say?"

"They say the Spaniards at the great rivers have fled, and Palma has their horses and their cattle."

This was staggering news.

Then Garcés remembered the meeting of the day before.

"What did those Indians whom we met yesterday say?"

"They are not men I know, and I have no way of knowing whether they spoke the truth," Sebastián replied, the line of his mouth tightening as it had tightened when on the way to California he had been asked about the route across the great sand dunes.

Garcés looked long at him, but he knew that before the journey was over, he might have to draw on all the reserves of confidence Sebastián had. So he said nothing more but rode back to the company. But, as the men of the party rode back and forth to consult on the little incidents of the road, he kept one ear alert for any scraps of conversation. Sebastián hardly spoke all morning to any of the soldiers, and not at all to the two other Indians. And yet by noon, the corporal was at his side, asking him to ride ahead with him for a moment.

"Your Reverence, have you heard what the Indians are saying?"

"You mean the Yuma and that Cajuenche we picked up on the way to

California?"

"Yes, Sebastián is very close-mouthed. And the Yuma is not much better, but the Cajuenche will talk if you can make out what he is trying to say. He says those Indians said the Monterey party has been killed."

Again, Garcés felt the chill at his heart, but he paused. Suppose it were true, how long would it take for the news to find its way to the river? Was there time? He stared, unseeing, at the corporal. Marcial Sánchez was a little man, fussy and self-important, but by no means unintelligent. The men were tired now, and he did not want the fear he felt at his own heart to spread. They were almost at the river now—soon they would meet Indians whom he had met, and could talk to for himself.

"You know how these stories go up and down the trails, and how they grow," he began. The grave face before him relaxed, and the soldier scratched his head.

"Have the Indians told this to the rest of the party?"

"No," said the corporal self-importantly. "I told them not to."

"That is good," said the friar, and the little man stood taller. "Keep your ears open, and if you hear any talk, report it to me."

The rest of the afternoon the friar rode back and forth among the company. They were tired from the strain of the desert-crossing, and the disappointment of not going on to Monterey had returned to some of them. As the hot afternoon passed, it seemed to the anxious friar that a repressed uneasiness seized upon the party. If it had been a company of monks, he would have said that half of them had heard the rumor and were trying to conceal their knowledge from their companions.

Just before sunset they came to the top of the river bank and looked down upon the green river bottom. A new impulse of life came into the whole party, and the horses plunged ahead, sniffing at the steaming air. Quietly, Sebastián rode ahead with the Cajuenche, and a few minutes later he shouted that he had found spring water.

Garcés was the first to reach the spring, and, under cover of the crowding around the water, he drew Sebastián aside.

"The corporal knows of the story of the killing of the Monterey men."

"It is that loose-mouthed Cajuenche," replied the Indian contemptuously.

But as Garcés watched the men gathering brushwood for the fire on the sandy river bottom, he decided that when they had all eaten, he would tell them the story. However, it was taken out of his hands by the arrival in camp, while they were still eating, of a couple of the Cajuenches whom Garcés had met on earlier visits, and who had travelled part way down the river with the company on its westward march. They were obviously bringers of news, and the friar went at once to the little knot of soldiers and Indians who had gathered around them.

While the other Indians held back, Sebastián began to question the strangers. There was so much repetition of the same phrases as the speakers canvassed the same ground over and over again that Garcés found he could follow the main drift of the conversation.

"Bad men tell bad tales," said Sebastián gravely, for at least the third time.

"What do they say?" asked the friar.

"The same thing," said Sebastián wearily. "The Spaniards have left the junction of the rivers and gone back to their own land."

There was no concealing it now. Half a dozen soldiers clustering about the spring had heard them talking, and they crowded round for more information. But apparently the Cajuenches knew no more than what they had said.

A couple of Indians from a neighboring village through which the party had passed earlier came up to the campfire while they were eating, and were warmly received as old friends. They had heard the story from a hunting party of their own people who had strayed into Yuma territory, but they knew nothing more. Then they added that everybody on the river knew it. But they could suggest no reason for the flight of the Spaniards, and even the rashest of the soldiers hesitated to suggest the obvious explanation.

But when the camp was quiet and Sebastián had lain down at the friar's feet, Garcés called softly to him.

"Yes, master," said the Indian, with one sinuous movement rolling from his feet to the friar's side.

"I think there is no question the Spaniards have left, Sebastián."

"They have left the junction of the rivers," said the low voice at his side.

"Do you think Palma drove them away?" asked the friar, dropping his voice to little more than a whisper.

But in the stillness of the night the Indian heard, for he whispered passionately, "Palma is no traitor."

"I do not think so, either," Garcés hastened to reassure him. "Do you think they heard that other story? The story about the Monterey men?"

"I do not believe that story either," said the Indian, and he slid quietly back to the place where he had been sleeping. There was nothing more to be done this night.

6

AFTER Mass the next morning Garcés addressed the assembled party. The men looked so anxious that he decided to lose no time in coming to the point, "You all know what is being said. The Indians love gossip as we do, and they do not spoil their stories. But something has happened up at the junction of the rivers. There is no use in frightening ourselves with speculation. We are going to find out what it is."

Then he briefly reported the instructions he had given to the Yuma and to Sebastián. Some of the men looked relieved that it had been brought out into the open; others looked anxious now that the fear had been acknowledged, and some looked simply sullen and oppressed as if this were but another burden that had been irrationally imposed from above. And there were one or two who looked excited, and even hopeful. So the friar hastily reminded the company of Anza's standing orders that nothing should be done to alarm the Indians.

He missed Sebastián as he rode to the dusty head of the cavalcade. But he had little time to think of the familiar mystery of what lay behind that seemingly impassive and yet suggestive face, for Corporal Sánchez rode up beside him.

"Do you think Sebastián is to be trusted?"

"Yes. Why not?"

"And Palma?"

Garcés faced his lieutenant. "What else can we do?" He was astonished himself at the defiance with which he spoke. He had not realized before how completely the easy confidence with which he had taken the road back had collapsed. He felt the astonished eyes of the soldier upon him. So, more gently, he added, "We shall know very soon now."

But the next day brought no sign of either Indian guide. That in itself was disappointing, but hardly surprising. Garcés, as he rode out at the head of the column, told himself that the Yumas would certainly need time to find Palma, and Sebastián would want to have more than the reiteration of the rumor to bring back. Time would seem much less important to him than probing the mystery. So he held in check his rising anxiety.

But there was one thing he could not shut his eyes to, and that was the fact that, although they had begun to pass a good many Indians on the banks above them, or in the thickets of green between their company and the river, none of them would come near the party. Sometimes when first descried, they were so close that they were clearly within hallooing distance, but in a few moments they had quietly slipped from sight. Nothing could be in sharper contrast to the friendly welcome of the journey out than this tacit avoidance.

And as he rode along, the friar could feel the silence and the vigilance of the men at his back. For a little while he toyed with the idea of riding on ahead, alone, to visit one of the villages he remembered in this country. But he knew he could not, for the men were beginning to show the strain of the uncertainty. Indeed, for the first time something like fear was coming into the air of the expedition. He wished for Anza to whip the fainthearted with his own easy confidence, Anza, who might even now be lying dead on the sand of the trail from Monterey. But that thought he rejected.

Then he became aware of a movement in the bushes ahead as if someone were looking through them. But he rode straight on, flinging his arms to either side that whoever was watching might see that he was quite unarmed.

Again, the bushes moved, and out of the clump stepped a single brown figure with arms upraised. It was Sebastián. But before the friar could speak, there was a clatter at his back, and he turned to face half a dozen of the soldiers riding posthaste with their muskets swinging in their left hands, ready for action when the headlong rush should be halted.

"Stop, you fools, and put those muskets back. It is Sebastián."

Not even Anza could have shouted a more peremptory command, the friar reflected ruefully, but Sebastián was at his bridle.

"Master, those thieves of Cajuenches forced me from my horse and rode off with it." It was hard to tell which it was, the walking or the indignation, which had left the Indian so exhausted-looking.

"Never mind the horse!" broke in Corporal Sánchez. "Tell us what you found out." On his horse he towered threateningly above the Indian, who on the ground would have towered a head above him. The friar saw the Indian's mouth tighten.

"Corporal, please leave Sebastián to me, and get the men on to camp. It is getting late, and we want to be settled before sunset."

With an ominous shake of his fist at the Indian, the corporal rode ahead. The friar let the bulk of the company pass on until the first of the spare horses appeared. At sight of a nearly fresh one, he signalled to Sebastián to take it. In a moment the Indian was on the bare back, riding along by Garcés' side, breathing deeply, and, the friar noticed, perceptibly relaxing.

"What did you learn?" he asked when he judged that Sebastián was comfortable enough to have forgotten the corporal.

There was no mistaking the unfeigned puzzlement on the brown face.

"Master, how shall a man know the truth?"

The friar did not smile, though irrelevantly he thought of some of the arguments of the theology class in his seminary days.

"What do men say?" he asked the simpler question.

"All men say, though most of them are lying Cajuenches—"

"Never mind who the men are. What do they say?"

"They say all the Spaniards have fled, and Palma keeps the horses and the mules and the cattle. Not a horse will Palma give away, and they say he is planning to make himself lord of all the villages along the rivers."

The friar considered. The holding on to the horses and the cattle might be susceptible of more than one interpretation.

"Why do they say the Spaniards fled?"

"They say men came from the north and said the Spaniards who had gone north had been slain and their horses taken."

But a sudden idea came to Garcés.

"What men do they say took the horses of the men who had gone north?"

"The Apaches."

Garcés stared, "The Apaches? But there are none on that route. They are to the east. I never heard of Apaches that far west."

"That is what they say."

"When do they say the Spaniards fled?"

"Ten days ago."

"Ten days ago," the friar echoed the words with such incredulity that Sebastián's mouth tightened again.

"Master, I speak the truth." It was several minutes before the friar saw the mouth relax again under his reiterated expressions of confidence.

But when he had sent the Indian ahead to be among the first to get water at the camp site, he returned to the question with Corporal Sánchez, "Of course, ten days is a round number, but we have been only fifteen days out of San Gabriel. The captain, for all his forced marches and his eagerness to report to the viceroy, can hardly be very far out of Monterey even now. When this story came to the men at the river, the captain had not even reached Monterey."

Together the friar and the corporal canvassed the possibilities of time and distance. But Sánchez refused to be reassured.

It was a very tired and a very tense little company that sat down around the campfire on the sand at the edge of the river. It was one of the narrower stretches of the Colorado, where the left bank towered high above their heads, and the night wind blew sharply down the darkening stream. After the desert the cool and the freshness of that river wind should have been welcome, but as it moaned lightly through the brush and the willows and the cottonwoods, the men clung closer to the fire.

There was a good deal of restlessness in the darkness, the river tumbling over itself in its narrower bed, the wind, an owl on the banks above, a loon in the bottom lands, all the familiar sounds of the night, magnified by the echoing walls of the banks above their encampment. And yet not a man but caught the stealthy crackling in the bushes at their back. It was the Yuma guide.

There was a shout from the group around the campfire, but the friar, who had observed that the Indian was panting, called for silence and ordered drink and food for the tired man.

While every pair of eyes in the firelight devoured him with impatience, the Indian drank and supped the pozole with quick fingers. Then abruptly he sat back on his heels.

"The Spaniards have gone back to their land, all but one. The one who keeps the mules has stayed."

There was a chuckle in the dark at this news, and in the chuckle it seemed as if all the anxious circle relaxed. "Trust Christóval not to give up his precious mules!"

"Where did you learn this?" asked the corporal in his skeptical tone, and the friar protested that this questioning of the Yuma must be left to him.

"I met men of my village down to trade a day from here." The Indian pointed up the dark river. "They will tell Palma we are coming. They said Pablo had been telling the villages down the river that the Spaniards were dead, and now is the time to make war on Palma. But they are afraid of the horses he has."

"I think," said Corporal Sánchez sagely, "that the sooner we come to Christóval's aid, the better. The Apaches will hear of those horses."

"Do the Yumas think the men who went to Monterey are dead?"

The Indian shrugged his shoulders. "The men of my village say that Pablo wants the Spaniards to be dead, for since Palma met the Spaniards and received that amulet he wears about his neck, he has been lording it over all men. But Palma says the Spaniards are not dead, that the great captain will come as he said."

"So Palma is faithful," said Corporal Sánchez solemnly.

But one of the soldiers in the shadows at the other side of the fire muttered, "Palma knows where his interest lies, the clever rascal."

"What do the men of your village say?" asked the friar quietly.

The Indian shrugged his shoulders. "What should wise men say? They say, 'Let us wait and see.'"

There was a laugh at this, and one of the soldiers slapped his knee and said, "Not bad for Indians at all."

"Well, they have seen now," said the corporal. And then as the Yuma said nothing, his voice rose impatiently, "Haven't they?"

There was a note of fresh confidence in the Indian's voice as he responded with great care, "They have seen half."

There was a roar at this, and Corporal Sánchez blustered.

"What are your friends doing now?" asked another of the soldiers.

For a moment, the Yuma seemed to be considering whether he should answer this question. Apparently, he decided it was a proper question, for he answered with great dignity, "The men of my village are going back to tell Palma what they have seen and what they have heard."

"Will Palma come to meet us?" asked one of the soldiers curiously.

But the Yuma only shrugged his shoulders. So the corporal stumbled to his feet and began setting his guards.

"These men around here," said Garcés quietly to the Indian when the others were stirring to make themselves comfortable for the night, "surely they will not make any trouble?"

"They will wait and see before they do anything," said the Yuma placidly. Then as an after-thought he added, "They are not fools."

Through all this talk Sebastián had sat quietly a little to the rear of the friar. Now he came forward. "Master, I think Palma will come to meet us."

"I doubt if he will think it wise," said the friar thoughtfully.

The next afternoon the friar had to admit that they were both right. For as they came up the river bottom toward the junction of the rivers, they were met by a party of Yumas, who came riding up to them without any effort at concealment. When they were still a little distance away, one of them rode forward, and the friar pushed out to meet him. It was one of Palma's headmen, and he rode ahead of his party, with one hand holding something against his breast. As soon as he dismounted, he offered his gift, what Garcés knew was for the Indians' meager supply, a generous gift of tobacco. As he took some, the friar saw that the other members of the party were similarly laden with gifts of food.

Even before the Indian made his little speech, Garcés felt sure of what he was going to say. Nor was he disappointed. The great king's servant, Palma had sent them to greet his brother servants of the great king and to escort them to his land. He had not come to meet them, for he was staying with the horses and the cattle of the king so that bad men might not be tempted. But when they came up to the meeting of the rivers, he would be waiting for them, and there he would make a great campfire for them.

"It is a trick," said Corporal Sánchez balefully, when the company was in motion again, and the friar could ride back to find the harassed soldier who had been using the halt to round up stragglers.

"No," said the friar, "he will be there."

And Palma was. As they came to the height below the junction, he came out to meet them, riding ahead of the company he had brought with him. He was wearing the precious medal on its red ribbon around his neck, and he was carrying himself with his usual dignity, but there was no mistaking his joy at the sight of the Spaniards.

"I said you would come back," he exclaimed with triumph. And then a leather-jacketed figure that had held back during the meeting rode forward to be saluted with yells of joy.

"Your Reverence," said Christóval, as he knelt for the friar's blessing, "I told those bastards they would be cashiered, but they wouldn't listen to me."

"But didn't the corporal order you to go, too?" asked the amused friar.

"Go and leave the mules and the cattle to these heathen, when the captain will be needing them when he gets back? What kind of fool do you think me, your Reverence?" It was clear that the faithful servant had expected better of the friar than that. But Palma was waiting, nervously turning the medal on his breast over and over again in his long brown fingers.

7

Palma was voluble in his explanations of what had happened. The rumor of the extermination of the Monterey party had come to the rivers. The men whom Captain Anza had left with the cattle and the saddle animals had believed the rumor. He, Palma, had not. He knew that bad men told bad stories, and, according to his account, he told the Spaniards that. But they had been frightened, and they had said they must go back to their villages before the murderers attacked them, too. He, Palma, had told them they had nothing to fear. If enemies attacked them here at the junction, the Yumas would defend their guests and their friends. But they would not listen to him. Two days after the story came, they went east. They took some of the cattle and the best of the horses. They assured him that if the captain were alive and ever returned, he would understand about the cattle and the horses, but Palma was clearly anxious about the trust which the captain had confided to him.

All this Palma told the friar again and again. In the various tellings, the emotional tone varied, and some of the dramatic details of the conversations reported, but the story was the same. It was quite clear to the friar that Palma was very anxious to impress him with his complete devotion to the interest of the king and the captain, that he was using the transaction to push his own cause. But it was, also, clear that in all this he was telling the truth.

But when Garcés tried to find out more about the story which had precipitated all the trouble, he found himself up against a wall of polite vagueness and complete inscrutability. The report had been brought into camp by some of Palma's own people who had been west of the river. That much was clear. But when the friar asked where they had heard it, the Indian was vague. He was vague, too, as to the circumstances in which they had picked up the report. And when Garcés tried to find out what sort of people had told the story, he could get nothing beyond the generic description that they were bad people. As to Palma's own attitude toward the report, the friar was puzzled. The Indian, for all his scorn of the story, was clearly uncomfortable about it.

So Garcés decided to find out what he could from Christóval. At first, the muleteer was inclined to be stubborn and uncommunicative. Some of the soldiers from Garcés' own party were loafing about the horses and teasing the muleteer. They now appealed to the friar, with a line of chaff that obviously disgusted Christóval.

The friar tactfully ignored the reported profanity, pooh-poohed the suggestion that Christóval had turned heathen while they were gone and made a pact with the devil, and then, seeing that the victim was nearing the explosion point, the friar observed to nobody in particular that doubtless the head muleteer would be glad of a little help currying and getting the horses in shape against the expected arrival of the captain. As he had expected, the soldiers lost no time in taking the hint. In a few minutes Garcés and Christóval were alone, the latter roaring with contemptuous laughter.

"A picked company, the captain said he had," he jeered.

"Christóval," said Garcés, coming directly to the point, "do you think there is anything in this story of the attack on the captain?"

"If you mean did those damned heathen kill the captain, of course, I don't. He's alive all right, and if he has half the sense he always had, he'll have the whole lot of them beaten soundly."

"I am sure he is alive, too," said the friar.

The muleteer's tanned face relaxed. "Your Reverence, it is a pleasure to talk to somebody who has some sense left. Of course, those dirty cowards would never outsmart the captain."

"But why," asked the friar, leaning on the rough sapling that made the top of the corral, "did the others run away?"

The brown face darkened, "The itching dogs could not keep away from their wives." He spat his contempt into the reddish-brown sand at his feet.

"But did they really believe that story?"

The muleteer laughed bitterly. "Of course, they didn't, but they thought that if he was having trouble with the Indians, it would take the captain longer to get back."

"Trouble with the Indians," repeated the friar wonderingly.

"Do you trust that windy Palma?" Christóval's astonishment was quite sincere.

"But it wasn't the Yumas who were supposed to have attacked the party."

"Oh, wasn't it? It was from some of Captain Pablo's men that these brown devils got the lie, wasn't it?"

The friar considered. "That I hadn't heard," he admitted cautiously.

But now it was the muleteer's turn to be judicious. "Well, that was what the interpreter said. Do you mean to tell me that Pablo would think of making trouble if Palma meant all this stuff he spouts?"

"Palma may not be able to do anything with Pablo," said the friar half to himself.

The muleteer looked at him now in unaffected surprise.

"Then," he said slowly, "he's not so godalmighty as he pretends."

But this notion the friar hastened to contradict at once. For it was no time to sow distrust of Palma.

There was nothing more that he could do until the captain came. So he set himself to get acquainted with Palma's village. He had been at first sorely tempted to use the time in pushing out to the north of the junction, but he had decided that the next fortnight, with a tired and, for all his reassurances, somewhat anxious party, was risky enough without his withdrawing whatever degree of control he could hope to exercise over these men. So with a sigh of regret for another lost opportunity he set himself to do what he could with the opportunity in hand.

Here he received an unexpected ally the first morning of his stay in the village. It was the little girl whom he had rescued, still wearing her necklace of shells. She was taller now, not so thin, a little more solemn and dignified, if that were possible. But she smiled at the friar and spoke a few quick words, which the friar could not understand.

Sebastián for all his habitual wariness looked startled, it seemed to the observant friar. "Here I am, master," he repeated slowly.

The friar laughed. "Tell her that I am glad to see her, but that as I have said before, she owes me no service." This Sebastián repeated, the amused, friar noted, with both alacrity and vigor. But the little girl shook her head and smiled a curiously wise little smile that made the friar wonder how old the child was.

"Tell her that a Grey Robe cannot have a woman for a servant."

Again, this was a speech which Sebastián was glad to translate. But the little girl made no answer. Only, as the friar went on to the Indian village, she stuck close to his heels like a shadow. Even for an Indian girl, she was small, but there was a curious effect of resolution about her small person. And though she walked demurely enough behind the friar, he soon noted that whenever they stopped at a brush hut, she contrived to emerge from behind his dusty habit and say a few words to the man or woman in the doorway, words that always produced, the friar was quite aware, a perceptible warming-up of the attitude of the Indian host.

With her large solemn eyes she missed no look or gesture of the friar, and she listened attentively to every word which Sebastián and he exchanged with the villagers. Presently, to the astonishment of the friar she began to venture a little Spanish herself, and when he tried to eke out her meaning for her, she was delighted and redoubled her efforts.

Garcés sighed, "If only she were a boy, what an acolyte she would make!" But, for all the inconvenience of her sex, the little girl trotted after them, her short bark skirt swishing briskly in their wake. And presently from much listening to the little talks which the priest gave on the basic Christian doctrines, she began to play the catechist herself to the amazement of her involuntary teacher. But Sebastián only shook his head and murmured darkly that this was no way for a woman child to behave.

So the first week of waiting merged into the second, and the second drew to its end. Garcés had begun to lose both his impatience and his anxiety. And the company of soldiers from days of swimming and riding and hunting and fishing and eating and resting seemed to be settling down to, if not contentment, at least patience. They were entertaining themselves, too, with the Indian women.

The friar had been quite aware of the risks of the cheerful dances in the late afternoon, with the whole village looking on from the sidelines. But while there was no denying the danger, he saw, also, that here at least the whole community was the witness of whatever happened, and from his side he could remind his charges of what the limits of decorum were. Grumbling, Corporal Sánchez consented to beat one young fellow who had obviously gone too far only when the friar had convinced him that neglect to do so might draw worse punishment from a couple of the husbands who were looking very darkly at that cheerful culprit.

The welcome which the friar received in the village that day was much more cordial than usual, but the next morning there were fewer soldiers at Mass. And when Garcés protested to the corporal, pointing out again that the Indians might be moved to take drastic action if the white leaders seemed indifferent to offenses against their dignity, the corporal grumbled that beating Christians and Spaniards over a silly matter of a hussy or two would never teach the Indian his place.

It was with great relief, therefore, that Garcés heard the first reports from a hunting party that Captain Anza and his company had been sighted to the southwest, a day's march away. With Sebastián he rode out to meet the captain, leaving the honors of the formal welcome at the junction to Palma himself.

In the joy and pride of that meeting all the anxieties of the last weeks fell temporarily away. The captain, having accomplished his mission, was in high spirits. He laughed at Garcés' anxieties over the story of his murder, but he admitted that he had been worried himself over the report of the flight of the Spaniards, which he had met on his way. His face darkened when he heard the facts, and when Christóval imparted his explanation of the flight, he swore that the runaways would receive a very different welcome from their wives, when the latter learned that they had forfeited their bonus.

With Palma he pronounced himself in every way satisfied, and the Indian chief carried himself like a prince in the glow of the captain's enthusiastic praise.

Anza was unstinted in his expressions of gratitude, for the fidelity of the Indian chief made possible the realization of a plan that had been in Anza's mind for some time now, the bringing of supplies to Monterey.

For a number of soldiers from the Monterey garrison had come with Anza to familiarize themselves with the trail from the junction of the rivers to the northern settlement. And now it was possible for him to send them back reenforced with cattle and horses that he knew were badly needed in Upper California.

But characteristically, he was full now of another project, nothing less than the leading of an expedition not of soldiers but of settlers to Monterey.

"Your Father Serra is a very wonderful person," he unbosomed himself to the friars in his tent that night after supper, "but those missions of his will never secure the country for his Majesty."

"That is not their primary purpose, you know," Díaz, who had come with Anza, objected gently. "They are first of all to convert the Indian and make him a good Christian, and so a good subject."

"Of course," Anza hastened to agree. "You don't need to argue that with me. But when the Indian is made a good Christian and a good subject, he must have a Christian community to go into. He can't live all his life in that school at San Gabriel or San Luís Obispo. You don't keep grown men in schools, at least not married men with families."

Garcés hesitated, "Of course, ultimately. But Father Serra says that it will be a long time before the Indian is ready to go into a colony of Spaniards and hold his own."

Anza frowned. "I don't know what you mean by 'holding his own.' He won't be the priest or the commander, true, but there will be things he can do in his own sphere, within the limits of his capacities. It takes all sorts of men to make any community. You need hewers of wood and drawers of water, if anybody is to do anything else. Now, that is something which Commander Fages understands quite thoroughly."

"But Father Serra is afraid Commander Fages—" the friar hesitated from a sudden accession of delicacy.

"Of course, they don't get on. Commander Fages told me all about it—"

But the Franciscans were not destined to learn what the commander had told Anza, for at that moment Sebastián appeared at the door of the tent, asking with considerable urgency for Father Garcés. The latter bade him come in and speak up in front of Anza. There was nothing he could talk about in this place that would not be of concern to the captain.

It did, indeed, concern him. Sebastián had just come back from visiting one of the villages to the southwest of the junction, and there he had heard the villagers talking of a raiding party which was that very day setting out to follow and ambush the men for Monterey.

"It is the old story," scoffed Anza, and then at sight of the Indian's agitation, he sobered and looked at Sebastián through narrowing eyes. "Whose village is it?" he asked after a moment's scrutiny.

"Pablo's."

"Go to Palma's camp and tell him I want to see him at once."

"He will be asleep," interposed the friar.

"He will wake up and settle this cock-and-bull business for once and for all," said Anza.

When two hours later Palma with two of his headmen appeared at the captain's tent, he did not make any effort to conceal his concern.

"He is a bad man, that Pablo," he said in the tone with which one complains of something irremediably disastrous like the weather.

"What are you going to do about it?" asked Anza sharply.

The Indian shrugged his shoulders.

The captain contemplated speculatively the medal around Palma's neck. Then he pointed to it. "Apparently, the king's representative here is not able to do the first thing the king expects all his officers to do, and that is to protect his servants when they are engaged in his service."

In his translation Sebastián must have made the veiled threat even plainer, for the Indian clutched the medal at his neck and glared at the translator. Then he turned to the captain, and now his arrogant eloquence seemed to have forsaken him, for a note of entreaty came into his voice, "Will you give me horses to do the king's service?"

Anza thought for a moment. Then he smiled. "Yes, if you need them. But suppose you try just sending word to Pablo that you have heard about his plans for the raiding party, and that if he does not give them up and report to you at once, you will fall upon his party and kill every man in it."

Garcés listened carefully to Sebastián's translation, and he was sure that just after the word "horses" he heard the Yuma word for guns. But before he could call Sebastián to account, Palma had begun very formally to give the message to the two young men who had escorted him. Again, the friar felt sure that he heard the word for guns, but the young men went off at once on their errand. And Palma explained to Sebastián that they would reach Pablo's village before the raiding party had got very far under way.

Noon of the next day brought a very sober-looking Pablo into the camp with Palma at his side. The latter undertook to do the talking. He had brought his own interpreter with him, the Yuma who had gone to San Gabriel, and through him he told the captain with great dignity that bad men had been telling lies to make trouble for the servants of the king. Pablo had just told him that there was no such party ever planned, and that nobody in all his village had so much as thought of interfering with the men for Monterey, for they knew they were the servants of the great king, and the brothers of the great chief, Palma.

The captain very coolly accepted Palma's reassurances at face value and invited both of the Yuma chieftains to dine with him. Then he added that he was very glad, for if any harm had been done to the party for Monterey, he would have been obliged to burn the villages of the offenders and kill all their men, and that would have been a pity when they were all brothers and friends. He said all this with a great air of ingenuousness, but it was quite clear from the look on Pablo's face that the Yuma interpreter gave a thoroughly competent translation of the main idea.

The friar said nothing when he saw Sebastián steal away quietly from the gathering in front of Anza's tent. And he made no comment when he did not appear for the feast that night. But he was not surprised when, just as he was preparing to lie down, the Indian returned.

"The party did not leave," he said reassuringly. "But those men are liars."

The friar brought that reassurance at once to the captain. The latter only smiled. Then he looked thoughtfully at the friar, "I think Palma means well, but he needs help."

"The mission—" began the friar eagerly.

But the captain lifted his hand before he could say more.

"Of course, that is the first thing. But for that we must have a presidio here, and still better a pueblo. We must have a new chain of presidios to bind up the whole frontier, but you are right—the key one is here. If the Yumas can be held, then we shall be all right. But the mission is not enough, whatever you say."

And then late as it was, he began to talk of the expedition that would bring the colony to Monterey. That was the next step.

✷ IV ✷

THE ROAD TO MONTEREY

I

It was, however, almost the end of that September of 1775 before Captain, now Lieutenant-colonel Anza, had his colony for Monterey under way. It had been a terrific spring and summer's work, he wrote to his friend, Father Garcés, for he had had to recruit his party and then outfit it with everything it needed from a forge to enable the blacksmith to take care of the horses' shoes to ribbons for the ladies' hair and dresses. But in the midst of this business he had not forgotten his friend's work. He had himself delivered the letter which Garcés had written to his superiors at Querétaro, asking for permission to leave his post, and he had taken advantage of the occasion to express the viceroy's and his own thanks for the very great services which Fray Francisco Garcés had performed on the expedition to Upper California, and to request the friar's services for the preliminary work on the mission for the Yumas.

Fortunately for his enterprise, the viceroy had already sent a messenger to Querétaro, asking the College of the Holy Cross of that ancient city to help him with the first plans for the great mission he looked forward to establishing at the junction of the rivers.

As Lieutenant-colonel Anza wrote to his Franciscan friend, the superiors of the College at Querétaro were no fools even in the things of this world. Of course, they were quite aware, as Bucareli well knew, that the expenses of the foundation which the viceroy would graciously grant them in the name of the king would come from funds already donated to the Church by the pious. But it was nonetheless pleasant to have authority, so often sluggish in affairs of the spirit, pushing for action. They had therefore with alacrity granted the viceroy the services of Fray Francisco Garcés for the work of exploration and peace-making that must precede the establishment of the mission.

And they had hastened to meet the other requests of Lieutenant-colonel Anza and his Excellency the Viceroy for spiritual help for the undertaking. A priest would be needed to stay at the junction with Palma and the Yumas while Father Garcés pushed his explorations. And, of course, the expedition itself would need a chaplain to go all the way to Monterey not only to minister to the needs of the colonists but, also, to keep a diary of the journey. Anza was not the man to tell another authority what to do in its own sphere, but to the partner of his dreams and his most intimate counsellor he clearly felt that he could express his misgivings without any qualms about loyalty. Whom did Father Garcés think his reverend superiors had given him for the two other positions?

There Garcés smiled. For he knew already the identity of one of the new colleagues. Fray Pedro Font, minister of San José de Pimas, had already been over to Bac to get Garcés' advice about preparations for the journey, and the latter had, as usual with his older and more dignified colleagues, felt that he made a very bad showing. His own preparations had always been of the simplest and the sketchiest. It had, for instance, been a last-minute impulse that had made him take the extra habit which he had given to Father Lasuén at San Gabriel. Ordinarily he took but the minimum of clothing or equipment with him, and usually he gave even that away somewhere on the road. Indeed, as the procurator at Querétaro had once grumbled, the only reason why he still had his breviary was that he had not yet run across an Indian able to read it.

As for food and drink, he had in the course of his wanderings learned to eat whatever food he came upon. But for Font, who in so many ways was the better religious, it was not, Garcés readily saw, so simple. His digestion was delicate, to begin with, and he was by temperament fastidious. As his fellow-friar readily guessed, it had cost him much more to come to the missionary frontier than it had Garcés. But when Garcés could give him little notion of what to expect in the way of food or what to take in the way of equipment, Font clearly felt that this vagueness and general unsatisfactoriness of his was of a piece with the unadorned church and the haphazard housekeeping of the mission of Bac, of which he had already had such a prolonged experience.

But whether or not he was adequately equipped or comfortable, Font would certainly serve Anza well. He would give a tone to the expedition that would do it good, and as Garcés knew from the reports of Font's which he had been allowed to read, he wrote beautifully. So Garcés smiled at Anza's dread of a chaplain who would doubtless try to keep him in order, too, because he knew the captain was really lucky to have Font for the expedition.

The other Franciscan addition to his party Anza was uneasy about for very different reasons. Fray Thomas Eixarch seemed to him disquietingly young, with the uncompromising innocence of the novitiate about him. Clearly, the captain was afraid he might shock the young Franciscan. Garcés could remember little of Eixarch except that he was regarded as exceptionally promising, zealous, and tireless, obviously a model religious in the making. Lieutenant-colonel Anza was afraid that he had better not tease him the way he was accustomed to tease another Franciscan of his acquaintance. That seemed to Garcés a prudent conclusion. Fray Thomas Eixarch would undoubtedly learn a good deal in the next few months.

The harvest was coming in just then, and Garcés knew that he must think of the winter. It would be well into the new year at best before he would be able to return, and the least he could do would be to leave his flock physically provided for.

It was, therefore, with a very modest sense of triumph that Garcés rode into Caborca toward the end of October. The harvest was in, and it was abundant. Miguel Dominguez had looked resigned rather than reproachful this time, and Captain Sotélo when he heard that this trip was just to the beginning of the new year, had given the friar the best horse in the guard's corral, "just to make sure that you do get back," he explained with his usual gruffness.

But, once in Caborca, Garcés reined up his horse and stood stock still. He had expected that the party would be there ahead of him, and he had known that it would be a very different sort of party from the former expedition. But he was quite unprepared for the spectacle that met his eyes in the main square of the town, in front of the two-towered facade of the old Jesuit church. It looked like a cross between a fiesta and the day after an Indian raid.

The whole square was filled with packs and bags and boxes of luggage scattered, quite without design, across its gray cobblestones. And over this luggage sprawled and straddled and stretched and climbed the most varied assortment of humanity of all ages that the Franciscan had ever beheld. Men sat smoking and staring doggedly into the dust of the cobblestones between their outstretched legs, women sat fanning themselves, then quick eyes following every move in the thronging square, little boys chased each other over and around the piled-up luggage, and little girls, their small brown fists clutching tiny skirts, leaned against their mothers' knees, watching with big eyes all the excitement of the scene. But the friar's eyes went at once to the fountain in the middle of the square, which was obviously quite the center and focus of all the activity of this amazing scene. Here muleteers were dipping their wooden pails and carrying them dripping in the foaming dust to their charges, braying thirstily by the walls of the surrounding buildings. Here the women were bobbing up and down in their broad-beamed skirts and splashing gobs of white linen in the washing trough at the base of the fountain, while others reached down shining dippers of water to half-clad children. Here and there a woman sluiced the contents of a dipper over a squirming head, while a couple of her neighbors firmly held their naked offspring under the stream of water from the topmost jet.

"They are always doing that, and I can never see that it does the little brats the least bit of good. In five minutes they're as dirty as ever."

It was Lieutenant-colonel Anza, laying a warm hand on the arm of the watching friar. The two friends greeted each other, and the friar congratulated the commander on having his expedition so well under way.

The latter flushed a little under his weather-bronzed skin, but he laughed gayly enough. "Those women certainly have things in hand. They are always washing and scrubbing, and it never seems to end."

"I suppose it is like the priest's work. It is always to be done over," said the friar thoughtfully, "and yet if it isn't done continually, the mess is pretty bad."

The commander laughed. "Well, at that I am not sure but the women are better employed than the men. Half the men are in the canteen now, drinking up all the aguardiente in the place. If I don't rout them out pretty soon, you'll have plenty to do, my friend, with the resulting quarrels."

But the friar shook his head, "I'll leave that to the commander who let them have the aguardiente in the first place."

"What can you do? I've held the rein pretty tight so far, and you know this is the last stop in civilization," Anza protested with a marked undertone of injured innocence.

"I know," said the friar sympathetically. "A little won't do any harm, but the day is going pretty fast now, and you don't want them too foozled for that early-morning start tomorrow."

There was a slightly stubborn look on the commander's face, and the friar sighed as he read in that expression the usual layman's conviction that the priest, living his privileged and protected life, can have little notion of the problems of a practical man who has to deal with the world as it is.

"I'll tell you what," Garcés said presently. "I'll ask Father Díaz here to let us have vespers. Perhaps he can rout out a few of his choirboys and give us some music. The women will like that. And then you can tell the men that their wives would like to have them come in, too, and offer a few prayers to the Virgin for the journey. Nothing gives a good woman so much pleasure as to see her man in church, and it certainly won't hurt the men," the friar added with a smile.

The sullen look had left the commander's face. "You friars do know what to do with the women." And then as the friar smiled at the time-worn jest, Anza's face relaxed. "You know, Father Garcés, Font tried to get me to have the canteen closed as soon as we arrived. And when I wouldn't listen to his nonsense, he went off in a huff to the church where he no doubt is still, praying for my sins."

But the friar shook his head, "He has his job to do, too. And," he smiled at the indignant commander, "Font is really a very good priest. His prayers won't hurt you."

As he expected, Anza's sense of humor came to the rescue, and he started off for the canteen. The friar tethered his horse, asked a couple of little urchins prowling around obviously in search of something to do, to water the horse, and not to tease it. And then he went up to the fountain to tell the women that he was hoping to arrange for vespers so that they might be ready when the bell began to ring.

The first woman he came to was one who had already caught his eye, the wife of Vicente Felix, one of the soldier recruits. She was obviously very near her time, and yet she had been struggling to clean up a whole brood of husky children. Finally, a couple of her neighbors had good-naturedly made her sit down on a stone at the foot of the fountain while they ducked a couple of disheveled little boys for her.

Now as the priest spoke to her, the large dark eyes looking so cavernous in her thin white face lighted. "I am so glad," she murmured, and the priest seeing the fear in the tired face, gently blessed her.

"I will pray specially for you, and so will all your neighbors," he tried to reassure her, and that scared animal look in the depths of her eyes seemed to go back into its hole.

Later, when vespers were over, and the rosary had been said, the friar told the commander about the frightened woman.

"Would it perhaps be wise to linger for a day or two?" he asked.

But Anza shook his head. "You see, there are several others. We'll have to stop a bit when the time comes any way."

"She seems afraid," said the friar, worriedly.

"She has had six others and no trouble, her husband tells me."

The square was now bubbling over with excitement, for the women were preparing the supper of corn gruel over little fires of thorn and mesquite root, and the children and the men were milling around expectantly.

Slowly, the friar pushed his way through the cheerful crowd until he found the little party he sought, the woman seated on a low box, with two little mites of humanity leaning against her tired knees.

"The vespers were nice, father," she said. She looked even more worn now, but calmer.

"You have nothing to worry about," said the friar. "I am sure you have been to confession."

"Oh, yes, and he—" nodding after the soldier's back—"has been, too."

"Then you have nothing to be afraid of," said the friar.

"I know," she said softly. "But it isn't for myself, father." And she suddenly put out her thin hands and caught the two children at her knee close to her. The children squirmed uncomfortably, and in a moment they had broken loose from her weak clutch.

She looked up imploringly at the priest. He sat down beside her, and in a low voice he began to reassure her, "That is something you must leave to God and Our Lady. You may be sure that God will not let any ill come to them when you have loved them and cared for them so well."

Again, the fear crept back into its lair in her dark eyes, and she wiped a tear away. "I know, father, I must be braver."

"Don't try to be brave," said the priest. "Don't try to do anything about it. Just leave it to Our Lady. She can do better with it than you or I can."

"It is a hard business for the women," said the friar later as he sat at supper with the commander in the guardhouse at Caborca.

"You don't need to tell me that," retorted Anza. "Of course, I'd rather do it with just the soldiers, but you can't have a colony without the women."

2

NOTHING showed more plainly the difference between Anza's first expedition and the second than the morning start. Garcés, as a rule, said his own Mass early and then helped to prepare for Father Font's Mass, which was the official Mass for the company. But often between the two Masses there might be some free minutes which the friar would spend walking through the camp.

When Font sounded the bell for the community Mass, most of the women hurried their children to his tent where a chest had been set in front of the lifted flap. Some of the men came, too, but most of them were still taking down the tents or lacing the loads on the mules, bracing one foot against the side of the animal, which always stamped and plunged in the hands of the man who held it for the loading. Usually, the result was a good deal of noise and confusion which would last until the striking of Anza's silver tankard, which Font used as a bell on the road, brought most of the company to its knees in front of the tent.

The first time Garcés saw the scattered expedition fall to its knees, he was deeply moved. The second experience, today, was still more impressive, for now the friar had a profounder sense of its meaning. It was not only the most solemn moment in the noisy and distracted day, but it was, also, the one time when the disparate fragments of the whole expedition were pulled together into one unified consciousness and intention. There was no mistaking the earnestness of petition in all those eyes drawn like steel by a magnet to the Host in Father Font's hands. A moment before, they had been so many individuals, hurrying through their own morning chores, fussing over their own children, their own pots and pans, their own bags to be packed; now they were one in a single act of common worship. The spell would be broken in a minute. There would be a scramble for the last-minute push of the dilatory or the inefficient; there would be much noise and confusion as they scrambled on their horses and mules; there would be some wrangling as they jockeyed for position in the line of march. There would be all the pulling and hauling of any group of more than a hundred and seventy human beings suddenly hurled into the closest day-long intimacy. It was that way yesterday; it would be that way today, perhaps even more so as the inevitable repetitions of petty annoyances and rivalries and exacerbations intensified the strain of the common life. But for those few precious moments the basic intention of the enterprise had been realized, and the solidarity of the Christian community vindicated.

Again, as yesterday, the high moment passed, and the kneeling group rose to wait for the "Ite, Missa est" with the poised alertness of the worshipper who, meaning not to fail in his duty, is yet resolved to be among the first to get out of the church. And then the stillness broke into the uproar of the morning departure.

Under cover of that excitement the commander beckoned Garcés aside. "Vicente Felix has just told me that his wife's labor has begun. So I have excused him from his duties today so that he can hold her on the horse in front of him."

"Pray that your flight be not in the winter," the friar murmured softly.

But the commander shook his head. "Don't forget that it is the chance of a lifetime for her and for the youngsters, too. A soldier's pay does not go far with that brood. And if they had stayed in Sonora, they'd have nothing but a little patch of ground to go with it. Here the whole world is before them. A house, as much land as they can use, and all the chances of a new community."

"I suppose that is what has brought most of them here," said the friar gently.

"Well—" Anza hesitated for a moment. "Of course, some of the single men are seeking their fortune. You remember Juan Miguel—well, he is scouting out Monterey to see if that girl he is always mooning about will like it. She probably won't, but she will make Juan Miguel brace up, and it will do him a world of good. Most of them, though, are—" At that moment the officer of the day came to tell the captain that he thought they could safely fall in line. There would be some stragglers as always, but there was no sense in delaying any longer.

It was well into the afternoon before the captain could return to the friar. But at once he plunged into what was clearly a favorite theme of his. "You were asking this morning," he began, while the friar blinked to recover what it was they had been discussing, "about what brought all these people on the road."

And then before Garcés could even begin to look intelligent about the morning's conversation, the commander drove ahead. "Mind you, we selected them carefully. I told the viceroy that I did not want any jails emptied into my colony or any village scolds or adventuresses dumped into it. And I told them to check up on the records of these people. No ne'er-do-wells or slatternly housekeepers or gadabouts."

"It does take checking-up," the friar assented encouragingly. He had said the day's office, and the rosary for Vicente Felix' wife, and he had ridden down the line to visit and encourage one or two others of the party who had seemed ailing or dispirited. Now he was quite ready to humor his friend.

"It takes very careful checking-up," said the commander in his most authoritative manner. "But there are able men among the poor."

At this the friar blinked quite awake. "But, of course," he said in astonishment.

The commander was not in the least abashed, however. "I used to think that in a new country like this a man had only himself to blame if he did not prosper. But I don't think so any longer. The king's service makes few honest men rich, and there are plenty of men who just jog along in the rut who might do something better if given a chance."

"And I suppose there must be many energetic women married to such men who might do even better," said the friar.

It was now Anza's turn to be a little stiff, "But surely a woman's place is to be content with what her husband gives her?"

Somewhat drily the friar agreed. He was thinking of Juan Miguel's Rosalía, when a soldier rode up to say that Vicente Felix had sent him to report that his wife's time had come, and he must get her under a tent at once. As Anza rode to the head of the line to give the signal for stopping, the friar rode back.

It was amazing the speed with which the long line stopped and men and women jumped from their horses and mules. And it was still more amazing the speed with which the women of the party converged upon the tent which the soldiers had already erected. Not all of them by any means could crowd into it, but the rest stood outside with that air of closed solidarity which the friar had observed women assume on such occasions, an air which makes even the most self-confident male suddenly feel embarrassed at his own irrelevance. It was curious how the whole aspect of the party had changed. Except for the bustling of the women, the entire scene seemed to hang suspended in the still air of the late afternoon.

Vicente Felix was leaning against a heap of luggage, smoking. Half a dozen of his fellow-soldiers were smoking with him. So the friar went over to the commander's tent. There he found Anza with his coat off, washing his hands in a basin of water and soaping them again thoughtfully.

"The women say the baby is coming the wrong way; so I am going over to see what I can do. God, if only it were a broken leg, or something like that!"

The friar and the commander went over to the tent, the commander going in, the friar lingering outside.

Only a few feet away two of Felix' older children were tossing a ball to each other. The boy, a chubby, slow-moving figure, the girl, smaller, thin and agile as a gnat, pitched their ball to each other, as if completely unaware of what was going on.

The friar called the boy and bade him take his sister to his aunt, who was gathering in the little flock some yards down the road. But the boy moved so sluggishly and indifferently that before they were out of hearing, a piercing scream broke from the tent and then failed as if for want of breath, so that the silence that followed was more dreadful than the cry. The little girl down the road began to clutch her brother and whimper, while the latter stood open-mouthed.

Then there came a sudden cry, sharp and explosive and indignant. The whole suspended air broke into a hearty laugh.

"Nothing wrong with that young rascal!" exclaimed one of the soldiers and started up the road for the father. The whole camp was suddenly laughing and talking. In a few minutes one of the older women emerged with plump arms akimbo on her broad hips. "As fine a boy as I ever saw in my life, even if he did come feet first," she announced triumphantly to the whole world.

Then she caught sight of the friar, "No need to baptize him now, father. You can do it properly tomorrow with the whole camp for sponsors."

So Garcés started back for the commander's tent. On his way he met the proud father, wiping his forehead as he walked along, escorted by a dozen of his comrades. The friar gave him his felicitations and went on his way. But he had barely settled himself on a chest in the commander's tent when Anza came in.

"Thank God, the boy's all right, but I don't like that woman's looks," he said wearily. For a few moments he stood there uncertainly, looking at the friar. Then he sat down on the chest. "Thank God! If the boy hadn't come all right, all the women in the party would be blaming me for not taking that dirty old harridan of a midwife down in Horcasitas. I'd have taken her, too, but I was sure she would die on my hands without her aguardiente."

"And Señora Felix?"

The worried look came back to the commander's face, "I don't like the way she looks. I wish you'd go over and see her. You've seen enough to know—but don't let her get sight of you, if you can help it. She's scared enough without making her think you've come to give her the last rites."

The friar said nothing. How little the healthy can guess about that strange midway world of the dying where all the signposts of health and morbidity are changed!

The patient seemed asleep, breathing with the heavy slowness of exhaustion. The priest went over and looked into her face. It was very still and expressionless, but there was no mistaking the almost luminous pallor of the thin features. The priest shook his head and sank to his knees by the low cot.

As he left the tent, one of the women followed him. Again, he shook his head, "You'd better watch her. If there's any sign of change, or if she wakes, you'd better call me." He saw the alarm on the woman's face, and he hastened to add, "I'm not a doctor, you know; so it may not be so bad. But it won't do any harm to watch closely."

Outside, he told the little throng, already beginning to celebrate, that the mother was asleep, and it was very important that she be not disturbed. One or two of the women looked alarmed, but the men had had their aguardiente, and the holiday mood was on them. Good-naturedly they moved off, as the friar made his way to the little knot where Vicente Felix presided over the barrel.

The proud father poured a little brandy into a small cup and held it out to the friar. The latter sipped at it with the proper good wishes, and then he returned it to the soldier. He at once raised it to his lips, but the friar laid his hand on the man's arm. "I don't think you had better, either. Your wife may be needing you before the night is over." He saw the man's weatherbeaten face pale, and he quietly nodded to the sudden fear in his eyes. But the birthday celebration still went on.

It was still continuing when long after dark, the commander came to Garcés' tent. "Will you come and see Señora Felix? She's awake, but she does not know what is going on."

The friar lingered only long enough to stop at Font's tent and tell him that he had better get the oil for the anointing ready. Then he followed the commander to the sick tent. Candles had been lighted there so that now the woman's face looked even more luminous in the soft light. Her eyes opened for a moment as Garcés stood over her, but they were as expressionless as the rest of the alabaster face. The friar sank to his knees and began the prayers for the dying.

When the last blessing had been given to the still unconscious woman, the commander ordered the tent cleared of all save the baby in a basket in a corner and the two women who were serving as nurses.

Garcés sat down on a couple of saddlebags that had been heaped for a seat by the low camp bed. The noise of singing, warm on the quiet night air, checked as if its throat had been seized. All the movements and stamping and talking ceased abruptly, too, and in the stillness the friar caught the voice of a cricket, sharpening the uncanny quiet. Then he heard a gulp and looked up to see Felix standing by his side.

With a swift movement the friar rose to give up his seat, but with an even swifter movement the woman caught his hand in a cold clasp. She was talking, too, in a low, hurried voice. He sank back and listened, with the keenness of hearing of one who has often listened to the faint confession of the dying. "All I wanted was to have us all together," she was saying as if explaining something that had been misunderstood. "I didn't want to be rich. I just wanted my husband to do what he wanted, and the children—" the voice trailed helplessly.

The priest took the cold hand and began to chafe it lightly.

She seemed to find strength again for something that desperately needed to be said, "You will ask Our Lady to take care of them, won't you?"

The priest held her hand firmly and bent down so that he was speaking into her ear, "You will ask her yourself, and she will listen to you, and do it."

The look of anxiety vanished. For a moment the eyes opened and looked steadily into the friar's. Then the white face relaxed, and a little sigh of contentment fluttered through the pale lips.

3

THE commander and the soldiers, who were used to the desert burial, often enough without any priest within reach to say Mass over the worn-out body, and the solemn requiem on the return, wished to bury Señora Felix by the roadside. But the women of the party were unanimously horrified at the idea. In vain, the commander explained that they would dig the grave deep enough so that the wolves would not find it in the winter rains. And they would smoothe the surface and put brush over it so that no wandering Indians might be tempted to desecrate it. His very reassurances but increased the women's indignation.

"Leave her where her children will never be able to light candles on All Souls' Eve and say a prayer for the repose of her soul?" Their indignation but thinly masked their horror at the idea.

In vain Font quoted the exquisite words of the dying Monica to Saint Augustine, "Lay this body anywhere…this only I request, that you would remember me at the Lord's altar, wherever you be." These were no cosmopolitan sophisticates, adept in the mystical speculations of a thousand years. These were illiterate peasant women, hardly wrenched from the parental farms, seeing all of life in the sanctities of the family and the village. Font owned himself beaten. After all, as the priest of all men should know, it was the women's sense of what was right and fitting that would be the cornerstone of whatever civilization they would establish in the new land into which they were going.

Anza was indignant at Font's failure to support his authority. But Garcés shook his head at the commander's protests. And presently he had a practical suggestion. They were now out in the country between Caborca and Garcés' own post at Bac. There was a rough trail from one to the other that the friar had often ridden to save time. Why not let him take the body that way to his mission, and when the party arrived the next day by the main road, they could have the funeral there.

"You, too," said the commander in disgust, but he was too old a soldier not to know when he had better give in. Still he grumbled, "It will lose us two good days before we are through. And you know I don't want to take too many chances with those mountains. It will be past November as it is."

The friar put a sympathetic hand on his friend's shoulder. "I know how careful you are in your planning, but there are things that always upset our plans, and this is one. Don't forget, too, that good spirits are better than good weather for travelers, and you are providing the good spirits now."

The captain's scowl relaxed, and something of the quizzical look with which he so often regarded the friar came into his tired face, "That sounds suspiciously like a hint, my friend." And he stooped down, and from a small leather-covered chest at the foot of the low bed, he took out a squat flask. "I think we both need this."

The friar nodded and took a fiery sup that coursed lightly into his veins. He handed the flask to the captain, who drank deep.

Then he looked up at the friar, "I don't think anybody could have saved that poor woman." It was a statement, but he looked at his friend with obvious hunger for confirmation.

"I am sure not," said the friar quietly. "You know I have always considered you one of the best surgeons I have ever seen in the field. And though this is a different sort of thing, still that woman was pretty far gone before ever the baby came. By the way, the baby seems husky enough?"

The captain's face lighted, "Even the women who grumbled about my not taking that midwife say that the boy is a fine one. And they admit it was a real job to save him." Again, the tired face shadowed. The friar sat down on the camp bed by his friend. Now that it was a matter of something to be done at once, his fatigue-muddied brain had mysteriously cleared.

"You know," he said, thinking aloud, "it would be just as well to get that poor body to Bac as soon as possible. Then we can have her laid out in the church properly when the party arrives, and they can say the rosary and the rest. Then early in the morning we'll have a proper funeral."

"That will be the next day?" objected the captain, but his tone was speculative.

"Yes," said the friar, "but after they have had their dinner, we can take the road again and get on a fair piece before we have to stop."

As he rose, the commander rose, too, "That is good of you," he said, and then as if seeing his friend's face for the first time, he added with sudden solicitude, "Are you sure you can start tonight? How about some sleep?"

The friar smiled, "It will not be the first night I have ridden, and I have good people at Bac who'll take care of everything for me so that I can sleep when I get there."

"Then," said the captain, "I'll rout out four of the soldiers and let them get the horse-litter slung, and the women can wash the body. Will you be ready in, say an hour or two?"

The friar nodded. Then he went to Font's tent where he found his colleague still sitting up, his breviary open in the candlelight.

He looked up as Garcés came in. "Are you going tonight?"

The younger friar nodded.

"It is wise," said Font gravely, as if his approval had been asked. And Garcés was conscience-smitten. The commander was so accustomed to fighting over his problems with Garcés that he had quite forgotten that this time he should be taking more official counsel. How many things to remember, the friar sighed. Then his mind raced ahead to the plans at Bac. Suddenly he looked up to find Font's eyes on him.

"You know, I was just thinking of the choir for that Requiem Mass. I've never been able to get my boys much beyond what you did. I'm not good at music, as you know," he said humbly. "I was wondering if tomorrow as you come along the road, you might not rehearse some of the boys and men on the *Dies Irae* at least."

"That," said Font, obviously mollified, "is a good idea."

Then Garcés explained the night's plans. He dwelt for a moment on the satisfaction a proper lying-in-state in the church would be to the women, and his plans for the rosary, and then, parenthetically, he mentioned the matter of a little feast.

Font scowled, "But surely at a time like this we might leave out that heathen nonsense."

"Of course, no drunkenness," said Garcés hastily, "but our women will get a bit of supper ready, and the captain of the garrison will want to give the men a little aguardiente. They can all talk about their grandfather's funeral, and how their favorite aunt died with her first child, and it will all feel more homelike and more like one village."

Font said nothing, but sighed lightly as he often did at the contemplation of human folly, and his companion rightly took the silence for a tacit admission of the cogency of his argument. Then he went out into the night to look for the litter.

But he had no trouble finding it, for the soldiers had lighted torches. And as the friar came up, they handed the torches up to the men who rode the horses between which the litter was slung.

"They thought it more respectful to the dead," explained Anza drily, as he handed the bridle of the friar's horse to him. And then aloud he added, "Vicente Felix wants to go with you, of course."

The friar went up and shook hands with the bereaved husband, and he found the usually strong hand moist and trembling.

"I'll ride by the litter, to see that everything is all right," said the friar, maneuvering his horse into place, and then, as Felix hung back respectfully, he urged him to ride on his other side. So they started off into the night.

The wind had risen and was wailing softly in the palo verde and the scrubby mesquite of this half-desert region. There was no moon nor any stars to be seen, and it was still, the friar knew, a good hour to the whitening of the dawn. But the torches flaring in the darkness gave enough light to find the road between the fringe of brush and low shrubs, which now and then took fantastic life and shot up alarmingly in the unsteady flare of the torches. Poised between the horses, the low-piled litter seemed to assume motion of its own and swing away from the horses' legs.

Once the friar put out his hand to steady the litter, and the hind horse stopped with a jerk. As the rider leaned forward to tighten a strap, the friar could hear the man's teeth chattering.

When the litter was again swinging rhythmically between the hoof-beats, the friar spoke very quietly, "She was a good woman, and she died to bring a man into the world. So she may even now be at Our Blessed Lady's feet praying for us all. But we'll say a rosary for her just the same. If she doesn't need it, Our Lady will give it to some poor soul who does." And in a clear, steady voice he announced the first of the sorrowful mysteries and began to say the opening prayers. By the time they had finished, the dawn was whitening in the east, and the worst of their journey was over, although they all knew that it would be well into the afternoon before they could reach their destination.

As Garcés had promised, the mission of San Xavier del Bac plunged into the business of the funeral with enthusiasm. The fate of the poor mother, dead in childbirth out in the desert, struck every frontier heart with pity, as the friar had known it would. But there was more than pity to the zest with which the whole of Bac plunged in that day. The harvest was in, and there was material plenty. There was, also, something of that lassitude which overtakes men when a big job is completed, and the imagination, no longer harnessed to the pressures of the moment, is free to roam a little over the wastes of the day's routine. It is at such times that the smallest cloud of excitement on the horizon is welcomed, whether it be for joy or for sorrow.

So while the friar slept against the day's later demands, the mission of Bac surpassed all his promises and expectations. The wives of the guard, headed by the captain's wife, who usually kept very quietly within her patio while her husband stormed through the pueblo, took charge of the body. By the time the friar had roused himself enough to think of the preparations that must be made, Señora Felix was lying in state in front of the altar.

As one of the soldiers' wives explained to the friar when he came to look at the figure lying before the altar, the captain's lady had given one of her old silk gowns and a worn lace mantilla for the burial. The result was undeniably fine. The thin white face, now quite serene, seemed very peaceful in the frame of lace, and even the work-roughened hands looked delicate, with a rosary and a late-blooming rose, softly pink, between the bloodless fingers.

"It is very proud she would be, if she could see herself," said the woman, and then she drew back respectfully as the friar knelt down before the altar.

Presently, he heard a stamping of horses' hoofs in the plaza in front of the church; so he hurried out to greet the arriving party. They were already dismounting when he opened the church door, but he saw at once that the usual cheerful bustle of the camp arrival was missing. Even the children were looking sober, and a bit frightened, too, the little ones with finger in mouth, clinging to their mothers' wide skirts, the older ones waiting quietly in the middle of the piling luggage.

But the whole company looked up when the first of the Indian women appeared with a basket tray of tortillas, to be followed by another woman with a steaming pot of chocolate. The soldiers' wives came out, too, to invite the women to come into their quarters and rest and tidy up. The first of the visitors to emerge from one of the little adobe houses came out in clean blouses with whatever bits of finery they had brought with them, long earrings, a necklace, a shawl. The effect was distinctly dressed-up-for-church, and presently every woman in the party had freshened up and decked herself as well as she could.

The commander joined the friar on the steps of the church, to which the latter had returned to open it for the party to come in. For a moment they looked at the company, very solemn still, but not nearly so frightened-looking. And, presently, the grave look on the face of the commander relaxed, too.

"It is an amazing thing the way these women contrive with their clothes. They all were given precisely the same outfit when they started, and my wife assured me that they would hate looking all alike, but look at them now. If you can see anything like a uniform there, you can do better than I can." There was admiration as well as amusement in the captain's tones.

But the friar, who recalled the half-amused complaint of an aunt who was reverend mother to a whole convent of nuns that the same veil could be pinned on twenty heads according to the same rules, and there would be twenty different effects, only smiled. For it was time now to open with prayers the lying-in-state of the soldier's wife. So he threw open the doors of the little church of Bac and bade them all come in for the prayers for the dead and the rosary.

It was quite dark within after the autumnal brightness of the plaza, and the candles made a pool of soft light at the end of the nave. The whole building was sweet now with cedar boughs, and there were some bright spots of color where one of the women who had decked the church had put some bright berries under a picture or at the foot of a statue. But it was the still figure, radiant in the soft light of the candles, that drew all eyes. And, presently, Font's stately presence loomed up behind the lights, and the sonorous beat of the Latin blessing filled the hushed silence, and the sweet smoke of the incense floated into the pool of light and made it a luminous haze.

When the rosary was finished, all the women pushed to the front of the church to gaze in admiration at the splendor of the dead. Señora Felix had made no figure in their group when she was living, tired, apprehensive as she was, always looking around anxiously for some straying member of her brood, always preoccupied with the nameless fussing of the mother of a large family. But now all eyes were fixed on her, and the praise of her marble loveliness was on every tongue. And she whose new clothes even had soon been clawed and pulled into smudged wrinkles now shone in fine clothes that drew the eyes of every woman in the church. Perhaps the strangest thing of all was that she who had never even in her shy girlhood known much of the world's attention, not to say homage, seemed to take it all with the serene indifference of a queen, lying there in their awed midst like a being from a more splendid world, the light of which still clung like a halo to this momentary visitation of a lower realm.

4

THE rest of the program at Bac went through as it had begun. And Father Garcés gave thanks for the generous energy of Indian and Spaniard alike. The supper which the women served to the party in the plaza brought freshly boiled and roasted meat and chili to give welcome relief to the daily fare of atole and jerked beef and bean porridge. And then the kindly women of the garrison produced little cakes and sweets to regale the women while the men drifted over to the canteen of the garrison where Captain Sotélo had broached a keg of well-aged aguardiente.

But it was a sober company that met in the church in the morning, and an even soberer company that with the long-drawn periods of the *Dies Irae* in their ears streamed into the little churchyard of Bac and laid the body of Señora Felix in the sandy earth under the shade of the sweet-smelling mesquite trees. And it was a still soberer company that rode out into the environing desert afterwards. But there was something different in the party that the friar was perhaps the first to be aware of, and the commander to find words for. It was first seen when they paused to make camp that night. Vicente Felix tried to round up his forlorn little family, but one of the women who already had a half dozen of her own, bade him bring them over to her flock. She would see that they got fed, and she would put them to bed in her tent. Even as she spoke, three or four others chimed in with invitations for the morrow, while the widowed soldier, mopping his brow with relief, went off to have a quiet supper with some friends who had no children to remind him of his increased responsibilities.

It was seen, too, in the little knots that gathered from neighboring tents to kneel down by the campfire and say the rosary for the repose of the soul of her whose body they had left in the graveyard at Bac. It was seen all the weeks that followed not only in the helpfulness that cared for the orphan baby and his older brothers and sisters, but still more in a spirit of intimacy that beguiled the long rides with stories and songs and jests and, presently, those endless speculations in which women love to put their heads together and while the hours away.

"It is as if they had lived together in the same village for years," said the commander one day when he had fallen back to ride with the friar at the back of the party.

"Yes," said Garcés, "even on that long march yesterday they never stopped talking and laughing. The women seem to meet the endless rides as cheerfully as the men, and it must be hard on them with the children to think of."

"And yet," said the commander, who never could bear even the remotest approach to a reflection on his men, "the men are better than I would have thought. You've noticed there is hardly a one of the married men who hasn't a child up in front of him, and some of them have three or four. Indeed, I have been worrying about the punishment some of the horses are taking."

"Have you noticed, though, how well-fed those horses are? For whenever they stop, the children are out plucking grass and weeds for their horse, even before they think of their own suppers."

"This is what they need out in California," said the commander with satisfaction. "You get a colony of these people out there at Monterey, and you'll have something like a civilization. There will be some place for the Indians to go when they have been made Christians."

"Will the Indians find their place in that colony?" asked the friar.

The commander looked at his friend in surprise. "Of course! There isn't a man but is talking of the land he will cultivate and the cattle he will breed. They will need all the Indian help they can get. And the women are always talking of the Indian women they will have for their kitchens. There will be plenty for the Indians to do, I assure you. Once, of course, you friars have trained them."

"But will the Indians want to do it?" persisted the Franciscan.

"Well, you saw yourself how they are learning to do things at San Gabriel? And at Carmelo they are already making great strides. We shall all have reason to bless you friars when we have made that desert bloom."

The commander looked puzzled when his friend made no reply.

Garcés was trying to think how he could put the thought that was troubling him into words. Presently, he had an idea.

"Look at this party," he said. "Back there in those towns in Sonora, if you had looked at those people there, would you have guessed that they would think of owning land and raising flocks and the rest of it? They seemed born to be underlings to their masters, and now they are thinking of being masters."

Anza gazed in astonishment at his friend. "But the Indians—surely they are not thinking of being anybody's master?"

The friar smiled, "I don't think they are, but I don't think they are thinking of being anybody's servant, either." He stopped. He had put it very badly. The commander was staring at him in frank puzzlement.

But before he could ask the friar what in the world he was thinking of, the officer of the day rode down the line to tell the commander that some Indians were coming around the foot of the peak ahead of them. So both Garcés and Anza rode ahead. They were coming into the land of the Gila Pimas, and the commander, who was anxious to see again some of the chieftains who ruled in the villages along the river, had sent couriers ahead to notify them of his approach.

"They look as if they had been out hunting," said the friar, watching them straggling along.

"But they are marching slowly," said the commander, "as if perhaps they were weary from fighting."

The two friends pushed ahead, followed by a couple of the soldiers. Looking behind for a moment, the friar saw the first of the colonists rein in as if uncertain of what lay ahead. He waved reassurance to them and an invitation to come on, and then he rode on to overtake the commander.

As the Indians drew near, it soon became apparent that both the friar and the commander were right. A couple of them were carrying on their shoulders the carcase of a big-horned sheep such as was to be found in the mountains. But ahead of them walked two men who bore aloft on poles what looked like two fragments of meat with the hair still adhering.

"Scalps," murmured one of the soldiers, instinctively taking a firmer grip on his musket.

"Steady," said the commander. "They are coming toward us as friends." And in a moment he gave a glad cry of recognition. For the two leaders were seen to be men whom they had met on the earlier expedition. At the moment of recognition the two Indians shouted greetings in Pima, and rushed forward with their gory trophies.

When he had embraced the Indians, the commander pointed to the scalps, "We have women and children with us this time. So won't you put them out of sight for a while?"

"But," protested the leader, "they are Apache scalps."

"Apache?" The commander's eyes flashed. "Where did you meet them?"

"Over there," the Indian pointed away from the river to which they were heading, and the commander relaxed. "We went out hunting, and a party of them fell upon us, but," proudly, "we were better than they, and we hit these two with our arrows."

One of the Indians who now gathered around the Spaniards exhibited a gash, half stopped with clay, and the surgeon in Anza looked grave. "It is nothing," said the leader. "You should have seen those Apaches run."

"A pleasant sight, I am sure," said the commander with feeling, and the soldiers laughed. Meanwhile the leader of the Indians was proudly exhibiting the scalps to the soldiers who gathered round. There were one or two little squeals from the women and the girls, and the men laughed.

"You'd squeal more, my girl," said one of the men, "if that fellow were coming at you with that lock standing up straight on his head." And the rest of the company laughed good-humoredly.

"What savages they are!" exclaimed one of the women. "They are little better than animals."

They were at the river now, and the commander gave the signal to stop and make camp. With relief the long line halted, and those to the rear began to drift forward while the first-come pressed to the river for water. It was still a perfectly cheerful and good-humored company, but it was also a very weary one. Garcés walked slowly along the little groups scattered at random over the river bank.

"I certainly could do with one of those half dozen Indian girls you were talking about right now," one woman called to another.

The friar paused for a moment to help a woman who had dropped some shelled corn retrieve her treasure.

"Remember what I said, though. You'll have to train them. They never lived in a house before," the neighbor called back.

"Father," said the woman, when she had thanked the friar for the recovered food, "do you think we really will have a half dozen Indian girls to help us as they say?"

The friar hesitated. And the woman looked up at him anxiously. "Or do you think they will be too stupid to learn how to do things the way we want them?"

The friar still hesitated, but he saw that here was a chance to plant a seed of thought in at least one not entirely closed mind. "Do you do things more cleverly when you are doing them the way you want to do them, or the way somebody else wants you to do them?" He saw the woman flush a little, and he guessed that perhaps before her marriage she had been in service.

He went off and discovered the commander still with his Indian guests, eating in front of his tent before a little fire of dry shrubs. The friar apologized for the interruption, and went on to ask if the captain had noticed how tired the party looked. The captain said nothing but waited as if he knew more were coming. Then the friar reminded him that there was till a good distance to cover before they would reach the Yuma camp and another chance to rest. Here there was pasturage as good as they were likely to find at this time of year, and an abundance of water.

The captain's eyes lighted. "These friends of ours," he nodded to the Indians, "have just been telling me about some very interesting remains of ancient times, a little way from here. If we stay here tomorrow, it will give the women plenty of chance to rest and do their business, and we can go and see these remains."

So the next morning after breakfast the captain and the priests and the Indians started out. The men of the party were still for the most part sleeping in their tents, but the women were already at the river with heaps of clothes. Garcés thought of the Indian girls they were dreaming of, but Font was talking with much eagerness of the site which they were going to visit.

"You see," he explained, "it's a well-known place. Father Kino mentioned it in his writings, you will remember, Father Garcés. It is a palace of their ancient rulers, he was told, but he was told, too, that it had belonged to another nation of men than these Gila Pimas who live here now."

As a matter of fact, Garcés did not remember. But Font's eyes had lighted as they lighted when he listened to music well-performed. And, as they rode over the desert away from the river, he told of the shards of fine pottery which Father Kino and others had noted in the desert, red and blue and white painted ware of finer workmanship and design than any which the Indians now used in this part of the world.

"Perhaps," suggested the captain who had been following Font's disquisition with great interest, "they were a different people."

"Father Kino reported that he had heard that," said Font cautiously.

Anza asked the leader of the Gila Pimas whether it was his people who built the great house they were going to see. The commander spoke in the Pima tongue which he had much less occasion to use than Garcés, and he had difficulty making the Indian understand. Presently, the Indian seemed to grasp what had been said to him, but he appeared disinclined to answer. Finally, he said a couple of words twice over. The captain looked at the friar for help.

"He says the ancient ones built it."

With that they had to be content. The friar suspected that the Indian believed that his own ancestors had built it, but was disinclined to use anything but the vague terms in which the Indian usually referred to the dead.

What astonished Garcés more than the great house itself was the series of broken walls and fragments of towers and houses which lay about it. Where their horses were now picking their way among stones and brambles and cactus thorns, a thousand miles from any sign of present urban life, must once have stood a considerable city. And here and there was scattered débris, the shards of the past, washed out of the sand in the recent rains of the fall perhaps, or kicked up by the passing feet of horses and men. There were some bright glints of color among the fragments, and presently they came upon a well-made disc of stone, finely finished, and a metate or grinding stone quite like what the Indian women still used, but much smoother. Was it because of greater skill in the maker or the slow abrasion of the weather, so refining in its action on the unyielding elements of life? It was a finer city that had stood here five hundred years ago in the land of the Gila Pimas than was likely to stand in Monterey for many a day.

But Font was exclaiming over the Casa Grande itself now; he was praising the noble and elegant proportions of the clearly-discernible ground-plan, still very much as Father Kino had described it seventy-five years ago.

"Those rooms were large enough for the viceroy's palace," he exclaimed. "And they were made out of timber and clay," he added in awe. So they scrambled in and out of the ruins, Font measuring and exclaiming, with delight, Garcés following more slowly, often stopping to watch the inscrutable faces of their guides.

"I wonder what the furniture was like?" asked Font.

The Indians looked puzzled when Garcés repeated the question in more specific terms. "What was in the houses?" he asked. "Jars for water, baskets of food, blankets?"

The Indian who answered shrugged his shoulders indifferently. "What more should there be?" he asked.

"But he must have been the great prince who lived here," said Font. "Surely, he would have this house furnished splendidly."

When Garcés repeated this in Pima, the Indian leader agreed that the man who had ruled the country in old days had lived there. He was called the Bitter Man, for he had killed a good many people and changed them into the saguaros which they now saw everywhere in this desert land. He had lived in this great house, of that the Indian felt sure, but he had clearly no notion of what was in the house beyond what he had known as the normal equipment of an Indian hut.

"I suppose they were bare like Greek houses," said Font, reluctantly surrendering the imagined pomp of a Pima Escorial.

"Those were windows up there?" asked the commander pointing to some round holes high up in the east and the west walls.

The leader of the Indians looked puzzled again.

"Did one look out there and watch for an enemy perhaps?" Garcés tried to make his question as particular and as dramatic as possible.

The Indian shook his head. "No, the Bitter Man looked out there"—he pointed to the wall facing the east—"to the sun when it rose, and there"— pointing to the opposite wall—"to the sun when it set."

"What did he say then?" asked Font. Dubiously Garcés translated the question.

The Indian looked a little surprised, and then he looked at the Spaniards, Garcés thought, a little contemptuously, "What does a man say to his god when he looks at him?"

The Spaniards looked away, and no one spoke. Presently, they caught their horses, mounted them, and turned away from the great house. As the horses picked their way through the brush and cactus, Garcés caught sight again of the beautifully smoothed metate. Poor women hoping for relief from their drudgery, he thought pitifully.

But in the month that followed, the friar had little time to worry about the problems of the future. For those of the present were pressing enough. Font was unquestionably ill. He had complained of indigestion at the start, and the food on the road did nothing to improve it. From time to time he suffered, too, from agues that would leave him shivering in the sunshine of high noon, and burning in the cold of the night. He was even more exacting with himself than with other people, and insisted on saying Mass every morning when it was possible, and on visiting the sick, and fulfilling all the duties of the chaplain of the expedition. But even his devotion to duty could not always master his infirmities, and more and more Anza leaned on Garcés for the help which the Church could give in the strains of the journey.

On the first expedition the friar had been immensely impressed by the unremitting watchfulness with which the captain tried to anticipate the emergencies of the road and to provide for them. The constitutionally haphazard and casual friar had been even more impressed by the astonishing success of these plans of Anza. Sometimes he had wondered if the far-sighted captain had not found the answer to the capriciousness of fortune.

But this time, though the commander had planned even more elaborately and painstakingly for every conceivable need, it seemed as if all his plans were at the mercy of an incalculable factor which had not played much of any part in the history of the first expedition, health. From the time they left Tubac there were never less than eight or ten of the company ailing in some degree. At first, when a soldier came to Anza's tent in the morning and reported that his wife was too sick to travel, the commander had grumbled that women, having no other excitement, were always imagining themselves ill. But the memory of Señora Felix was too constantly present in his thoughts for him to risk not going to see the woman.

And always he found the same story. This was not the first day of her illness, the other women who shared the tent would protest. She had been looking poorly for a couple of days before she complained, and then she had persisted in riding on although her neighbors protested. But now even that slow donkey, her husband, had seen how she was and been frightened. By that time the commander-surgeon himself was beginning to be alarmed and was sending back to the medicine chest in his tent for the best remedy he could recall from his medical studies.

Too often he had to cancel his marching orders at once. Early in the month he had to remain for three days in the salt lands at Laguna to give two dangerously sick women a chance to recover. At Opasoitac the aftermath of a miscarriage, which now nearly took the life of the mother, delayed them for two days more. A birth later in the month kept them waiting in freezing weather for three days more. And only a few days after that he had to stop again for a day to save another woman from a miscarriage.

"What a trouble we make coming into the world!" he groaned to the friar that night. And the friar dryly reminded him that baptisms were much less time-consuming, to say nothing of depressing, than funerals.

Then, too, there was the problem of clothes. The commander thought he had done very well with that, providing every woman with the same garments so that there would be no room for rivalry and emulation. But, as many men have found in the world's history, he presently discovered that in his preoccupations with decency and modesty and comeliness, he had neglected the problem of comfort. The jackets and skirts and shawls he had provided would have done very well in the villages which the women had left, where, when the weather was bad, they would have clung to their own firesides. These garments proved completely inadequate when unprecedented rains fell early in their progress down the Gila River. In vain, the anxious captain gave orders that all the blankets of the party should be used to wrap up the women and the children. The women were still wretchedly exposed whenever they had to come out from their wrappings to take care of the children. And Anza swore to the sympathetic Garcés that never again would he attempt to lead a colony with women in it. Any number of Apache raids, but not that.

But the sorely-tried commander admitted that in general the party stood all these delays and vexations extraordinarily well. Only once did he feel any real concern about their spirits. It was early in their journey down the Gila River. Several things had gone wrong, one after another. To begin with, just when he was counting on recovering a little of the time they had already lost, by some rapid marches down the bottom lands along the river, most of the party were deprived of a good half of their night's sleep by the Indians' friendly celebration of their arrival.

The next day, as they started forth, a little glassy-eyed from the night's reveling, it was discovered that some of the best of the saddle animals had gone astray in the brush. Precious hours were lost in rounding up the stragglers. And then, when the men and the animals had at last struggled wearily into camp, there came a drenching rain that lasted a full hour, and that was followed by still longer, and, if possible, even drearier hours of steaming clothes and shivering bodies and ever-dampening spirits by the roadside fires.

When the commander finally was able to leave the tent where the invalids had been assembled and start back for his own, he came upon a very dreary and bedraggled company huddled shivering around the smoky fires. He was nearing exhaustion himself, and the sight of all the glum faces and the limp figures depressed him. So he flung himself down on his camp bed, hardly glancing at Garcés, who had been waiting to see whether any of the patients were likely to need his services or might be left to seek a much-needed sleep.

"I have never seen such a drowned-rat effect in my life," the weary commander shuddered. "They are sitting out there around those damp fires looking as cheerful as if they were waiting for the last trumpet to sound. I am not feeling so cheerful myself that I can stand the look of them much longer."

"I'll go out and see what I can do," offered the friar, starting wearily to his feet. Two of the more adventurous lads of the party had become so engrossed in trailing some straying cattle that afternoon that they had got lost themselves, and the friar had had compassion on their mother's worries and gone out and dragged the scamps in.

"You look fagged yourself, at least for you," amended the captain, reflecting on a second look that this was still the serenest face he had seen for some hours. "Where's Father Font?"

"In his tent—it's the ague again. Father Eixarch is trying to keep him warm."

"Do you know what I would like to do? Give them enough aguardiente to make them drunk and forget their troubles," said the commander with the closest to a conspiratorial air which his friend had ever seen on that candid face.

The friar shook his head. "You know you would have more trouble than you have now. But I do think a little aguardiente, just enough to warm up and not enough to fuddle them, would be the best medicine you could prescribe tonight," answered the friar cautiously.

The commander's face lighted up.

"Mind you," said the friar, "be sure how much of that aguardiente goes into each cup, and have the rest brought straight back here."

Anza promised, and Garcés feeling slightly uneasy, went back to the tent which he shared with Eixarch, devoutly hoping that the unexpected warmth would send the party promptly to bed. But he was hardly half through the hitherto neglected day's office when an unmistakable burst of song rose in the stillness of the dark and rainy evening. It was certainly not a hymn tune, that.

With a sigh he closed his breviary and picked up his hat. When he struck the main trail on which the largest of the campfires had been built, he saw that a very considerable crowd must be still around the fire, to judge from the shadows that moved about it and the volume of the now slightly disordered singing. He went straight to the commander's tent. But there was no answer to his greeting. Lifting up the flap, he went in, and saw in the candlelight that Anza was still stretched on his camp bed, snoring heavily. There was no sign of the aguardiente barrel.

The singing was getting unmistakably noisier, and he judged from the thin wail of the violin that came in on a gust of wet wind that they were dancing now. For a moment the friar thought of strolling down himself. But some of that singing suggested that there were members of the party too far gone from sobriety for any one to be sure that in the heat of an interruption they might not say things which on the morrow no one would want to have said. So quietly, avoiding any chance of running into the firelight, the friar took his way to the tent of the corporal supposed to be responsible for the guard. He, too, was asleep, but the friar had no compunction about waking him.

At first, the man had been sullen at the disturbance of his slumber, but when Garcés grimly advised him to listen to the singing, he hurried on his jacket and thanked the friar for waking him before Anza was aroused.

As he had feared, Font was quite awake when Garcés looked in upon him again. He was sitting up on his camp bed, his fine eyes blazing with indignation out of his blue-white face, and his teeth chattering with the chill. Eixarch was obviously trying to keep him from rising and, sick as he was, going down to quell the rowdies.

"It is all right; they'll be stopping now," Garcés hastened to reassure him.

"All right!" spluttered Font between his chattering teeth. "Roistering when they should be down on their knees praying that we may come out of this morass alive!"

There was no question that the next day the party was in much better spirits than it had been for some time. But it was a very difficult day for Garcés. When in the morning Father Font was seen to be at least better enough to mount his horse, Garcés tried to explain to him that he was at least as much to blame as the commander for what had happened, for he had consented to a little drink to warm up the drenched party. But Font refused to listen. It was, he stiffly pointed out, quite impossible for Father Garcés, who was neither the commander nor the chaplain of the expedition to assume a responsibility that could not be his.

Anza, on the other hand, affected to think lightly of the whole business. Wasn't the party in much better shape today than it had been last night? If a little drunkenness were necessary to affect such a change, then wasn't it justified? Clearly, Father Font had chosen a bad moment for his protest, and the commander was unexpectedly stubborn and even sullen when Garcés tried to make the peace. However improved the aspect of the party, that day was a very hard one for its leaders, spiritual and temporal.

But, fortunately, the next day brought its interest, strong enough to drown out the memory of that ribald singing. For a host of the Opas and the Cocomaricopas flocked to join the travelers, and, while they examined the party with fingers as well as eyes, and the party dodged and stared at them, their leaders assured Anza of their undying fidelity to him and his king, and their willingness to keep the peace with the Yumas and make peace with all the other Indians of the great rivers. It was an immensely heartening experience for the commander to find that the diplomatic efforts of his former expedition were already bearing such promising fruit. And he soon became quite his old self as with the help of Father Garcés, he planned for a great meeting of the leaders of these tribes with the Yumas at the junction of the rivers.

And then, with his arm in the friar's, he asked the Indians if they were ready to receive missionaries and learn the things they must know to be saved. They answered that they always wanted to hear the things that were true. Then Garcés brought out the banner which he had already shown to so many of the peoples of that part of the world, the banner with the Blessed Virgin and her Son in her arms on one side, and the terrible picture of the lost soul in the flames of hell on the other. And they all nodded and said this was the picture they had heard about, and it was as men had described it. And then the friar sat down in their campfire circle that evening, and he talked to them of heaven and of hell, and of the love of God, who wishes all men to be saved who will listen to the truth when it is preached to them.

And Father Font, moved by this evidence of the commander's devotion to the missionary objective of the expedition, forgot his grievance of the past day and sat down beside Anza at the fire. He understood nothing of the language of these people, and only with difficulty did he follow the Pima tongue in which Garcés was talking to their interpreter, but it was impossible to miss the deep sympathy with which the latter friar spoke and his Indian friends listened.

Font, seeing his colleague squatting there in the circle of Indians, turned to the captain and said in clear tones that carried to the other side of the fire, "When one sees Father Garcés sitting there so contentedly among those Indians, surely it seems as if God had created him just for the purpose of sitting there and talking with them."

And when Garcés heard the warm laugh of the commander in response, he knew that peace had been made in the party, too.

6

As soon as the expedition came into the Yuma country, Anza sent four of the soldiers ahead with an interpreter to notify Palma of the impending arrival and to invite him to meet his Spanish friends on the way. But before the party could have reached Palma's village, a messenger from Palma arrived to announce that the Yuma chief had been waiting for four days at a point some twenty miles from his village where he felt sure the commander must come. He had now returned home, but only, the messenger assured Anza, to make preparations for their proper welcome there.

Two days later Palma was as good as his word. The welcome he gave the commander left no doubt of his delight at the arrival of the Spaniards, for he embraced that dignified soldier with a warmth that clearly surprised him. Then with an even more astonishing formality he inquired for the health and well-being of the great king and his viceroy. The courtesy enchanted both Anza and Father Font. But Garcés found himself wondering if perhaps the Indian had not misunderstood the accessibility of the first of these earthly powers. For he went on to express his envy of the commander, who had had the great privilege of standing in the presence of the king and listening to his high words with his own ears.

But there was no misunderstanding the report which he now proceeded to give as to what he had done to fulfil the commands which he had received from Anza on his first visit. He had made peace with his neighbors, and he had formed alliances with them, and he had persuaded them to refrain from going to war with their old enemies. With a good deal of dignity Palma pointed out that this had been a real sacrifice for a warrior of his spirit, but he had made it to prove his friendship with the king of the Spaniards.

To all this, Anza nodded with unfeigned pleasure and approval. But at one item in Palma's speech, the commander called a halt and asked the interpreter to repeat what he had said. It was quite clear what he had said, however, namely, that in his making of peace he clearly excepted the people of the mountains to the west, for they had invaded the California settlements to steal horses, and they had killed one of the Spaniards. They were bad men, and with them he would not make peace.

But though that piece of news, heard for the first time, made the Spaniards look at each other, there was nothing but reassurance in Palma's entire oration. He had, clearly, done all in his power to keep his promises to the commander. And now, equally clearly, he looked to the commander to redeem his promises in turn, for, he lost no time in asking whether this party had brought the Gray Robes and the Spaniards with guns and horses whom the commander had promised to ask the viceroy to send to stay in his country. Indeed, as the eloquent Indian orator warmed to his task, he offered all his lands to the king that the commander and his party might stay with them and give them the religion which he had promised.

It was both a magnificent and an urgent invitation. Listening to it, and watching the dark face of Palma glowing like the face of one who has become possessed with a vision, Garcés thought wistfully of the slow and devious ways of authority, both secular and ecclesiastical. For once to seize the moment when it was hot, and to do the thing in hand without waiting for the slow-moving wheels of empire to grind out this tiny fragment of a universal plan—the friar involuntarily sighed.

But the commander, though his dark eyes kindled at Palma's enthusiasm, responded with becoming sobriety. All this which Palma had said was good, very good. But the Yumas must understand that just as promises to send missionaries and soldiers and settlers had been made to them, so these same promises had been made to other people even before they were made to the Yumas. And these soldiers and settlers whom they now saw before their eyes were going to those other people so that Palma might see for himself that these promises were kept, in their proper order.

Clearly, as he listened to this explanation, Palma was straining at the leash, and the friar's heart went out to him in sympathy. But before Garcés could say anything to Anza, Palma was answering this measured explanation with matching gravity. He could understand, he said, that the great king had many plans, and they could not all be brought to pass at once even by his power. So they would wait, but if the promised establishment of the mission had not been made when the commander returned from this expedition of his, then he, Palma, would himself go to the viceroy to urge the fulfilment of the promise.

There was nothing threatening in the voice or manner of Palma as he said this, but there was no mistaking the earnestness with which he spoke. The commander with equal solemnity agreed that he would be glad to conduct Palma to the viceroy on one condition. Again, the eye of the Yuma chieftain lighted. That condition was the obvious one, that the tribe should consent to Palma's going away for the visit. For, as Anza proceeded to remind Palma, he would have to travel a great distance, and this would take time. His people must understand this, too.

To all of this the Indian agreed, but Garcés felt sure that though he was trying hard to control his impatience, he was finding it hard to assimilate the immediate disappointment. The friar found himself wondering, too, what impression the conference had made on the solemn-faced Indians sitting in a circle at Palma's back as he talked. Clearly, they were impressed by their leader's dignity and his eloquence in holding parley with the strangers. But how far did they share Palma's hopes? That they with their beady eyes never leaving the speaker's face must sense his disappointment, he felt quite sure.

That night Anza decided to hold a little ceremony in front of his tent where the light of the campfire would make it possible for all the Indians to see the honor he did their leader. The viceroy had sent an especially magnificent suit of clothes, with a gold-braided and embroidered cape which would have done credit to his own court, as an official recognition of the king's captain.

All this Anza carefully explained to the Indian chieftain, and then he presented the glittering trophy. This the Indian received with fitting solemnity, and at once donned it, and strutted around in the firelight to the great admiration of his followers. Indeed, it was impossible for the Spaniards themselves to withhold their admiration of so princely a figure.

Then, as one official confiding in another, the commander told Palma of the plan for leaving the two friars with the Yumas to begin preparations for the religious foundation which would be the core of the establishment he had promised. He did not hesitate to represent them as the actual first step in the direction of the realization of his promises, and he asked Palma to accept them as such.

This Palma readily agreed to do. He had already embraced Father Garcés as an old friend, and he now greeted Father Eixarch with warm promise of every help. In his cordiality of welcome he offered to receive the friars into his own house, but Anza hastened to decline this suggestion as too much of an imposition. As he did so, he avoided the eye of Garcés, who would have accepted the doubtless crowded and malodorous lodging at once as the readiest way to his objective. And the commander went on with great cordiality to suggest that the Yuma captain could keep the two friars under his special protection in the house which the Spaniards would build for them.

This Palma promised with enthusiasm, assuring the king's commander that he would consider the two friars and their safety as his personal responsibility which he would delegate to no one else. And these assurances Anza solemnly accepted on behalf of the viceroy who had sent the missionaries to him. Then the commander addressed himself to the friars, bidding them select as soon as possible the site for their house so that he might have as strong and comfortable a lodging as possible constructed for them before he went on. To Garcés the precaution seemed a little superfluous. He had never worried much about the problem of shelter, but Eixarch warmly thanked the commander for his care, and hastened to remind his colleague that it was not primarily a matter of housing themselves but of having a proper place to say Mass and to begin catechetical instruction. So rebuked, and with justice, Garcés promised to select his site as soon as possible.

But the days that followed brought so many demands that Garcés had little time to think of that promise. First, there were the sick to be visited and to be comforted. And then, when they were able to ford the stream and make camp between the rivers just above the junction, there was the throng of friendly Indians to be greeted. And then there were the settlers to watch and help in the hours that followed. For the Indians of Palma's village thronged around their guests, pressing upon them all sorts of food, wheat, maize, calabashes, beans, watermelons, until the Spaniards, weary enough already of their road rations, thought they had come into the land of plenty.

Some of the settlers had already the fine art of receiving a respected host's gifts, but there were others who had had little occasion in a hard life to learn that most delicate of arts. Some were simply stupid with astonishment and took the gifts without any word of thanks. They, however, did not worry the friar, for he suspected that the sincerity of their amazement would give their warm-hearted hosts an adequate enough sense of appreciation of their generosity. The ones who really worried the friar were those who received the gifts as the tribute of the savage to his superiors, and made little effort to hide their condescension. And then, of course, there were those who were simply greedy and took what they had a chance to take with little sense of the finer implications of this hospitality.

There were guests, too. Some of the Jalchedunes whom Garcés had met earlier came into camp to report that they were ready to make peace with the Yumas. This news pleased the commander, and he came and sat down with them in the campfire circle with Garcés, who had taken the responsibility of entertaining them. Courteously, he asked their leader for the news of their land. With perfect soberness that worthy launched into a long story of an Indian of the land beyond the high mountains to the west. He had fled from the changes that were happening in the lands to the sea, the Jalchedune put it tactfully, and he had been killed and his body burned by some of the peoples whom he had visited. But he had come to life again, and now he was travelling with a viper in his hand. He was a sorcerer, and he was killing people in the Jalchedune villages, and there was a great fear in all their land.

"I think, Father Garcés, the sooner you resume your travels, the better," said the commander dryly. "Tomorrow, you let me see where you want that house."

Although it was a couple of miles to the southwest of Palma's village, the hill still drew Garcés' imagination. Indeed, he found time to ride down there and survey again the magnificent view from its majestic height. But when he returned to camp, he found the commander and his brother friars deep in conversation with some of the Yumas who had just returned from an expedition into the desert toward the mountains.

Apparently curious as to this fresh evidence of the invisible linkages of the Indian world, Anza had inquired about the news they had picked up. They had replied a little vaguely, looking uncertainly at Palma as they answered. Stung to anxiety, the commander told them that he already knew there had been trouble between the mountain people and the Spaniards in Upper California, and that he would be glad of more news of that. Then he appealed to Palma, telling him that any interference from hostile Indians would seriously delay his return to Monterey.

Palma at once bade his men tell the commander frankly whatever they had learned. So adjured, their leader admitted he had heard news of the trouble Anza referred to. The bad people of the mountains had fallen upon one of the settlements for their horses, and they had killed one of the Spaniards, a Gray Robe, they added. But they had been driven off.

There was horror in the little group and wonder as to which of the priests whom they had met had become the first martyr of the new foundations. Was it Serra, Garcés wondered. He most deserved that greatest of honors, and yet he was the man they could least spare.

But there was no time now to wonder about that. The disaster in California had, if anything, increased the urgency of starting the mission for the Yumas. That height there above the river—but even before he asked the commander about building the house on the height, he knew what the answer was. Anza said, "No," a flat "no" that did not leave any room for argument. Later when they could make the proper establishment with a garrison and all, Garcés should have his mission on the height. That was settled. But for now, they must build where Palma could watch over their safety. Garcés might covet martyrdom, but it was the commander's duty to hold it off as long as possible.

There was a touch of dry humor to the last, but there was clearly nothing to be done for the present. And Father Font finally capped the commander's argument by pointing out that it was not Father Garcés who was going to be left alone in that house but Father Eixarch. And at that Anza laughed aloud, pointing out that Father Garcés would be quite out of it all in the safety of the wilderness. So there was nothing more for Garcés to say.

But for all their jesting, the shadow of the California martyrdom had fallen over the pleasant sunshine of the Yuma land. The commander spoke of it several times as he came back to see if the building of the little house for the priests were going on as he had ordered. It was little more than a rough timber shack, thatched with arrowweed, but the captain took pains to see that it was water-tight and that it had a strong door which could be barred in case of need. And when the party left the two friars alone at their house and disappeared down the river bank, to the surprise of Garcés it was of the martyrdom of the still unidentified California missionary that Eixarch at once began to talk.

"It seems to me that martyrdom is the greatest privilege that can befall a missionary," he said at last.

"Yes," replied Garcés, his thoughts still with the commander and the party going down the river. It was his own choice that he should stay for the expedition among the neighboring peoples. Indeed, it was his judgment that peace among all the adjoining tribes was essential to the protection of the bridge to California, that had led the viceroy to order him to stay. Still his thoughts had been so closely involved in the least of the interests and anxieties of the commander and his charges these last weeks that for the first moments after the last of the cattle had straggled around the bend in the road, he had felt strangely bereft and alone.

But Eixarch was still talking. "I should feel that God had really accepted my sacrifice, if I could have the privilege, wouldn't you?"

"All the great writers of the order have so taught us," said Garcés, vaguely groping back to the memory of certain discussions in the novitiate at Querétaro.

His young colleague must be thinking of such discussions now, for he went on almost enviously, "Of course, I shall never have the opportunity for martyrdom you have."

"I?" Garcés asked in such complete astonishment that the younger friar hastily suggested that perhaps they ought to make sure that all the supplies the commander had left them had been stored away properly before the Indians should return from escorting the party down the river.

But when the next day Garcés stopped on his way down the river with

Sebastián to look out from the hill of his dreams over the rivers, the conversation with Eixarch came back to him. Garcés tried to remember his own novice days. He had been thrilled by the stories of the great missionary martyrs which he had heard read at that time, and he had burned to undertake their adventurous labors. But it was the things they had done that he had dreamed of doing, that he might be able to bring in those miraculous drafts of souls which they had been able to take in their nets. As for their ends, he had always been sure that he was not of the stuff to embrace such sufferings.

Once he had been worried about his own incapacity for such high heroism, and he had asked the novice master if he thought one who was clearly not made of such material should dare to attempt such labors. The novice master had questioned him closely. No, he felt no doubt of his vocation. He felt sure that this was the work which God had given him to do in his very limited way. And he had no thought of drawing back because of any risks he would run. Only he was afraid that if he should be left face to face with the ultimate test, he would not be strong enough for it. And he would not want to disgrace the order just because he was weak.

The novice master had been patient, and finally, he had reassured him. He had said that no man except a very few like our blessed father Saint Francis had been sure of themselves there. Indeed, many of the bravest martyrs had felt as he had, but they had found that when their time came, God had given them strength enough to meet it. He felt sure God would not give him the test of martyrdom without giving him His grace, too. With that Garcés had to be content.

And, presently, he had become so much concerned about other matters that he had forgotten about it. In these last years he had had some narrow escapes, but they had never been of a character important enough or significant enough to be dignified with so high a name. Indeed, they had but confirmed his suspicion that the chances of his life were altogether of a much humbler character.

He had reached the height now, and as he looked over the beautiful expanse of mountain and river and canyon and sandy river bottom, he thought of how Saint Francis had exclaimed at the height above Lake Trasimene, "This is a holy place." But he smiled at himself as he had smiled at Eixarch. His task was to start the cabin on the height which later would become the mission. If he succeeded, then better men than he could make it as meaningful a place as God had made it beautiful.

He watched a bird fly out from the crag, and its shadow fly before it as it moved. He was wasting golden hours maundering here, when there was work waiting to be done. And his spirit blew free from the tether of thought about himself, and flew joyously to the journey ahead.

$$* \quad V \quad *$$

THE SEVEN CITIES OF CIBOLA

I

It was almost a month later when Garcés returned with Sebastián to Palma's village. It had been a very satisfactory month for him, traveling down the river and back again, visiting old friends and making new. Everywhere he had received a cordial welcome, for the story of the Old Man with the brightly colored banner had gone ahead of him, and men and women rushed out to meet him when they heard that he was coming near their village.

It was beautiful winter weather this second journey of his to the peoples of the Colorado. The air above the sands was wine-like in its crisp freshness, and the radiant blue sky cloudless in the vibrant sunshine. Even the dry stubble of the maize fields rustled with life in the quickening breeze from the mountains. And the river shone with cool brilliance in the dappling of the wind. But most wonderful of all, when the terror of the summer heat was recalled, was the soft warmth of the sun in the cool air, bright and kindling and life-giving. The words of Saint Francis' "Hymn to the Creation" came easily to his lips as he rode down the river bottom lands with only Sebastián for company, and he found himself chanting over and over again: "Praise to our Lord God in all the works of His hands, praise to our Brother Sun, shining on all earth's lands."

And now he found himself in his preaching speaking of the beauty of the world which God had made and which man by his sin had defaced. Only it was like Garcés that he said more of the beauty than of the sin. And everywhere he found willing listeners, who, when he had finished, would nod their heads and say, "These are good things which the Old Man tells us."

It was with great content, therefore, that he returned to Palma's village to tell Palma that nearly all the peoples down the river would send representatives up to the junction to make their peace with the Yumas and each other.

But things had not gone so well with Eixarch. It was much colder on the upper Colorado, so cold that sometimes, the friar confessed, much as he had wanted to say Mass he had not been able to. And the rains had come, finding out every crevice in the thatch and every crack in the thin walls. Indeed, the river was unmistakably rising, and Palma was preparing to abandon his house and make his camp on one of the islands in the river. Eixarch was disappointed at the prospect of having to find a fresh site and start over again without the help of the commander and his men. Of most of the Indians he had no complaint whatever on the score of hospitality. Palma himself had been the soul of attentiveness. When the commander came again, he could certainly report that the Indian chieftain had more then kept his promise that he would constantly watch over the friars who were left to his care. Indeed, one of Eixarch's main troubles was that that promise had been kept too literally. His little house had been continuously full of Indians coming and going, and, above all, staying. It was so cold that he had had to keep the door of the little house shut, and—well, Father Garcés knew as well as he the habits of the Indians. By nightfall the stench of his house was like that of one of their lodges. Sometimes, shivering as he already was, he had had to open the door and the window and let the night air in while he swept and washed.

Garcés had sympathized, "A nose is a luxury which a missionary can hardly afford."

It had been said in all kindness, but for a moment Eixarch felt rebuked, for he added hastily, "You understand that I love them, don't you?" And Garcés had hastened to reassure him. For there was no mistaking Eixarch's enthusiasm for the work he had undertaken. And Garcés knew that now after the weeks of silence he was only opening his heart in sheer relief at having someone to whom he could talk without having to estimate the effect of every word and gesture, someone to whom he could complain without compromising his basic loyalty. So the gates being down, the flood came.

Now it was that scoundrel, Pablo.

Garcés raised his eyebrows. "But the commander had such good hope of him. You know he half suspected that the tales we heard of his villainy were due to rivalries we did not yet understand. Indeed, he asked me once if I did not think that Palma was just a little bit playing up the wickedness of Pablo to set off his own virtue."

But Eixarch shook his head with the exasperation of long-suffering patience that has had to be patient too long. "For all his ugliness Pablo is a dashing rascal, the sort that would appeal to a soldier, even to so wise a one as the commander. And then when the commander was here, he came to Mass, and he came to the rosary in the evening, and he behaved as if he were as eager as Palma to have us stay. You know what hopes the commander had of Pablo!"

"Yes," said Garcés. "Father Font asked me if I thought the commander was afraid that Palma might take himself too seriously, and wanted to have some counter-weight or check to him. But I thought the commander simply wanted to have as many chiefs as possible supporting our project, for the Indians do not lean on one man so much as civilized people do."

"No," said Eixarch after several moments' consideration. "It is simply that the commander has been deceived in the man Pablo."

"What has he done?"

"He has not been to Mass or to the rosary for weeks now." There was no mistaking the indignation of the young friar.

He had had a hard time, Garcés reflected, looking at the thin face, usually so eager, now so tired and even severe.

"You know," he said gently, "one must expect that until they have been instructed and understand."

"But he promised the commander!"

The older friar smiled, "You know backsliding is not unknown among seasoned Christians. Remember Pablo is not yet baptized."

"Backsliding!" repeated Eixarch contemptuously. "That is only the beginning. He is an inveterate heathen, he is almost an apostate, for he has had a chance to learn better, and now he is back to the worst of his ways."

Garcés tried to bring the face of Pablo before him. Captain Feo or Chief Ugly-Face, they had called him when they first came into the river country. Certainly, he had nothing of Palma's good looks or dignity of bearing or eloquence. Squat of figure, flat-faced, scarred, slovenly of carriage, there was nothing in him that at first sight would inspire trust. But there was a very intelligent, not to say shrewd look in his small eyes, and though he said little, he was soon found to be quick of understanding and possessed of a real gift of coming to the point when he did speak. And as the commander had found, when he undertook to do something for the visitors, he had been both prompt and efficient.

"Of course, there have been stories," Garcés admitted, "but there has been nothing to them, we have found out afterward."

"But there is to these stories. Palma has been telling me for weeks now that Pablo is a wizard, and Palma is right."

"Have you noticed that it is always from Palma or Palma's men that we get these stories of Pablo?"

"But this I know," said Eixarch, coming to the point. "The other night I was down near Pablo's house. He had a sick man who had been brought there that day, and I heard Pablo singing in a low, melancholy voice, and as he sang, I could hear him slapping and pounding the sick man."

"What did you do?" inquired Garcés anxiously.

"Nothing, then," answered Eixarch a little stiffly. "But this morning I went in to see the sick man when Pablo was away. He was so sick that I was considering whether I should baptize him when Pablo came in. He must have guessed what I was thinking, for he began to cry out, saying that if I baptized him, the man would surely die, for all the people I had baptized had died."

"I suppose that is true enough," said Garcés with a sigh.

Eixarch's face flushed, "Of course, I should not dream of baptizing anybody I was not sure was going to die. There has been no time to give anyone, not even Palma, sufficient instruction."

"I know. That is the difficulty."

"But Palma!" The tired face lighted. "Palma told Pablo that if it were his daughter who was ill, he would let me baptize her even if she should die, for then he would know that she would go straight to heaven."

And the young friar, having freed his breast of his grievances, proceeded to develop his favorite theme, the virtues of Palma. To these Garcés turned a grateful ear, for the severe look vanished from the face of Eixarch, and something like his wonted enthusiasm came back to warm his voice and light his face.

The next morning Garcés had a chance to see for himself. For the sun had barely risen when Palma came to the door of the little house. The Indian paid no attention to Garcés when he slipped past to go outdoors to get fresh water to bathe. When the friar returned, he found Palma kneeling in front of the door, his hands clasped, and his eyes riveted on Eixarch, who was just beginning Mass.

The little room was crowded. The two Spanish servants whom Anza had left for the mission, the muleteer, the Indians who served as interpreters, Sebastián, and half a dozen of Palma's principal men left almost no room for Father Garcés except in the corner between the end of the altar table and the wall. It was a devout little congregation, but Garcés had soon to admit that the focus and center of that devotion was the Indian, Palma. He was the first to kneel, the first to stand, the first to strike his breast and bow his head, the first to lift rapt face to the contemplation of the raised Host. Alone of all the group he never took his eyes off Father Eixarch. It was as if he were a fragment of steel pulled to the magnet of the celebrant. Garcés found himself deeply moved by this intense concentration of devotion.

And then as Eixarch was distributing the Communion to one of the mission servants and to the boy who was serving the Mass, a strange idea came to the watching friar. For he noticed that the Indian was following each motion of the priest as he said the words of the prayer and laid the Host on the communicant's tongue with the same absorption with which he had watched the consecration itself. And this same minuteness of observation extended even to the priest's washing of his fingers when the distribution was finished. It was then that it occurred to him that Palma watched Eixarch as if he were expecting some day to perform the rite of the Mass himself.

Later in the day when Garcés had said his own Mass and the two friars had breakfasted, he suggested this idea to Eixarch. But it seemed only to shock him. "But he is married and he has children, and he knows that we do not marry." And then a sorrowful look came into his face as if he felt that his colleague were looking for some pretext of objection to his star pupil.

They had no time to discuss the conversion of Palma any further, for at that moment Sebastián came to tell Garcés that some of the Jalchedunes whom he had visited on his return from Upper California had arrived with some of the Cocomaricopas to visit Palma in celebration of the peace which had been made between their peoples. The rest of the day Garcés had to spend attending the visitors on their tour of Palma's village, for both host and guest had been very insistent on his presence. This had been burdensome to the friar and puzzling as well.

It was not until well into the afternoon, however, that he received his first clue. During the course of the day a large proportion of Palma's tribe had gathered together to welcome the visitors, and now they were all sitting by the fire to smoke and to exchange formal greetings. It was then that Palma rose to his feet and, striking a commanding pose, began to speak. He was wearing the viceroy's suit, and he gave a curious effect of sophisticated splendor among his almost naked fellow-tribesmen, huddling together about the fire for warmth against the damp winter air. As he began to talk, Sebastián squatted down at the feet of the friar, prepared to interpret.

But Garcés needed no interpreter to understand the wide gesture of embrace with which Palma began his speech. And he hardly needed Sebastián's help to understand his first words, "We are all brothers now, ye men of the Jalchedunes and the Cocomaricopas. We who were enemies from old time are now brothers. It is because of the Old Man and the commander and the other Spaniards that I have laid down my arms and do not make war any more. It is not because I am afraid. My people are many, and I have many firm friends. The Cajuenches, and the Quemayás, and the Yabipais, and the Jamajabs, all these peoples are my friends."

There was a little rustling of pride in the ranks about the fire, but the visitors sat there listening quite impassively. And Palma went on, more proudly now, it seemed to the watching friar, "Men have told me that the Jalchedunes are not such faithful friends as these others. And foolish men have said that the Jalchedunes might break the peace which we have made."

Garcés held his breath as Sebastián repeated this with mounting excitement in his voice. There was no mistaking the defiance in Palma's haughty figure as he went on, "Well, then, let the Jalchedunes come out with their bows and arrows. With the Spaniards to help me I shall give you the punishment you deserve."

"So that is it," he said to himself, with a cold feeling deep within. But the Indian was going on with even greater dignity and assurance. "For who shall make any stand against the Spaniards? They are to the south, and to the east, and they are beyond the mountains to the sea. Who shall be strong enough to oppose them?"

All of Palma's people were sitting very quietly about the fire now, and it occurred to the friar that perhaps these last references to the approach of the Spaniards were not intended for the visitors at all but for Palma's own people. At any rate, no one said anything. And, presently, Palma was making a conventional speech of welcome and of friendship, and the visitors were responding in kind. But Garcés hardly heard what Sebastián was saying, for he was thinking over Palma's words about the Spaniards.

That night when he returned to the mission, he repeated them to Eixarch. The latter's eyes sparkled in admiration when Garcés had finished his report, "Indians are not such fools as some men think. He apparently has grasped Colonel Anza's plan very well."

Garcés stared at him in astonishment. "Do you still think the spiritual advantages of our friendship are the ones Palma most seeks?"

Eixarch looked at his colleague coldly in the candlelight, "Do you think we should be suspicious of this instrument which Providence seems to have raised for the conversion of the peoples of the rivers?"

To that direct challenge Garcés made no answer. He was tired, very tired. And he was not entirely clear even in his own mind as to just what it was that made him so uneasy when he should have been like his colleague, confident and happy.

2

But he had little time to wonder about Palma in the weeks that presently stretched into months after that January day. For they proved to be among the most crowded and strenuous of his life.

It all began simply enough. The success of the two expeditions had more than vindicated Anza's faith in the possibility of linking up the old frontier-mission world and the new. But the experiences with Pablo and Palma had brought home to him the truth of Garcés' contention that such a perilous and extended line of communication was defensible only by the friendship of the Indian peoples along the route. Of the tribes to the south and the southwest both Anza and Garcés felt as sure as any mere visitor could be. But the peoples to the north and the northwest were no less important both for the new settlement among the Yumas and the settlements on the California coast. Both of the friends, however, were still a good deal in the dark about these peoples. Garcés thought that the key to their friendship was to be sought in the Jamajabs up to the north, for he had come upon them often enough on the trade routes between the mountains and the coast. If he could win their friendship, it would mean both guides and allies for the route to Upper California.

Garcés had been pondering over this problem for some time when about the middle of February a couple of the Jamajabs happened to come into camp to see Palma. The latter, apparently, lost no time in showing off his new allies, and one of the guests immediately invited the Old Man to come to see

his people and volunteered to serve as his guide. Garcés made a hasty calculation. It was the middle of February now, and he and the commander had
estimated that the escort to Monterey should be able to reach the Colorado
again by the middle of May. That left him still three months, plenty of time,
he decided, to make sure of the peoples to the north.

So with the one volunteer guide and Sebastián, Garcés set out to visit the
lands of the Jamajabs. His plan was of the most general sort, to see as many
of the villages and people as he could reach, and to find out all he could of
their connections and alliances, pushing as far to the northwest as possible
in the time he had.

At the very beginning of his journey the friar had a piece of unexpected
good fortune. It came in the form of a party of some eighty Jamajabs who
were on their way down to see the Yumas. They had heard news of good
things happening among the Yumas, they explained to Garcés' guide, and
they were going down to find out more about these things. At another time
the friar would have been curious about the nature of these reports, but now
he was concerned to see that the Jamajabs not only had their weapons with
them, but that they had been fighting on their way. For they had prisoners,
two frightened women, who were now pushed in front of the warriors.

The women said nothing as they stood there, and the friar saw that they
were young, and he thought of his little Yuma friend. The interpreter, noting
the friar's interest in them, explained that they were Jalchedunes.

For a moment he watched the Indians crowd around his horses and pack
mules, for he had brought two extra horses for the inevitable vicissitudes of
the road. Then he proposed to the leader of the Jamajabs that he let him have
the two women in return for the poorest of his horses and some shells and
tobacco.

He saw the man's eyes light greedily, and then a look of calculation came
into them. The captives were two wives; should he not have two horses to
give to the young men who would not have the wives? But the friar held firm
to his proposal, and, presently, the captain of the party not only gave up the
women, but volunteered to accompany the friar into his land. And this he
did, sending all but three of his companions on to the Yumas.

✳ They were coming into the mountains now, and the fast traveling in the
cold and over the rugged ground of the mountain passes was obviously hard
on the women. So the friar proposed to the Jamajab guide that he should
take them back to their land, free, as a gift to the Jalchedunes and a pledge

of peace to be made between the two peoples. And he explained briefly that the reason he had come into these lands was that he wanted all the peoples to be at peace with each other that they might hear the good things he had come to tell them. To his delight, his guide at once volunteered to take the women to their land while the captain took the friar to the Jamajabs. To this the captain agreed at once and proceeded to tell the old man what he should say to the Jalchedunes.

It was a long and eloquent harangue which he delivered to the interpreter, but the main idea was simple. He bade the old man tell the Jalchedunes that he brought the women back to them as a pledge of peace. And then the captain lifted up his arrows and broke them and threw the pieces on the ground, bidding him tell the Jalchedunes what he had done, and inviting them to do the same. For now they were friends.

But great as was the happiness of the friar in this moment's success, it proved but the prelude to an even greater triumph, for when they had gone over the mountains to the north-northeast, to the first of the Jamajab villages, the whole village flocked out to meet them. It was still cold weather, but the naked men came running out, with the short-skirted women and the children not far behind. Altogether, there must have been about two hundred of them. They were quite as tall and sturdy-looking as the Yumas, and it seemed to Garcés in that bright moment as if they were handsomer. They gathered around the friar's little party, embracing even his horses in the warmth of their welcome.

Then came an Indian who was obviously a person of consequence, not so haughty or so dramatic as Palma, but dignified enough, with a certain easy confidence that was not to be mistaken. Indeed, as the captain who had escorted the friar hastened to explain, he was the captain general of all the villages of the Jamajabs. Like Palma, he was very well able to speak for himself. He made a long harangue which the Jamajab captain who had met the friar translated into Yuma, and then Sebastián repeated more slowly and briefly in Spanish. But the substance of it was unmistakable.

The Jamajabs had heard of the coming of the Spaniards to the people of the rivers as they had heard of their coming to the people of the coast. They had heard of the good things which had been said to the Yumas. And now they wanted the Old Man to know that they were ready to hear the good things which he had to tell them, and to do the good things which he should ask them to do. Again, as so often, the friar ached to understand the words themselves that he might guess at the feeling of the man who used those words and guess at what still lay unsaid in his mind. But he had to be content with the words of Sebastián, and they were quite enough to raise his hopes for the future of these friendly people.

Now they listened to the friar's preaching with the help of Sebastián and the brightly colored linen banner of which they had heard, and upon which they gazed with deep interest. And they crowded around the friar, examining his habit, and looking with awe upon his rosary and his crucifix, and his breviary, and his compass, of all of which they had apparently had some previous report. As they nearly smothered him, the friar wondered what they had heard of these familiar things, but there was no mistaking their friendliness. And before the first meeting broke up, they had ratified the pledge of friendship with the Jalchedunes and had promised to make all the friends of the Old Man their friends. For he was the first Spaniard who had ever come into their land, and of him they had heard only good things.

Never had the friar enjoyed a warmer welcome, or a more successful visit with a new people. But there was more even than this in the triumph of that first visit to the Jamajabs. For when the friar told them that he could not stay with them but must go on to the fathers who lived to the west near the sea, the captain nodded at once, and said they knew all about the Gray Robes on the coast. And they would be glad to give him a couple of guides to go with him. That news gave the friar satisfaction on two counts. It gave him hope of finding a more direct and accessible way to the coast, and it gave fresh evidence of the correctness of a theory he had for some time held, namely, that the Jamajabs possessed extensive relations that might be of vital importance for the consolidation of the road to Upper California.

So encouraged, he decided to put the theory to the test once and for all. He accepted the offer of the friendly Jamajabs, and together they lost no time in setting forth in the direction of Upper California.

From the start that journey more than fulfilled his expectations. For the friar and his three Jamajab companions had been on the road hardly a week when they fell in with a party of Jamajabs coming from the mountains. They greeted the friar in friendly fashion and explained that they had heard there were other men like him on the other side of the mountains. They had brought with them some baskets full of sea shells, which they showed him as great treasure, and from which they gave him some of the blue-white shells as a friendly gift.

Again, some ten days later, they fell in with another party of Jamajabs, similarly laden with shells. And these greeted the friar and his party with even more cordiality, for, as they told him promptly and proudly, they had seen the Gray Robes at San Gabriel. And they produced a basket of parched corn which they said the Gray Robes had given them for their journey. They were full of the wonders they had witnessed at San Gabriel.

It seemed as if every day brought some fresh proof of the friendliness of the Jamajabs. But when the friar tried to get his guides to turn from the southern direction which they were now taking as they came to the mountains, he had no success. He explained that he did not want to go to San Gabriel but higher up on the coast, to the more northern missions. But they swore that they knew of no other way than the one they were following.

Sebastián, also, said that there was no other way through the impassable mountains. So there was nothing for it but to go to San Gabriel. Once the disappointment was accepted as unavoidable, the friar consoled himself with the thought that when he arrived at San Gabriel, he could push north by the royal road to San Luís Obispo, and then to the east to explore the marshy region, the Tulares, of which Font had already given him a report, and see if perhaps there were not some way back east through there to the Jamajabs. And now that it was inescapably in the line of duty the friar could without fear of self-indulgence look forward to the pleasure of seeing his fellow-missionaries there. But that brought a shadow into the sunshine of March that not even the high spirits of Garcés could quite shake off. For his guarded questions, and the less restrained questioning of Sebastián had put past any shadow of doubt the story of the death of the Gray Robe. No one, of course, knew his name, and no one would hazard a guess as to the identity of the murderers beyond the generic description of "bad people"; still less would any of the Indians they met suggest any suspicion as to the cause of the trouble.

When he first saw the woods and fields of San Gabriel mission, it was impossible to think of disaster, for every step the horses took made it clearer that the work of the intervening year had prospered. The flocks in the meadows, the newly-planted fields, the well-fed-looking Indians fishing in the creek, the clustering of tule Indian huts opposite the log-and-tule shed in which the fathers lived, all gave evidence of prosperity. It was the feast day of the patron of the mission, March twenty-fourth, a wine-like day of golden sunshine and still cool breeze, the height of the California spring, and the fiesta was in full progress.

The warmth of the friar's welcome gave him no time to bring up any shadows; nor did the tour of the mission upon which his proud hosts insisted on taking him as soon as he had given thanks for his journey and eaten. For it was a triumphal procession in which the friar found one cause for admiration after another.

And then with great pride the friars set out the dinner for their guests. For they had not forgotten the thinness of the welcome of the year before, and they were anxious to atone with the plenty of the present. It seemed to Garcés that the cooking had improved, too, and he ventured to compliment Cruzado on the progress they were making in training the Indians.

"It is Father Lasuén you have to thank for that," the young friar replied seriously. "He said that there was no excuse for not having things clean at least, and he watched the kitchen when he came over for a visit last winter."

"I am glad to hear he is safe." The two friars stared at him in amazement.

"What did you hear?" asked Father Paterna sharply. Briefly Garcés summarized what he had heard from the Indians.

"It was Fray Luís Jaume," said Father Paterna simply.

"Fray Luís Jaume!"

The two friars of San Gabriel nodded.

"But when I was in San Diego last year, I thought he got on especially well. He was learning the language, and—"

"That had nothing to do with it," said the older friar. "He was the one who rushed out to see what was wrong, and they fell on him. They probably never looked to see who it was, if they knew the friars at all."

"Then it was the savage tribes from the mountains as the Yumas thought?"

"We do not really know," said Father Paterna quietly. "Of course, some of the mission things were found up in the mountains. There was not much to steal, but what there was went far enough. What was in the village came back fast enough, of course, when it was all over."

"You mean the Indians in the village?" Garcés suddenly felt sick. And he knew from the miserable look on the faces of the two friars that that bitterest of all possibilities was what they believed.

"San Diego never had a chance," said Cruzado with sudden passion.

"That is part of it, but only part of it," said the older friar judicially. "It would have been different always at San Diego if they could have gathered their neophytes into a proper mission such as we have here. But they never had enough to manage it," he sighed miserably.

"It was runaways, then?"

"Partly," said Father Paterna. "The fathers at San Diego say that the ring-leaders were some of the restless spirits in their mission group who ran away and stirred up the wild heathen who live toward the mountains. It was not hard to do it—love of booty, love of a raid even."

"But the neophytes?" asked Garcés.

The older friar spread out his hands. "You may take your choice. Disinclination to discipline, though it was easy at San Diego. That is part of it in all probability. But," he paused and lowered his voice, "there is always the possibility of a wizard—the Indians are easily frightened by their threats and stories. And then—" he hesitated.

"There is no use in our always trying to hide it," Cruzado broke out passionately.

The older priest looked calmly at the younger friar, and sighed, "Perhaps, you're right," he said surprisingly, "but I do not see what else we can do. After all, the viceroy insists that we must have a soldier escort."

"They make trouble, no matter what we do," Cruzado was less explosive now, but his indignation was even more moving for his effort to suppress it. "Christians, a fine example of all our teaching!"

"Hush," said Father Paterna wearily. "We have trouble enough as it is with the captain."

"Which captain?" asked the friar curiously.

But the superior shook his head, and with an effort he smiled, "This is scandalous, telling you all our troubles on San Gabriel's day, instead of praising God who has given us so much, and our glorious patron to whose intercession we ought to be so grateful." And as he spoke, he went to the door and threw it open so that the warm afternoon sunlight streamed into the little whitewashed room.

3

BUT a shadow had fallen over that glorious spring day. And it only deepened when later that afternoon Garcés began to talk over his plans with the San Gabriel missionaries. For he soon realized that they were hardly listening to him. They were looking at each other intently, as if uncertain whether or not they should speak. Finally, the older father began rather shamefacedly, "We ought to tell you that the Upper California commander, Don Fernando de Rivera y Moncada, will not approve at all of your work to link up the Indian tribes."

"But what do you mean? Commander Anza has been most eager to see the tribes brought together."

"Don Juan Bautista de Anza is a very different man from Commander Rivera, we can tell you," said Cruzado grimly.

But Paterna shook his head, "I think he is mistaken, too, but we must not forget that he is still anxious about San Diego."

"I think he ought to be," interrupted the younger friar. "The man on watch at the presidio saw the flame of the burning mission and says he thought it was the moon; so he did not sound the alarm, and the soldiers slept through the whole assault."

Paterna, however, would have none of it. "We cannot believe they would be such cowards."

Cruzado shrugged his shoulders.

"Anyway," the superior continued, "that is not our worry just at present. What is troubling us now is that the commander does not want any intercourse between our Indians and the Indians outside, especially the Indians to the east. You see, he believes that it was the savage Indians in the mountains who were responsible for the attack."

Cruzado leaned forward. "He gave orders that peaceful Indians who came to trade for shells should be seized."

"What did you do?" asked Garcés.

"Fortunately, they had just left when the order came. You may have met them. They are the same people as those Indians of yours. Jamajabs, I think, you said?"

"But they are friendly. And they were grateful for the food you gave them."

"I wish you could tell that to the commander."

At the moment neither of the mission priests nor Garcés thought there was any chance of that. But, as it turned out, Garcés was not able to get away as promptly as he had hoped. Neither the captain of the guard at San Gabriel nor the captain of the guard at San Diego would give him supplies or escort for the journey north. So Garcés was still debating what he had better do when Commander Rivera stopped at San Gabriel on his journey north. He was still indignant at the escape of the Jamajabs whom, he asserted, the friars had help to get away. So he was far from pleased to find Garcés there.

"Don't you have a mission post of your own?" he asked rudely.

"I am charged by the viceroy to visit all the Indian tribes along the new routes and to do all I can to make peace among them," replied the friar calmly.

The soldier shook his head. "I cannot understand his Excellency. He believes everything you friars tell him. Now, if he would ask me, I would tell him that this is a soldier's business. Let me have enough men and supplies, and I'll make a peace that will stick. But so long as all this wandering about goes on, what can you do? All this gabbling about campfires will lead only to mischief."

It was hard for Garcés to restrain his indignation. "It is in that talking about campfires that the friendship of the Indians is secured, and stable alliances are worked out that will secure the new routes and protect them from the intertribal wars that might wipe out our remoter settlements."

The commander nearly exploded with impatience. "That is what I cannot make you friars see. You do not understand it at all. Of course, they will make alliances and all the rest of it, but it will be to attack us. Look at what happened in San Diego. These Diegueños are a poor lot who would never make any trouble on their own if they were left alone. And the same is true of the Indians here. But bring in these Indians from the mountains and from the desert and from the rivers, and you have a different story."

"But you can't keep them out. These trade routes over which the peoples of the desert come to get shells are centuries old. The law of nations demands that trade should not be disturbed when the people who want to trade are honest and friendly."

Rivera stared; then he slapped his leather-booted leg with heavy laughter, "The law of nations for these savages! That is good. Only a priest could think of that."

But the friar stood his ground, "The laws of the Indies say expressly that the natural rights of the Indians shall be respected."

But here Rivera exploded, "I have had all I want to hear about the natural rights of these sub-human savages. It is of a piece with all this constant complaining about the way the soldiers behave with the Indian women. I'd like to hear something about natural rights for them, too."

There was nothing to be gained from further talk. Garcés announced that since he could get no other escort, he would go north on the Camino Real and strike east when he reached the Tulares. The commander retorted that he would unquestionably be bogged in the marshes if he were not scalped in one of the savage rancherías. His manner implied that it would not be a bad thing, either.

When the friar asked if he might at least have a horse, Rivera ungraciously replied that he might if he would take himself off at once, but he would not allow any of his own men to risk their lives on such a wild-goose chase.

However, the hospitable friars of San Gabriel gave him food for the journey from their stores, and they secured two volunteers from their own Indians to serve as his guides. One of these latter was a good Spanish student; so it would be possible for the friar to do some preaching as he started north. Thankful for this aid, Garcés started northwest along the edge of the mountains with his little company of the Jamajabs and Sebastián and the two Gabrieleños.

The first couple of days went better than he had dared hope. The first day's march was very short, but it brought the little party to an Indian ranchería that greeted the whole company with great cordiality. The Indians seemed thoroughly content here, and with the help of one of the Gabrieleños the friar preached to them, and was listened to with nods of approval and sympathetic interest. And when the next morning the two Gabrieleños declared somewhat unexpectedly that they must return home, one of the Indians of the ranchería volunteered to see the party on its way.

But the very next day the shadow of San Diego fell upon the little expedition. They had reached another ranchería and been welcomed in a somewhat reserved fashion, but welcomed nonetheless. As Garcés with the help of the Indian from the neighboring ranchería began to talk to his hosts, he became aware of a certain caution that seemed to be relaxing as he talked, mainly with signs. And as he went on talking, showing his compass and his breviary and his crucifix and giving his little gift of tobacco, he tried to guess what was wrong. He scrutinized the people who came and sat around the campfire with a good deal of curiosity. There were plenty of men, and there was the usual abundance of children and women, old women in plenty. And then he knew—there were no young women in sight.

Finally, as they began to eat supper around the fire, he thought he saw the chief of the ranchería give a signal to one of the young men. And then with the help of the Indian interpreter from the south the chief explained to his guest that the young women had gone into hiding when they heard there were Spaniards around, for they feared they might be soldiers.

"But do the soldiers pass here? I thought this ranchería was well away from the main road?" asked the friar, still puzzled.

There was obvious hesitation on the part of his hosts. Then an old man answered, speaking very slowly and cautiously. They were some distance from the road over which the Spaniards traveled, but they had occasion to go down to the shore every so often, and from the people dwelling there they had heard of dreadful things which the Spanish soldiers had done. So when they heard Spaniards were coming, they sent their young women away so that there might not be any occasion for trouble.

The old man must have guessed from the expression on the friar's face with what a heavy heart he heard this news, for he hastened to add that they knew now that their present guests were good men, even if they were Spaniards. And after a moment's pause he added that the young women had been sent for and were on their way now. With that obvious proof of the impression which they had made, the friar had to be content for that night. But a sick feeling lingered in the back of his mind as he thought of all the little villages in this country to which such reports must have come.

That was discouraging enough, but there was worse to come. It was two weeks later, and they had now come up into the mountains. It had been pleasant to travel again in a world of pines and oaks and other trees which the missionary had known all his life, but it was heavy work pulling one's self up the mountain crags, where the horse could hardly be trusted, and scrambling down the grassy slopes of innumerable canyons. So the friar was glad when some of the Jamajabs whom he had picked up on the road volunteered the information that they were not far from a ranchería where they had stopped before on their travels. To save trouble, he decided, he would send one of the Jamajabs to tell their friends of his coming.

At first he thought he would keep for company the two Jamajabs who had come the whole trip with him, but they seemed disappointed. So remembering the Indian love of going along in a crowd, he bade them go, too. As he watched them scampering off, he smiled at the curious figure his two guides made among their naked tribesmen. For they still clung to the clothes he had given them to protect them against the mountain cold on the way to San Gabriel.

The ranchería was made up of a number of specimens of a new type of dwelling, larger and more substantial than anything he had yet encountered. Square, apparently, made of palisaded sides with mats of rushes to cover the bow-shaped roof, it looked something like a blockhouse. But to his surprise, as he came up to the group of houses, only an old woman, followed by a number of other old women, came out to meet him.

Presently, the Jamajabs appeared from among the houses, talking vigorously with many gestures to a couple of old women, who seemed rather puzzled. As the friar watched, one of the latter returned to the house. Presently, she reappeared with food and drink, of which the most promising-looking to the Spaniard was a basket of seeds. The Indians were quite friendly now, and they sat down to watch the friar eat with good-humored satisfaction. But still there was no sign of anybody but the old women.

The friar thought of the well-concealed fear with which these old women had stayed behind, knowing well that they were the least valuable part of the tribe, the part soonest spared and therefore most readily exposed. If he could not express his admiration for their pluck, at least he could thank them for their hospitality. He arose and called to Sebastián and the Jamajab guide who had conversed most easily with the Indians of San Gabriel.

But all the Jamajabs came at once, laughing and calling out to him. From Sebastián he learned at last what the joke was. The people of the ranchería had seen them coming, and they had thought that Sebastián and the two Jamajabs who had worn the friar's shirt and blanket must be Spaniards. For who else, they argued, would wear anything but his own skin in this fine spring weather? So they had all rushed off to the woods to hide, leaving only the old women in the houses of the ranchería.

To the Indians, including even Sebastián, it seemed a good joke, but to the friar it was still a shock. So obvious was his distress that when he begged the Indians to ask the old women to call their people back, they hastened to comply. And soon the men and the young women and the children were running out of the woods and crowding around him to examine his clothes and his rosary and his crucifix with friendly curiosity. Finally, the leader of the village arrived, and he began to talk to the friar with great cordiality.

It was not always easy for Garcés to follow the far from complete translation of the Jamajabs to make out just what it was that the old man was saying, but the main drift was clear enough. The Jamajabs had told him good things of the Spaniard. They had told him that he was not one of the

Spaniards from the west but a Spaniard from the east, and everybody knew they were good men, the Spaniards from the east.

Involuntarily, the friar winced, as the Jamajabs said that, and the chief seemed to conclude that his guest was in need of further reassurance, for he went on to say that the Jamajabs had assured him that they did not think of the Old Man as a Spaniard but as a Jamajab. It was perhaps the biggest compliment that the friar had ever received, but he was in no mood to appreciate it.

However, there was no time to repine at what could not now be helped. So Garcés deliberately put his mind to the morrow's work. And he talked of his mission north with such effect that when he asked for a guide, the chief himself at once volunteered to escort him to the next ranchería. And when the next ranchería gave so grim a report of the people to the north, the Nochis, that even the Jamajabs refused to go any further, the old man spoke with such conviction of the excellence of the guest and the message that he brought that an Indian of the Nochi nation who happened to be present, volunteered to take the friar to his own people. In vain, Garcés tried to persuade the Jamajabs and Sebastián that they would be safe. They were, for the first time since they had refused to go above the line of San Gabriel when they crossed the mountains, adamant. They were worried enough about the rashness of the friar, but they would not themselves go any farther. They had no arms, they said, nothing wherewith to meet hostile men. So there was nothing to do for it but to leave them with their friendly hosts and push on alone.

But it did not prove so simple. Almost the first Indians they encountered refused to respond to their greetings, although his guide assured Garcés that they were Nochis. When the friar tried to approach them, they retreated precipitately. They had been out hunting, and now they stood clutching their booty of squirrels as if they feared the stranger might try to take it from them. Garcés' guide still shouted reassurance, and the friar tried to make them see that he had no arms and could do them no harm.

Presently, one of them relented so far as to fling a couple of squirrels to the stranger. The Nochi guide picked them up, and the friar flung back a couple of strings of white shells that he had been given from the fathers' store at San Gabriel. One of the Indians darted forward and snatched up the shells and then ran back to his companion, who had stood the while watching the friar. But they would come no nearer, and presently the friar decided that they had lost enough time on a quite hopeless interlude.

So it was with a good deal of misgiving that at the end of a couple of days Garcés found himself in the neighborhood of the first of the Nochi rancherías. Indeed, he took the precaution of sending his Nochi guide on ahead to explain the purpose of the impending visit.

But even as he waited, wondering what sort of welcome he might look for, a crowd of Indians came running out to greet him with noisy friendliness. Immediately, the friar began to distribute his small store of shells and tobacco. But before he had got far, one of the Indians, speaking in broken Spanish, asked for paper that he might roll up his tobacco into a cigarette. The astonished friar finished his little distribution of gifts, and then while the women were bustling about some cooking, he addressed himself to the Spanish-speaking Indian.

The man might be a runaway, but he was quite cool about it. For he told Garcés readily enough that he was from the coast where there were other white men dressed like the friar. And when a little later Garcés took out his crucifix to show to the Indians crowding around him, the supposed runaway took it into his hands with obvious veneration and kissed it repeatedly.

But much as the friar wished to solve the little mystery of this Indian, his attention was immediately diverted by the arrival in camp of some strange Indians, still, he found out presently, another branch of the Nochis, this time from farther north. They were much interested in the presence of the friar, and they examined his clothes and his small possessions with great interest and much chattering among themselves, as if these were things they had heard about and had been curious to see. Then with the help of the Indian who spoke Spanish they urged him to come to their land in the north.

But the thought of Sebastián and the Jamajabs waiting with growing anxiety made the friar resist that temptation. So he said no, that he had friends waiting for him to the south, and he acted out what he said so that his refusal might not seem rude.

Thereupon, the friendly Nochis, apparently with no thought of anything beyond giving him a picture of the country he could not see, settled down to tell him about some Spanish soldiers who had come into their land. Apparently, there had been just two of them, and the friar soon guessed they were some of the deserters from the discipline and the monotony of the life of the mission escorts whom he had heard about as one of the worries of both friars and officers. They had behaved very badly with their women, the Nochis said, their faces darkening at the memory. So they had killed them, and they had torn their bodies to pieces and scattered them on the earth. This last they described with appropriate gestures that made the friar shudder.

But it was quite clear that the Indians felt only the satisfaction of a bad business well cleared-up and the friar's shudder they accepted as a tribute to the efficiency of their methods. So Garcés gravely assured them that the Spaniards, too, were accustomed to punish those who did such wrong things as these men had done. But the thought of those hapless wretches torn into bits stayed with the friar, and that night as he lay awake in the Indian house, listening to the breathing of his housemates in the little rooms all about him, he thought, too, of Fray Luís Jaume who had done only good to the Indians and who had been so terribly beaten and cut to death. The shadow of San Diego was a long one, stretching the length of the whole coast.

4

BUT the friar had little time to think of the disappointments of his northern journey. It was days later than he had planned when he turned back; so in spite of unusually steady pushing ahead and the discovery of a number of short-cuts, he did not reach the land of the Jamajabs until the end of May. There he found letters from both Anza and Eixarch. They told of the safe return of the escort from Monterey, and bade him hurry to the land of the Yurnas without delay so that he might return with the party to Sonora. But the date which both writers had suggested for the latest possible meeting had passed two weeks ago, and he felt sure that the party must have gone by now. Garcés had hardly finished reading his letters when a hunting party came into camp. They had been in the Yuma country, and there they had heard of the departure of the Anza party. They reported, also, that there had been a story at the meeting of the rivers that the Old Man had perished in his travels.

That report went to the conscience of the friar. For he hated to think of the needless anxiety his dilatoriness had caused, was still causing. All the paper he had was the soiled and mussed sheets on which he had written the rough notes for his diary. So he set himself to writing a message on the blank space of the commander's letter. He gave a brief account of his trip, reassurances as to his well-being, and congratulations on his friend's achievement. The date of his return he left vague, largely because he did not feel capable at the moment of figuring out times and distances.

He was soon to be glad he did. For the Jamajabs, who had given him a royal welcome, were now crowding around him as he finished giving his instructions to the messenger who was to carry his letter to the Yumas. At once he knew that they had some mighty plan in hand. So, tired as he was, he prepared to give it his courteous attention.

As the captain of the Jamajabs came up to the friar, the noisy mob subsided for the inevitable speech. So cordial was the exordium that it was not hard to smile and make the proper responses. Garcés had already guessed when his Jamajab guides asked for leave to go ahead and inform their people of his arrival, that they wanted to tell their story so that the whole tribe might prepare a fitting welcome for their guest. To judge from the account he now heard, they had told their story well. And in the telling, as the friar learned to his amazement, they had not omitted any of the evidences of friendliness which the Old Man had shown them. For the Jamajab captain recounted in detail how he had given his clothes to his friends when they were cold in the rainy days along the river, and how he had shared all the food he received, and the tobacco and the shells, and how twice when one of them was ill, he had suspended his journey until the sick man was strong again. The captain finished this recapitulation of the journey from the Indians' point of view with the verdict that the guides had done well when they said the Old Man was a Jamajab, and so would all the people of the Jamajabs ever regard him.

The friar was not quite clear as to what was expected of him at this point, but the swift progress of the captain's oration left no doubt in his mind that they had not yet reached the climax to which all this eloquence was leading up.

"And that night when the guides had finished their speaking," said the Jamajab captain, "I slept, and a dream came to me."

And now from the way in which the Indians leaned forward, the friar knew that the captain had finally reached the point of all this oratory. "And that dream was that I stood here in our village, and I saw the Old Man come into the village, even as the guides had said he would. And then when the Old Man had sat down and I had greeted him, and he had looked at his papers, and he had written on his papers and had called a messenger and sent that messenger away, I saw a great many people coming into the village. They were men from several peoples who came into this village of ours. They were Yabipais Tejua, and Walapais, and Chemehuevi, and Jalchedunes, and they all came into this village. And they sat down in the presence of the Old Man, and they talked of many good things, and they feasted, and they made firm the peace which we have all made at the bidding of the Old Man. And they feasted, and they talked, and they made the peace firm for eight days."

At this point the leader paused dramatically, and the whole company waited breathlessly with their eyes fixed on his face.

"And in the morning," the captain went on with rising excitement, "I awoke, and I said, 'This is a good dream,' and I summoned the old men of the village, and I told them this dream as I have told it to you, Old Man. And they, being full of wisdom, said, 'This is a good dream,' and to all the peoples of the dream they sent messengers, to the Yabipais Tejua, and the Walapais, and the Chemehuevi, and the Jalchedunes. And they said it was a good story that we told, and they would be here to greet the Old Man. And today, Old Man, this dream has come to pass. And men from all these people are waiting to come into the presence of the Old Man and make a peace that will stand firm. And for eight days shall we feast and talk, and the dream I dreamed will come to pass."

For the peace-making the friar had but to express the joy he felt, to commend the dream and the plans that had been made to bring it to pass. And this he did with a warmth and a sincerity that enchanted his hosts. But he had to tell them that the eight days of talk and feasting were impossible. They knew that the commander had sent him letters, and he had bidden him come on to the land of the Yumas. There was much of the king's business to be done, and he was bound to do all he could to further that business. For thus only could the missions be set up that would make it possible for all the peoples of the rivers to hear the good things which he had told the Jamajabs.

Though they were obviously disappointed at the thought of losing all the feasting and the talk, still they could not gainsay the force of the friar's argument. They had begged him too often to stay with them to cause any delay in the carrying out of the plan that would assure them of what they had asked for. So they assented to the change of program and began to make their plans for one night of talk and feasting that would, by token at least, bring their captain's dream to pass. And while the women busied themselves with the preparations for the feast, the men went out to bring in with honor the guests who were still arriving to see the Old Man.

The result was a crowding of the campfire on the edge of the village that exceeded anything which Garcés had yet experienced even at the junction of the rivers. For it seemed as if the whole Jamajab nation were coming into that one village to greet the Old Man. And now mingling with them were the visitors assembling in surprisingly large parties for such short notice. And the friar began to suspect that the plans for the peace-making must have been under way ever since the first of the parties of Jamajab shell-traders had arrived home with their tale of the company they had encountered on the way. For it looked as if half the Indians of the region were crowding into this one village.

The result was indescribable clamor and confusion, for the very men who padded so silently in the ranks of the Anza expeditions, now that they were with their own people on their own ground were full of laughter and chatter and shouts of greeting and even yells of high-pitched excitement. All the while they were milling around the friar, touching his clothes, feeling of his rosary, breathing on his crucifix, and nearly stifling him with the odor of their naked bodies and often strong breaths. In the noise and the stench and the crowding, it seemed to the weary friar that he would faint. So with difficulty he groped his way out of the mob and called to Sebastián to come and help him find a spot where he might sit down and catch his breath.

A couple of the Jamajabs of the village who happened to be standing by came to the rescue and escorted Garcés up to a little promontory on the river bank above the village. Here the exhausted friar sat down, and laid his reeling head on his knees, while the clamor below him sank to a dull roar as of water falling from a height.

He must have slept for a few minutes, for when he raised his head, it felt clearer. But in a moment he realized that he was not alone. With a sigh he turned around. A little group of Indians were sitting behind him, patiently waiting.

And then he realized what it was that covered the dark masses of their bodies and gave them so statuesque a look as if they were carved out of stone. It was the blankets in which they were wrapped, blankets of dark blue wool, the famous blankets of Moqui. He blinked, and all his weariness fell away from him. For now that he had seen the westernmost pier of the great bridge he had been dreaming of in the land of the Nochis, his thoughts had flown east to the other pier of that bridge, the land of the Moquis. His heart beat fast. He had heard of the men of Moqui, fierce, inscrutable, inaccessible in their white fastnesses between the desert and the sky, but he had never seen any of them, or met anyone who had really known them. Only in old books he had read—but as he looked at these men, waiting for him to speak, he realized that these must be some of the Walapais, who came from the east where, doubtless, they traded with the men of Moqui.

So he began to question them of the land to the east of the rivers, asking them how far they had gone. They had travelled far on embassies, these men of the Walapais, and they told him they had heard about the country to the east as far as Santa Fé. Courteously, he asked them of the lands of their people, and the number of their villages, and the lands where they hunted. And he expressed polite admiration at their tale of many villages, and of hunting grounds that went up into the sky, and of wolves and deer and coyotes and mountain lions brought home from their hunts.

And then he expressed his admiration of their blankets and asked them if their people wove them. But at that they were surprised, for they said they thought all men knew the blankets of Moqui.

The friar repeated the word, and asked if they went that far on their trading expeditions. But they shook their heads. It was the people who dwelt on the slopes and in the depths of the great canyons who went to Moqui and brought back huge packs of their blankets. It was from them that the Walapais got their blankets, giving in return shells which they had obtained from the Jamajabs and skins from the animals they themselves had hunted. And as Garcés mused how these ancient trails of barter bound up all the savage world, the Walapais asked him if he would not come with them to their country and show his banner to their people and tell his good news to them, too, even as he had to the people of the rivers.

Gravely he asked them if they would take him to Moqui if he came with them. But they very honestly said no, they would not be going that far. And then he asked them if they could get him guides from their villages to take him there, but they said no, again, and then seeing his eagerness, they explained that it was too far. They would take him to the people of the canyons if he wished, for they were good people, but he would do better to stay with the Walapais. For they would learn the good things which he had to teach them, and they would do as he bade them. For a moment he was tempted, but he remembered Anza's orders to go to the Yumas as soon as he could; so putting temptation away, he told them that he would come when he could, but that he had orders from his chief to go to the Yumas.

The peace-making feast lasted well into the night, with long speeches from various representatives of the parties to the peace. The heart of the friar was warm within him as he witnessed this tangible evidence of his labors, and as the wind blew the light of the flames high on the earnest, shining bronze faces, he felt a great thankfulness well up in his heart over the fullness of the hour.

So it was with a deep sense of content that the next morning he distributed his little presents of shells and tobacco. Especially did he take care to give the most generous present he could to the Walapais, for though he could not go to Moqui yet, he felt sure that one of these days he would be rounding out the bridge in that direction, too. For the sweetness of the triumph of the last night had driven out the cobwebs that had clouded his imagination since he had turned back from the land of the Nochis, and though he was still weary, he was already looking ahead to the next expedition.

But he had hardly got past the last brush huts of the village when he heard a wild yell from the river. With the echoes of the speeches of the peace-making still in his ears, Garcés could not believe that that was a war yell, but it came again, and again. The friar turned back to the village. There could be no mistaking that cry. Some of the Indians from farther away who had not been invited to the peace-making must have decided to avenge the insult and sent a war party. And yet who could be so mad as to challenge the Jamajabs on their own ground when so many of the tribe were gathered in one village? Garcés stood where he was, listening.

There was no mistaking the uproar from the river now. It seemed, too, that it was moving up from the shore to where the friar stood waiting uncertainly. For at the first cry Sebastián had slipped quietly from Garcés' side to see what it was that had disturbed their departure. Now he was running back, followed by two of the Jamajabs whom the friar at once recognized as leaders in the village. All three were breathless.

"It is some of our men. They recognized the slayers of their kin in the Walapais, and they were lying in wait for them when they took the river trail," explained the foremost of the Jamajabs, panting for lack of breath but astonishingly matter-of-fact in his explanation, as if he were giving a dispassionate report on some unavoidable accident.

The friar flared with indignation, "Faithless Jamajabs! Is it a Jamajab trick to invite men to a peace-making, and then when you have all talked and eaten together, ambush them?" His indignation burned on the quiet river air, and the Indians shrank away.

But one of them still muttered, "It is hard for a man to see the murderer of his kin walk in the sunlight."

"He should not invite him to a feast then. Good men do not lie in wait for those who have just risen from their campfire," he lashed at the Indian in bitter contempt, but the man only shrank away with a shrug of the shoulders.

"The Old Man is right," said another voice, and the friar looked around to see the captain of the Jamajabs. Behind him a crowd of Indians were bringing along a half dozen of their number held firmly so that they might not run away, and after them came the Walapais with whom Garcés had been talking the day before.

Now they all stood around Garcés, and the captain briefly told the story which the friar had already heard, and when he concluded, he bade the culprits stand forth that the Old Man might see them. They were still angry and defiant, but the friar could see that the first warmth of their violence had left them, and they were becoming a little uncertain of where they stood. Garcés made no effort to conceal the scorn with which he looked upon them, "Do you think such treachery worthy of the Jamajabs?"

And then he turned to the captain, "Do you think any man will ever again break arrows with the Jamajabs when he knows that the Jamajabs have waylaid guests leaving their campfire?"

The guilty Indians tried to mutter something, but the captain of the Jamajabs raised his arms for silence. "The Old Man is quite right. The Jamajabs do not kill their guests. Let the men of the Walapais depart for their own country."

Now it was the turn of the Walapais to push their way to the friar and to shout that they did not dare to set forth for fear that the Jamajabs would waylay them farther on where there would be no Old Man to whom they could appeal. They shouted their fears loudly enough, but there was no mistaking the fright in their eyes. And as his anger cooled, a sick disgust washed over the friar.

<h1 style="text-align:center">5</h1>

GARCÉS thought of the Yumas waiting for his return and of the summer work at Bac. And then he looked at the frightened faces of the Walapais and the smouldering sulkiness of the Jamajab culprits. One more outrage such as this, and the work of months of peace-making along the rivers would go up in smoke. He would be late in his return, but he would see that land of the canyons that he had heard of, and he would at least make a beginning on the road to Moqui.

"I'll go with you," he said at last, and the grateful Indians embraced his mule in their relief.

But at the last moment Sebastián refused to go any farther north. Apparently, he had heard terrifying tales of the people in that region and of the spirits that dwelt in the canyon land. Hastily the friar reminded Sebastián that now that he was a good Christian he had no reason to fear the spirits which any bad men might invoke against him. He had only to say his rosary as a good Christian should. It was in vain, and so much of the friar's weariness had now returned to him that he was in no mood to take the chances of a sullen and fearful companion. So he bade Sebastián wait with the Jamajabs only for a few days, and then if his master had not returned, he was to go down with the Jalchedunes to their lands and wait there.

Several times the first hours of that pleasant trip along the river bottom Garcés thought with amusement of Sebastián's fears. But, presently, he began to realize that this was a very remarkable country into which he had come.

For the ground on either side of the stream was beginning to rise, and the river bottom to grow narrower and sandier. Soon the earth was washing away from the banks until presently only the reddish-brown of the sandstone was to be seen on either hand. And before long even that color seemed to bleach out into a weather-beaten yellow and gray, and presently, in the bright sun of high noon, the banks rose almost white. The river was running faster, too, and the wind was rising. High above their heads could be seen the green of the trees and bushes along the top of the banks, a green that looked dazzlingly fresh and bright to eyes accustomed to the desert.

A few days later the travelers left the river course and by precipitous paths found their way up into this green world. Whatever regret the friar may have felt at losing the dramatic river route was soon forgotten. For a night of camping in the pine-sweet coolness of the forest brought back fresh life and energy, and this sense of exhilaration lasted. For even as they pushed their way through the wooded country, the friar perceived that they were constantly climbing higher. Sometimes the rise was by almost imperceptible stages as they trotted up an open slope of sweet mountain grass. Again, the trail shot up in a precipitous jut of thinly-earthed rock with the pine trees and the junipers clinging uncertainly to the brown edges. Always it seemed to the desert veteran as if they were traveling on the green roof of the world in an intoxication of freshness and coolness.

And then when from days of travel Garcés had become thoroughly accustomed to this mountain-top world, the scene changed again. First, he noticed that they were running more frequently into canyons and ravines. And then he realized that the path along the river was growing steadily wilder and more precipitous.

The crisis came one afternoon when for some time they had been riding along the rim of what seemed an endless labyrinth of canyons and mountains. For once, Garcés' terror of the depths beside his path was yielding to the delight of the color when suddenly he noticed that the foremost of the Walapais had found a nick in the firm rim of the canyon, and was fast disappearing from view down an invisible path. Even as Garcés watched him in astonishment, one of his other guides came up and explained hurriedly that he must give up his mule. The Indian assured him that the mule would be taken to his still undisclosed destination by another and longer way. The friar hesitated for one last look around the incredible panorama, turning in the slanting afternoon light, even more incredible shades of maroon, and purple, and orange, and mauve gray, astonishingly soft and lovely in the melting air of the fading day.

Then he dismounted, and addressed himself to the dark plunge into the bowels of the earth. As he tried to keep pace with the sure-footed Indians filing down the narrow, twisting trail on the side of the precipice, he soon became so absorbed in the momentary hazards of the descent that he forgot everything else. Only when they halted on a ledge of naked rock overlooking still vaster depths below did he have leisure to peer over the edge of the canyon again. Now he was almost blinded by the blaze as the sunset thrust one sword of many-hued flame through the riot of color, and then slowly faded.

The friar had little time to look out at the terrifying splendors of the canyon in that sharp descent into the bowels of the earth. But when he could for a moment's rest take his eyes from the narrow path at his feet, he watched in admiration how the silver ribbon below widened until, as they set their feet on the last drop high over the tree tops below, they heard the roar of the water rushing down its rocky bed. And then he saw that it was now almost the breadth of the stream they had been following all these days and immeasurably more boisterous in its rock-hemmed strength.

But there were many more minutes of anxious descent before they caught sight of the first mat-covered huts in a green pool where the dark rocks drew back in what was almost a hollow circle. There before the darkness of the bottom of the world quite blotted out sight, they descried moving figures and knew that here in the depths of the earth men still lived. By the time they had at last found solid ground under their feet, the cheerful glow of a campfire came through the darkness and the roar of the river with a cheerful promise of human fellowship. Never had traveler given sincerer thanks to Saint Christopher and Our Lady than Francisco Garcés gave that night as he followed the Indians, a little unsteadily, to that welcome blaze.

The world Garcés woke to the next morning was even more surprising than the world on which he had slept. For it was no trough of sand or stone on which he looked but a green valley with willows and cottonwoods and sycamores along the rocky margin of the river. It was still too early in the day for the remote sun that lighted the heavens to penetrate into these depths; so the walls of the canyon hung all around in somber fastnesses of darkness as if the night still kept its clutch on those congenial shadows. But where a splinter of sunshine shot through a break in the nearer of the eastern canyon walls and splashed into a field of corn, it turned the dark green blades into translucent light, as if they had been made of glass. And all around was the cool freshness of a world of living and growing things filling the bottom of this kettle of rock.

Even as the friar looked, the far-off rim of the mountain tops warmed into life, the dark rocks foaming into rose and gold under his eyes. And then he rose wearily but cheerfully.

For once he blessed the Indian's love of loitering sociably with friends, for the five days that followed in the green world of the Jabesúas gave him a sorely needed chance to rest. Even at the end of that period he was still a little dizzy whenever he thought of the terrible way by which they had come. He would have liked to linger even longer with the friendly folk of the canyon, who seemed never to tire of fingering his clothes and his compass and his rosary and his crucifix. But the Walapais were anxious to show him still more of the wonders of their land, and though the friar for once felt that he had had his fill of the strangeness of nature, he knew that he would never find his way out of this canyon unaided.

Even with the help of the Indians it was a long hard pull to the rim, and many a time the Spaniard looked enviously at the lithe brown forms scrambling so steadily and apparently so easily up the invisible toe-holds of

a seemingly perpendicular wall. For all the wonder of the changing colors of
the mountain walls, the friar was not sorry when they reached the top and
came out on a slope of dwarf-pine-covered earth. There his mule was waiting
for him. As he climbed with relief on its back, he laughingly told his guides
that he had seen quite enough of the boasted wonders of the canyon country
and was quite willing to take their word for the rest.

But they only stared blankly until finally one of them gravely assured
him that the greatest wonder of all was yet to be seen. That he could not
believe, but he saw that it was quite useless to argue the matter. He was,
therefore, completely astonished when the next day the Indians more than
made good their boast.

It was well past high noon, and the white glare of the sun was softening
a little when they emerged from the forest and came out on a rocky plateau
with a great sweep of clear sun-bright air before them. After the shadows of
the canyons it seemed as if the whole world of the upper air opened there
before them. And the friar drew a deep breath as he gazed out upon that
radiant space. But one of the Indians was speaking and pointing. The friar's
eyes dropped, and then he started in astonishment.

For not a dozen feet from where he stood, the earth fell away sharply. He
ran forward and looked down into the shadows, and then he looked around.
In every direction but the wooded slope at his back, the earth fell away, and
now he saw they were on a sort of spur over the edge of the precipice. They
stood on a great mountain—and then he looked out into the vast space before him, and on the opposite side, he saw that another mountain, no, a great
plateau rose. And then he looked down again.

The Indians were smiling and gesticulating at him, and suddenly he
knew that this was the great canyon of which the Walapais had been talking
in the camp of the Jamajabs. But it was something more than any canyon he
had ever seen, even if it were magnified many times. For within that great
gash in the earth's surface rose whole ranges and chains of mountains, in
rows and in swirls, piled one on top of the other, as if the Maker of the Universe had assembled in this great trough of the earth all the models for all
the earth's many-piled surfaces. Every kind of rock seemed to be there, too,
from the black volcanic slag at his feet to great ribbons of rose and yellow
and grey, and brown and fire-red stone, band upon band as if all the world's
earths had been pounded into each other. But even this seeming order was
a delusion, for he soon caught sight of a place where the ribbons had been

stood on end like the columns, of an ancient temple, and just beyond an even more startling effect where in a sudden fantasy they had been twirled so that they bulged and receded like the colors on a child's top. It seemed a veritable nightmare of geological fantasy, where all the possibilities of creation had suddenly been unleashed in a flaming gash down the green side of the world. And yet it was strangely lovely, too, in the radiance of the air, in the majesty of the assembled shapes, in the long rhythms of the banded colors, in the new worlds of light and shadow that came into being as if momentarily born of this marriage of sun and space.

The friar looked harder at the great depths of this subterranean world, and suddenly far below he caught a flash of silver, like a ribbon of light fallen from the upper air and turned by the shadows to a lunar evanescence. But for that ribbon at the bottom of those mountains he would have said that the canyon had no bottom.

"That is the great river up which we have been traveling," said one of the Indians, and Garcés stared incredulously.

"Come and see," said the Walapais. And before the friar could answer that for his part he was quite content to take any man's word for it, rather than plunge into that world of falling precipices, the Indians were trotting along the rim of the great canyon seemingly unaware of the overwhelming impression which it had made on their guest's imagination. For he was accustomed to meeting the vast panorama of his endless journeys, piece by piece, as far as a horse might cover in a half day's time, or a man walk in a day or two. But here it was as if all the impossible trails he had ever been on had been hurtled together in a nightmare from which he expected to wake at any moment.

6

IT was, therefore, a great relief to come again into an ordinary small Indian village, this time of friendly Yabipais, old allies of his Walapai guides, who made the party warmly welcome. But before the friar could begin to talk with his hosts, he became aware that other visitors were coming into the village.

As they came into the circle of the firelight, Garcés' heart leaped, for the new arrivals were wrapped in dark blankets. There were four of them. Two sat down in the front of the circle where some of their hosts had made way for

them in the warmest part in front of the fire, but two of the blanket-shroud-
ed figures did not come forward. Instead, they remained a little behind as
if perhaps they did not have the same confidence in their welcome as their
companions.

"These are men of the pueblos," explained one of the Walapais.

"From Moqui?" asked the friar as calmly as he could in his excitement at
this first meeting with the men he had come so far to seek.

But the Walapai shook his head. "These," pointing to the men by the fire,
"are from Zuñi."

"Zuñi!" And with that word, the unattainable and the remote and the
dreamed-of became the still remote but the already known and attained. For
there was a priest at Zuñi, and the men of that pueblo, if still remote from
the realm of the King of Spain, were already within the fold of the Church.

And this sense of reassurance was strengthened when the Indians began
to examine the crucifix which he passed around the circle. For the Walapais
took the crucifix in their hands with awe and seemed to breathe from it.

But the men from Zuñi took it into their hands with reverence as if they
understood its meaning, and kissed it with familiar devotion. So much pleasure did the sight of this give the friar that he stared at them, devouring with
hungry eyes every least look of these remote Christians.

Then he remembered the two men who would not come to the fire,
and he turned to look for them. And then he saw that one of the Zuñis was
holding out the crucifix to the blanketed figure behind him. To the watching friar's astonishment this man shrank back into the shadows, refusing so
much as to touch the wood of the crucifix.

When the crucifix had returned to the friar, the circle around the fire
broke up, and some one threw more pinon logs on it so that a bright and
fragrant blaze illumined the whole place. In that light the Indians crowded
around him to examine his clothes. The two men from Zuñi came up to the
friar and kissed his hand and asked for his blessing, kneeling to receive it
while the others looked on with large eyes. But when Garcés looked for the
two who had come with them, he saw that they were still standing on the
edge of the circle, and though it was dark where they stood, the friar was
quite aware of the attitude of repulsion in those somber figures.

So taking a little tobacco and some shells in his hand, he went over to
where the men stood and proffered his gift. For a moment, the man who had
refused to touch the crucifix looked at the friar and then muttered something

which the latter could not understand and turned away, going now into the firelight where Garcés could for a moment see his face, unmistakably sullen and hostile. Astonished, the friar turned to his companion. He kissed Garcés' hand, and hopefully the friar offered his gifts. The Indian took the shells and tobacco, examined them, and then, still without a word, pushed them back into Garcés' hands and turned away. The friar came closer and held out the shells so that their precious whiteness gleamed temptingly in the firelight, but the man pulled his blanket around him and turned his face away in a gesture of repudiation impossible to misunderstand. And while the friar stared at him, one of the Indians who had knelt for his blessing came up to him and spoke in hesitating but unmistakable Spanish, "They are from Moqui, father." And the Indian looked at the friar as if that answered all questions.

Scarcely able to control his excitement at that magic word, Garcés turned again to the two men on the edge of the circle, but they had vanished.

And now the weariness of the day washed back over the heart of the friar. For the hope that had galvanized the aching limbs had yielded to the grief of a rebuff which went to the heart of his innermost loyalty. In the morning he would make one more attempt; he would ask the men from Moqui to show him the way. And perhaps in the long hours on the trail he might be able to pierce that sullen hostility.

But in the morning the men from Moqui had vanished. The friar thought of the friendly Zuñis, but when he inquired for them, he found that they, also, had left before dawn. So he asked the Walapais to go on with him to Moqui, but they refused, explaining that they must go back to their own village. And they went on to ask why the Old Man did not come with them. They were good men who would listen to him. Had he not seen how the men from Moqui had turned away rudely from his magic? Again, the friar said he must go on to Moqui. But the Walapais only repeated their invitation for the Old Man to come with them. And, presently, it became quite clear to the friar that there was no persuading them. It was not simply that they wanted him to go back with them. They were unwilling to go into the pueblo country.

During Garcés' conversation with the Walapais, some of their Yabipai hosts stood by listening and watching without intervening even when the Walapais made certain disparaging generalizations about all the people in this part of the world. And they said nothing when finally the friar announced that he was going on alone. But he was hardly out of sight of the village and into an open country of mesquite and pinon when he became aware that someone was behind him.

For a moment he hesitated, and then his mind went back to the little group of Yabipais who had listened to his talk with the Walapais that morning. He had barely noticed it at the time, but now he remembered that they had been holding various bundles and burdens in which he had not been interested enough to identify even roughly.

Now when he turned, he found it was, as he had guessed, a trading party of seven or eight Yabipais coming down the trail behind him. As he stopped, they stopped, too, and one of them came ahead to greet him. It was an old man whom he had spoken with the night before, a man who had traveled often to the east, and had learned a little Spanish from some of the mission Indians.

With a sudden accession of hope the friar waited for him to come up.

"They are men of poor heart, those Walapais," said the old Yabipai gravely.

"They do not know the people of the pueblos, I think," ventured the friar. "I do not believe such evil of them as they speak."

The Yabipai considered while his fellows caught up with them. "Some of the men of the pueblos are good men who will be glad to see the Gray Robe. But some of the men of the pueblos will not give up the old ways; they will not hear of Jesus and they will not come to the long prayer of the Christians."

"Why?" asked the friar.

For some minutes there was no sound but that of the sandals of the Indians slip-slipping over the sand of the trail. The sun was high in the heavens now, and the colorful half-desert world had flattened into a whitish-gray that stung the eyeballs of the traveler so that he was glad to fix his eyes on the gray-green sagebrush that fringed the almost invisible way. The friar had given up any hope of an answer when the old Yabipai without preamble said suddenly, "Some men cannot forget the bad things that happened in old days."

"What things?" asked the friar. The Indian said nothing. Only when the friar had given up any hope of having his question answered did the Yabipai break the heavy silence. "Do you remember Popé and the cords with the knots that he sent out from Taos to all the pueblos?"

"Do you think any Spaniard forgets Popé in this country?" countered the friar.

The Yabipai looked at him as if measuring him.

"Popé did great wrong," said the old Indian.

The friar smiled gently, "I shall not deny that. Four hundred Spaniards died when those ropes of Popé were untied."

"Some of them were Gray Robes, too," said the Yabipai with a side-long look.

"Only they were black," said the Franciscan. "But it does not matter what color the martyrs wear. It is all red in the end." He thought of the words which Father Serra was said to have spoken when he learned of the death of Luís Jaume. "Now that the ground has been watered, we shall have a harvest." Twenty-one of Garcés' brother Franciscans died in that uprising of 1680.

The Indian was speaking again, "The priest at Zuñi did not die."

"That," said the friar with a smile, "is to the glory of the men of Zuñi."

"He was a good man," said the Yabipai thoughtfully.

"They were good men who died, too."

The friar's voice had sharpened, and again the Yabipai looked at him.

"That is true," said the Indian gravely. "When the war cry sounds, the good and the bad die alike."

The friar said nothing. And for some minutes they walked on quietly. It was hard to think of anybody having energy enough to raise the war cry in the heavy stillness of this greenish gray world, bleaching in the flinty sunlight.

"Men died, too," said the Indian, as if there had not been any interruption to their conversation, "when they came back and hanged Popé's followers."

"That is true," said the friar slowly. "But those men had given their faith and had broken it. At least," he added, justly, "some of them had."

"The men of Moqui gave no pledge," said the Yabipai thoughtfully. "They broke no pledge, and they lived."

The friar was shocked by the seeming finality in the flat conclusion of the Yabipai's sentence.

For some time the friar had been watching a low bank of cloud-like gray come out of the indeterminate horizon. Now it was clear that it was a mesa of some extent, almost directly in front of them. Neither the Yabipai nor the friar said anything about it, but the friar watched it come nearer, growing darker and beginning to assume a rough shape, as if it were a wave of the desert floor washed up in some vast upheaval and frozen there in its muddy gold between the earth and the sky. And now as they came closer, the friar saw that it was, indeed, a pueblo with the grayish-white walls rising out of the rock of the mesa as if they were a part of its aboriginal structure, spattered with patches of reddish stone where the plaster had worn through. The sky-line was curiously jagged, but the main plan was unmistakable.

"What pueblo is that?" asked the friar.

"It is the pueblo of Moconabi," said the Yabipai promptly for once, as if he had been waiting for the question.

"Moconabi?" repeated the friar thoughtfully. "What men live there?"

"The dead," answered the Yabipai. The friar looked at him, but his face was perfectly composed.

So, though he knew the answer, the friar asked the inevitable question, "How did they die?" For here in this land where the memory of things long past was still the most living of actualities, he clearly must know what it was that men remembered.

Again, the Yabipai seemed to consider. Then he answered very slowly, "Old Man, all men say that the Old Man is wise and speaks good things. The Old Man does not need me to tell him that man does harm to man, and the man who believes he is injured kills the man who hurt him, and then the kin of the slain man kill again, and so the war cry is never silent for very long. And who shall say who did the first wrong, and what wrong shall be the last?"

"Only God," said the friar. "And that is why he said, 'Vengeance is mine,' and His alone it is."

"Then we shall leave it to God," said the Yabipai.

They were now abreast of the ruined pueblo. Great shadows gaped from the gray face, where the rain had washed away the adobe from the reddish stones, now blackened by the years, and they had come tumbling down to pile up the heap of débris at the fool. One could see the ends of the wooden beams of the ceilings in one place, and they were still black in spite of the rains of a century. There were holes in the walls, too, holes that looked as if they had been made by cannon balls.

And now as his eyes traveled around the torn height, the friar could see the broken towers of the church. One was nearly intact, and in the shadows one could almost see the silent bell hanging. But the other was cut away clean so that only the lower part of the open space remained like a window against the radiant blue sky. Through some freak of the now slanting sunlight, that frame was snow-white against the soft yet brilliant blue of the sky. It seemed to Francisco Garcés that he had never seen anything so majestically serene as that broken window on the cloudless sky of the desert.

Filled with the perfection of it, he sighed lightly.

The Yabipai broke the silence, "The pain of the dead is over. It is only the living who remember grief."

7

THE visit to Oraibe, the first of the Moqui pueblos, began inauspiciously enough. When the party was still seven or eight miles from the mesa on which the Yabipais said Oraibe was located, they met a young man journeying alone, in a wool shirt and good sandals. The Yabipais hardly needed to tell the friar that this young man was from Moqui. So Garcés rode forward and saluted him.

The latter returned the greeting with a casual gesture, but when the friar held out a handful of tobacco, the young man shrank away and would have nothing to do with the gift.

About a league further on, two riders appeared, likewise coming from the direction of Oraibe. They, too, looked more like Spanish soldiers than like Indians of the desert, for they wore substantial leather garments, and they sat astride good horses. Again, the friar rode ahead of his companions to greet them, but at sight of him they drew up, and the only reply they vouchsafed to Garcés' friendly greeting was to make unmistakable signs that he should go back. This time, however, the Yabipais decided to take a hand. For when they saw the friar coming back, they rode ahead, and the leader of the Yabipais engaged the two men from Moqui in conversation. Apparently, he was trying to intercede in some fashion, for he stayed with the strangers for several minutes, talking with a good deal of animation. Then, he returned to the waiting friar.

"They are asking what you will do," said the Indian somewhat uncertainly.

"Tell them," said the friar resolutely, "that I am going on to Oraibe, and if they will not receive me there, I shall keep on my way to the Spaniards at Santa Fé, for I am a Spaniard."

However, the Yabipai leader did not ride back to the Moquis, but stood there awkwardly, scratching his head as if he could not decide whether or not that answer would do any good. Garcés knew that the Yabipais could not be much interested in his errand. After all, they had come to Oraibe to trade, with their loads of mescal and skins and other stuff of their country, and they were not likely to welcome any difficulty that would interfere with that.

They were now, the friar knew, within a few miles of Oraibe; so on a sudden impulse, he left the group and went on.

After a few minutes the old Yabipai and one of the boys followed him, leaving their companions with the Moquis. These two were enough to give Garcés the immediate help he needed to find a path up the steep slopes of the mesa. The way itself was so narrow and twisting and precipitous that it engaged all the drought of the friar to get his mule safely up that path. About halfway up, they paused to draw their breath at a sheepfold built on a ledge of the slope, and in it the friar saw some large black sheep that might well have made a Sonora shepherd envious. Then they resumed their climb to come out on top of the mesa.

It was sandy here, with no sign of grass. So the friar pushed on until he came to a slight hollow where he saw some very fine peach trees, and then past some garden patches of onions and beans and squashes to the spring, spilling out into a small pool that was the obvious source of the water for all this cultivation.

Now there was no mistaking the well-worn path, running downhill a little and then abruptly turning to end flat against some old stone and adobe houses, doorless and windowless, blindly masking the entrance to the pueblo behind them. A few more steps, and they were in Oraibe, and the friar was standing in the entrance of a straight, wide street, surveying the most remarkable town which he had ever entered.

The first impression was of something very casual, half-finished, and in bad repair. The second was of very careful contrivance and well-seasoned planning. The street in which Garcés stood was both broad and straight, with side streets entering it at precise right angles. But the houses that rose on either side were of varying heights and sizes, so casual in their adobe blocks that it was easy to believe they were but outcroppings of the cliff from which they sprang. And yet as the eye searched their planes of light and shadow, it was soon apparent that they were very ingeniously contrived. For each level consisted of a series of patios, each one completely walled off from its neighbors, with anywhere from two to three apartments opening off it.

Yet again the pattern was broken, with the patios opening at various angles, and short ladders leaning against the walls, and baskets, and looms, and chicken coops, and brightly painted water jars, and all the tools of a busy craft and agricultural life in evidence on these open-air patios, mounting up to the sky for two or three stories. It was a ragged effect, that of the yellowish-gray housetops against the bright blue summer sky, and yet a very solid one that gave a sense in the weathered stones of something long-enduring and indescribably ancient.

But Garcés had no more time to take stock of his surroundings just then, for the housetops were thronged with women and children, staring at the newcomers. One of these women, the old Yabipai recognized, and he called a friendly greeting to her, where she stood on her housetop. Then the old man took off one of the heavy packs from his horse and started up the ladder. The friar hastened to follow his example. But the woman on the housetop called out some order sharply to the old Yabipai, who was now standing beside her. The Yabipai came to the edge of the roof, and, looking down at his traveling companion, he shrugged his shoulders and made an expressive gesture of repulsion. The friar stretched out his free hand to the woman on the roof, but she shook her head.

So Garcés looked around. Behind him was a little blind corner of masonry where the walls of adjoining houses met. There he unsaddled his mule, and looked around uncertainly. In a minute the old Yabipai was at his side to take the bridle of the mule and lead him off to a small sheep-corral at the end of one of the side streets. Then he came back to where the friar stood watching him.

He shrugged his shoulders. "You'll have to stay here alone. These people will have nothing to do with you. They're a bad lot."

But now the women and the children were coming down from the housetops to stare at him. At first, he thought that he could turn their curiosity to friendliness. For they kept coming up from all angles to look at him, and then they would run away, and then come back again. Presently, some men appeared from the entrance to the village, with children tugging at their hands, as if perhaps they had run out into the fields to find them. Hour after hour they kept coming and staring and talking to each other in low voices. But none of them would come near the stranger. In vain, he spoke to them and smiled and made signs. In vain he offered them some of the white seashells which all desert men so much prize. He saw the dark eyes glitter, but none would put out a hand to the shells. Not even the children would come near, but clung to the black dresses of the women, still gazing with big eyes at the stranger.

So it went on all day. The friar was tired and thirsty and hungry now. Fortunately, he had filled a gourd of water at the spring. So he gathered up some of the cornstalks that strewed the street, and with the burning glass he carried he struck fire to the little heap. Usually, Indians were fascinated by the burning glass, but though these people watched every move with wide eyes, they gave no other sign of interest. So he took out a small pot and set some porridge to heat.

It was evening now, with the softening of light that turns everything to iridescence in the desert. The men were coming back from the fields, carrying their hoes and dibbles and hatchets. But though they all looked at him with bright eyes, they gave no sign of greeting or friendly interest. In the softening light the stone walls of the houses seemed less alien and forbidding than these expressionless faces, with only the brown-black eyes inscrutably and dangerously alive in the wooden countenances.

Not until the street was dark and empty in the sudden stillness of nightfall did anyone come up to speak to him. There was still light enough for him to see that the man before him was bent, and that he was bowing still lower as he spoke with the thin voice of age. The grateful priest hastily took some shells and some tobacco and gave them to the old man. To his astonishment, the Indian responded in quite understandable Spanish, "May God reward you."

But before the friar could question him further, there was another step approaching, obviously a far more vigorous one. As another Indian came up, the friar greeted him, and held out the same gift of tobacco and shells. And this was followed by the same acknowledgement, and now he offered his crucifix, and the newcomer took it into his hands and kissed it.

To his astonishment the young Indian began to talk to him in quite comprehensible Spanish, "Father, these are wild men here at Oraibe. They do not want to be baptized. But I have been baptized at Zuñi. We have a father there, and all the people of my pueblo are good. We know that all who are baptized go to heaven."

"Has the priest of Zuñi been here in Oraibe?" asked the friar curiously.

"Oh, yes," said the Zuñi, "but he was glad to come back to us. He said that these are bad people, and they will not let themselves be baptized."

"It is a pity," said the friar compassionately. All around him he could see dark shadows moving in the street and on the house-tops, and he could hear the hum of conversation, and the rustling of dried cornstalks, and the light thumping of ladders where they touched the walls.

The Zuñi was speaking again. "Father, you can do nothing here. You had better come with us. There are three of us, and we start at sunrise. Before noon we shall be at the first pueblo, and we shall spend the night there. Then we shall travel the next day and the following night, and we shall be at Zuñi."

The friar made no answer to that invitation, but he asked the two Indians from Zuñi if they could get the captain of Oraibe to speak to him.

The young man seemed to shrug his shoulders in the dark. "It is clear that the captain does not want to come here. Who can tell where he is hiding?"

There was nothing the friar could say to that, but he could feel all about him in the dark a considerable crowd of people whispering and listening. So he contented himself with entreating the young Zuñi to tell the people about that he was a priest of the Spaniards in Sonora and of other Indians like themselves, that he had come through the lands of many peoples, and that he had come to tell them the things of God. He heard the Zuñi speak very quietly to the bystanders in their language. But Garcés could form no notion of their response. Only he could hear them going away, and presently, above his head, he could hear people settling for the night on the housetops. Some talked noisily, others sang, and through it all came the sharp sweetness of a flute.

The friar listened to all this bustle, so familiar from nights in Spanish villages, with a deepening sense of loneliness and strangeness. He had fallen asleep, however, when he heard a shrill voice speaking. As he struggled to consciousness, he realized that a single voice was haranguing the night, and while it was speaking, there was deep silence. But when, after what must have been a lengthy oration, the voice ceased speaking, the noise of the night resumed. Then another voice broke out into speech, and there was the same stillness. And then again the muffled noise of the night, gradually sinking into silence, as the heavy darkness closed down. But for the friar there was no sleeping. For the cold had him in its grip, and a certain sharp tenseness possessed him as if that unearthly flute were still playing on nerves deep within his body. He must have slept a little, for presently the old Yabipai and the boy were standing over him, asking him what he was going to do.

In a low voice he told them that he was going to Zuñi. There was not enough light to see their faces, but there was no mistaking the alarm with which they hastened to assure him that they would not go with him.

Feeling their dismay, he took out some shells and offered them to the Yabipais, asking them to go and buy some corn from the Moquis so he might have food for his journey. But they pushed the shells back at him. And they explained anxiously, as if they must make him understand, that the Moquis would not sell him any food even for so great a price as he offered. This was grim enough for the friar, standing there alone in a corner of the hostile village, but there was worse to come. Even as they were talking, two of the young Yabipais who had been his traveling companions yesterday came up and handed back to him the shells he had given them on the road. Evidently, they not only had not succeeded in convincing the Moquis of his friendliness, but they had had their own suspicions awakened by the warnings of the men of Oraibe.

The friar was stiff from the cold of the night and the hardness of his bed, and his head was tense and yet heavy for want of sleep. But he knew he must decide what to do at once. The trip to Zuñi, seen in the chill light of this grim dawn at Oraibe, was clearly impossible. Without escort it would be madness to return to Moqui from Zuñi. Even if the Zuñis brought him back to Moqui, they would hesitate to take him on to the Yabipais, for they were not friends.

So he slept fitfully, from sheer exhaustion, until he was finally awakened by the sound of singing and dancing in the streets near him. He thought of the crowd on the housetops and in the streets the night before. It was a little past daybreak now, and he could see the rout breaking out of the canyon between the houses ahead quite clearly now. In a moment they were passing by his retreat, and he could see that among the Indians were some who were painted red, with feathers stuck in their heads. As they came by, he could see their instruments, too, a tray-like kind of drum beaten with small sticks, and the flutes on which the players threaded the heavy throbbing of the drum with their piercing sweetness. All around him the walls reverberated to the beating of the music and the stamping of many feet and the clapping of many hands on the housetops and in the streets. The whole pueblo seemed alive and throbbing to the pulse of one great rhythm.

And now the sun was really up so that he saw quite clearly a crowd of people suddenly break away from the main procession and start for his refuge. For a moment he thought they were going to rush upon him, and with a thrill in his famished stomach he knew that it would be but a few minutes before he would be overwhelmed by their sheer numbers. The picture of Fray Luís Jaume beaten and cut past recognition flashed into his mind. In a wordless prayer he commended himself to the Master in whose service he had come into this hostile world, and he braced himself. But just before the mob reached him, four of the men whom, by their confidence and dignity of appearance, he judged to be the leaders of the rest, stepped forward, and the tallest one made a grimace, and addressed the friar.

Garcés understood none of the words which the Indian orator used, but he grasped clearly enough the meaning of gesture and intonation. He was asking him with signs why he had come, and without waiting for an answer, he was bidding him be gone with the now familiar gestures of repudiation and repulsion.

The friar caught his breath and with signs invited the four Indians to sit down. But they refused to move. Then he arose so that he was facing them, and he lifted up his crucifix, and began to address them. In his anxiety not to let this last chance of possible communication pass, he began to talk in every tongue he could lay hands on, in Yuma, and Pima and Jamajab and Yabipai, and when those tongues failed, in his own Castilian, all the while making nervous gestures to convey his meaning to the now attentive Indians.

But though his voice rose until it trembled in the passion of his endeavor to reach their minds and hearts, the faces still gazed at him with the same blank-wall expression which he had encountered during the past days. Only one old man made any response, and he cried out in a high, cracked voice but in unmistakable Castilian, "No, no."

For a moment, the friar paused with his crucifix still held aloft as if he were hanging on that hostile air. But even as he gazed at the speaker, he knew that the whole silent crowd and the waiting walls around him had found tongue in that voice. Still the old man was screeching, "No, no." The friar's hands fell to his side, and he bowed his head. Then he made a sign for his mule to be brought, and he stooped down and began to pack his cloak and breviary and crucifix into the saddlebags.

He would have said that the crowd behind him did not move or make any sound, but when in a couple of minutes he turned around again, he saw the Yabipai boy who had already been so faithful appear down a side street, leading the mule. The friar thanked the young Indian, who backed away hastily. But the crowd lingered as the friar saddled and loaded his mule, and then with as much calmness as he could muster, he started back the way he had come two days ago. The whole assembly followed him to the edge of the pueblo, and there, having seen that he was on his way, they turned back, leaving him entirely alone.

It was almost sunset when he reached a little rise of ground to the northwest of the desert over which he had been traveling all day. Here he paused to rest and to let the mule browse after the climb. Away to the southeast he could see the mesa country, one strange table-land rising up behind another like rock-fast islands out of the sea of the surrounding desert. The glow of the sunset in that clear air turned those distant rock walls to mother of pearl and alabaster.

Garcés thought of Fray Marcos de Niza gazing from a similar height across a plain very much like this at the same time of day, and seeing the first of the Seven Cities of Cibola glowing in the wrecked dreams of two and a half centuries ago. But instinctively his mind shied away from the reawakening pain of that thought, and he took refuge in the more distant memory of Moses gazing on the Promised Land which he was never to enter. But Francisco Garcés had entered into Oraibe, and he had been thrust out. And at the thought of that his mind in its sad groping thrust back even farther to the beginning of things, to that last vision of the angel-sworded garden from which Adam and Eve had turned for all the wilderness of this mortal world. And for the first time in his life the usually optimistic friar knew that he would not come this way again.

8

THAT defeat at Oraibe was still bitter in Francisco Garcés' memory when something over a year and a half later he sat down in the mission house at Tubutama to make a final draft of his diary for the viceroy. Nothing could have been in greater contrast to the pain of that moment than the serene and ordered peace of the freshly white-washed room in which he now sat writing. The window over the table was open, and through it he could look out to the snow-capped mountains shining against the radiant sky to the north of the city. The wine-sweet air of the desert January came in the window, too, incomparably exhilarating with a tang of the distilled fragrance of the mesquite in its cool freshness.

Ordinarily, that breeze would have whispered to the friar of the sagebrush trail and the river canyons and strange men living over the curve of the horizon, but today he was content to sit here, slowly pushing his quill over deserts of paper. He was surprised at himself. But here he was slowly putting together and copying his notes hour after hour. Perhaps it was the example of Font whom he found writing out his diary when he arrived yesterday. Font had only recently taken refuge at Tubutama. An Indian uprising had wiped out his own church and mission, and he had barely escaped with his life. But there was nothing in his manner to indicate that his settled calm had been even ruffled by the harrowing experience through which he had just passed.

Last evening Garcés had sat here in the little study and read his breviary, while he watched Font writing steadily and easily sheet after sheet of his beautiful script. At first, it had been the steadily moving hand that had taken his companion's eye from the page of his book. And then it had been the look on the other's face as seen in the candlelight. It had been a look of concentrated and yet serene absorption that marked the features of that stately face. And yet there was a certain light in the look that did not come from the candle. It was rather as if the candle had struck the light already behind those radiant features.

He had been surprised, too, by another thing. When Font had first sent his invitation to Bac, Garcés had hesitated. He had always stood in awe of Font, had always felt a little uncomfortable in his presence. It had only been because Font had stressed the urgency of getting their materials into form for the eye of the viceroy that he had finally decided to come. And now to his astonishment he had found the ordered peace of Tubutama a delight.

Garcés was tired. The last eighteen months had been hard at Bac. For the long absences of the missionary had borne their fruit, as Font had long ago warned Garcés they must. The Indians had grown lazy, and Miguel Dominguez had waxed tyrannical, and then the Indians had turned sullen and still lazier, with deceit now added to laziness. The Indians who had grown accustomed to coming into Bac to see the Old Man had kept on coming, but the young friar who had been taking the missionary's place had not known what to do with them. So they had hung around the plaza and pestered the soldiers and their wives until the captain ordered that they be driven out. And then the Indians of the mission grew still more sullen, and they lost their pride, until presently they were slipping out into the mountains and into the brush across the river, and rumors drifted back of neophytes' taking part in the old heathen rites.

When Garcés came back to his post that September day and received the full impact of the disaster, he knew who was to blame. And resolutely he put every thought of the bridge between the old mission world and the new out of his mind, and set himself to picking up the pieces of the work which had been given to him and which he had let slip through his too careless hands.

At first, it had been hopelessly uphill work. There were days when not more than half a dozen Indians responded to the call for help. The captain offered the services of his men to round up the idlers, but the friar asked for time. And he worked with those faithful Indians and the women who came to his rescue, setting a pace that for very shame they strove to emulate. And then when the day was done, he saw that the workers had each man his share of what food was to be had, and he led them into the church for the evening prayer. And in the hearing of all of them, speaking their own language he solemnly gave thanks for those servants who were found faithful. It was slow work. And the captain, who was now limiting his consumption of aguardiente under the friar's friendly eye, was generous in his offer of suggestions for speeding up the reform. But the friar said that he would let the lash and the raids on heathen villages wait until they had seen whether other methods would not work.

It was a year and a half before the captain gave over making his suggestions, and the friar dared to think that his battle was won. But the Indians who had stayed in the mission were coming to the services and working steadily, and the Indians who had strayed were beginning to drift back again and sheepishly to take their old places. If the call to the promised mission to the Yumas should come, the mission of Bac could be handed over to Garcés' successor with some prospect of a chance for a good man to get some real work done.

It was then that Garcés learned that the mission on the Colorado had been authorized in Spain, and that authority was considering ways and means. That, Anza wrote bitterly, might, as things went in New Spain, mean any number of years more of delay. There had been a reorganization in the administration of the viceregal powers, and now it was another man, commander general of the interior provinces of New Spain, Croix, whom they would have to put in possession of the considerations that had won Bucareli's support. But that, Anza reminded his friend, was the inevitable lot of anyone who tried to do anything in this hierarchical world of theirs. He was himself writing to Croix about the importance of the mission to the Yumas, but he was sure from the experience he had had with the colony for Monterey that the mission alone was not enough. They must plant colonies like Monterey all along the line just as soon as they could get the right people and the supplies to do so. But, as the friar read the captain's letter, he could almost see Anza shrugging his shoulders—what business had he writing such things? It seemed to be God's and his Majesty's pleasure as revealed through vice-regal order that he should spend the days of his prime chasing Apaches.

It was the day after he received Anza's letter that Font's invitation came. Garcés went to the shelf on which he had stored his notes. He tried to think of the junction of the great rivers and of the people who lived on their banks. Palma's face came to his mind, and Sebastián's, and, curiously enough, the face of the little girl whom he had sent back to the burned village. They were like the faces of the dead, seen in an aching moment of remembrance, and then melting into the shadows. He felt as if he who had spoken to those people and moved on those sands were dead, too.

But, for the first time in months now, he remembered that Bac was not the whole world. The night Font's letter came he spent a long time kneeling in the dark church, with only the flicker of the light in the sanctuary to remind him of any life but the teeming life of his mind. It was not of the mission on the Colorado, or Palma, or Anza, or San Gabriel that he was thinking, as he knelt there, but of Oraibe, of the thin sweetness of the flute, the whispers of the night, the dark faces, and the inaccessible height turned to gold against the sunset.

And it was of Oraibe that he was thinking now as he gazed out of the placid window of the study at Tubutama. His fingers took a firmer grip on the unfamiliar quill, and soon they were moving so quickly and so fluently over the page that he forgot the hated labor of writing. For he was setting down what had happened at Oraibe, from the man from Moqui who would not look at the crucifix in the camp of the Yabipais to that last look at the forbidden mesa in the sunset. As he wrote, the old hope and the old dream and the old pain came back, and his hand quickened, and he wrote in his sprawling, ill-shaped scrawl as fast as ever Font had written in that exquisite penmanship of his.

Never in his life had Francisco Garcés written so quickly or so easily, or tasted so fully the bittersweet magic of the pen. And when he had finished, he set the quill down and sat there staring at the last page he had written. It was there now, all the glory and the grief of it, but as he gazed at the work of his pen, he saw that it had all been taken away from him, as if it had always been an alien thing. And he saw that in some way he could not understand, the bitterness of it had been exorcized, and he contemplated it as if it were something which had happened a long time ago to some man who was now dead and whose grief no longer cried for assuagement.

And yet he was not entirely free of it. There was something else. The bell was swinging in the tower outside the little study, and he felt its vibrations in the quiet room. And yet he would not have moved, had not Font looked in just then and asked him if he were not coming into the church for vespers.

But even in the church, chanting the familiar responses to Font's measured prayer, something stayed alive in the back of his recollection. It stayed there through supper as he listened to his host's gracious speech of Anza and the great expedition which they had shared. It was like the wind stirring in the palo verde and the sage-brush on the edge of a night camp in the desert. And it brushed at the edge of prayer as he read his breviary by candlelight while Font again wrote happily at the table before the now shuttered window. It was Oraibe still, but not the hope, or the disappointment, or the dream, or the grief of it. It was, rather, a wonder, the beginning of a question.

There was nothing of the speculative about the mind of Francisco Garcés. He was by profession, and by nature even, a thoughtful man, but in general his thinking was specific. The world of his mind revolved about definite people and definite situations. He was quite without interest in abstract philosophy, and although he had had an excellent theological training in Spain, for him as for his founder the love of God was the main of his theology, and the desire to open the hearts and minds of his fellows to the wonder of that love his ruling purpose.

Living so absorbedly in the demanding present, he had felt no need of the past. What of the past, like the life of his Master, entered into his present did so with no awareness on his part of temporal distinction. The timelessness of eternity was to him a thoroughly congenial concept. He had been surprised when he was making his theological studies to find that men had argued about the idea of eternity; it had seemed to him self-evident like the goodness of God. And the relations of past, present, and future had seemed to him analytical abstractions without appeal to his instinctive sense of the fullness of God in the present.

But now as he thought of that pueblo world in which the things that had happened over two centuries ago were still living memories in that clear air, in which the fears and loves and hates of men whose bodies had long ago fallen into a dust that only the Judgment of God could sift from the sands of the desert, still moved the hearts and minds of living men, for the first time he saw the past in a new light. For the first time, he saw that to understand the present enough to do anything with it, one must know something of this past that so brooded over it, that so haunted the brightness of a summer noon in the vast lucidity of the desert. And for the first time there came into his mind a dim awareness of some pattern in the loose texture of day-to-day experience, and for the first time a yearning to find the dim lines of that pattern. For, although he could not yet have put it into words, he felt that if he could understand Oraibe and what had made it, he would be better able to do his part for the planning of the mission at the meeting of the rivers.

Even this came clear but slowly in his mind, much as a mountain gradually draws near the foot-traveler in the desert. But it came back to him the next day, when he returned to the study, and his eyes fell on the bookcase against the wall opposite the sun-drenched window. He had seen that bookcase before, but he had had no leisure or real inclination to explore its contents. Now moved by a new need, he scanned the shelves.

They were familiar enough from distant school and seminary and novitiate days—Virgil, Cicero, Vitruvius, there was nothing on that shelf. Thomas, Bonaventura, Suarez—nor on that. But at the next his eye lighted. For the shelf began with José de Ortega's *Apostólicos Afanes de la Compañia de Jesús.* That he had on his own brief shelf of books at Bac, for he had brought it as a guide for his own travels. The *Rude Ensayo,* perhaps—but here was a book he remembered from novitiate days. It was a history of the conquest of New Spain, and beside it a large book on the martyrs of New Spain. These two books he set on the table and pulled up the chair and began to read.

It was characteristic of Garcés that he began with the story he best remembered, the story of Fray Marcos de Niza. For he had done something of the same sort of work Fray Francisco Garcés was now doing, scouting and path-finding for Coronado nearly two hundred and fifty years ago. And he had come to so inglorious an end. Garcés had always felt a profound sympathy for the friar who had seen a golden city in a pueblo village, partly because he had always been sure that those who saw in his famous misreport merely the compliant lie of a self-seeking romantic were wrong, and partly because he had guessed even the first time he heard the story that Fray Marcos had been moving dimly in a world he did not begin to understand. It had always given him the same feeling whenever he heard that story alluded to, a chill wonder if he would himself have understood any better in Fray Marcos' place. Now he was going to see if he could find out what that world was which his fellow friar of two hundred and fifty years ago had so signally failed to understand.

When hours later that day Font found his guest still reading, he picked up the books on the table and looked to see what had so absorbed his unliterary colleague's attention. He smiled when he saw that they were history, and he murmured that history was the recreation par excellence for the man of action. And then when he saw the wistfulness with which his colleague laid down the book he was reading, he ceased to smile and gravely offered the volumes to his guest to take home with him. And Font marveled at the eagerness with which his guest accepted the offer.

So Garcés' diaries were dispatched with Font's to Mexico City, and Garcés returned to Bac. Although the aspect of that mission was very different from what it had been when the missionary last returned after an absence, there was still much to do.

Yet the thought of Oraibe persisted, and often in the evening when the last visitor had gone, and he had finished the day's office, he would trim the candle and take down one of the Tubutama books from the shelf over his head and read. And then, the next day as he walked to the fields on some errand, or as he ate his parched corn for supper, he would think over what he had read, chewing the cud of it slowly and carefully. So he got the story of Fray Marcos de Niza quite clear in his own mind. He had certainly believed too easily the stories which the Indians told. But why? The friar of two centuries and a half later thought he knew how his predecessor had come to make that mistake.

He had cared nothing for the wealth which his military colleagues sought. He had not cared enough about it to enter fully into its meaning for their minds. He doubted if Fray Marcos had ever quite realized until it was too late that this was not just greed on their part, but a passion of seeking, a passion for achievement, just as dynamic for their thinking as his thirst for the conversion and the saving of the Indians' souls was for his. He had not seen what terrible labors they would willingly embrace for the hope of satisfying that passion, and how terrible would be their despair when they found it baseless and all their hope of honor frustrate. He was as incapable of any intended deceit in this as in any other undertaking of his life, but he was equally incapable of any understanding of what the discovery that the Seven Golden Cities of Cibola were but ordinary Indian mud villages meant to Coronado and his soldiers.

$$* \text{ VI } *$$

THE MAKING OF DREAMS

I

He had reached that point when Lieutenant-colonel Anza rode into Bac one fine day in March. Garcés had not seen him since that day, now so long ago, when he had watched him ride off from Palma's village with the men from Monterey.

He looked tired as he settled himself on the one rough chair in Garcés' little house and leaned comfortably on the cottonwood table. "It is thankless work, this chasing Apaches. If we had enough men and the viceroy would give us the supplies and the equipment, we could clean up the frontier. This is just plugging holes. You raid one Apache village, and they have fled. You burn it, and they wait a while, and then they are back. We just haven't enough men to hold the frontier properly."

The friar considered, "But surely there are many men in the villages and the towns of Sonora, and, as I remember, there are enough poor fellows never earning enough to feed their families back in Spain."

The captain smiled at the friar's ignorance. "How many of them would last three months in the desert? And those who are any good, do you think they want to leave their homes and their families for a soldier's pay and a soldier's chances?"

"But think of those men who first came into the country with the conquerors?" The friar was thinking of the story of which he had been reading the night before.

The commander smiled dryly, stroking his dark brown beard. "You forget that that was the beginning. It was all new, and a great adventure into a unknown world. The Apaches are an old story now. And then"—something of the old teasing look came into Anza's face—"there was the hope of making one's fortune. I shouldn't need to remind you what you friars have done to that from Las Casas down."

"You think the colony is the answer, I know," Garcés replied, with too much compassion for the tired captain to argue just now.

The commander's face lighted. "Yes, Monterey is doing famously. I wish you could have seen those people getting at their houses. It is like being born anew for some of those men, and for the women, too." And then the mobile face shadowed, and he gnawed his lip for a moment. "But there you have it again. You can't go out into the wilderness and gather up a colony, or even into the city. It takes money and supplies and planning and troops, and all the rest of it."

"But I understood from my letters," said the friar, "that the despatches from Spain had given authority for colonies."

The commander shrugged his shoulders. "Men complain of the slowness of the mills of God. They ought to try bringing their grain to the viceregal mills. It will be done, and let it be done, but is it ever done?"

"Of course, on the Colorado it will be better to wait until the mission is set up."

The commander snorted. "The mission on the Colorado? What makes you think that that will be any easier to get than the colony?"

The friar explained about the command from the viceroy to send the diaries to Mexico. At the mention of the labors of the Tubutama visit, the soldier smiled sympathetically. "I am glad to hear even that much evidence that the matter has not been completely forgotten."

"But didn't they promise them to Palma when he was with you?"

The smile faded from the captain's face, "They promised so much to Palma that I am not sure they remember what it was now."

It was the friar's turn to grow grave. "They should be more careful."

Again, the commander smiled. "Didn't you make a lot of promises to Palma, yourself?"

"They were spiritual matters," said the friar firmly.

"Of course. But are you sure where spiritual matters leave off in Palma's mind and other matters begin?"

The friar winced, but Anza was so absorbed in his own problems that he had no eye for the perplexities of his friend.

"You knew they baptized Palma and gave him another cane?" He seemed a little uncertain still as to where to begin.

"Your letter and a letter from Querétaro told me that, but tell me about it. Just what happened?"

It was all the commander needed. He lighted a cigarette and began to talk, as if the mere talking were a relief, and then presently all his old eagerness came into the tired face, "Just as soon as I had told the viceroy about the expedition, I asked for permission to present Palma to him. You know how these Spanish grandees are. They read treatises on the noble savage, and they are always looking to see those treatises come to life and walk into their reception rooms. I could see that he had been drinking in all we had said about Palma's dignity and eloquence."

"But that is all true," said the friar firmly.

"Of course," said the commander, a little impatient of the interruption, "of course. But you and I know that Indians are, well, Indians. The dignity and the eloquence are there all right, but that is a long way from being the whole story. You and I know that we don't know much about the rest of it," he considered for a moment, and then he added hastily something that gave the friar a shock that made him stare at him in astonishment, "at least I don't. You know more about it than anybody I ever heard of." He did not look at his companion or see the distress on his face. But he kept on steadily as if he were talking to himself "But I at least know that it is there even if I can't make anything of it, but the viceroy thinks that what he sees on these state occasions is the whole thing."

He paused and watched the smoke from his cigarette curl up to the bare timbers of the ceiling. "Mind you, I am not denying that Palma was impressive. He wore that suit that we gave him, and he carried himself as haughtily as if he had just come from his Majesty's court in Spain and knew already that the viceregal court was but a poor affair. The viceroy gave a reception for him at the palace—"

But now the friar had forgotten his own shock, "A palace reception for Palma?"

The commander smiled a little, "Yes, again the reading. But Palma bore himself very well. When the ladies curtsied to him standing there by the viceroy, he bowed very gracefully. But he would not kiss any hands, or even touch a lady's hand."

"I wonder what he made of it," said the friar softly.

Anza shrugged his shoulders, and, again, his careless words struck to the heart of the friar. "You'd know more about that than I would, and I wish you'd tell me. I have been wondering about it ever since, when I had time to think about it."

"How did he look?" asked the friar, drawing his breath sharply.

And, again, the commander considered for several moments before he tried to answer, and then he seemed to give up the effort to sort out his ideas. "He was impressed, all right. I am not sure how much he understood, of course, and all the decorations and the fine clothes, and that sort of thing must have seemed very strange. A formal reception at the palace *is* impressive, you know. The funny thing is that it was the etiquette, the ceremony, that I think most appealed to him. I have an idea that meant more to him than the looks of things, though it sounds funny when you say it."

"How about the baptism?" asked the friar.

"Oh, they made a big thing of that, too. Palma asked for that right away when he saw the viceroy. So they had him make a formal application, telling about his life, and his religious views, and his desire for instruction in the mysteries of the faith. It was an impressive document when he got through."

"But who wrote it out, and where did he get it?"

Anza laughed. "I am sorry you weren't there. I suspect the books had their part in that, too. For Palma said he had but the most vague ideas about a great spirit that rules the world, and now he wanted to know the truth." He looked at the friar.

"Did Palma say that?"

The commander shrugged his shoulders again, "I tell you I wish you could have been there. I don't know what Palma said to Father Eixarch, but that is the way it came out. He read it to Palma in the presence of the Archbishop of Mexico—"

"The archbishop?"

"No less. I tell you that they did everything in a grand way. And don't think that Palma did not appreciate that part of it. Savage or not, he has an instinct for it. The archbishop wore his finest robes and his best archiepiscopal manner, paternal and gracious, and yet Saint Peter at the gate of heaven would not be more authoritative. I don't believe you could manage it, Father Garcés," added the captain with an affectionate twinkle, "but the archbishop did, and Palma loved it. I think the archbishop appealed even more to him than the viceroy. When it comes to that sort of thing, Palma, noble savage or not, has the right taste."

"I suppose they made a ceremony of the baptism, too?"

"In the cathedral, and a company that did honor to the occasion, but everybody agreed that no one played his part more worthily than the neophyte."

"And then?"

"Oh, what you would expect—a reception, a feast, more presents, speeches, and then Palma went back to his huts on the Colorado, to tell his naked tribesmen about it all. That I confess I should have liked to hear, but those Apaches made it impossible for me to give him the honor of my escort."

"And the viceroy promised the mission to Palma?"

"Mission, soldiers, colony, everything. And he confirmed Palma in his authority over his people and their lands."

"I wonder what he expects," said the friar half to himself.

"God knows," said the commander without any tinge of profanity. "I have thought about it a good deal, and sometimes I think we shall be very fortunate if Palma has not told his people that something like the cathedral and the viceregal palace are coming to the Colorado with the archbishop thrown in for atmosphere."

But the friar shook his head firmly, "Palma is an Indian. I doubt if he saw much of the cathedral or the palace at all, and the things that take our eye within both structures would most of them be simply things not to stumble over. But he will expect something very grand to come to the Colorado, and it will not grow smaller as he thinks about it and talks about it."

The commander looked at the friar humbly, "You know more about that part of it than anybody else. All I know is that the sooner we get something to the Colorado, the better it will be for all of us."

But it was not that familiar worry about the slowness of the revolutions of the wheels of officialdom that kept the friar awake that night long after the commander was snoring peacefully on the hide bed in the corner. It was the sudden realization that he was supposed to know more than most men about the thoughts that flickered in those dark eyes and the feelings that beat behind the mask of those calm brown faces. For if in a crisis men should look to him for that understanding, and there should be no better understanding than his, then where would they all be? And what did he know more than Fray Marcos de Niza who in his day had loved so much, and striven so valiantly, and in the end had so terribly misunderstood?

But Garcés had very little time to think about these things in the days that followed Anza's visit. For the present was much too inexorable in its demands of the faithful missionary to leave him much time to brood on the past. The resurrection of the spring was at hand, and the missionary was not yet sure enough of how his new majordomo would carry his new honors to leave the fields long unwatched, as the Indians of the mission toiled at the spring planting.

But the desert was in flower now, with great patches of purple and flame and white and gold, that here and there washed up on the lower slopes of the mountains so that even from the fields he caught a glimpse of their splendor, and on the afternoon breeze the cool fragrance of the brief flowering blew in on the sunny air. And sometimes when he had seen that the labor of the fields had been fairly distributed and was proceeding steadily, he would walk out beyond the meadows into the open country and for a half hour drink in the wonder of the returning life of the world. Then his thoughts, hitherto tethered to the little tasks of Bac, would open out on the bright air, and he would be thinking of the open trail and of the lands beyond the still snow-capped mountains.

2

It was from such a walk as this that he was returning one day in early May when some of the Indian boys of the mission ran out to meet him in great excitement. They should have been about their little tasks of picking up stones in the fields or conning their lessons in the sacristy. But he let them tell their news of strange Indians come into Bac to the church and asking for the Old Man whom they said they knew.

"But why all the excitement?" asked the friar, reflecting that, for a schoolmaster, his discipline left much to be desired. "Don't we have strangers coming into Bac all the time? What is so remarkable about these men?"

But they urged him to come and see. These were not, they were sure, men from the neighboring desert or the mountains but men from far away. They were tall men and very—the boys were at a loss for the word. One of them, a lithe young wretch with a gift for mimicry that had already got him into trouble with the Captain of Bac, drew himself up very haughtily and made a motion of throwing a blanket about his shoulders and then, strangely enough, clutching a stick very firmly.

The friar shook his head, "Remember, Tómas, that it is very hard to save boys who make dignified people look funny, from a beating."

"But, father, I was not laughing at him, for he is not funny at all," and the friar saw that the lad was quite serious. And then he knew who it was who had so impressed the by no means impressionable young rascals of his choir.

It was Palma, sitting now on the stone doorstep of the church, with his gold-braided blue cloak pulled haughtily over half his face and a shining cane in his hands.

When the proper greetings had been exchanged, and Palma had eaten the parched corn and dried meat that was the friar's best at this time of year, and had solemnly accepted a reedful of his host's tobacco, he sat down comfortably on a sheepskin that Garcés had kept from a gift of some visiting Indians for just such a distinguished guest. The friar settled himself comfortably on a low stool, and for some moments the two men smoked quietly, the Indian with content, the Spaniard with growing impatience.

"I have been to Altar," Palma began at last. And then he paused. "They said I might find the commander there."

"Did you?" the friar asked, leaning forward encouragingly.

"The commander was not there when I arrived, but men said he would return. So I waited, and they sent men out to find him."

Fortunately, somebody at Altar had had sense enough to realize the importance of this visit. The attention was obviously something which the Yuma chief remembered with satisfaction. Now as his face relaxed, the watchful friar realized how tense and anxious it had been when he began to speak.

"The commander came home again, and he greeted me as a friend makes a friend welcome. And we ate and we smoked, as we have done here." Again, Palma remembered these simple things with satisfaction.

And the friar thought with a moment's rueful amusement that, doubtless, the commander had feasted his guest much more generously than the missionary had been able to. But all he said was, "Commander Anza thinks a great deal of you, Salvador Palma."

"He is a good man," said the Indian with satisfaction.

Again, Palma smoked for some minutes in silence. Presently, he seemed to have made up his mind. "What I told the great captain I will tell the Old Man. I was baptized in the great house in great village."

"My warmest congratulations, Salvador Palma," said the friar earnestly.

The Indian expressed his pleasure in the congratulations with dignified appreciation. Then he went on, "I am a Christian now. And I want my people to be Christians. I told this to the great king's man in the great house, and he said it would be done. He who speaks for the great king said it would be done. The great priest said it would be done. They all spoke good words there in the great city, and I believed them. I believed them, and I took them away in my heart, and I told them to my people, and they believed them. For they are good men and like to hear good things. There were some men who are not good men, like that Pablo, and they said, 'We will wait and we will see!' But the others said, 'We shall see great things done, for the great king's man has promised them to Palma, and Palma has told them to us.'"

Palma spoke slowly at first; then his voice sharpened with mounting passion. The friar admired the way in which he condensed into those few sentences the substance of what he knew had been many talks in Mexico City and on the banks of the Colorado. And he admired the way in which, even as the passion broke through his measured speech, he still managed to keep it so firmly leashed.

He had laid the reed pipe down on the floor beside him, and he had clenched his hands firmly around the silver-headed cane.

"I told them these things, and they believed me, the good people, but have they been done?"

He turned sharply to the friar.

The latter was not entirely surprised. He knew that this question of the broken promise must come up sooner or later. And he had been thinking what he should say. Now, without having quite decided, he said very simply, "The commander and I have been distressed, too, that the mission has not been established. But the viceroy has just this last month sent for my diaries and for Father Font's diaries that he might take counsel for the planning of the new settlements."

But the Indian shook his head, "That has been said before, 'Be patient; we are planning.' I have been patient, but where are the plans?"

"It takes time, you know," said the friar. He knew it sounded feeble, but for very compassion he could no longer keep silent.

The Indian shook his head. "When I say I will make a plan, I make it, and then carry out that plan. I am only one chief, and the king is chief of many chiefs."

The friar smiled sadly. "That is the trouble, Palma. It is like the commander's expeditions. When I travel alone, I do not worry about where I shall find water or grass, for one man and one horse can always manage. But when you have a hundred men and three hundred horses, then you must plan, and it takes longer to plan than to go ahead. The more you have, the more difficult it is."

The Indian stared at him with puzzled eyes, "I do not understand," he said at last quite flatly. "One man has so much strength. Have not a hundred men a hundred times as much strength?"

The friar shook his head. "A hundred times as much strength, yes, but they cannot act so fast or so easily as one man. You can take my word for it. I found that out when I traveled with the commander. If one man gets lost, then he can lie down and go to sleep, and in the morning, he will wake up, and he will get back on his road without much trouble. But if a hundred men get lost, it may be disastrous. If it is good, the hundred men will make it better, but if it is bad, the hundred men will make it worse. The viceroy cannot get things done so easily or so fast as you or I could."

The Indian had listened to this explanation, half fascinated and half bewildered, and totally unconvinced, but now he seemed to have an idea. "Then suppose you do it?"

The friar smiled. "Do you mean for me to come up alone to the junction of the rivers?"

Palma considered. "Could you not bring some horses and some guns with you?"

The friar held his breath and stared at the Indian. There was no guile in the dark face before him. The question had been asked apparently in simple faith.

Hastily, the friar decided to answer it as it had been asked. "I have nothing to do with the guns, or with the horses except when the commander gives me one to ride on. I am a priest. I have to do only with the prayers and the sacraments and the teaching."

The Indian was obviously striving to sort these ideas out. "But the king's man said that all these things would come together to the river."

In his anxiety the friar seized upon the obvious way out, "But that is the trouble. It is because all these things will go to the junction of the rivers together, that it takes so long to get it all planned and done. If it were just a matter of sending me, it could be done much sooner."

"Then you come and tell them," said the Indian with the first hint which the friar had perceived of calculation in his manner; "come now with me."

The missionary put out his hands to indicate the room in which they were sitting and the church to be seen from the window, "I am responsible for all this here, and I cannot leave it until I hand it over to some one who is sent here to take it I cannot just go when I choose. I am not a chief. I must wait for the orders of my superiors."

The Indian thought this over. The denial was plain even if the reasons were not entirely clear. "But Pablo and his men say that the Spaniards are telling me things that are untrue, that we may wait and see, and the Spaniards will not come. They say I have been telling lies to my people, I, Palma, and they say they are fools to listen to me."

"Pablo is a troublemaker. Your people know that. They will not believe him, and the Spaniards will come, and they will see that you have told them the truth," said the friar stoutly.

The Indian looked at him wistfully as if he would have believed it if he could. Then he said very thoughtfully, "My people who are good believe me, but Pablo keeps on saying these things, and the good people look troubled, and the bad people look happy."

There was no mistaking the reality of his anxiety or the fear, that with all the waiting, was coming into his own soul. For very compassion the friar could do nothing but comfort him. "The Spaniards will come, Palma. Don't worry. They will come, and then your people who have believed you as they should will see how right you were, and Pablo and the rest of them will be laughed to scorn as they deserve."

The Indian's eyes opened wide, and they kindled as the friar spoke. And then he looked down to the silver-headed cane in his hand. "See this cane! The king's man gave it to me that I might rule in the name of the great king. And he gave me clothes like his own, worthy to stand in the presence of the great king over the sea."

"They are very fine," said the friar gravely.

"The king's man gives good gifts," said the Indian with sudden complacency. "And he says the Spaniards with their horses and their guns will come, and they will bring great gifts to the people of the rivers."

Palma's eyes were shining now, as if they had recovered sight of a vision which had been long hidden from view. He stroked the shining silver top of the cane as if it were earnest of some great felicity to come.

The friar hesitated. He was thankful enough that the Indian's anxiety had been even temporarily alleviated, but an old fear had stirred again in his own mind. He took up the crucifix which he wore on his breast, and, as his fingers tightened on the smooth bone, an idea came to him. Palma was a Christian now—but before he could speak, the first straining of the ropes of the bell in the adjoining bell tower came to his ear, and in a moment the little house was shaking with the first peal of the Angelus bell. It was time to get ready for Vespers. They were a little late tonight.

In the service that followed, the friar still thought, in the interstices of prayer, of Palma. Every time he turned to face the people, he saw him standing or kneeling there, a brown pillar among the crouching figures of the women and the children and the old men who were too feeble for the fields. Some of the soldiers had come in late, and ordinarily they would have been in the forefront of his consciousness. But now he had no thought for any of his congregation but Palma, for none watched every movement of his, listened to every word, with such rapt attention. Again, the curious thought came to Garcés that had come to him on the Colorado, that the Indian was trying to take the rite into his mind and his very body that he might himself repeat it. It was fantastic, he knew, and he resolutely tried to shake it off and fix his mind on the intention of the petitions he was reciting.

But his first thought when he had completed the service was of Palma, and when he had taken off his vestments in the little sacristy, he hurried round to the door of the church to find him. For he knew now what he must tell him, the idea that had first come dimly to him when his fingers touched the crucifix. He must tell him that for the Christian the crucifix and its lesson was the important thing, and not the things that Christians possessed. Not horses and guns, but the crucifix, and the lesson that it never failed to preach even to groping and forgetful fingers.

But before he could reach the door, several people stopped him, as always happened whenever he tried to go anywhere in Bac.

So when he reached the church door at last, he found the church was empty. He hurried to the little house, but Palma was nowhere to be seen. He would have a couple of hours yet to sunset, and he must be anxious to get back to the river with his reassurances. The friar clung to that explanation. But a thought came that he could not put out of his head. Palma had talked more freely than his wont of his anxieties, more freely perhaps than he had meant to talk when he decided to stop at Bac on his way back to the river. And now that he had exhausted his desire to talk, perhaps even now, his pride had reasserted its wonted empire over his mind, and he had fled from embarrassment or temptation.

That night Garcés wrote a letter to Fray Diego Ximénez, now the father guardian at Querétaro, and he told that cautious but by no means slow-minded or timid potentate that in his judgment the delay in the establishment of the mission on the Colorado was putting in jeopardy the whole project of the conversion of the Yumas, and so the whole program for the conversion of Upper California. Then he went on to give a very brief but incisive account of his conversation with Palma. He said nothing of his wonder about the picture of the conversion in the Indian's mind, but he stated quite definitely that Palma was worried about his ability to hold his influence over his people in the face of his rivals' taunts about the untrustworthiness of the Spaniards' promises. He would have liked to talk with Anza first, but he felt that the time had come for more drastic action.

3

Apparently the father guardian lost no time in using Garcés' letter to the utmost, for the harvest was not over before a messenger came to Bac with a letter from Querétaro. The letter was brief enough. It expressed with the formality characteristic of the father guardian's correspondence the deep consolation which Fray Francisco Garcés' zeal and activity in exploring the possibilities of the mission field had given to all the brethren at Querétaro. It proceeded to inform him that Fray Juan Díaz had been appointed as his colleague for the projected missions, and it predicted that both missionaries would doubtless be summoned very shortly by the new commander general of the interior provinces of New Spain, Don Teodoro de Croix, for the discussion of plans. The letter concluded with a command to Father Garcés to hold himself in readiness for such a summons.

The friar read the father guardian's missive with a good deal of satisfaction. Certainly, that reverend official had lost no time in informing secular authority that the Franciscans of Querétaro could hardly be expected to assume any responsibility for the missions on the Colorado if their success were made quite impossible by the continued delay. And secular authority seemed at last to have been aroused, for the new year was hardly under way before the summons came from Croix to see him at Arizpe. And a few days later came a letter from Díaz asking his old traveling companion to meet him at Arizpe that they might join forces for the crucial interview with the commander general.

At once, Garcés began to prepare in his mind for the differences of point of view to be expected in such a conference. But when he met his old road companion in Arizpe that bright January day, he found to his surprise that Díaz regarded the impending conference with the commander general as but a matter of form.

So confident was he that finally Garcés felt moved to interpose a word of caution. "But suppose Croix wants to set the mission in motion and yet cannot find the means to do so?" he suggested as delicately as possible. "After all, Bucareli cares as much about the missions as anybody could. And yet he has not been able to find the means to get them started." For the moment he forgot all his own impatience in the simple desire to do justice to a good friend.

The face of Díaz took on a very grave and judicial expression. "The viceroy has been most generous, but he has been hampered in his good intentions by the inefficiency of all the frontier administration. But all that has now been changed. Croix has made efficiency the watchword of his administration, and he is determined that all the laziness and procrastination that have characterized frontier affairs shall be eliminated."

Garcés stared at his colleague. And then he looked through the open window before which Díaz was sitting and out to the bell tower of the church that had always fascinated him. It was a very heavy sandstone affair, square and solid with a pyramidal cap on top. For a moment the friar played with the fancy that if that cap were pushed but slightly askew—but the very presence of Díaz was a rebuke to such levity. In reality, he was trying to think as seriously as he had ever thought in his life. But what could he say to Díaz, sitting here and talking of what was now mounting into years of waiting as if it had been nothing but feckless inaction?

"Have you talked to Commander Anza?" he asked at last.

"Commander Anza?" Díaz raised level eyebrows. He was a grave-faced man, not much older than Garcés himself, who was taking his new responsibilities seriously. Clearly, he was in no mood for digressions.

"About plans, the things that need to be done before we can start for the Colorado." It was a very lame explanation, and Garcés knew it.

"Commander Anza has written to Querétaro," Díaz conceded. "Of course, he is disappointed that he has had to put so much time on the Apache business. And naturally"—there was ever so slight a tinge of patronage in the voice of Díaz—"the commander is disappointed that he should not be free to go on with the new settlements that he has done so much to promote." The official look deepened on Díaz's calm face, "I need not, I am sure, remind you, Father Garcés, that it is our place to work with whatever agencies his Majesty's representatives see fit to give us. We cannot play favorites, you know."

The friar bowed gravely to the rebuke, "Of course, but not all men are as skillful as the commander at this very difficult work."

Díaz agreed casually, "Very likely," and then he went on to the theory of which he had obviously been thinking a good deal in these first days of his new undertaking. "But it is the part of a good administrator like the Caballero de Croix to so organize affairs that whatever man he delegates to the task may be able by following directions to accomplish it."

But before Garcés could say any more, there was a tap on the door, and one of the soldiers of the commander general's staff appeared to announce that the commander general was at leisure now and would be honored if their Reverences would come to his headquarters. As they went along, Díaz reminded Garcés that this was no time to raise unnecessary difficulties. Garcés could but stare in bewilderment. All the thinking and the planning of weeks now had been lifted up into a realm of complete unreality, and he found himself overwhelmed with a sudden sense of futility as if he were walking in one of those dreams in which the protagonist strives vainly to avert some dimly-seen menace and suddenly finds himself unable to lift a hand.

Nor did the sense of unreality leave him when he found himself in the presence of the commander general. A handsome man, with a certain casual ease of manner that suggested a personality thoroughly at peace with itself, the commander general had even more of the air of official confidence that had baffled Garcés in his talk with Díaz. And he began to speak with a certain light graciousness of manner that still further bewildered the friar. "I have seen your letter to Querétaro. His Reverence, your father guardian, was good enough to let me see it. I agree with you that this delay has gone far enough. Indeed, those missions should have been despatched long ago. So now I ask you to set at once about your preparations." He addressed himself to Garcés, but the latter could only find words to murmur his thanks.

It was Díaz who stepped easily and confidently into the conversational breach. "I want to assure you that the Franciscan fathers of the College of the Holy Cross at Querétaro are most sensible of the great honor that is being paid to their house in this distinguished commission," said Díaz, rising with surprising ease to the occasion.

The commander general nodded graciously. "You will need certain supplies," he said, instinctively turning to Garcés.

"Mainly horses and rations and the implements of the divine service, and of course some simple presents for the Indians," said the friar, relieved that the exchanges of officialdom had at length descended to a level on which he could make his modest contribution.

"Presents?" repeated the commander general with an indescribably light underscoring of surprise.

"Just the usual things, beads, tobacco, some clothes for the leaders, nothing of much cost but of great value to the recipients in that they have been looked for, indeed, expected as promised."

"But I was very definitely given to understand that Palma's intention in all this is entirely spiritual," said Croix, and now the friar thought that he caught a slight undertone of raillery in the well-bred inflection of surprise.

The friar smiled. "Your Excellency, even more seasoned Christians than Salvador Palma like to see their spiritualities gilded with a little remembrance of the natural man. And your Excellency realizes that this enterprise will have for all of us its quite lay aspects as well as its spiritual."

The commander returned the smile with easy cordiality, "Oh, yes, the settlements, of course. But that is a different matter over which your Reverences do not have to worry yourselves, happily for you," he added with a flattering look of half-envy.

Díaz instantly looked sympathetic, but Garcés studied the pleasant face in front of him. He remembered his colleague's warning not to borrow trouble. But the miasma of unreality was again strong in the air. He must make at least one attempt to dispel it.

"Lieutenant-colonel Anza had hoped to lead the settlers to the Colorado. After seeing what he did with the settlers for Monterey, one could not imagine finding one better suited to the task than he." Garcés could feel the shocked eyes of his colleague on him, but he finished the sentence stoutly.

The commander seemed quite unaware of any embarrassment. "Quite," he said with the same almost light easiness of manner. "But unfortunately, the great commander is a man of many talents, and just now he is needed to deal with the Apaches. We shall have, I am afraid, to be content with something less than absolute perfection as so often happens in this world of ours."

Díaz hastened to assure the commander that all the fathers of Querétaro quite understood, and that they would be happy to cooperate with anybody whom his Excellency should designate. Again, the gracious head bowed in understanding. And then Croix turned to Garcés.

"I understand that in Upper California there has been some difficulty with the escorts. So I am empowering you to select the members of your escort yourself so that you may feel that they are men whom you can trust. I am having the papers drawn up now in order that you may take the men from any garrison you wish."

This time Garcés had no trouble in expressing his thanks with sincerity.

"And again, I want to repeat, I am anxious to have this get under way at once. Indeed, I should think you ought to be established there on the Colorado in plenty of time for the fall planting."

"It is January now," said Garcés with sudden caution. "That would mean July at latest if we are to be settled before the Indians scatter for the harvest and the planting." His mind was settling to the slow business of ways and means.

"But surely," said the commander, flicking an invisible speck from the lace ruffles at his wrist, "that is plenty of time. We have all been thinking of this Colorado business long enough. It is action that we need now."

Clearly, it was not the first time the commander had said something like this, but if there were any echo in his ear, it did not offend his good-humored complacency. For he rose now as if all the difficulties had been settled as they should have been long ago.

"We are very fortunate to have a man like this on the frontier," said Díaz as they came through the door of the commander general's modest headquarters fronting the church.

Garcés looked up at the quaint cap on the top of the bell tower. It was impossible to imagine that ever slipping into any frivolous fantasy. But the curious sense of unreality was settling down again.

"Now we can really get things going," said Díaz, forgetting official decorum and rubbing his hands with honest pleasure. His companion rather vaguely assented.

"What is the matter?" said Díaz sharply as they stood before the door of the little sandstone priests' house beside the church. "Here you have been moving heaven and earth for years for these missions on the Colorado, and now that you have them, you begin to raise doubts and hang back!"

"It is not that," said Garcés hastily. "It is simply that"—he reached for the words, but they hung in the air out of reach—"well, it is not so simple as his

Excellency seems to think."

It was Díaz's turn now to stare at his companion in utter bewilderment. Only when, that afternoon, the two friars settled down to the work of planning for their expedition did the curious sense of unreality lift a little for Garcés. But he still found himself in the strange position of imposing limitations upon the too facile imagination of Fray Juan Díaz. Especially was he skeptical of his colleague's plan for getting most of their escort from the presidio of Altar. But Díaz insisted that the abandonment of Altar had long been mooted. With the new presidios on the Colorado, the whole presidial line would be swung forward. That had been in Croix' mind for some time, everyone knew.

Delicately Garcés replied that this was outside of his view of the Colorado settlements. The missions were his affair, and the missions alone. He said this very simply, even apologetically, as if he were aware that he might be accused of taking too narrow a view of the matter. But Díaz flushed a little and hastened to say that, of course, he had no thought of going beyond his own province, but, after all, were not the presidios designed for the defense of the missions? Anyway, what other plan could Father Garcés suggest? Two or three from this presidio, and two or three from that, with the likelihood that each presidio would embrace the opportunity to get rid of its proved trouble-makers?

Garcés had to bow to his colleague's arguments. If only Lieutenant-colonel Anza had not already gone to his promotion in New Mexico! Even a letter to Santa Fé would take time that they no longer had. And then the friar reproached himself for being so ungrateful as to cavil at the chance for which he had been praying all these months, even years.

Croix was receiving a messenger when they returned to his headquarters that afternoon. The door was open, and they could see that the serene official of the morning was completely transformed. He was berating the messenger, and the man was feebly reminding his Excellency that he was only a messenger who could not guess the contents of the letters he carried, still less be held responsible for their tenor.

Catching sight of the two friars with the roving eye of indignation, the commander general called them into his office and laid the offending paper, which the messenger had obviously just delivered, before them.

"That, your Reverences, is what any man who tries to serve his Majesty on the frontier these days must expect to have happen. These two Creole magnificoes, the Marqués de Aguayo and Don Lucas de Lasaga, have been complaining to the king that their land in Coahuilla is suffering from Indian depredations because, forsooth, I am holding all the troops idle on the frontier. A fine pair, scions of bankrupts and beggars, both of them, who have made their fortunes out of the country. They sit there snugly enough in Mexico, and when I try to raise some taxes to support a flying squadron to protect just that region in Coahuila, they refuse to pay a peso, swearing that they have always been able to defend their own without troubling his Majesty. That is the story with all these upstarts of magnificoes in this country. They seize every bit of land that will feed cattle, and then they put armed ruffians in charge of their vast haciendas and rush off to Mexico City. And so long as the silver flows to Mexico City, they will not spend a peso or lift a hand no matter what happens to the land. Someday a fire will start that will burn down the whole frontier, and then where will their precious haciendas be?"

Now that he had freed his mind to the sympathetic friars, his anger had obviously spent itself. So he bade the relieved messenger betake himself to the garrison canteen for refreshment, and the secretary to write Inspector General Galvez a full account of the matter. That done, the commander settled back to listen to the plans of the spiritual wing of the great frontier enterprise. Here, at least, the calm expectancy on his face seemed to say, one could happily relax in the certain knowledge that the greeds and the passions that animated the Creole landowners would not spoil the noble order of a great enterprise.

But he shot up in his chair readily enough at the first mention of the possibility of transferring the presidial forces at Santa Gertrudis del Altar to the new presidio on the Colorado. And he hastened to put the startled Díaz right, "Of course, there has been mention of that possibility in times past, but that is definitely out of the question now. There is no need of going into all the reasons at present. But it is enough to say that for all the years this project of establishing a presidio on the Colorado has been under discussion, no one has been able to find the proper site for it."

"But we know now," interposed Garcés, "that the junction of the two rivers affords a spot admirably suited to such a presidio. You will remember how Commander Anza"—he began carefully.

But before he could find words that would not seem to invoke the example of the popular commander against his superior, Croix interrupted, "But surely, my dear Father Garcés, I do not need to remind you of all men how changed everything is since you and Commander Anza made that expedition of yours. At that time everyone had hopes of securing the men and the means to pursue a more vigorous frontier policy. That opportunity"—he seemed to be choosing his words carefully—"unfortunately was not embraced. Now"—he threw his hands wide—"you know as well as I how Indian disorders are increasing throughout the country. It would take many more men than we have ever been able to put into the service of the king to just hold our own on the frontier. If these settlements on the Colorado should realize our expectations, then some of the pressure would inevitably be relieved on the frontier, and our whole task would be easier."

It was Díaz's turn to look bewildered. "But surely, your Excellency, you are not thinking of setting up those missions on the Colorado with no presidios to protect them."

For a moment Croix looked at the friar. Then he smiled coolly, "Your Reverence is not serious, I am sure, in suggesting that we could even think of asking the missionaries to take any unreasonable risk. I have said that you and Father Garcés are to secure such an escort as seems suitable to you. My orders for this are already drawn up. As for the reinforcement of this initial escort, I think your Reverence may have confidence that the civil and military power will not fail to do its duty. Just as soon as the arrangements for the missions are made, you may be sure I shall have the other arrangements ready to communicate to you."

The commander general arose, and with a charming smile assured the two friars that he was quite at their service in any of the plans they should make.

4

THERE was nothing they could do but take their leave. On their way out, the secretary stopped them to present their appointments to the new missions to be established on the Colorado, and to furnish them the necessary authority to take whatever soldiers they should desire for their escort. It was with difficulty that Díaz restrained himself until they reached the street and were out of hearing of the guard at the door.

"It sounds as if he were going to back down on the presidios," he began, with an appalled look at his companion.

"Not necessarily," said Garcés cautiously. "He may be thinking only that we shall make a better start ourselves without them, and then when we have things in hand with Palma, the civil arrangements may be consolidated. You know how well they have done at San Gabriel."

"But Anza and Rivera and the rest of them all have insisted that the Upper California pattern is not enough. There must be settlements as well as missions, and, surely, that means there must be presidios to protect both." Díaz made no effort to conceal his anxiety.

Now it was Garcés' turn to be confident and reassuring. "Those are matters that we have never presumed to meddle with. The missions are our field."

"But those other settlements have a good deal to do with the success of the missions," Díaz still worried.

Garcés, however, was beginning to feel a certain freedom. The missions were going to be theirs to set going as they knew how. Those first beginnings would be the simple cooperation with the Indians which he had been studying all these years on the trail and in the campfire circle. This was what he had been learning how to begin to do, and now he had his opportunity to set about it. For a moment he thought absurdly that he would like nothing better than to start out for the rivers right away. But he did not suggest it to his companion, for he knew that he must think of vestments and of the sacred vessels for the Mass and for the other rites of the Church that he was bringing to these new neophytes. And beads and tobacco—

But Díaz was still looking worried over the incomplete plans.

"We shall set about doing what we have to do, what is ours to do," Garcés said gently. "That is all God asks of us just now."

Díaz smiled, but even that was shortly to prove more than enough for the courage of the two friars. For the very first thing they tried to do, the raising of the company of soldiers for the escort, was soon enough discovered to be almost impossible. They had agreed that Díaz should go to Horcasitas to select a group of soldiers there, while Garcés was to stop at Altar on his return journey to Bac. Both friars had agreed that they would have only men who could be counted on to set a good example to the neophytes. They had seen enough of the scandal which certain supposed Christians could give to observant converts.

Garcés had hardly delivered half of his little appeal, before the captain of Altar, a friendly man whom the friar had long known, threw up his hands in despair. "My dear Father Garcés, you would like to talk to a dozen of my best men? So would I. So would every other presidial commander on the frontier." At first, the friar thought this must be a rather extravagant version of the conventional commander's despair about his forces. He had already heard some pretty lurid speeches from the captain of Bac these last months. But to his astonishment he found, presently, that the captain of Altar was not exaggerating his predicament. For he proceeded to particularize with an energy that left the friar breathless.

"What is the matter?" he repeated the friar's sympathetic query. "Everything. The Seris raided the horse herd last fall, and I haven't half the horses I need even for the men I have. I am so tired of the profiteering of these Sonora horse-traders that I swore I'd breed my own, but you know what the pasturage is around here. I haven't proper mounts for half, no, a quarter of my men. Then you should see their clothes. The leather-jacket group haven't half a dozen decent jackets among them. The rest are soggy rags that smell to heaven. Shoes, breeches, hats—the same story. Saddles and equipment— even worse!"

"But surely the commander general—"

The captain of Altar shook his head. "Father Garcés, I'll believe any miracle you promise to perform with those Yuma savages of yours sooner than I'll believe you'll get any equipment out of the royal exchequer."

"But I thought the soldiers were paid enough so that they could buy their own equipment," said the friar.

The captain stared at him with mock incredulity. Then he sighed, "I suppose convent finances are different. They must be. What do you think happened to the garrison's wages last fall? The paymaster went to Chihuahua with a saddlebag full of lists of things the men wanted. I looked at the lists— they were all right. And what do you think that wretch did when he got the garrison's wages? Gambled half of it away in one of those gambling dens that still survive in spite of all the assurances we have been given, and then some of those devils of merchants helped him drown his sorrows, and when he got back here, he had a quarter of what had been ordered, and that so ill-assorted and so shoddy that it was all but useless. Of course, I jailed him, but what good does that do my men? This spring's wages had to go for food and some cotton cloth to cover the nakedness of their children."

The friar expressed his pity, but the sympathy seemed only to stimulate the flow of indignant eloquence. "What sort of work do you think I've got out of those men all winter? Only half of them had decent carbines to begin with, and they neglected them so badly during the winter, while I was down to Arizpe trying to get some help out of the new administration, that when I got back and tried to check up, I found half of them ruined past any hope of repair. And the men will not drill or do maneuvers or anything but gamble and hold cockfights. The only action I got out of them all winter was when they went out to do some hunting to fill the pots at home."

The next day the sympathetic friar went over the establishment at Altar and found that the distracted captain had hardly exaggerated. Even as he was surveying with compassion the decay of the garrison, a report came in that some of the tribes to the north of the Gila had been pressing the Cocomaricopas to join them in a raid on the Pápagos.

"That is all I need, a nice little Indian war to make my cup full!" exclaimed the commander bitterly. And he rushed off to gather a small party to go out and investigate the rumors.

But Garcés had hardly reached Bac before there came a messenger from Díaz. The letter he brought was brief and to the point. Díaz had barely reached Horcasitas when the Seris took to the war path. The sudden alarm precipitated a crisis which must have been building up for some time. For the men, half-starved from a hard winter, almost completely lacking in fresh equipment or, indeed, any equipment at all, had nearly mutinied at the prospect of an Indian raid. Díaz had got promise of some men when the threat from the Seris was over, but he could hardly wait for that. So he was going to Buenevista to see what he could do there. He was sure Garcés had done better than that; so he would come straight to Bac from Buenevista.

It was then that Garcés sent word to the commander at Altar that he would be glad to take any half-dozen soldiers he could send who were not known to be scandalous. He received three, and with them he went on to see the captain of Bac, who had sworn that losing a rational man for missionary was bad enough; not a man would he give to that chimera on the Colorado. In the end he gave three. The friar was feeling pretty discouraged when Juan Miguel Palomino arrived smiling. He was now a corporal and married to his Rosalía. He brought a letter from the captain of Tubac.

"It is not Juan Miguel himself, you understand," wrote the captain, "that I would bank on, but there is nothing he is likely to meet that he is more scared of than Rosalía's tongue if she should think he had not borne himself creditably. So I think you can count on him not to let you down too badly."

Garcés laughingly agreed, and sent an Indian express to tell Díaz to hurry, that he had a commander for the escort at least. But it was well into July before Díaz appeared rather sheepishly with six recruits whom he had pried loose from Horcasitas and Buenevista. With that pretty miscellaneous dozen the two friars had to be content. But it was August before they were able to set forth for the rivers even with this makeshift company.

Neither of the friars had any illusions as to the probable consequences of this delay. At best the road from Bac to Sonóita was an arduous one. Now a real drought had reenforced the normal dryness of the season, and the result was apparent from the start in the thin dry pasturage and the almost empty water holes. Only the fact that their company was so small gave them any chance of getting through at all.

But it soon became apparent that, small as the company was, it had yet taxed the resources of the frontier for horses and equipment. It was the old story of the first Anza expedition on a smaller scale. Very few of the horses were anything like good enough to meet the rigors of this summer season. Indeed, it soon became clear from the comments of the men that the frontier commanders had this time not even made a pretense of giving anything but those winded and spent creatures that they felt could be spared from the real business of the frontier for the inevitable Indian feast.

And what was true of the horses was true of all the equipment. Broken straps that spilled precious supplies in the dust made even Garcés scrutinize the gear of the party with new attention. The general flimsiness and shabbiness of it all made him at last ask Juan Miguel why he had not checked up on the equipment sooner. Weren't the men supposed to provide their own gear? Surely, self-interest, if nothing better, should have made them demand better stuff than that.

But Juan Miguel who had been trying desperately to flag the drooping energies of his command now unexpectedly sprang to the defense of his men. "Father, how can these men provide new gear when they get such low pay and have all the expenses of their families out of it? And everything they buy in these presidial towns is so high. They say it is the price of the carriage, but it is the greed of the merchants. And when they have paid for new gear, what do they get? Second-hand things discarded in the cities of Mexico, good enough for the frontier, they say, no doubt, and flimsy things that the merchants pick up for next to nothing. Is it any wonder that the men have no stomach for any real action, and the wild Indians go on unchecked?"

"You must not let the men hear you grumbling like this," said Díaz sharply. He had ridden up in the middle of the conversation and had been shocked at what he heard. Juan Miguel fell back, hurt and angry and ashamed of himself, all at once. Garcés felt sorry for the man so anxious to do his best with his first real opportunity, so worried over its obvious handicaps. And he felt annoyed at the unnecessarily official attitude of his colleague.

For there was no question of the justice of Juan Miguel's complaints. It was only with great difficulty that they reached even Sonóita. And there they had to stay for several days while the men rested, and the horses ate and drank of the relative plenty of that green spot. So refreshed, they started out with renewed hopefulness.

But beyond Sonóita the road steadily worsened. By the time they reached the rock tanks on the other side of the fiery sands beyond Sonóita, days beyond any rational schedule, their supplies of food for the horses were exhausted, and there was no possibility of replenishing them. As for the men, once they had watered the horses and mules, they collapsed among the rocks, hugging any patch of shade in their ragged pile.

Díaz surveyed the blazing scene.

"We'll stay here tonight, and tomorrow we'll start back."

But Juan Miguel protested, "There is nothing for the animals."

"We'll give them some of our corn," said Díaz. "We can get more when we get back to Sonóita."

"And Palma?" asked Garcés when Juan Miguel had vanished with more alacrity than any of the company had shown for some time.

Díaz shrugged his shoulders. "He'll have to wait again, I'm afraid."

"How long do you think he will wait with all the trouble we have been hearing about to the north here?"

"What can we do?" There was no mistaking the challenge in Díaz's voice.

"This," said Garcés quietly. "Let me go on ahead to tell Palma we are coming. My presence will be an earnest of more to come."

"Alone with these reports of trouble among the river people?"

"That is the safest way to go," said Garcés.

"Palma will not believe that you have come to stay," said Díaz shrewdly.

"There is something to that," his companion agreed sadly.

In the end it was arranged that Garcés should go on with a couple of the soldiers, and one of the Indian guides to help with the finding of water and to furnish any interpreter's services needed. It was, Díaz said in spite of Garcés' protests, dangerous; so they would ask for volunteers.

They were all sitting around the fire after supper, and there was silence when Díaz had finished. Then three men spoke almost simultaneously, Juan Miguel, the old man, Cayetano Mesa, and young José Martinez. Juan Miguel Garcés rejected at once. He must stay with the party, for it was his responsibility. But the other two the friar accepted with enthusiasm.

When, later that night, Díaz started to commiserate his colleague on the way plans were working out, Garcés cut him short, "They are the two I would have picked. Cayetano Mesa is not young any more, but he knows how to use his resources intelligently. He will never fall to the buzzards. José is rash, but he is young, and he will learn."

Díaz looked intently at his colleague, but the latter seemed perfectly confident.

"Now then for supplies," said Díaz, "we'll give you everything we can spare."

"No," said Garcés, "we must travel fast if we are to get there before Palma loses heart over the report of the party's turning back. That means that we must travel light. Just the food and the tobacco and vestments that we can carry on our own mounts and the spare horses."

"You can have mules for the packs," said Díaz.

But Garcés stuck to his original plan. To travel fast they must travel light. Once Díaz had had a chance to rest his party and obtain fresh horses and supplies in Sonóita, he would try the desert again. They could see now that they had not made sufficient allowance for the exhaustion of the journey across the Papaguería. The weather would be a little easier, too, and everybody would know where they needed to hurry, and where they could take their time. For his own dash to the rivers Garcés had no fear. They could always find water and pasturage for so small a company.

5

THE smaller party proved an advantage for other things beside the water supply. Indian hunting and trading parties that would have hesitated to approach a large company of Spaniards did not hesitate to come up to the small one. Twice they shared the kill with the travelers, and the fresh meat helped to renew flagging energies. They had suggestions, too, as to where pasturage and water could be found. And, perhaps most important of all, they brought news, news for the most part of restlessness and friction among the peoples of the rivers. Especially was there trouble among the Jalchedunes and the Yumas. A small hunting party of three Yumas had been fallen upon and slain. It was a group peacefully engaged in their own business, said the first party, a company of Pápagos from the seacoast, who told the story. In their version, it was the Jalchedunes who had been at fault. But when, two days later, a hunting party of Cajuenches told the same story, it was the Yumas who had been making trouble, and this killing was not the beginning, but a well-deserved punitive action.

To the friar feasting on the roasted antelope of the Cajuenches the question of initiation did not seem so important as the fact that there was trouble where he had thought he had made peace. The only comfort beyond the roasted antelope was that, as they talked over the details of the story, the Cajuenches were worried about the attitude of the Yumas. Obviously, people who hoped to hold up their head in the river world would take prompt measures of revenge. But something seemed to be holding the Yumas back, and even the friendly Cajuenches were beginning to wonder if they were afraid of the Jalchedunes.

Sitting there by the camp fire, they canvassed the situation quite frankly.

Several of the party had met Garcés on his visits in the land of the Cajuenches, and the others had heard of him as an old friend of their people. But the friar smiled rather ruefully to himself when they began to discuss the part which the friendship of the Yumas with the Spaniards played in all this. For either they had forgotten that he was a Spaniard, or they took it for granted that he had little to do with the determination of Spanish policy, an assumption he was not at the moment disposed to dispute. At any rate, they calmly weighed the relative strength of the Jalchedunes and the Yumas, admitting that, alone, or with their prospective allies, the Jalchedunes would clearly outweigh the Yumas, but if the Yumas had the Spanish guns and horses at their backs, then they could make vengeance bitter for the Jalchedunes.

Clearly, the conversation around the fire was taking a direction which no Christian could allow to pass unchallenged. So Garcés interrupted this thoroughly statesmanlike discussion to point out that the Yumas had asked for missionaries and were going to become Christians. Christians did not raid for vengeance. Of course, he added hastily, feeling the rather appalled silence in the dark, Christians did not allow anybody, friend or foe, to commit outrages without seeing that justice was done on the malefactor. But justice and vengeance were two different matters.

There was a respectful silence when the friar had finished his little sermon. He was very tired, and he did not think he had done a very good job of it. But there was, presently, a little murmur of approval, and then the oldest member of the hunting party, for whose word the others were obviously waiting, delivered his verdict, "It does not matter what you call it—if the Yumas have the guns and the horses of the Spaniards, the Jalchedunes will be sorry they killed those Yumas." Obviously, the sermon had not covered all the necessary ground, but the friar was too tired to do more that night.

But the reports of trouble among the river peoples worried him as they pressed on to the north. Suppose the Yumas had been holding off with the Jalchedunes in hopes of support from the Spaniards, how, then, would they receive the certain rumor of the turning-back of the party? As he whispered to his horse, and urged it on, he told himself that he was foolish to be worrying about this when, before another day was over, they would be coming into the land of the Yumas and would be in a position to know how much there was to all this rumor.

Twice that day, in fact, they caught sight of small parties of Indians crossing their path at some distance, but neither party gave any sign of having seen the strangers coming across the plain to meet them. That this failure to see the approach of his company was deliberate, Garcés felt quite sure, but he was puzzled as to its meaning. This was the season of the fall planting of wheat and barley, and the season for the harvest of all sorts of seeds and nuts and desert fruits. Yet it was not like Indians to give up the excitement of a party of visitors to their country for half a day's work. They might, of course, not be Yumas at all, but this was too close to the Yuma stronghold for strangers to be moving about so casually.

Garcés' companions, therefore, paid little attention to the Indian guide's third announcement of men in sight. Even the friar himself scrutinized the small figures in the distance with remote curiosity. But, presently, the guide cried out that they were drawing near, and he proceeded to go forward to meet them, for there were only two coming down the road. Still without much hope, Garcés watched the two spots grow into men on horseback, and then his heart gave a leap, for one of them was a tall-looking man riding his horse with confidence. Certainly Yumas; perhaps—but it was too much to expect Palma to come out on a rumor of a party that had failed even in its approach. And then, as the two Indians rode into clear view, Garcés gave a glad cry, struck his horse's flank, and dashed ahead. It was Sebastián.

In the joy of that meeting Garcés had no disposition to ask any questions. But once he had flung his arms around his master, Sebastián was, for him, extraordinarily eager to talk.

"They said, those lying Cajuenches, that the Pápagos told them the party of Spaniards had gone back. But Palma said if the Cajuenches had it from the Pápagos, then they could laugh at it. For who ever paid any attention to what the Pápagos said, anyway? He said the Spaniards would come. He said the great king over the sea, and the great king's man in Mexico had said it. And the Old Man had said it, who, they knew, spoke only the truth."

Carefully, Garcés explained what had happened. Sebastián listened with surprising pleasure to the recital of what seemed to the friar a very doleful tale. And at the conclusion, he slapped his thigh with satisfaction. "That is just what I told Salvador Palma when that second lot of Cajuenches came into camp with their story that they had seen the party going back with their own eyes. Pablo, the evil one, laughed, and said, 'There are your Spaniards for you, Palma. They can't even get their horses across the plain of the Papaguería. That is the last you will hear of them!' But I told Salvador Palma that even if all the rest went back, the Old Man would not go back. So he gave me his best horse, and this, his favorite nephew, to ride with me, and here I am."

The friar hastened to welcome the Indian who had just ridden up with leisurely dignity, a solemn youth, almost as stately in manner as his uncle, but with a certain look of hard sense in his eyes, that caught the interest of the friar. This impression was immediately confirmed by his behavior. He announced formally that he had seen the Old Man, of whom he had heard so many good things, and he would go at once to tell his uncle in order that he might come out to meet him. In vain, the friar pointed out that they would soon be making camp, and they would want him to stay and sup with them. The young man said that it was for this purpose alone that he had come, and he must go back at once. Sebastián would show him the way to Palma's house if the friar had forgotten it. The last might have been a jest, or it might have been a taunt, but the Yuma said it quite dispassionately.

Sebastián, Garcés judged, was not sorry to see him go, for now he rode beside the friar, speaking with even more freedom. It was not like him to be so eager to talk, but Garcés gladly assumed that it was pleasure at seeing an old friend that had loosened his tongue.

It was soon clear, however, that there was something else on Sebastián's mind. He was, to begin with, anxious to explain that his failure to come into Pimería Alta to seek his good master was not due to any lack of loyalty.

"I was quite sure of it, Sebastián," said the friar cordially. "After all, I left you, to go where you felt you could not go, and I told you that if I did not return within five days, you were to go back to the Papaguería. So you did what I told you to do."

But Sebastián was anxious to tell his patron how he had found his way back to Palma, and how he had stayed with him. Palma had been generous to him, and had told him that he was free to go to Pimería Alta to seek the Old Man. Apparently, Palma had been a little puzzled that Sebastián did not embrace this opportunity. Once he went so far as to tell Sebastián that if he had not been chief with a cane from the great king's man, he would himself have gone to San Xavier del Bac to see the Old Man and to hear him say the long prayer.

Garcés wondered if Sebastián were afraid that Palma would try to raise some doubt of his loyalty; so he assured him that he had not expected him to come, that each man must follow his conscience, that he was not a slave but a free man. It was then that Garcés saw the first shadow of a look of relief on Sebastián's. The flow of words seemed to have been checked, too. For he said very simply and directly that he would be glad to do anything that the friar asked him to do. But he did not like to work in the fields with an overseer who would complain if he sat down to rest, or with soldiers who would feel free to beat him at pleasure.

So that was it? Sebastián would be happy to roam the country with the friar, acting as his servant in all things, but he dreaded becoming a cog in the mission organization. With a sigh, the friar wondered how many neophytes, stolid and uncomplaining as they usually seemed, felt that way.

But before he could go far on that gloomy line of thought, Sebastián was talking again, "He has been saying bad things, that Pablo," he resumed indignantly, and the friar closed his eyes, making ready to listen patiently to the gossip and intrigue of the Yuma nation. After all, Sebastián was a man living without family or personal tie, among a people not his own. It was, perhaps, only to be expected that he should come to watch the pool of village life with a dramatic curiosity.

But Garcés opened his eyes wide at Sebastián's next remark, "He has been saying that Palma has ceased to rely on the strength of the Yumas. He does not go off and attack the Jalchedunes as a Yuma chief should, but he is waiting for the Spaniards to come with their horses and guns and fight the Yumas' battles for him. Pablo says that is a shame such as the Yumas have never known."

"But, surely," interrupted the friar, "Pablo knows as well as Palma that the Spaniards want all these tribal disorders to cease. They certainly are not going to encourage these ruinous wars among the peoples of the rivers."

Sebastián looked queer at this. His companion could not decide whether it was disappointment or surprise or just bewilderment. Apparently, he decided to lay hold upon the simplest thing which the friar had said, "As for what Pablo knows, that I cannot tell. But I know what Pablo says."

The friar said nothing, and Sebastián went on with something like his old confidence, "Pablo says that Palma is waiting for the Spaniards to come with their horses and their guns, and he asks, 'Where are the Spaniards with their horses and their guns?'"

Now the friar was indignant at the reiterated taunt, "Look here, Sebastián, are you sure of what you are saying? Have you heard Pablo say these wicked things, heard him with your own ears?"

It was Sebastián's turn now to resent the friar's skepticism, "I am no Cajuenche, Old Man. Everybody in Palma's and Pablo's villages knows that Pablo says these things."

With that the friar had to be content. But, as he rode along with the now silent Sebastián, he found himself turning the story over in his mind. It all came back to the old question. When he and Commander Anza and Bucareli made those promises, what exactly did they mean to Palma? What was in his mind as he listened to them? At first the friar had been disappointed to find that the Indians were so scattered on his arrival, but now he consoled himself with the thought that he would have an easier time finding out what was in Palma's mind if he could get him alone or in a small group.

As Sebastián had promised, Palma came out half a day's journey to meet the friar. And with him came a half dozen of his chief men. Nothing could be more respectful or more enthusiastic than Palma's welcome, nor more ceremonious. If he found anything disappointing in the sight of the dusty, travel-stained friar and his two soldier companions, there was no hint of it in his manner. He declared that this was the day for which he had prayed and lived ever since the Old Man had left his land, and that his return to stay with them forever had filled the bowl of his happiness full. And behind him his chief men listened with that curious impassivity which never failed to fascinate the friar, who could never make up his mind whether it meant that they were really impressed or were simply maintaining official dignity.

But there was no time to wonder about that now. In simple but respectfully measured terms Garcés expressed his gratification at the welcome of the great Yuma captain. He told how Fray Juan Díaz and he had started out with a proper escort for the new mission, and how the drought-stricken condition of the country had turned them back. But he had not been able to bear the thought of delaying any longer; so he had pushed on with these gallant companions to assure Palma that the mission was being founded, that the Spaniards were coming to set up the permanent establishments they had promised.

Again, Palma expressed his joy and his thanks. And then they adjourned the formal welcome for the business of making camp for the night. Palma apologized for the small number of his people who had come to welcome the Old Man. It was the time for the fall planting and for the gathering of the ironwood nuts and the opuntia fruit and until the last day they had not been sure from the reports when the party would arrive.

Needless to say, the friar declared himself honored enough for any man by the welcome of the great chief, and rejoiced in the opportunity to listen to his words of wisdom, undisturbed. And that evening at the campfire he settled himself comfortably to smoke with his host and to exchange the formal greetings and good wishes fitting to such an occasion. Then, when these formalities had been concluded, he began to make courteous inquiries about Palma's family and the welfare of his people in general. On the former, Palma was clearly without any concern but his pride in the growth of his young son and his married daughter's children. On the latter, however, he was clearly less secure, for he sighed and said that the Yumas would be the happiest of men if all their neighbors were good men like themselves. But, unfortunately, there were bad men to the north of them, the Jalchedunes, whom, doubtless, the Old Man remembered for their savage and treacherous ways.

Garcés with some difficulty suppressed a smile. It was difficult to think of his Jalchedune fellow travelers in the desert as either savage or treacherous, and he recalled some difficulty that he had had in persuading them that the Yumas were the gentle characters whom he had found at the meeting of the rivers. But he remembered the story of the slaying of the three Yumas and listened soberly enough, while Palma gave an account of the Jalchedunes that

clearly made them the origin and fountainhead of all the world's wickedness. It was not difficult to register the proper shock at the enormities which
Palma retailed as the history of their ways back to their fathers' fathers' days.
According to Palma's account the Yuma nation had been a model of patience,
slow to anger, tireless in searching out the truth, and modest in their visita-
tions of justice.

"But they swore in my presence to keep the peace," said the friar at last.

"What are sworn words to the Jalchedunes?" asked Palma with noble
contempt.

"I shall go up to their land and ask them what they mean by breaking
their word."

"But not alone?" Palma was aghast at the suggestion.

"Why not?" asked the friar. "I have visited them, and many of their men
have kissed the crucifix."

A look of shrewd consideration now came over the face of Palma. "But
that was before the Old Man had come to live with the Yumas. Now the
Yumas should go with the Old Man."

Palma was quick to notice Garcés' hesitation. "Then would it not be better to wait till the soldiers come with their guns and horses?"

For a moment Garcés said nothing. He was sick with disgust, and indignation, and fear, and he did not trust himself to speak. Finally, he thought
he could hold his voice cold and steady. "I have come to make peace and not
war."

"Of course," said Palma calmly, as if he had no inkling of the turmoil of
feeling within the friar's mind. "But those who would make peace sometimes
find themselves in the middle of the fight, do they not? Is not that why the
soldiers will come with their horses and guns?"

For a long minute the friar stared at his companion's face, seen only in
profile against the fire. "The soldiers are to obey the king's orders and protect
good men from bad." Too late he realized that this simple truism would
probably convey more to the Indian than he ever intended.

But before he could qualify or explain, Palma was asking with unmistakable eagerness, "Will the Old Man say the long prayer tomorrow morning? I
have waited many moons now to hear that prayer again."

So with his mind in inextricable confusion the friar lay down on the bare
earth with his head to the fire, and when he had done nothing more than
commend his new mission to the Master who had sent him, he fell into the

dreamless sleep of complete exhaustion.

6

IN the morning Garcés had plenty of reason to repent his suspicions of the night before. For Palma was at his side as soon as he awoke, and he watched the friar intently as he unpacked the vessels and vestments for Mass. And throughout the Mass that followed, the celebrant was constantly aware of those hungry eyes watching every move he made. When, finally, the friar turned for the last blessing and looked straight into Palma's face, he found it impossible to doubt that almost ecstatic light on the Indian's face.

But at breakfast, although Palma spoke again of his satisfaction in the arrival of the Old Man, he said nothing more of the long prayer but went on talking with ease of the harvest now under way.

It was, as Garcés suspected, not a very successful harvest. For the drought had stunted the corn and dried the pumpkins on the vines, and the wild seeds and nuts and fruits were meager and scarce. And, of course, the game was far from fat even when the hunt was successful. It had been necessary, too, to keep watch in the borders of their land against raiders. Altogether it was a hard time for man and beast. And then, as the friar was listening with the absorption of complete sympathy to the Indian's recital, Palma said a surprising thing, "It is a pity that you did not come sooner. We need your magic."

The friar winced. "Salvador Palma," he began gravely, "it is the knowledge and love of God I bring you, and not magic."

But the Yuma chief did not seem to be paying any attention to what he was saying. And one of the young Indians of his company was listening with a look of astonishment on his face as if he were hearing something he had not expected. And then Garcés saw that some more Indians were approaching very quietly through the long grass.

Palma spoke to one of his young men, and he loped off. Then the Yuma chief turned to the friar. "It is Pablo come to see whether I told the truth."

Pablo came up with half a dozen of his men behind him, and greeted the friar. His welcome lacked the warmth of Palma's, but it was quite correct and even gracious. He took the crucifix which the friar offered him readily enough, and, even if he did not kiss it as Palma had, he yet held it to his face and breathed on it. It was the same gesture which the missionary had observed before in the heathen Indians he had visited, and, recognizing its undoubted reverence, he had not hesitated to accept for the kissing of the Christian. Now, looking into the ugly, shrewd face of Pablo, he wondered.

It was perhaps the first time he had ever gazed directly into that notoriously ugly face, and he saw that report for once had not exaggerated. It was a gross-featured face, with a large, thick-lipped mouth, and flat, spreading nostrils, and slightly bulging eyes. It was scarred and pitted, too; yet there was a look of intelligence in it, and even of easy-going humor. The owner of that face would be a very good man to have on one's side, and not at all an easy man to win, the friar suspected. Now Pablo was returning the friar's scrutiny with a certain amused coolness of mien that fitted oddly the threatening character of his face.

"Are these all who have come with you?" he asked finally.

The friar saw Palma's face darken.

"Yes, the drought made it necessary to go back to Sonóita to get better horses and supplies. We came ahead to let you know that the king's men are keeping their promise."

"When will they come?" asked Pablo.

"Just as soon as it is possible," said the friar, and he turned back to help Sebastián pack his saddlebags. For some minutes Pablo stood there watching them work. Then Palma called out sharply to him, and he went away at a tantalizingly leisurely pace.

Clearly, there was no time to be lost.

In silence Garcés helped Sebastián finish securing the load on the spare horse. Then he took the bridle of his own horse and started across the stretch of thin grass on which they had been camping. As he came near the Indians, he heard the voice of Palma sharp but indistinguishable, and then the voice of Pablo, clear and quite unmistakable, "I'll believe it when I see it." As he came up, however, both Indians fell silent and turned toward him. There was a knowing look on the ugly face of Pablo, but Palma looked distinctly annoyed, as if his patience had been tried a little too much.

So the friar began to talk in an easy, confident fashion of the preparations to be made for the founding of the new mission. The first thing to do, he said, was for Palma to gather the Yumas together and tell them why the Old Man had come.

As he had guessed, this beginning caught Palma's imagination, and he forgot his irritation in the prospect of the great meeting of his people. In his enthusiasm he even turned to Pablo and began to discuss the plan with him.

"The men to the north will not dare to leave their lands till they have made the harvest secure. The danger from the Jalchedunes is too great," objected Pablo.

"But I will go to them," interposed Garcés, "and tell them that we wish them to come to the junction of the rivers and to make peace with you and with us."

Now the look of mingled complacency and malice on the face of Pablo was unmistakable, "It will take more than a little tobacco and fair words to get the Jalchedunes to think of peace, or"—he paused a moment—"the Yumas either." In vain Palma protested; Pablo shrugged his shoulders at the suggestion that he had been rude to the Old Man. He had but answered as any true Yuma would, he maintained, and, now acting as if he were the affronted party, he rode off.

For some time the little company rode along in silence. Garcés burned to ask Palma what had happened to the peace which the Jalchedunes and the Yumas had made and celebrated with so much solemnity, but every time he looked at Palma's face, he judged it better to wait. Presently, Palma seemed to have mastered his anger a little. So the friar asked what had happened to the little house in which Father Eixarch had lived and said Mass when he spent the winter with the Yumas.

"It has fallen to ruin," said Palma, but the mention of that winter with its associations of old triumphs was clearly a happy one, for he looked at Garcés now with something of his former interest. "But we shall build you another house to live in right away, a better house."

The friar smiled, "I was not thinking of a house to live in, but of a house to say Mass in when the rain and the cold comes. That is all I really care about."

"It will be done," said Palma with his habitual confidence.

Afterwards, Garcés had reason to be grateful that he had suggested the house, for it was the only one of Palma's plans that it was possible to make any beginning on. Actually, it was little more than a rough shelter made of cottonwood trunks and willow saplings laced together, but it promised to fulfil its purpose of sheltering the celebration of the Mass. Yet even the construction of this very primitive shelter was intermittent and spasmodic, for in spite of Palma's promises it proved impossible to bring the Yumas together.

The necessity of supplementing the meager harvest with natural fruits and nuts was the reiterated excuse of Palma, but as a week passed and then ten days, the friar began to wonder if that was the whole story.

He had not been idle during this period, but had wandered up and down the riverbanks on either side, visiting the people as they worked in their little garden patches or fished or hunted or trapped. There was no question that the labor of the harvest was going forward, but there was no question that it was not anxiety about the harvest that was uppermost in their thoughts. Always their first question after they had greeted him was had he brought the Spaniards with the horses and guns with him. And always, when he said that he had come ahead to start work on the mission, and the others would come later, there was obvious disappointment, and, still more alarming to the friar, obvious anxiety. And then, when they went on to answer his questions about their well-being since he had last seen them, there was the recurring talk of the crimes of the Jalchedunes. And now and then there was complaint of the Cajuenches, too. Apparently, the Yumas were experiencing a very bad spell of nerves over the intentions of their neighbors.

It was after a day of such conversations that Sebastián said one evening as he made porridge at a small campfire on the way back to Palma's house, "Pablo is telling the people that the reason Palma does not call all the people to meet the Old Man is that he is afraid if they once meet together, they will start to attack the Jalchedunes without waiting for the Spaniards, who are not coming anyway."

"Who told you that?" asked the friar sharply.

"One of Palma's men," was the vague and somewhat sullen answer.

"I think all this fuss over the Jalchedunes is unnecessary, anyway," the friar added with what for him was unusual severity. But that evening before the friar and Sebastián had finished their supper, he had reason to change his opinion.

It all began when two strange Indians who had been watching them for some time from behind some bushes finally decided to emerge and come and sit down by their fire. They greeted Sebastián and the friar in perfectly fluent Yuma, but the latter felt sure they were not Yumas. Garcés looked at Sebastián, but the latter was staring into the fire as if he had no interest in the strangers whatever.

Presently, one of the Indians asked Garcés if he were not the Old Man of whom they had heard from the people down the river. The friar agreed, and Sebastián looked up quickly from the fire and away. Garcés waited for the man to go on, but he seemed to be weighing the answer before going on. Presently, he went on to say that he had heard that other Spaniards were coming to the rivers. Again, Sebastián looked up sharply, but the friar said quietly that that was true. Then, deciding that he could hardly be judged rudely inquisitive by a man who had asked so openly for information himself, he inquired if his guests were not some of his good friends, the Jalchedunes.

At this direct question all three Indians looked at him in alarm. But the friar went on to add that he would like to see their land again and the good people who lived in their villages.

The response was gracious enough for a king's ambassador, "Our land would be honored with the feet of the Old Man in its dust, and all our people will come to see the Old Man and listen to the good things he has to tell us."

It was the moment to strike. While Sebastián stared at him with scarcely concealed alarm, Garcés asked the Indians if they would take him to their country now.

"This night?" asked the Indian who had spoken most freely.

"Tomorrow morning," said the friar with a smile.

"It is impossible."

"Impossible? That is not a Jalchedune word," said the friar.

The thrust went home. The Indian sat up very tall, "We are Jalchedunes in the land of the Yumas."

"What of that?" retorted the friar. "The Jalchedunes are good men, and so are the Yumas."

"The Yumas! They are treacherous thieves and murderers. They kidnap, and they waylay. They seize upon peaceful traders and hunters—" now even in his indignation the Jalchedune seemed to remember that he was in the land of his enemy.

"They will not hurt you if I am with you. Tomorrow we shall go to Palma who is their chief and our friend, and I will ask him to give us guides to your country."

But both of their guests were now clearly frightened. "They will seize us even as you ask him." In vain the friar argued. They not only would not accept his reassurances, but they clearly grew more frightened as the conversation went on. Finally, they both slipped back into the bushes.

It was getting dark now, but Garcés could see the gleam of Sebastián's eyes in the firelight as he spat, "Spies, they are."

Startled, the friar looked at his companion. Then he said very calmly, "I think we had better say nothing to our Yuma friends of these men. They may, for all we know, be peaceful traders only. After all, they had their baskets."

But next morning when Garcés had finished saying Mass, he went straight to Palma, who had lingered as usual to talk, and told him of the two Indians who had come to his fire the evening before. Palma listened in silence. He spoke only when the friar repeated the Jalchedune's refusal to lead him to their land for fear of the Yumas.

"He had sense, that man," he said quietly.

The friar looked at him steadily.

But he had no time to think any more about Palma, for just then he caught sight of the two Spanish soldiers waiting for him.

"Some of these Yumas are pretty scared of the Jalchedunes," José Martinez began.

"I don't think there is any real danger," said the friar, recognizing the familiar symptoms of the soldier who is beginning to spoil for some action.

"There wouldn't be any if you would let us take our guns and horses and join a party of Yumas who want to go up there and clean them up a bit."

For a moment the friar stared at the young soldier. "Are you mad?" he asked, and then he turned to the older man. "Why have you let him talk this nonsense and not said anything to stop him? Surely, you know, there wouldn't be enough of you left for me to give you Christian burial if you ever got mixed up in one of these tribal wars!"

Cayetano Mesa considered, "I did tell him he hadn't a chance. But, father, do you think you have a chance of getting anything done the way things are here now?"

The friar said nothing, and the veteran went on doggedly, "We are getting short of supplies, too. And we aren't saints to be able to stomach that food Palma hands out at his campfire."

"Let me think," said the friar wearily. It was the beginning of the great enterprise he had dreamed of and prayed for all these years. He helped Sebastián put away the vestments with the Mass vessels in the saddlebags, and all the time he was praying for some light on his problem.

"I don't like the looks of things, and that's a fact," said Cayetano Mesa, obstinately dogging the friar's footsteps as he gave the saddlebags to Sebastián to take up to Palma's house for safekeeping.

"It's time the rest of them were getting here," he went on.

Garcés looked at him. "Would you two be willing to go back with a letter to Father Díaz? I shall tell him what you have said, and you can tell him, too."

"And leave you alone with these heathen savages?" Cayetano Mesa's face slowly turned red.

"There's nothing to that," the friar reproved him. "I know these people; they are my friends, and Palma is a good Christian."

The old soldier stared, but in the end José persuaded him that the friar was right. They would not hurt him of all men, and they could do nothing till the others came. So Garcés with a heavy heart went to write his letter to Díaz. But what should he say that would not alarm his colleague unnecessarily and yet would hurry things up if official procrastination were again playing its usual part?

In the end he wrote a very brief note saying simply that there was trouble between the Jalchedunes and the Yumas, not disastrous so far as he could judge, but quite enough to make it impossible for them to get anything done. He still thought that the prompt arrival of Díaz and the rest of the escort would reassure the Yumas enough to make them feel like beginning on the mission.

When the letter was sealed, he went off to tell Palma what he was doing. The latter was enthusiastic. "Good. Tell them I can hardly wait to welcome them." And then he gave orders that food should be prepared for the soldiers' journey. The friar was amused at the faces of the two Spaniards; so he told Palma that if he would give them some ground corn for atole and some dried meat, that would be enough. This was soon done, and the two soldiers sent off with more food in their saddlebags than they had seen for a long time. It was pleasant, too, to see the sparkle in José's eye as he waved his ribboned hat in farewell. But when all the excitement of the departure was over, Garcés was suddenly sad at the thought of the days of waiting that must still pass before he could hope even to hear from his colleague.

7

As it turned out, however, Garcés was able to turn this month to very good account, visiting the people who were now drifting back to their winter villages along the rivers. Everywhere, even in Pablo's village, he received a warm welcome as a known friend who had come back to visit them.

Everywhere the Yumas pressed him to stay the winter with their particular group. And when he said he must hurry back to the house of Captain Palma, they made him promise to return, and they loaded him with food for his trip and to spare.

Sometimes in the villages the headmen would ask when the Spaniards with the horses and guns would come, but the general run of the people were clearly not especially concerned about that. Now and then some unusually candid or, perhaps, unusually articulate soul would say cheerfully that it would be good to have the power of the Spaniards in the land of the Yumas, but the terms in which this anticipation was expressed were so general that the friar could not be sure that much more than friendly welcome was intended.

Yet there was unquestionably a restlessness in the people along the rivers that even the outsider could not miss. Garcés noticed that whenever there were fresh marks in the sand outside the villages in the river bottom, the responsible men of the village would look carefully to see who made them. Any smoke in the distance was sure to be investigated unless the location were known to be that of a neighboring settlement. When some men from a hunting party brought in an arrow different from their own make, there was much talk about the campfire that night. And when, as happened twice, trading parties from peoples to the east who had been to the coast for shells stopped on their journey at a village campfire, there was a marked constraint in the usually friendly air, and afterward when tobacco had been smoked in the reed tubes, and conversation resumed, the friar was conscious of a good many leading questions asked about the movements of their neighbors so far as they might be observed by visitors.

It was after following such a cautious conversation for over an hour that Garcés decided to appeal to one of the old men who happened to be present. He was a man with whom he had often talked about the customs of various peoples, for he was a Jamajab who had settled down with the Yumas when he married the sister of Palma's father. Perhaps it was the fact that he knew two ways of doing things that gave this old man a certain awareness and a certain power of definition of awareness that most of his fellow-tribesmen did not have. Although the old Jamajab had never shown any interest in being baptized, Garcés had said he would call him "Gerónimo" for his wisdom, and he had good-naturedly accepted the new name. Now the friar asked Gerónimo why the Yumas were thinking so much of their enemies these days.

The old man smiled. "I have watched men for a great many years," he said, "and I have heard them tell of their dreams. And I have noticed that when they are well but the belly is empty, they dream of food. And when they have food, but cannot eat because they are sick, they dream of being cured. But when they are well, and the belly is full, then they dream of power, and they see themselves carrying the feathered staves into the field, and all the old women dancing around the scalps they have taken."

But more than that the old man would not say, for at that moment he saw his wife, who was the sister of Palma's father and a notable woman, looking at him, and Garcés judged it wiser not to press his friend at that moment.

He had his reward the next day when he came across the old man watching his wife weaving a rabbit-skin cape. He was sitting there with the composure of a man who knows that his wife is doing something that is within the reach only of a woman who has a man of substance for her husband.

He greeted the friar warmly and invited him to sit down on the sand with him. Then when they had sat there for some minutes in silence, the Jamajab began to speak as if he were thinking aloud, "You noticed yesterday that men's thoughts are turning to their enemies. I hear that Pablo is dreaming again." He stopped for a few minutes as he watched his wife twist the strands of furry skin more tightly together to slip over the cord of rolled willow bark. Then, as Garcés waited in silence, he went on, "But no one thinks that there is in him anything like the power that there is in Palma."

The friar rubbed the toe of his sandal into the clean sand on which the old woman had set up her loom. "Do you think Pablo wants to take Palma's place?" he asked, without looking at his companion.

"What do you mean, 'take Palma's place'?" The old Jamajab was frankly puzzled.

"Well, be the chief captain of the Yumas himself instead of Palma?" It seemed pretty bald, put so, perhaps even blasphemous, for the friar had long known that there was something religious in the position of Palma, though he did not know what it was.

Gerónimo looked past the friar over the river. The hills beyond were red and purple against the deep blue sky, but there was a slight darkening in their splendor all the somberer in its prophecy because the blue of the sky was so unusually sharp and clear for this river country.

It was minutes before he answered slowly, "The only way Pablo could take Palma's place would be to convince the people that his dreams have more power than Palma's. It would take more than words to do it. Success in battle would do it."

Garcés caught his breath. "Is that why Palma wants the horses and guns of the Spaniards?" He realized that there was a doubt of Palma's sincerity implicit in the question, and he was afraid that Gerónimo would resent the insult, but the old Jamajab considered the question with quite unemotional objectivity.

Indeed, for some minutes he seemed to have forgotten his company. Then he turned suddenly to Garcés. "The horses and the guns are not the power of the Spaniards. They show the power of the Spaniards. It is the power itself which Palma wants."

"When you use that word 'power,' what do you mean?" asked the friar.

For the first time, it seemed to him, the old man was a little uncomfortable as well as puzzled, for he sat very still without moving, as if he were reconnoitering something suspicious. Then he pointed to the friar's crucifix and to the sky above, "When you dream of that man there, and you talk to us, you have the words, have you not? And the words are good. How do you get the words? Who shall say? That is power."

The friar tried to think of what he might say to the old man. Apparently, the Jamajab misunderstood his silence, for he suddenly leaned forward, and touched his friend's breast, "It is not the horses and the guns but what is there that is important. That is what Palma wants."

A warm joy surged into the troubled heart of the friar. The spiritual, then, was what Palma sought. But Garcés had hardly reached that conclusion before the old man was adding, as if to himself, "The horses and guns come from that." With sickening speed the tide of joy ebbed, and the friar stared at his friend. But he had said all he was going to say. The warmth of the day was over, and his wife was ready to leave her weaving.

But Garcés had no time to worry that night, for to the evening campfire came a Pápago whose sister had married a Yuma, to bring her a present of game from his hunting.

Almost at once he began to talk about the Spanish soldiers who were coming from the south to the river.

"Have you seen them?" asked the friar.

The Indian shook his head. "The trading party saw them, two, three days' journey away," he said vaguely. In the little circle around the fire, there was the usual interest in prospective visitors. And though it was hard for the friar to be sure of the significance of the look on Gerónimo's lean, brown face, it seemed to him that the old man was smiling.

But this was still clearly not all the Pápago had to say. And, presently, as the circle about the fire settled back into the quiet contemplation of its own thoughts, the visitor went on to tell how the news of the approaching Spaniards had come to his village, and how some of the young men had wanted to waylay the visitors and take their horses.

At this the whole group around the fire stiffened, Garcés with alarm, the rest of the group, he suspected, with that excitement with which men hear that the event which they have long been anticipating has at last come to pass.

It seemed to Garcés as if the whole company hung in a sort of suspension upon him, waiting for him to speak. "I think," he said very quietly, "that we can rely on the good sense of your wise men to see that your young men do not do anything so foolish." The Pápago looked at him but said nothing. Nothing was said in the circle around the fire. It seemed to Garcés that a light sigh ran through the group, but it might have been the wind rising down the river.

But the next day when Garcés went across the river to see some people who were sick in one of the villages he had already visited, he heard of the Pápago raid again. This time it was reported to have taken place, and the booty was said to have been fifty horses, no less. Nothing was said about the soldiers or their guns. The friar listened to the story without excitement, and at its conclusion, he assured his informants that he did not believe a word of it. He did not, however, deem it wise to share the grounds of his certainty, namely, that he very much doubted if Díaz would have been able to raise any such number of horses.

But when a week later the party did arrive, looking very tired and dusty, Garcés was not so sure. Palma had not been able to accompany him at the last moment; so Garcés had been able to ride out alone with the scouts. As soon as the company and the scouts had made camp for the night on a little knoll across the river from Palma's village, Garcés came straight to the point, for in the festivities of the morrow's welcome, there would probably be no chance for the two friars to talk to each other.

"We heard rumors of trouble," he began, "but I gather that nothing came of them."

"Plenty came of them," replied Díaz grimly. "One of those Pápagos came into Sonóita while I was trying to see if I could not get some men. It looked as if I might be able to get a dozen more, and then this fellow came in with his tale that some of his nation had taken to the warpath and were going to ambush us as we went along. You know what happened. The men who had not completed their enlistment drew back as fast as they could, all but two, and the others did everything but desert!"

"I shouldn't have thought the delay would have helped with that," said Garcés gently. "What was the trouble?"

"Trouble?" The voice of Díaz rose a little as he repeated the question. Then in a lower tone, he resumed, "It was horses, clothes, food, everything, literally everything. Finally, I appealed to Croix at Arizpe. But he was ill, and some council was acting in his absence. They sent it as their opinion that since everything looked so unpropitious, we should give up the effort for the present and wait until proper provisions could be made." He sighed.

Garcés murmured his sympathy.

"I sent a messenger with a letter to Querétaro, but I knew that if I waited for an answer, everything might slip through our fingers, including Palma's patience. Anyway, the more I thought about it, the surer I became in my own mind that I could not turn back."

"I cannot imagine what made those people at Arizpe suggest what they did."

Díaz shrugged his shoulders. "It seems to be the way of courts and chancelleries all over the world. Postponement is their one answer to a difficulty. I am sure that when the angel Gabriel blows his trumpet, they will send in a petition asking for a month's delay."

"But you did start," said Garcés with warm pleasure.

"Yes. When it came to the scratch, the dozen you see here decided that they did not want to miss the chance. They have really been very good about all the trouble of the journey"—and Díaz's calm voice warmed—"you know, these soldiers have their points. They love to grumble, but they are very patient when it comes to the hardships of the road. Indeed, a friar might well take example from them when it comes to patience."

In the flickering light around the fire Garcés smiled at the sincere awe in Díaz's voice. He was learning fast, Garcés thought, and then he was ashamed of even the patronizing thought of a better man than he would ever be.

A similar impulse of compunction must have struck Díaz, for he said quickly, "But here I talk of us all the time, when you must have had a much harder time here all alone."

"No," Garcés smiled at himself now, "I didn't have the vagaries of the so-called civilized official mind to contend with. I have been exploring what I suppose they would call the primitive mind."

And he proceeded to give a quick sketch of his experiences of the last month. Once or twice Díaz interrupted. He made him repeat the conversation with the old Jamajab, and for some minutes he said nothing. Then when Garcés was beginning to wonder if he had fallen asleep, he spoke again with admiration, "One need never worry about you, Fray Francisco Garcés. You will turn any mischance to good account."

Garcés laughed, "You'd better tell that to Father Font. He will tell you quickly enough that I am simply indulging my curious tastes. But, seriously, don't forget I have been among old friends."

Nevertheless, it was a comfort to talk in one's own language with a man who knew the sense in which one used a word. It was pleasant to bring out the abstractions again, and to be able to imply, and to suggest, and to smile a little over one's anxieties.

He needed that respite, for the next morning he had hardly finished his thanksgiving for the great privilege of being able to offer the sacrifice of the Mass again, when there was a little stir on the fringes of the camp where the soldiers were, already loading their horses and mules. He had not raised his head, when he heard a voice from the bushes behind the improvised altar ask in Yuma, "Are these all who have come?"

He rose from his knees, and looked straight into the ugly face of Pablo. Even as he came forward to greet the friar, the latter fancied that he saw in the bright eyes a sparkle of malicious satisfaction. But he dismissed the thought as unworthy of the high perfection of this day, and he returned the greeting with simple friendliness.

✳ VII ✳

THE PROMISED LAND

I

JUAN Miguel looked as grave as ever and as anxious when he first arrived, but the completion of their journey had given him a certain assurance. So as soon as he was settled at his new post, he looked around him to see what could be done to get on with their undertaking. The soldiers, he decided, could manage with their tents for the present, but the fathers should have a house where they could say Mass and where the vestments and the sacred vessels and the papers of the foundation could be protected. The mind of Juan Miguel was strong on good order.

He managed, too, to communicate his steady purpose to his company, and they set to with a will to fell trees and to cut logs. Palma was delighted, and at once suggested that the house should be built on the height which they had long ago selected. And so those early October days Garcés had the joy of watching the first structure rise on the height of which he had so long dreamed. Of course, there was no possibility of a bell, perhaps for a long time to come, but the square log building rising before his eyes was evidence enough of a dream come true.

The little house would not hold many people, perhaps a dozen or fifteen; so Garcés asked if something like an Indian "shade," or porch of boughs laid across uprights, could not be added at the front. Then in fine weather it would be possible to say Mass under the shade for a larger congregation than could ever get within the house. This suggestion Juan Miguel accepted with his usual conscientious readiness, and before the week was out, the first mission building stood completed.

Then under the direction of Díaz, who was better than his colleague at anything that involved paperwork, Juan Miguel and his men set about constructing a table that might serve as an altar, a chest to hold vestments and the sacred vessels, and a shelf for the missal and the few books the friars possessed. Another small shelf was built above where the altar table would be placed, to hold a little wooden statue of Our Lady which Díaz had brought all the way with him from Caborca. An old lady in that city who was a complete invalid had given it to him. She had never walked since her husband was scalped in an Apache raid, and she had hated the savages with a great bitterness, but when Díaz told her about the plans for the missions on the Colorado, she had changed her mind and had given him the statue. It was old and angular, made by Indians in Mexico, and it was brown from the smoke of countless votive candles, but it was her greatest treasure. Now Díaz set it above the altar table with a small candle in front of it and a single pale winter rose which one of the soldiers had found in a sheltered corner under the height.

Palma shook his head in approval when he saw the statue, and said, "That is good." And that day the two friars and the Yuma chief and Juan Miguel looked out over the river and began to talk again of the future. It was a clear day, so clear that the high hill down the river on the right seemed little more than an arm's reach away.

"If we follow your example, Father Garcés, and choose a height for the second mission, wouldn't that be a good place?" asked Díaz.

But any worry over the plans for the second mission soon proved absurd. For the immediate difficulties of the first claimed all the waking thoughts of the friars and presently began to haunt their sleep. As usual they were of the simplest sort, and Díaz wondered how they could ever have failed to foresee them.

At first, the friars were very much encouraged to have parties of Indians on their way back to their villages from the autumn harvest of wild fruits and nuts come up the height to see the new house. For it gave the missionaries the most natural opportunity possible to see old friends and to meet new. It was certainly a much less laborious way than Garcés' expeditions. And once they were there, nothing was more natural than for their hosts to tell the visitors about Palma's long prayer, and show them the vestments and the vessels, and tell them the story of the Virgin and Child, and explain the meaning of the crucifix.

Indeed, so impressed was Juan Miguel with the interest of the Indians in all these things that of his own accord he asked Garcés if it would not be better if he and the soldiers built another house for the friars to live in, and then the present house could be kept as a church with all the additional impressiveness of the house that was reserved strictly for sacred purposes without any distraction of the everyday business of the friars' life. To this the Franciscans gladly assented, and the building of the second house was begun.

But it was barely under way when the two friars realized that they were facing a problem that would tax all their resources. For the visitors after they had been shown the simple treasures of the house and had listened to the instruction did not go away.

At first, the friars thought little of it, even though the soldier who served as cook complained about the amount of corn porridge, with a little jerked beef cut up into it for flavor, that the visitors consumed. For many of the visitors brought presents of seeds, which Garcés knew represented much labor in the gathering and pounding and kneading into dusky-looking cakes, and even dark, sticky lumps of mashed locusts which were offered as the great delicacies they were to the donors, and, more welcome to the soldier cook, rabbits and deer and fish from their hunting. For these were by no means empty-handed beggars, but friends coming to visit friends, bringing delicacies, and taking for granted that they would be invited to share the staples of their hosts' cooking pots even as they had invited the wandering friar to share theirs, times without number.

Palma sent up presents of corn and beans in quantity, for as the chief of the village he was used to keeping open house for not only visitors from other tribes but for widows and orphans and for the poor when they could not manage to feed their families, and he readily understood the problem on the height. But even these supplies were soon exhausted, and replenishment was uncertain, for Palma was away a good deal. So Díaz was very soon inquiring into the question of just what supplies they had in prospect for this unanticipated development of their program.

The cook declared with the vigor of long pent-up indignation that it was about time they began to think about how they were going to feed the whole river. And the friar was forced to admit that as things were going now, the angry prediction did not seem so preposterous, for they were only at the beginning of the winter season in which an expedition to visit the new arrivals on the height with their famous curiosities would make a very welcome break in the monotony of the season for any of these travel-loving villages. Soberly Díaz took stock of the supplies on hand, so many bushels of beans, so many of peas, so many of corn, and so on.

When he had completed his calculations, he and Juan Miguel stared at each other. With the present rate of visitors, they would be able to get midway through January. Garcés found them working over their figures. Both men looked up at him as he entered.

"What are the chances of buying supplies from the Indians?" asked Díaz.

Garcés shook his head, "They are going to have a hard enough time to take care of themselves. I told you the harvest was much less abundant than usual."

"We can send the men out hunting," said Juan Miguel.

But again Garcés shook his head. "Game is not abundant in this country. And there are always risks in hunting parties."

In the end there was nothing to do for it but appeal again to headquarters. Garcés sat down and wrote the letter to Croix at Arizpe. He gave a very measured account of their arrival and what they had been able to accomplish, but he added that they had every prospect of winning the people of the river if they could have even the minimum means to do it. With food to take care of visitors through the winter, and seeds and tools for the planting in the spring, he thought it would be possible to attract enough of the Indians to settle around the height to cultivate sufficient food to make a real beginning on the mission next fall. After that he thought that they would be able to make even faster progress than San Gabriel, which he had seen in Upper California. But if the relief and enforcements which they had been promised, and on which they counted, did not arrive soon, Garcés feared that all they had accomplished would be lost, and Palma and the other Indians completely disillusioned and alienated. Díaz himself wrote an even more candid and immeasurably more authoritative letter to Querétaro, in which he made no effort to conceal his growing distrust of the intentions or the capacities of officialdom.

When the two letters were completed, they were entrusted to two of the soldiers, with instructions to ask Croix for official post for the letter to Querétaro.

It was, however, the letter to Querétaro that brought the first response. It came in January in the form of a small party including the two soldiers and their Indian guides and a young friar whom Garcés had never seen, but whom Díaz greeted warmly as a promising student of his at Querétaro, where he had for a term served as a teacher. The party brought some supplies, fresh wine for the altar, brandy for the winter chill, vestments, altar breads, some tobacco which the friars had ordered for diplomatic purposes, some chocolate and sugar and jerked beef. But of the much-needed staples they brought only enough to feed the Spaniards themselves about two months, with nothing to spare for hospitality.

But one thing they did bring that was of priceless value to the two tired men marooned on the rainy height above the rising river, and that was the personality of Fray Juan Antonio Barreneche. He had been ordained only recently, and the wonder of his new priesthood was still strong within him. He was a warm, friendly young man with curly dark hair and large eyes that in his thin face made him look younger than he was. He was obviously tired from his journey, but he was bubbling over with excitement over the new world in which he found himself.

The thick blanket of rain lifted a little the day after his arrival; so Garcés took him out to the edge of the bluff in front of the mission and showed him the river view still shortened by mist, and gray with the turmoil of storm-stirred waters. Even so muted and attenuated, the prospect was a noble one, and the face of the young friar glowed.

So Garcés began to tell him of the peoples up and down the river, and of the mission bell which he had dreamed of hearing calling them all to the Angelus prayers. And then he went on to tell of the other mission that was to be built down near the highest of the peaked hills just below them. He told of all the Indians who had come up to visit them, and of the wonder with which they had looked at everything there was to show them, and of the interest with which they had listened to the things they had been told.

To all these things the young friar had listened with wide and glowing eyes, until it seemed to Garcés as if the river mists had cleared away and the warm sun were shining again.

But the young friar was appealing to him now with great earnestness, "Father Garcés, will you teach me to be a good missionary?"

"I?" asked the friar, stepping back in astonishment.

"You see," said the young man, with the persistence and the self-absorption of the young, quite unaware of the incredulity on the face of the man beside him, "I am not a born missionary like you. I wanted to be a teacher like my professors in the seminary. I never thought of being a missionary. Of course, I had heard stories, but they sounded to me like the stories of the early martyrs of the church. It never occurred to me that I could do anything like that. Then I heard one of the missionaries from Querétaro talk at our seminary, and I knew that I must go."

Garcés smiled at the simple narration, and Barreneche concluded that he had not made himself clear. For he thought that the older man was giving him an approval he did not deserve. So he went on even more earnestly than before, "You understand, I did not think I should ever be especially good at it, and I am not sure I very much wanted to be a missionary. But I felt I must." He was looking very anxiously at the face of the older friar.

"And now?" asked Garcés.

The anxiety vanished, and the face lighted. "I am so happy to be here I cannot see how I ever thought of doing anything else."

When they arrived home, they found Díaz waiting for them. As they entered the little house, he set down his breviary and took up a sheet of paper on which he had been working when they went out. "Now that you are here, Father Barreneche, I think I can go to Arizpe myself. The letter you brought from the father guardian told me to use my judgment and not to hesitate to see the commander general myself if the full expedition delayed much longer. We have had no answer to Father Garcés' letter; the soldiers who took it never got to see anybody who could do anything. So I am going to tell the commander general that either the expedition comes with proper supplies, or we return to Pimería Alta. I have the authority here in this letter."

The face of Barreneche had gone white with the shock, and he stared blankly at Díaz. The latter misunderstood the look on the young man's face for disapproval.

"If this rain continues, and the Indians cannot come here to eat our stores, we have enough to get to April, perhaps. But one or two good weeks of visits, and we'll be running short in March," he said with almost harsh finality.

And now there was impatience in Díaz's voice as he asked the young friar, "Didn't they tell you anything of this in Querétaro?"

The cold look on Barreneche's face warmed a little. "Oh, they said I must expect to find things hard here. They told me how Father Garcés had gone up and down these valleys—"

But Díaz interrupted with an exasperated look at Garcés, who was again blushing with embarrassment. "This is a very different thing from going up and down the valleys. This is having the valleys go up and down you."

And then, in spite of his irritation, he smiled at the reddening face of

Garcés. And patiently, like a teacher explaining to a slow class, he addressed himself to the young friar, "This is not the romantic hardships of missionary life as the novitiate reads it and dreams about it. This is trying to build a house quite literally without any clay or straw to make bricks. It is not a matter of personal hardship at all, but of getting the indispensable supplies to do the work we have come to do. We could sit here and starve, and lose all these people and any chance of converting them while we did it."

It was Barreneche's turn now to flush with embarrassment, "I am afraid I did not understand."

The grim look on Díaz's face relaxed a little, "That is the secret of the whole business, I am afraid, and for heads older and supposedly wiser than yours."

He smiled at the young friar as he spoke, and Garcés was relieved to see the smiling young face come slowly to life again.

But now Díaz was speaking to him, "I wonder if perhaps you would not do better with Croix than I would at that. He knows—"

But Garcés interrupted with a flat denial. Croix had his letter, and what good had it done? Croix would discuss the theory and the abstractions and the things which Díaz would handle better than he. But he saw that he was only confirming the opinion which Díaz had had all along, and that was all he had wanted.

2

It was early in April before the first report came of Díaz's return. Supplies had long ago run short, and Garcés had used the last of his store of beads and tobacco to buy corn for the mission. The soldiers had been out scouring the hills and mountain slopes in the neighborhood for game when the weather would permit. Garcés had feared the possibilities of conflict with the Indians always latent in such undertakings, but he had finally yielded to Juan Miguel's pleading. Even those risks were preferable to the already apparent results of idleness and hunger. It had been a long pull; so that the first rumor of the return with its promise of relief sent a new thrill of hope through the men on that remote height.

The men were talking now about their homes, and they kept asking Garcés if he thought that Díaz might perhaps be bringing back some of their wives with him. Again and again, the friar explained that the bringing of the families would not be possible until ampler resources for the actual starting of the settlement had been secured, and that would take time. Barreneche, who had been putting in the months of waiting learning the language of his prospective neophytes and coming to know as many of them as he could, was a little inclined to be good-naturedly impatient of the men's homesickness.

Garcés smiled at his ardent young colleague, "We mustn't blame them. We are trained to live alone; they are not. Indeed, they are expressly trained not to live alone. And then we have our work here now, no matter what happens. But they cannot begin theirs until the settlement arrives. It is really hard for them."

The young friar laughed ruefully, "Of course, you're right. I suppose it is simply that I am getting a little tired of hearing so much about Rosalía."

"She is an old friend of mine," said the older friar. "And, I suspect, an ally to whom we have more reason than we know to be grateful."

And then, as the young friar looked thoughtfully at his colleague, the latter went on, "Don't forget the Lord likes variety in humanity. Not even the saints are all alike."

"But the variety makes it harder to manage," said the young friar wistfully.

"Quite," said Garcés dryly, and then he smiled at the puzzled young face, now even thinner than when it came to the river, "but don't forget that it also makes certain that not everybody will have my faults."

Barreneche laughed, and the older friar was glad to see the sun shining in that bright face again. But he thought of their conversation the next evening when the long-anticipated arrival of Díaz became a fact.

It had been a heavy half-day's work getting the men and the horses and the bags and loads across the flooding river on the rough raft which Juan Miguel had had built against their coming. But Díaz had brought a carpenter and a blacksmith for reinforcement of their company, and, best of all, he had brought what seemed to them in their want abundant supplies of corn and beans. So even the labor had been a triumph, and now the company could be heard singing joyously in their log hut across from the little house in which the three friars had just sat down.

"Not much question, is there, what Juan Miguel has done with that new barrel of aguardiente?" asked Díaz, shutting the door behind him wearily.

"The men saw it," said Garcés. "This flood weather has been pretty hard on them. It's a long time since they had anything to celebrate."

"Anything to celebrate?" The weary friar looked up sharply, and Garcés waited. Even in the first excitement of the welcome on the other side of the river, with the soldiers cheering and Palma watching with shining eyes, Garcés had seen that his colleague looked not only tired but anxious and over-watched, with dark circles under his eyes, as if for too many nights he had lain awake when the rest of the company slept.

"Don't you want to go right to bed?" asked Garcés, even in his sympathy for his older colleague catching the look of disappointment on the eloquent face of Barreneche.

The gray-faced friar shook his head, "I'll sleep better for talking a little. And you have to know sooner or later."

"Are they going to give it up?" asked Barreneche, his anxiety breaking through his habitual respect for his elders.

Díaz smiled bitterly. "That would be a piece of clear thinking of which they are incapable, I think."

Garcés stared at his usually calm friend. "Did you see Croix?" he asked finally.

"Oh, yes, he is recovered enough to take hold again, a firm enough hold, I should say." Díaz still seemed at a loss how to begin.

"Wouldn't he listen to you?" asked Garcés, while Barreneche waited, his curiosity obviously turning to alarm.

Again, the bitter smile came to the lips of Díaz. "Oh, he listened with perfect courtesy to everything I said, just as he had listened to Governor Neve and Lieutenant-governor Rivera before I got there."

"What is he going to do?" asked Garcés, fixing the tired eyes with his own steady gaze.

Díaz shook his head as he yielded to his colleague's plea to come to the point. "The most original creation in the history of the Indies. A settlement which will include three different elements all in one, a mission for the Indians, a presidio to hold and to push out the frontier, and a pueblo of colonists to take possession of the land, all in one."

Garcés stared in unbelief. "All in the same place, here?"

"His Excellency is generous; there will be two of these hybrids, one here, and one wherever we want to locate it, say down at the Cerro San Pablo."

"But," Garcés still sounded incredulous, "all three in one?"

"All three in one."

"But who will be in charge? What will be the main objective?"

Díaz lifted up his hands as if in protest, and then he let them fall wearily into his lap. "Be sure I asked the commander general just those questions. All I could get was the nice neat answer, 'The military will be in charge of the military operations, the settlers in charge of the farming and the work of the pueblo, and the missionaries will be in charge of spiritual things with no worry about temporalities.' In short, we'll be in the golden age again, quite out of this sinful and distracted world."

Barreneche sighed, and Garcés realized that he was thinking of all the last months' worry over corn and beans. "It will be nice to have nothing to take care of but our religious duties," he said gently.

"Very nice, indeed," said Díaz. "Have you thought how you will take care of them?"

And then, as he saw the young brother's face flush, he added more gently, "That is just the trouble with all these catchphrases. They don't enter into the labor of ways and means. I told Croix how we began here, and how they did things in Upper California."

Garcés broke in, "I am afraid he has been listening to Neve without consulting Serra. You know all the trouble there has been. Neve is always saying that by the laws of the Indies, the Indians are not to be held in any bondage. Of course, they must be converted, but once they are converted, they are to enjoy the freedom of any Spanish subject. Serra told me he had told him again and again that you do not take a child and turn him loose in a company of men, and tell him that he is to fend for himself without any help or protection. The Indian needs the school of the mission that he may learn how to live like a civilized man and a Christian."

"Yes, he had been talking with Neve all right. He agreed with the school argument, but he said Serra thinks the Indian should always remain in school."

"That is not fair," said Garcés warmly. "The order was glad to turn the Sierra Gorda missions into parishes when the Indians were ready for it. Serra was one of the leaders, perhaps the man who did most to make that possible after Father Kino himself. But it took years and years of steady missionary work even after the missions were reestablished. And those Pame Indians were more intelligent and more advanced people than the Indians of the coast. Does Neve think that what took so many years with people like that could be done in a third of the time with poor and backward peoples like those of Upper California?"

"Do you think I did not urge all this on our commander general? But like Neve he has been reading Rousseau, and he has no real idea of the gulf between the life of these Yumas here and the life of the Spaniards in Arizpe, say, and no notion of the labor it takes to move even the most willing men from one to the other."

For several minutes the two missionaries stared at each other, while the young friar looked from one to the other. Then Garcés sighed. "I don't think that either Croix or Neve understands that the way the Indian lives is all tied up with his religion. They have certainly found that out at San Diego. They have preached and taught just as well there, but their Indians are always slipping off to the dances and the other rites of their pagan fellows. But at San Gabriel they can learn to live a Christian life."

"That I urged, too, but all Croix would say was that from your account and Anza's these people are used to a more settled life, and we won't have that trouble. Besides, living right here between the two Spanish pueblos, and seeing the respectable life that goes on there, they will be attracted into the pueblos to share their benefits. So we shall be able to make good Christians out of them."

Something in what Díaz had just said reminded Garcés of an old worry. "By the way how are those pueblos going to support themselves?"

Díaz shrugged his shoulders, "I thought I told you that in the beginning. On the land. Croix understands from you and Colonel Anza both that the land is very fertile here, and he is quite sure that with proper management the land will support the three groups very handsomely. Anyway, the land is to be divided between the three so that each group will have its share."

"But this year with all the land, the Yumas have been put to it to find food. Does Croix think that with a third of the land they will be able to manage?"

Díaz laughed in his weariness and his exasperation. "I asked Croix that, and he said that I was taking no account of the progress that would be made. He rather implied by his tone and manner that as a priest I could hardly be expected to appreciate the possibilities of progress. So far as I could make out, he expects the colonists to take over a good part of the land and plough and plant it more systematically than the Indians have ever done. He thinks that will attract the Indians into the service of the colonists, and that as laborers on their farms those who would not be good enough farmers to take care of themselves will fare better than they would in the state of nature. He is a great seeker of the happiness of his fellow men, a great humanitarian!"

"That is the vision Neve has had for some time, and Father Serra says that before they are through, it will mean simply that the land will be in the Spaniard's hand and the Indian will be doing all the work of cultivating it. That will be slavery, indeed."

"That I told him, too," said Díaz, "and he solemnly reminded me that according to the laws of the Indies slavery is forbidden, and he will enforce the law."

Díaz took his head in his arms, and Garcés stared at him, for the moment paralyzed by an overwhelming sense of helplessness. Then, overcome by pity for the weary man opposite, he looked away as if to seek help from the bare sapling wall. So his glance fell on Barreneche, whose presence the two friars had completely forgotten in their preoccupation with the visit to Croix. His eyes were wide, and the thin face was frozen in a look almost of horror.

Garcés put his hand out and touched his arm, "Father Barreneche, forgive us for not remembering that you were here. These are problems with which we have wrestled a long time, and we shall a long time yet, I am afraid. We shouldn't have let them all fall on you at once. Now we'll all go to bed and say no more until we are rested." Like a sleepwalker, the young friar rose and made ready for bed, without saying a word.

For a long time Garcés lay awake that night, listening to the young friar turning and tossing on his hide bed. Once he thought he heard him weeping. They had been brutally careless to dump all their anxieties on the younger man's inexperience, and now the least he could do was to respect his pride. But concerned as he was for the young friar, he was still more anxious about Díaz. Never had he seen the dignified calm of his colleague so disturbed. All those weeks of worry without anyone to share his anxiety had broken even that serene poise.

When Garcés awoke the next morning, Díaz was already astir, tired, with great circles of shadow still under his eyes, but he was himself again, calm and self-possessed. Quite without embarrassment, he greeted Garcés and then went into the chapel to prepare for the morning's Mass of thanksgiving. Barreneche was gone, too, and when a few minutes later, Garcés entered the chapel, he found him helping his older colleague.

Not until Mass had been said, and Palma greeted, and various Indian visitors welcomed, did Garcés have a chance to speak to his colleagues. They were breakfasting on fresh tortillas and hot chocolate, and the good food had made all three relax a little around their rough board table.

"I am going to write to his Excellency today to tell him why I think his plan will not work out as he expects, and I shall send a copy of the letter to the father guardian," he said as easily as he could.

Díaz's eye flashed, for he well knew how Garcés hated all the slow labor of the pen, "I am glad to hear that. Your word will count for a good deal with the commander general."

Garcés shook his head, "I do not think it will make any difference, but I think I should do it."

His friend nodded, but he said nothing. When he had finished his bowl of chocolate and said grace, he excused himself to go out and see how the men who had come with him were.

It was only after he had gone that Barreneche ventured to address Garcés, and there was an earnestness in his voice that arrested the latter's movement to the cupboard for paper and ink.

"If he will not change, what do we do?"

Garcés could feel the uncompromising thrust of that challenge, and he was surprised at the coolness of his own voice, "Then we just do the best we can with the settlements as they are given to us."

"Even though you know—"

"Even though we know." And then as the solemn young face gazed at him, he smiled a little. "We shall win a few souls anyway even with our dreariest expectations. And who are we to put any bounds on the mercy of God?"

The young man drew a deep breath, and a slow smile warmed the drawn features to life, "I am glad. I thought last night you were going to leave the river."

3

Garcés completed and despatched his letter to Croix, and then the three friars sat down and calmly took stock of the situation. Now that he had said what he had to say on the underlying principles of the plan, Díaz presented its details to his colleagues quietly and dispassionately. Its basic difficulties were no less glaring in this objective scrutiny, but now they were viewed not as something that might be changed to some preferred alternative, but as the ground plan on which they must work as well as they could.

The first fact to be faced was the continued delay. The political and military command of the new establishments had already been given to Don Santiago Yslas, first ensign of the presidio of Santa Gertrudis del Altar. He was known as an able man, energetic and ambitious to make a name for himself, but as both of the older friars knew from their experience with the Anza expedition, it was going to take some time to recruit the twenty families of settlers from Pimería Alta and equip them for the new settlement. There were, also, the ten or a dozen laborers who were to work on the building of the new pueblos and take care of the herds, who must be found, and their families equipped. And always there were the families of the soldiers already on the Colorado to be outfitted for the expedition, for, after all, upon them depended the presidial function of the new settlements. And there were still the additional soldiers to be recruited if the detached pickets assigned to the protection of the settlements were to be adequate for the uncertain future. And always there was the problem of horses and cattle to be gathered from the meager stocks of the frontier. On the basis of what they knew of the task ahead of Don Santiago Yslas, it would be summer at best before the party would be ready to start. And with so many women and children to take care of in that desert country, no responsible leader would think of starting until the worst of the summer heat was past.

"It will be fall before they come." It was Díaz who concluded their estimates, and the friars stared at each other.

But their anxiety over the continued delay was nothing compared with Juan Miguel's when later that day Díaz and Garcés communicated the result of their analysis to him.

"Fall!" he echoed dismally.

The sympathetic friars nodded.

"Rosalía will be wild at the delay."

Before Garcés could reassure Juan Miguel, Díaz was saying quietly, "I think not. Like the sensible woman she is, Rosalía is doubtless making her plans and her preparations for the trip very carefully. Would it not be a good thing if you did the same and had your men do it, too?"

But a stubborn look came into Juan Miguel's face, "Soldiers are very different from women."

"Of course," said Díaz briskly, "but there are houses to build, aren't there?"

Juan Miguel rubbed his thin beard doubtfully. "They have done a good deal as it is, with the chapel, and the priest's house, and the guardhouse, and the storehouse. They say they are not skilled builders, and where are those laborers that they were told were going to do the building and the other work?"

A slight shadow of impatience passed over Díaz's face as he looked at the bewildered officer. "Those things are as much a part of their duty as mounting guard and keeping their arms in shape, and you know it."

But Garcés smilingly interposed, "Tell them, Juan Miguel, that these houses are for their wives and their children to live in. I don't think they will object."

Juan Miguel's pale face cleared, and he looked at the friar with more life in his tired eyes, "That is true, father. But then"—and the good-natured friar began to sympathize with Díaz's irritation as he saw the chronic trouble-hunter cast about for a new grievance—"what will we do for food until next fall? It has been bad enough getting the men fed this winter."

"Oh, that!" said Garcés cheerfully. "I am going to ask Palma if there isn't some land we can have to sow corn and beans for next summer and fall. Before we are through, we shall have to feed ourselves, and we might as well begin now."

Tacitly Díaz and Garcés had already divided the work of the mission between them. Things like the selection of the sites of buildings and the management of the soldiers Díaz with his organizing and executive ability undertook, while anything that involved the help of the Indians was left to Garcés. Now he started out cheerfully on the sort of errand which he could best do.

But on the way down hill he passed the church. And to his surprise he saw that the heavy door was standing open, and a cloud of dust was blowing out into the bright spring sunshine. When he looked in the door, he saw it was Sebastián sweeping the packed earth floor vigorously.

"Good!" he said cheerfully, "After all the crowd in here yesterday I was thinking of doing this myself."

Sebastián's face had lighted at the praise, but now he shook his head severely, "A master who has a good servant does not need to do such work."

"Come now, rest a moment, and give me your advice. We don't want to have all the trouble we have had over food again if we can help it. Do you think that if I got a couple of soldiers to show them how to do it, we could get some of the Yumas to sow it for us? The soldiers will supervise it and take the responsibility."

With astonishment the friar saw the dark eyes widen, and he caught the quickening of the Indian's breathing. He had been leaning easily on his cornstalk broom; now he straightened up and held the broom almost as if it were a weapon for defense. "The soldiers will *make* the Indians work."

The friar smiled. "Not *make*, Sebastián. Don't you think they will be willing to do it for us?"

But the Indian did not relax. "For you, father, of course. But the soldiers will beat us. That is bad, father."

"Listen, Sebastián, the soldiers will not beat you. I will not let them."

The friar grew sober at the look Sebastián gave him, for he saw in a flash that while the Indian had no doubt of his will, he had no confidence in his power. Then, without a word Sebastián resumed his sweeping.

"I'll see Palma now," said the friar to himself, but he had hardly got beyond the church door before he heard a respectful call behind him. It was Juan Miguel running to catch up with him.

"Look here, Juan Miguel, have you been having any trouble with the soldiers and the Indians that you haven't told me of?"

There was complete astonishment on the now curiously flat face of Juan Miguel. "But that is just what I was going to tell you, father," he exclaimed, pausing to catch his breath.

"What is it?" asked the friar, anxiety sharpening his voice in spite of himself.

Juan Miguel coughed. "You remember what you said about the need of watching out with the soldiers since they did not have their wives with them?"

"Yes."

"Oh, I've been careful, but that José has been sly."

"José!" The friar stared in complete incredulity.

"Oh, I know, he assists your Reverences at the Mass in the morning, and he is prompt enough in his duty, but he has been hanging around the house of the Jamajab who is married to the sister of Palma's father."

"Oh," the friar lifted his eyebrows, "my little friend Teresa. She has been baptized, you know, and she comes quite faithfully to Mass every morning."

"She's a naked savage just the same," said Juan Miguel stolidly.

"I can't imagine my old friend would let anything improper go on in his house. She is a relative of his wife, and her grandfather left her in their care when he died."

"But José takes his guitar and goes down to their house and leans up against a pole and strums it as if he were under a balcony at home in Buenevista."

Juan Miguel was such a picture of indignant respectability that the friar had a hard time to keep from smiling, but he checked the impulse, for Juan Miguel was only doing what they had all urged him to do. Still the picture of José strumming his guitar at the Jamajab's door—the friar sighed. "He is not betrothed to any of the young women who are coming, is he? I forget how he happened to get into our party in the first place, for you remember we specified that all the escort should be married men who could bring their families."

Juan Miguel scratched his head thoughtfully. "Well, you see, father, in a way it is my fault. He is a sort of cousin of Rosalía's, and he coaxed her to ask me to take him. He wanted to seek his fortune, and there's no question he needed to. His father and mother are dead, and an uncle brought him up. He was a drunkard and not much good, either. Nobody in Buenevista would want their daughter marrying into such a business, but the boy's all right; at least he seemed so until this."

"José is all right," said the friar firmly. "I'll see Gerónimo, and until then don't say anything to the others."

It was at last Juan Miguel's turn to smile. "But they all know it. That was how I learned, from their nudges and jokes. José was furious when they began to talk about it, and when one of the men said he was going over to the house of the Jamajab, José told him that he would kill anybody who dared to speak to Teresa."

"The Jamajab would do the same, I suspect. So you had better tell the others to leave this alone. I'll see Gerónimo, myself."

But as he started down the road to the river, the friar felt less sure of himself. He had had very little experience with marriages. The land business with Palma was much more in his line; so he decided to tackle that first.

It was even simpler than he had hoped for. Palma said at once that there was a piece of land which would not be planted because the owner had died, and his wife and sons were quite well-off. So the Yumas would sow it for the friar when they sowed their own. Obviously, Palma saw nothing to worry about in that inquiry. But there was, equally clearly, something on his mind. The friar lingered, and, presently, Palma asked him if there were anything else he wanted to see him about that day. At once Garcés replied that he had thought of going on to the house of the Jamajab. That seemed to please Palma, and he said, "Good," and with that seemed to lose any concern about whatever it was that had been on his own mind.

Still more uneasy, the friar went on his way to Gerónimo's house. And as he went along, he began to wonder if the Indian village would still keep its wonted position sprawling over the low ground along the river a couple of miles to the northeast of Puerto de la Concepción. To a casual eye it looked as recent and as make-shift as the tiny cluster of huts on the top of the height. And yet the friar felt sure that for countless generations the Yumas had made their home here, moving to securer ground on the islands in the river when the April and May floods came, and then, when they subsided, moving back.

The Jamajab welcomed his visitor with grave pleasure, and his wife went at once to bring some corn gruel and dried venison. When the gruel was warm, she sent Teresa to serve their guest. The girl smiled up at Garcés shyly as she presented his bowl to him, and he asked her how she was. She had grown a great deal since he had rescued her from the Cajuenches, but she had the same winning gravity and shy dignity of manner. She could hardly be called pretty, the friar supposed, but she had a natural grace and poise that many a Spanish lady might have envied.

Not until his guest had finished the food, did the Jamajab speak of anything but the promise of the river bottom for the new crops. Then both of the women disappeared.

"You have heard perhaps?" asked Gerónimo.

"I have heard that the soldier José has been singing at your house. I am sorry you have been annoyed."

"It is strange music," said the Jamajab critically, "but I am not annoyed. I am only puzzled. José has asked for Teresa."

"What have you said to José?"

The Jamajab laughed. "You were a wise man to refuse to take Teresa. It is what I should say to Teresa that puzzles me."

Then he explained. It had been simple with José. He had said that he wished to make Teresa his wife in the church as a good Christian should. The Jamajab had then told the young man that when a man married a woman of another tribe that was friendly, he thought there was less trouble if he went and lived in her village. It was not what men usually did, perhaps, but it was what he had done himself, and he had been content. The young man had gulped at that, the Jamajab recounted with a smile. They had said no more, for another visitor had come just then, Sebastián, and when the young Spaniard had gone, he, too, said he wished to make Teresa his wife. And when the Jamajab made his little speech, Sebastián said he would be glad to live in Palma's village.

"That would seem to settle it," said Gerónimo, "but Teresa tells me that she will not look at Sebastián, and she will have José, or she will never marry, like the woman for whom she is named."

"Perhaps she can persuade José to settle in her village. Of course, they would have to wait till he is released from his service."

The Jamajab smiled calmly, "I do not know about that. There is no need to. She says she will live in his village as a good Christian wife should."

"I wonder," said the friar thoughtfully.

Gerónimo smiled. "There is nothing to wonder about, I am afraid. Teresa is very clear, and she is very stubborn."

"I think I had better talk to José," said the friar uneasily.

"It would be much simpler than talking to Teresa, I assure you, and I should be much obliged for any help you can give me."

But it did not seem at all simple to the friar when the next morning he asked young José, who had just served his Mass, to wait and have breakfast with him. For the very invitation to stay and see the priest had brought an embattled look into the face of the young man that boded no good for the conversation. Garcés judged it wise to come to the point at once.

"When do you want to be married?" he asked quietly.

"As soon as can be," said the young man firmly.

"Of course. But where will you live?"

The obstinate look gave way to one of boyish perplexity. "The old man says I should live in the Indian village, but Teresa will not have it. She says she will not have me shamed before my friends. That wretch Sebastián has apparently told her what people say about soldiers who run off to live in the wilds with Indian women."

"You are not contemplating turning Indian, then?"

The young man flushed, but his host's voice was so friendly that he forgot his injured pride and leaned across the table eagerly. "I want to take her for my wife just as if she were a Spanish girl in the pueblo. I am sure she will make me just as good a wife, better in fact."

"So am I," said the friar, "but you will have to help her."

"What do you mean?" There was a suspicion of the sulkiness returning.

"Wait till the other soldiers' wives come. She can watch them then and learn how to make your home the kind of home you want."

"But—you have been talking to her?"

"No. Is that what she has been telling you?"

"Yes, but—"

"She is a wise woman," said the friar.

"But Juan Miguel says we shall have to wait till fall. That is a long time."

The friar smiled wearily, and José flushed. "I am afraid I have been thinking only of my own affairs, father."

"It is hard not to," said the friar gently. "Only remember that everybody else is finding it long, too."

4

IN spite of the universal disappointment over the delay in the arrival of the settlers, the weeks of that spring flowed with unexpected swiftness into summer, and summer into fall. Perhaps the fact that the crops were good that year helped, for the plot that the Indians cultivated for the soldiers and the friars put the basic beans and corn of their diet beyond anxiety. But the thing that helped most was that Díaz succeeded in giving the company a vision of the pueblo that they were building for the future. The rough huts and cabins that they were now working on would yield presently to proper adobe houses with patios and gardens and a fine church and a barracks for the soldiers, all surrounded by a good wall that would make them secure against any disturbance. This was just a start.

So these men, who were not accustomed to the monotonous grind of laborers or skilled in working with their hands, set themselves to the task of building the first rude shelters that would protect their families and their new neighbors until they could begin to build in earnest. A good many of the Indians came up to watch the work, and, as the weeks passed, they began to lend a hand, hauling and lifting and digging, and, presently, trying out some of the Spaniards' tools for themselves. The friars talked to them, too, about the new settlement, trying to give them a feeling of partnership in the enterprise.

And they began to suggest to some of the Indians who came most faithfully to the morning Mass and instruction that they, too, might like to move their homes into the security of the pueblo where they would not only be safe from their enemies but close to the church. It was Díaz who took the initiative with this. For he was more at home with the black and white lines of plans than Garcés.

But there was another reason why Garcés left the explanation of the pueblo plan to his colleague. It was a reason of which he was ashamed but quite aware, and he did confess it to Díaz. It was simply that he could not see how it would be to the good of the Indians that they should come into the pueblo and live there. Díaz was astonished when he first heard this rather haltingly from the lips of his colleague.

"But surely you want them won from this beastly existence of theirs to a rational and Christian life?" he protested.

"Of course, in a foundation just for them—"

Díaz shrugged his shoulders, "But we know we can't have that, and we have agreed that we should not give up our work here. It is our duty to do all we can to make it succeed. The commander general has expressly asked us to do everything we can to attract the Indians into the pueblo."

"We can let them see the pueblo, and then they can come in if they want to."

Díaz smiled. "You agree with the commander general that the spectacle of the respectable life of these pueblos will be potent enough to lure the Indians into them?"

At the look on Garcés' face, he dropped the tone of grim bantering, and his voice became almost pleading. "Of course, you know as well as I that the Indian will not give up his way of life unless he is at least urged to."

"But it is what we are offering him that makes me hesitate to urge him."

"It is the chance for his salvation," said Díaz firmly.

Garcés could only agree, but it was Díaz who went to tell Palma about the plans for the pueblo. To his delight the Yuma chief not only listened to him with great interest but at once declared that he was ready to bring his own family into the new establishment. "When the harvest is finished, I will build my house on the river just above the great height," he told Garcés the next day when he came to talk over the plans with him. "Then my family and I will hear the bell ring from the tower, and we will come up to pray."

"Is not the Old Man glad?" he asked when the friar said nothing.

Garcés hastened to reassure him. "Of course, I am very glad, Palma. You have certainly kept your promise to the king."

"And the king will keep his promise to me, now," said Palma.

"God grant it," said the friar half to himself.

But as the harvest came and passed, and the first reports of the approaching party began to come to the river from Indians of other tribes who had seen them on the way, Garcés had too much to think of to remember his fears. There was, for example, Juan Miguel's problem. All his men were burning to go to meet the party. Juan Miguel himself felt that the dignity of the king's presidio demanded that they stay at their post. But he was upset by the pleas of his men, and the friar suspected that he would at a word dash off to meet his Rosalía. Poor fellows, thought the friar, here we do everything we can to make men build a home and cherish a family, and then we tear them away.

But aloud he said, "It isn't just a matter of dignity, Juan Miguel. The Yumas are not quite so excited this year as last about the Jalchedunes and their other enemies. But they are restless; indeed, there is a good deal of uneasiness among all the river people, especially now that a good harvest is in, and they no longer have to worry about food. I don't think it would be wise to let the word spread that the Spaniards had abandoned their camp on the river."

Juan Miguel stared. "Those savages do spread the worst lies, don't they?"

But though he was only half convinced of the necessity of paying some attention to the impression his actions might make on the minds of the Indians, he agreed that it was best to stay. And he contented himself with sending a couple of the soldiers, chosen by lot, to go with Palma's guides to meet the approaching party.

Fortunately, at this juncture Garcés remembered a lime pit he had seen below the height to the north, and he suggested to Juan Miguel that perhaps the soldiers would like to whitewash the interiors of the log-and-mud huts they had built for their wives and children. It was a happy inspiration that kept the men who were not on watch busy for the next few days, digging and slaking the lime and mixing it and sloshing it happily on the walls.

"Wait till my old woman sees this," exclaimed one veteran as he surveyed his handiwork. "She will say it is the first time I ever did it without being nagged out of house and home in the twenty years she's known me."

And when one afternoon Garcés stopped at Palma's house, he found that the Yuma chief had set all the women of his household, including not only his wife and daughters, but also the widow who was temporarily living in his house until she could be married again and her daughter, to grinding corn that he might have a welcome present for the women who were arriving.

So when at last the party came in sight, the whole region at the junction of the rivers was alive with activity. As the friar watched the Spanish and Indian settlements alike swarming across the stream on rafts, or in the case of the children on basket trays, or like most of the Indians, swimming with sure strokes, he found it impossible to remember his fears. For the exhilaration of this fulfilment of so many hopes swept up the whole area in one joyous rush to meet the newcomers. And then there was the glorious mêlée of the meeting, with almost every soldier disappearing headlong into a swarm of children while some woman flung her white-sleeved arms around his neck and clung to him as if she would never let him go.

Garcés felt his own heart beat, too, for already he saw in the people now beginning to come up the hill to the church the same phenomenon he had noticed in the second Anza expedition. It was the pulse of a mighty excitement, the excitement of a new hope in the hearts of those who had never had a chance to take their lives in their hands, and who now found themselves with their first chance to have a part in shaping their own destinies. Here, on these hills and in this river valley, the world was beginning again, and that fact sent a quiver of fresh energy through even the frailest and the most fatigued of the new arrivals.

And it swept through the next weeks. The low, shed-like structures that the soldiers had built to shelter the women and the children multiplied. They were better built now that trained hands cut and squared the cottonwood logs and the women helped to chink the interstices of the willow branches with the mud of the river bottom that they might be proof against the coming winter rains and cold. But the most striking feature of all was that they were now divided into separate rooms so that each family might have its own little house.

The friar drifted through the busy paths running down from the height of the Puerto de la Concepción to the river and then farther along the river bottom to where Palma was building his new house, within the bounds of the pueblo and yet away from the houses of the Spaniards. Not far from where he was building, Gerónimo and his wife were working on their winter house. As the friar stopped to watch the building, he compared it in his mind's eye with the work of the Spaniards which he had just been seeing. It was much more impromptu in its effect, much more ragged, for, after all, the house of the Indian might not be used for more than the winter's shelter, whereas the Spaniards realized that their temporary barracks would be useful for storage after the more permanent adobe houses could be built.

But the Indian houses were not without their advantages. They would, as the friar well knew, be quite weather-fast, and where the square of the Spanish houses stood up rawly against the sky above the height, these nestled into the pockets of the bluff as if they had come up out of the earth and already were part of its integrity. There was a tact, too, in the way in which they gravitated toward the aggressive new settlement and yet kept their distance, as if already they stood a little on their ancient dignity.

But of all the houses the one that interested the friar most was a very small one, actually one room standing alone, a little apart from the houses of the square and toward the Indian side of the settlement. Like the Spanish houses it had a rude chimney of stones from the river bed and a door in its doorway and a shuttered window, but it crouched lower to the ground than the Spanish houses, and it had the prevailing shade of the Indian dwelling extending from one end like a porch. It was the house which José was building for his Teresa.

But quite as moving to the friar as the building of the houses was the work of the women in settling into them. He never ceased to wonder at the way in which the moment a woman moved her brood into that little cell for which she had been waiting in the first shed-like shelter or in the tents by the river, she made it her own. It was not what she had to put into it that made the difference, for she had no furniture and only the barest of essentials of clothing and utensils to store there, and they were all of the standard patterns which the commander had bought in quantity from the traders who had flocked from Mexico to the headquarters of the expedition in Altar. But each woman, even the poorest, had brought some personal treasure with her.

It might be a statue of the Virgin holding her Child, with smoky hands and face, but with a fresh dress of the finest material the owner could buy for her needlework. It might be a statue of Santiago with bright leather shoes which its proud owner had embroidered for that much-traveled saint. Or a gilded and painted crucifix, or a brightly-colored print of Our Lady of Guadalupe with her brown face and her roses.

And there was treasure of this world, too, and here again, limited as was the basic pattern, the variety was astonishing. It might be a mirror, heavily banded with tarnished golden scrolls, gleaming brightly from the whitewashed wall. It might be a copper pot hanging splendidly in the small fireplace; or a pewter platter with its soft gray sheen on a narrow shelf above, or a bright pottery jug, or an embroidered coverlet or bright blanket, folded neatly on a heap of straw in the corner. Whatever it was, the friar admired it as a symbol of the housewife's devotion to the rites of her own daily craft.

And there was variety enough in the ways in which the women took possession of their new homes. Rosalía's bare little cell was as clean and as neat and efficient-looking as her own trim and resolute self. Indeed, she had already taken in a couple of a sick neighbor's children and was busily scrubbing them up, to their obvious surprise. She was a very tiny woman with quick, sure movements that seemed the unimpeded expression of a thoroughly certain and made-up mind.

Nothing could be greater than the contrast between Rosalía and her next-door neighbor, a large sloppy woman with a dozen children swarming around her. She whisked off the top of a rough bench by the fireplace with her apron and bade his Reverence be seated in a rough, warm voice, and produced a small jug, and over the friar's protests, she poured out a little aguardiente in a small tin cup.

"My man Mateo (he is the blacksmith you know)," she explained with obvious pride, "is no drinker, but he likes a sup when he comes in at night, and he wants it to be good."

It was the rawest of the frontier's aguardiente, but the friar took a polite sip, while two of the youngest began to struggle for his rosary. This his hostess at once stopped, shouting to the culprits that she would wring their necks if they did not treat his Reverence with the respect due to Holy Mother the Church. The startled friar expected the children to yell, but they seemed not in the least frightened, and scampered off cheerfully. It was then that he noticed that they were very clean and plump little creatures even if the house was as disorderly-looking as its mistress. And the friar wrote down in his parish inventory another strong woman who might help in quarters where Rosalía would be resented.

5

GARCÉS was doubly grateful for both when he went to call on Doña Francisca Manuela, the wife of Ensign Yslas, who had come in command of the expedition. The friar had given her a little time, for he had suspected that it might take her longer to get her household organized. He had heard that she had been too exhausted to come to the church on her arrival; and although most of the women of the expedition came to Mass in the morning, she had not yet appeared, but had stayed within the house which the ensign had appropriated for his headquarters.

Here she received the friar in a neat inner room which had been already equipped with a large and handsomely appointed bed, a rug, and a couple of folding chairs with embroidered seats. Not only was she an extremely pretty woman, but she gave an effect of sophisticated elegance that was in striking contrast to the appearance of the other women. For her dress was of silk, and she moved with a certain languid grace that was, he felt sure, some affectation of that world of fashion of which he had seen so little.

For all her air of rather sulky indifference she was looking at the friar with frank curiosity.

"I suppose you like all this," she began surprisingly enough, with a little wave of a very white hand.

Then, before the friar could begin to answer, she leaned forward, and without any sign of affectation, she said quite frankly, "I hate it."

"But—"

"Oh, I know, it's a promotion for my husband, and that's why I let him come. But if I could have guessed what it would be like, I would never have left Altar."

"Oh, come," said the priest gently, "you have hardly been out of your house long enough to see, have you?"

"You mean I have not been coming to church?"

"I was not thinking of that," he replied with a smile, "and I certainly meant no reproach. But the women of the party are having a very pleasant time making themselves at home here."

She smiled pityingly, Garcés was not quite sure whether at the party or at him. "Of course, it is better than anything they have ever known before."

"I think rather," said the friar gravely, "they are trying to make it better than what they have known."

She stared at her guest uncertainly. But before she could quite make up her mind about him, a barefooted mestizo woman appeared in the doorway with a steaming pot of chocolate. The pot was of silver, the friar noted irrelevantly, and then his hostess gave all her care to serving her guest.

When a good minute had passed, and he had still said nothing, she rallied him with a touch of mockery in the archness of her tone of voice, "Your Reverence seems very much preoccupied."

"I was thinking of how different this settlement here on the river seems to the different people involved, and how little they understand of each other's feelings. And yet they should be able to understand each other, for most of them have come with much the same motive."

The mockery deepened as the archness became less sure in her tone, "That is a curious thing for you to be thinking of, father, for they say that you have no thought but for those wretched savages of yours."

The friar hesitated for a moment, and then he said quite gently, "Well, that is my calling as a missionary, is it not?"

She nodded indifferently. "I suppose so."

But he was going on very gently, "They have their hopes of something better, too, from this settlement."

"Do savages think of such things?" There was obviously something here which had caught the attention of the vain and thrashing mind.

It was then that he saw his way clear, and he proceeded to tell her about the Indian girl Teresa. To his surprise she listened to the story with deep attention.

"She must be very pretty," she said presently.

"I am not sure I would know about that," said the friar with a smile, and she laughed lightly. "But," he went on, "José is satisfied, and that is enough for that. For my part, I am sure she is a remarkably intelligent woman."

Something of the old affected tone came back into her voice, "Remarkably intelligent women are often trying, and sometimes very dull."

"She will need all her intelligence in the days ahead," he said gravely.

"Oh, I don't know," she said with a certain judicial quality in her manner that surprised him. "Most of the laborers and their wives are mestizos as you have seen. And I have a couple of servants who are, too. In fact, they make better servants than people who pretend to be pure Castilian, as if Castile did not have its own riffraff."

The friar thought of José and the old Jamajab. But he said nothing.

"Will they be married in the church?" she asked presently.

"Oh, yes, she has been baptized. In fact, she comes to church quite faithfully."

The woman looked at him suspiciously, but there was no question that he had said the last quite without malice.

"Then she wears clothes like a Christian?"

The friar smiled, "She certainly wears clothes. But they are her own native costume, and not Spanish."

"You mean what the Indian women wear in the missions?"

"No, what they wear here on the river."

To his amusement she seemed shocked. "And you let them come into church?"

But the friar did not smile as he answered, "We had neither the clothes nor the authority to clothe them. And, as a matter of fact, the women behave very modestly in church."

"I shall give her her wedding clothes," said Doña Francisca Manuela with finality.

"That is very kind of you."

"It will give me something to do," she said candidly. "I'll send Maria Thomasa"—she nodded to the door from which the woman with the chocolate had appeared—"to see her in the next day or two. Where will she find her?"

"She lives in the house of Palma's father's sister, the one who is married to the Jamajab. Any of the Indians around will be able to direct her."

"You mean that man who made all the gestures and talked so long when we came? I was nearly ready to drop; so I did not try to find out what he was saying."

"Yes, he is their captain, and a very remarkable man."

"Do you missionaries find all savages remarkable?" she asked.

The friar laughed. "I think Don Santiago will tell you the same."

"Then she is some kind of princess?"

Again the friar smiled, "Not exactly, but it would do no harm to treat her as if she were one."

The pretty face looked at him with a certain shrewd intelligence breaking through the boredom. "Do you know, I feel a great deal better than when you came. Won't you come again?"

At supper that night Garcés gave his colleagues a running account of the day's visits. Barreneche listened with sparkling eyes, Díaz with a look of skeptical puzzlement, and the new friar who had been so busy with the invalids of the party for the first days after their arrival that he was only now beginning to become acquainted with his fellow-missionaries, with a look of complete astonishment.

"Would you mind telling me just what you are driving at?" said Díaz when he had finished.

"Why, nothing," replied Garcés with a look of surprise that took very little feigning.

Díaz raised his eyebrows, and the two younger men waited, one with admiring anticipation in his look at Garcés, the other with deepening bewilderment.

"This is what I mean," Díaz went on firmly. "I spent the day talking over the plans for the building of the pueblo with Commander Yslas and Juan Miguel. Now if you were to sum up your day in the same fashion, what would you say you had been doing—in a word, I mean."

"Getting ready for a wedding," responded Garcés promptly. And then he was surprised himself at what he had said.

Barreneche gulped, but he could not hide the delight in his eyes. While Garcés stared contritely at Díaz, the latter turned with a smile to the newcomer, "Father Moreno, you know the reputation of our brother here. There is not a man in the order, indeed not a man on this frontier, friar or soldier, who has gone further or learned more of what we need to know for the service of God and king. But his methods are like the ways of Divine Providence, past finding out."

But embarrassment sharpened Garcés' wits. "That is nonsense. You know how anxious we all are about the relations of the Indians and the settlers. Well, this wedding will give us a chance to make a little fiesta—"

"A fiesta! Since when have you found the provision of fiestas among the duties of a missionary friar? The next thing, you will be proposing that we arrange for an Indian dance."

"But, but—" Garcés stumbled a little in his haste to explain—"I am not proposing that we arrange the fiesta. There will be no need. It is simply that this will be the first wedding here, and—well, I think you can leave it to the women."

Díaz was contemplating his colleague with unusual thoughtfulness, "Father Font always says that you have a special vocation to the Indians. I think he would be surprised to think of you as a missionary to the ladies. But, seriously, granted that a fiesta for the women would do little harm, you know perfectly well that the men will enter into it after their fashion."

"You are coming to know Don Santiago Yslas well," said Garcés; "you can give him advice, and he will listen to you."

Díaz looked doubtful. "I am not so sure. Today I had my hands full enough. He seems to think of all Indians as enemies who must be held off until they can finally be beaten down."

In his anxiety to tell his fellow friars about the day's conferences with the new commander Díaz forgot about his colleague's preposterous suggestion, and Garcés was careful to say no more.

Nevertheless, the next morning when Mass was over, he asked José if he had thought how he wanted to be married. For the house was finished now, and Garcés remembered seeing the young man going to the north of the height the evening before.

José scowled, an unusual thing for his cheerful self. At first the friar wondered if the young man were not going to answer the question at all. Then he looked up at the friar suddenly. "Father, can you make any head or tail of women?"

"Well," Garcés considered, "so far as my professional capacity is concerned, I think they are as unreasonable as men, but I should hesitate to say more than that. What is it that Teresa wants you to do now?"

The disgusted lover smiled a little. "I wonder how you guessed. But never mind. You know, one of the things that made me love Teresa is that she has none of this nonsense that most girls have, or at least, I thought she hadn't, but now I am not sure. You know what she wants? I suggested that we could be married quietly after Mass some morning this week; I was going to ask you today. But she wanted to know whether that was the way Christians were always married, and when I said I supposed there was such a thing as a Nuptial Mass, she said we should have that."

"Well," said the friar, "that is what it is for. What is the matter with doing as she says?"

From the way in which José shook his head one might guess that more than the unreasonableness of women was in his mind. But the friar was waiting for his answer; so he plunged ahead, "But you know the other soldiers—the fuss that they make at weddings."

"Quite," said the friar dryly. "And I don't need to tell you that the Church would be quite happy to see half of it forgotten. But you're marrying like the two self-respecting Christians you are, and you want to stand up in front of your friends with your wife and let them all see that you are proud of her."

José stared at the friar. Then he rubbed his head doubtfully. "You think it isn't just a woman's vanity?"

"Under the circumstances it is far from a woman's vanity. You are going to have a very sensible wife, José; you'd better listen to what she says. And now you had better go and find Father Díaz and ask him when you can be married."

It was not until supper that night that Garcés learned that José had caught the friar on his way to the house of Yslas. Díaz was, therefore, quite prepared when the commander said that his wife was interested in expediting the marriage of the soldier and the Indian girl, to say that he had the date for the wedding for the next Thursday, subject to the approval of the commander. And when the commander observed that since it was the first wedding in his new command, he would like to give something to a fiesta, Díaz yielded to his fears only to the extent of asking that the ration of aguardiente be limited. This Yslas was quite ready to promise.

"The commander also said that he was especially grateful to Father Garcés for calling on his wife." There was a merry laugh at the supper table that night as Díaz thus made amends to his colleague.

So the celebration of the wedding of Teresa and José, like everything else that went into the making of Concepción, was compounded of many elements and many motives. Doña Francisca Manuela was as good as her word. Indeed, the next crisis in the plans for the wedding arose out of her well-meaning efforts. For when Teresa came to see her at her invitation, she offered the astonished Indian girl a full bridal outfit from high-heeled slippers to tortoise shell comb and mantilla. To her amazement Teresa courteously but firmly declined the whole thing. In vain, the commander's wife coaxed and cajoled and threatened and presently sneered and stormed. Teresa stood firm. And once she had persuaded Doña Yslas to listen to her, she astounded that lady by convincing her that she could not walk in the high shoes, and that she would feel naked in the brocaded skirt of the wedding dress. She had herself suggested the compromise of adding a plain linen jacket such as the commander's lady was then wearing to her grass skirt. For in this way the varying delicacies of both races would be conserved. The mantilla she accepted for sheer splendor.

So the wedding was held with the barefooted bride wearing her somewhat motley costume like a queen, and the full splendors of the Nuptial Mass to dazzle the Indians who filled half the little church and three-quarters of the space in front of the open door. And then, when the nuptial blessing had been given, and Teresa with her willowbark skirt rustling had walked with great dignity beside José in his dress uniform to the door of the church, there was a great cheer from both races.

It was a brisk early winter day, and everyone was glad of the great fires that had been built at either end of the pueblo square, with spots of stew and great hunks of roasting meat on improvised spits to make fragrant the clear autumn air.

By tacit agreement one fire went to the Indians and the other to the Spaniards when it was discovered that cooks from the two races were functioning at opposite ends. Juan Miguel himself took charge of the aguardiente in one of the rooms of the guardhouse with an assistant to keep the score of the drinkers. Commander Yslas issued an extra ration of tobacco for the Indians, so that there might be no disparity in hospitality.

And after the wedding feast was consumed, there was a drinking of toasts in sour country wine of which there was not enough to cause even Díaz any worry, and then there were speeches by Don Santiago Yslas and Palma and Díaz. And then when the speeches were over, there was dancing, beginning with long stately measures in which Commander Yslas led out Doña Francisca Manuela and almost everyone but the bride and groom danced. From that the pace quickened to the fandango and other dances in which only the young and the old who were anxious to demonstrate their prowess persisted. And then the Indians asked if they might dance, and they started one of their interminable rounds in which the whole village joined from little pot-bellied babies to withered grandmothers. And when it was over, both the pueblo and the village formed an escort, half procession and half mob, to bring the bride and groom to their home.

Díaz and Garcés watched the company go off in high amity, singing songs of which it was perhaps just as well that some of the words blurred in the now somewhat frayed excitement of the singers.

Then Díaz turned to his colleague, "With the Monterey people it was a funeral. Now it is a wedding. I should have remembered when you suggested it."

6

THE exhilaration of the first fiesta lingered into the early weeks of the winter rains. Garcés was aware of it as the women lingered after Mass in the morning chatting, as he found them visiting each other on his calls upon the sick, as he discovered one or two hardy souls like Rosalía and Barbara going down to Teresa's house to show her how to cook in the Spanish fashion. Above all, he saw it in the readiness with which soldiers and laborers volunteered to go over and build the first shelters for the priests and the settlers a couple of miles below the Cerro de San Pablo, the hill down the river. Something like a community spirit had come to the height of Concepción, and it was pleasant in the evening when the weather was not too cold to hear the people singing hymns together at the doors of their houses.

But the friar was not so sure of the other section of the pueblo. From the start there had been small difficulties which everyone had been too busy to pay much attention to. A mule had disappeared, and a couple of horses from the horse herd. These were commonplaces of all presidial stations and the commander shrugged his shoulders when he mentioned it one day to the friars.

There were various small thefts, too, a hatchet from one of the wood-cutting parties which had taken a siesta after lunch, a knife or two from the garrison, an iron pot from a house, some linen which a woman had spread out to whiten on the bushes back of her house. These petty thefts were reported to Yslas, and when Yslas got round to mentioning them to Díaz, Garcés immediately reported them to Palma. The result was that the hatchet and the iron pot were returned at once, for they were not easy to conceal in the Indian village.

There were various thefts of food, too, tobacco, jerked beef, chili, tortillas, and parched corn. Naturally, the housewives and the commissary complained, but Garcés explained that perhaps they should be charged to the account of involuntary hospitality. There was more irritation when report came that soldiers and settlers out hunting or working in the woods had come across Indians eating jerked beef in outlying rancherías. But it was only when a hunting party from the pueblo surprised a group of Indians around their camp-fire one evening, and when the latter fled, discovered horse bones in the fire, that anger really flared. The friars had a hard time restraining the indignant soldiers from going that night to Palma's house and demanding the immediate discovery and punishment of the culprits. And when in the morning Juan Miguel went with Garcés to see Palma, to the horror of the friar he seriously proposed that the thieves who had killed the horse should be apprehended and given over to the soldiers to be hanged for their crime.

Palma, who had at once agreed to see if he could find the culprits, protested the hanging. Juan Miguel, who was never brutal, wavered and looked at the friar, but the soldier who was with him was indignant. He declared that where he had served before, the company of the presidio had burned a whole Apache village for stealing horses. Palma said nothing to this tirade, but Garcés was not surprised when he reported two days later to Commander Yslas that he was satisfied that the depredations on the horse herd were the work of Pablo's village.

It was an awkward moment for such a charge. The settlement of San Pedro y san Pablo de Bicuñer was rising a couple of miles below the Cerro de San Pablo, in very close proximity to Pablo's village, and Díaz and Moreno were doing their best to secure the good will of Pablo. So the matter of the horse feast was dropped. But the week was hardly out when some Indians were heard approaching the horses in the night, and the guards fired. In the resulting mêlée all but one of the Indians escaped, but he was found under one of the horses which the shot had brought to the ground.

One of the herdsmen who had heard the uproar in a neighboring field rushed to the pueblo for help. So half the men of the settlement streamed out to the pasture. There in the flaring light of their torches they found the dead horse, and the Indian lying with one leg caught under it. He was dead, for his head had been bashed in by the end of a carbine.

Garcés protested the crushed head, but there was no support for his squeamishness. So he waited for morning, and then again he went back to the field. Palma was already there with a couple of his principal men, prowling cautiously around the field in which the horses were kept while the guards watched them with suspicion and obvious resentment. To Garcés' relief, however, Palma was not interested in the dead Indian. He was only a Jalchedune, certainly bent on no good in the territory of his enemies.

But it was clear that something was worrying Palma. And, presently, he seemed to have decided to confide in Garcés, for he took him by the sleeve, and pointed to the ground at his feet. The friar looked, but he could see nothing more than the stalks of a lot of little shrubs, half-cropped, half-trampled into the now muddy ground. Finally, he straightened up and told the Yuma that he could see nothing. But the Indian still pointed, saying only a single word, "Mesquite."

"Mesquite?" Garcés repeated puzzled.

"Men eat mesquite," said the Indian sternly. And then he pulled the friar on to look at more trampled ground. Slowly it dawned on the Franciscan what had happened. The finest and thickest stretch of mesquite in the neighborhood of Palma's village had been almost completely destroyed.

At once Garcés hurried to the house of Don Santiago Yslas. He found the commander waiting for him.

"What does that rascal Palma have to say to this?" he saluted the friar.

"It is none of his men. It is a Jalchedune. He thinks some spy, for they are old enemies."

"A Jalchedune!" cried the commander scornfully.

"Yes," said the friar gravely. "They found a bow and arrow with the man that I can say are not of Yuma make."

With a bad grace the commander admitted that he had to accept Garcés' assurance, but when the friar went on to report about the destroyed mesquite, he let go of his temper with relief. "You talk to me of trampled weeds when I have lost half a dozen horses, and might have lost more if that soldier had not fired! It is this constant coddling of the Indians, listening to their trivial complaints and accepting their lies, that keeps the frontier in a ferment and makes it impossible for the military forces to make any progress in establishing order."

There was nothing for the abashed friar to do but bow before the storm. But the condition of the mesquite field had opened his eyes to possibilities he had hardly dreamed of.

So he waited uneasily until the February flood had begun to subside a little. Now a considerable section of the jungle of arrowweed and other specimens of brush that fringed the muddy section of the river bottom was clear above the flood, while here and there patches of bare earth which had been almost gray with dust during the fall now were almost red from the rains. Already the Indians had begun to poke in these little parcels of moist land with sticks, and to thrust corn and melon seeds into them. It was at this stage that Commander Yslas remembered something which Garcés had spoken to him about shortly after his arrival, and sent for the friar.

"What was this you were saying to me last fall about burning some of the brush along the river? Of course, we had too much to do to think about it then, but I notice that it is drying out fast now," he began, much in the manner of a busy father who has just had some whim of his son's recalled to him, and for once has a little time to indulge him.

Garcés shook his head. "It is too moist to burn still, and it would be no use for planting this year, anyway. When you have burned it over, it takes the flood to clear it and level it a little. If we burn it over this summer, then next spring we can use it."

He made no effort to conceal his regret, for he hated to disappoint the commander when he was ready to cooperate.

But Yslas hastened to reassure him, "Oh, well it doesn't really matter. There's plenty of land around here that is already clear enough. They tell me that all that bare land we saw when we came here will be all right to plant when the river's gone down."

Garcés stared at the commander, for there came back to his mind the river as he had first seen it, with the Indians working in their gardens all along the water's edge. "But those fields belong to the Indians. They have planted them from time immemorial."

"Belong to the Indians!" Yslas repeated in astonishment. "Really, Father Garcés, I cannot believe that long as you have been away from civilization, you do not understand these things better than that. This pueblo has been given all the land adjacent to it by the ordinance of its foundation."

The friar tried to hold the anger that blazed within him at those calm words. His voice sounded remote and fatuous to his own ear as he asked dryly, "But what will become of the Indians?"

He must have succeeded in controlling his voice better than he thought, for Yslas replied in a cool, curiously pedantic tone. "I cannot understand what makes you missionaries so persistently suspicious of the intentions of his Majesty's servants. You sound as if you thought I were contemplating dispossessing the Indians. They will have their share in the prosperity of the pueblo just as you and I will. You told me last fall that they have been short of food, and I think it is clear from these depredations that we have been suffering that they are. When I hear of their planting with sticks in the river mud, I don't wonder. With proper planting and proper care, this river land will feed many times the people it has ever fed. That is the difference between barbarism and civilization."

"But they have their customs and their ways of dividing up the land. Won't you speak to Palma, at least?"

Yslas shrugged his shoulders. "I have other things to do than listen to Palma orate on Indian customs just now. Later, when I have time, I'll tell him my plans."

Garcés hesitated; then very carefully he expostulated with the commander, "Indians have their ways of doing these things. They like to sit down and talk them over. One does not get very far with just telling them what to do."

Yslas' eyes snapped, "Savage anarchy it is." And then a rather distant look came into his face, "I have always understood that a decent respect for authority is, also, the foundation of the Christian life."

Clearly, there was nothing more which the friar could accomplish here. Discouraged, Garcés went out into the late winter sunshine and looked from the bluff down the river. Already he could see the Indians at work in little patches of ground, high above the water's edge, where the winter rains still left the ground red and moist but where even the heavier floods of later spring would not reach. None of the Spanish settlers seemed to be watching them poking their sticks into the ground and dropping seeds. If any did, the whole process would look as haphazard and ineffectual as the commander had suggested, for the Indians were working with their usual casual leisureliness. Anyway there was very little he could do about it just now.

For there was difficulty at San Pablo with Pablo's people who were resisting Díaz's efforts to get them to come to church and Sergeant Juan de la Vega's to persuade them to help in the building. Garcés and Palma spent a good deal of the next couple of months going back and forth, trying to persuade Pablo and his people to give Christianity a chance, and Garcés came to suspect, to keep Pablo in check with regard to schemes which Palma clearly suspected but which the friar was never quite sure existed.

With his own work to do at Concepción and all this extra traveling, Garcés had little time to think beyond the day's immediate demands. But at the beginning of March the question arose again in a form which he could no longer evade. For Commander Yslas sent for him and informed him that he had been working on the plans for the assignment of the land for the spring planting.

"I have reserved certain lands for you to take care of for the Indians," he explained.

Apparently, he misinterpreted the friar's start, for he went on with the heightened graciousness of a man who sees that his generosity is appreciated, "That strip which the Indians planted for the church last year will be part of it. So will that strip which you had the soldiers burn off last year, and so will those fields on the other side of the river which you said had been only partially cultivated last year."

"But the rest of the land on the river bottom at the foot of the height here?"

"That will be the most suitable for the soldiers and the laborers. I have told the colonists that they will have to go farther afield. After all, they will have the leisure for it. It means that your Indians will have fully half of the land they had before, and, properly cultivated, it will yield quite as much." He seemed to be waiting for the friar's reply.

"Commander Yslas," said the friar gravely, "I do not want even to seem to question your good intentions for the Indians, but I must beg you to see Palma and tell him this before you let the pueblo folk do anything about the land. You know the Indians are used to doing things year after year in the same place and in the same way. They will not understand unless you give them time to readjust and give them your reason."

"But that," said Commander Yslas, "is exactly what I am asking you to do now, to explain this to them."

For a moment the friar stared incredulously at the commander. Then something snapped in his brain, and though the flame was still raging in all his body, he knew what he must do. And his voice was quite steady as he spoke, "This is not my field, Commander Yslas. If I tell Palma, it will carry no authority, for he knows that I am not in charge of the temporalities here. And I cannot undertake to persuade him that this is just, for I do not think it is."

"But it is just that making him see that it is just that I expect you to do. You are charged with the spiritual and moral government and instruction of this pueblo. I cannot think of any clearer exercise of that spiritual duty than to see that the king's subjects in this pueblo understand their duty and do it. And their first duty is obedience to rightfully-constituted authority."

But the friar stood firm, "It is precisely because I am sure that we have no chance of winning their willing submission if we lose their confidence in this, that I am begging you to see Palma before you do this."

The commander was losing his patience now, "Then, Father Garcés, if we do not win their willing submission, may I remind you that I am prepared to compel it? Where will your precious Indians be then?"

Garcés recoiled, and the commander smiled a little. The friar rose and stood before the soldier, "There are more than three thousand souls in the Yuma villages, and of them at least four or five hundred must be seasoned fighting men."

"Are you threatening me?" shouted the commander.

"No, I am only reminding you of the judgment of God if you do this great injustice." Even as he said it, the friar was astonished himself at the clearness with which he now saw it all.

7

IT was hard on the heels of this interview with the commander that the reply to Garcés' protest over the new arrangement arrived at last from Querétaro. The father guardian made no secret of the fact that he and the other members of the council of the college agreed with his disapproval of the new mission arrangements, and shared his fears. They had made their protests to the viceroy, and they had been told that nothing could now be done. The new arrangement was the best that could be had under the present circumstances, and it was a choice of either that or nothing. The council had decided that they could not now withdraw the friars; that would be to leave the settlers and the Indians without priests and to jeopardize their whole missionary program. The only thing the friars on the river could do was to put all their efforts into the spiritual work of their post. That, from all the father guardian knew of the frontier, would be enough to satisfy even the zeal and energy of Father Garcés.

Disappointed as he was, the friar smiled at the dry conclusion. Fray Diego Ximénez had always had a gift for putting a sting into the tail of a mild-seeming admonition. This time, Garcés admitted, it was not undeserved. He had been so preoccupied with the plans for the new settlement, so busy visiting with the Indians along the river, that he had not been doing anything like what he might be doing at home. It was, he thought ruefully, still holding the father guardian's letter in his hand, his besetting sin.

The next day Díaz arrived at Concepción to get his letters and his share of the supplies for the service of the church that had come from Querétaro. His letter was even more emphatic than Garcés'. Nobody pretended that the arrangement was a sound one, but it was his business to do the best he could. Significantly, the father guardian added that there would be no want of zeal in the missionary staff at the establishments on the river. What would be especially needed was prudence and sound judgment, and for this the council of the college looked especially to Díaz.

Díaz smiled affectionately at his fellow-missionary when he had finished this. "That is what one might call the official point of view. Everybody on the council knows that you are worth ten of me."

But at his colleague's embarrassed protest, he sobered. "It is quite clear they can do nothing, and are just telling us to make the best of it."

"God knows there is plenty to do," said Garcés vaguely.

Díaz smiled. "Well, there are some things that rather jump to the eye. To begin with, didn't we talk of getting a larger church here? Even for half the pueblo, this is too small. And if the Indians should get to coming in any numbers, I don't know what you would do."

"There is no denying that," said Garcés. "But," he added doubtfully, "that will involve getting the commander's cooperation, and after our interview two days ago—" he proceeded to tell his fellow-missionary about the failure of his efforts to save the land of the Indians.

Díaz listened gravely, but when Garcés concluded by repeating his doubt that the commander would listen to any proposals of his for using precious pueblo time and labor, Díaz did not hesitate to contradict him. "That is where you do not understand men like the commander. He will not listen to you when you talk to him about the distribution of the land here, but he will be delighted when you talk to him about a new church."

So it proved. Yslas received the friar with marked reserve when he appeared at the door of his office, but when the friar announced what he had come to discuss, the commander warmed immediately. "I was waiting for you to get round to that," he said with the closest to enthusiasm which Garcés had yet seen in the formal official. "As a matter of fact, my wife has been telling me for some time that the church is too small. That is why she does not go more. You know how these fine ladies are—the stench of the Indians and all that."

The friar remembered the last time that Doña Francisca Manuela had come to church. She had sat on a stool in the corner near the altar rail, with her two women servants and their husbands around her, fanning herself elaborately with a lace fan, and sniffing at a gold-topped bottle which she kept taking from her women. He had been preaching, and yet he had found it impossible to forget her flutter there under the pulpit, and so, he suspected, had half the women in the congregation. For a moment, he had been glad she did not come oftener, and then he had forgotten it all in the press of other, less personal matters.

But the commander was plunging ahead now on the theme of the church, "Just as soon as we can get the manufacture of adobes under way, we'll build a proper church for you. Of course, we shall have to wait a while yet for that. But there is no reason why a larger church of the present type should not be built now."

"That won't be necessary," said Garcés hastily. "I have talked it over with Father Díaz, and he agrees that if we take down the wall between the church and the priests' house behind, we'll have enough for now. At least, it will see us through till next fall, and it will not interfere with our Lenten observances."

"That is true," said the commander with approval; "a good Lent will be a good thing for this pueblo. There has been too much loafing and drinking among the men, and my wife says the women are settling down to their usual gossip. Lent will do them good, and there ought to be less of this constant grumbling about rations."

"The rations," began the friar slowly, "are not always adequate for the larger families, I am afraid."

The commander's easy geniality evaporated. "Don't let those women impose on you, Father Garcés. They are always grumbling about something. And they are wasteful; many of them simply don't know how to manage. You stick to the church, and you won't be led astray. I know soldiers and their wives. And when we get those new crops in, it will be much easier all around."

"I hope so," said the friar quietly.

"It will be," said the commander with assurance. "Now for your job at the church—I'll have a half dozen of the soldiers and the laborers there tomorrow, and I'll tell the commissary to let you have anything you want. Just you tell them what you want, and they'll do it."

The friar thanked the commander sincerely and took his leave.

But as he reached the door, Yslas called him back, "Remember, I'm as devoted to the Church as any man living. Just tell me what you need any time, and if we have it, it is yours."

Again, the friar expressed his thanks.

The commander was as good as his word. The soldiers and the laborers came, and they moved the altar and all the furniture of the tiny sanctuary, and they tore out the wall between the house and the church. Then they white-washed the interior of the frame and mud structure and put the altar back with the statue of the Virgin over it, and moved the rough rail to the new sanctuary. When they were through, the church was more than half again as big as it had been, and clean and shining white within for the Lenten season.

For Mass on Ash Wednesday morning the commander had the guard paraded into the church. The celebrant of the second Mass, Father Barreneche, was just entering the church from the tiny sacristy in the corner of the building, when they appeared. Garcés, who had said the earlier Mass for a handful of people, mostly Indians, motioned to Barreneche to wait for a moment. Very impressively the dozen soldiers of the garrison, headed by the commander, marched to the front of the church.

It was a fine effect, and Garcés bowed to the proud commander, who ostentatiously opened a missal. Then Barreneche entered the sanctuary, and the Mass began before the largest congregation which had filled the church since the wedding of José and Teresa. But Garcés had hardly given thanks for this evidence of cooperation when he became aware of something which he had not noticed before. The front of the church was entirely occupied by the people of the pueblo; the Indians, of whom a good many had come, were in the back.

What a contrast they made! In the front, there was a good deal of color in the uniforms of the soldiers, in the dresses of the women, in the jackets and ribbons of the settlers, and even in the Sunday best of the laborers. There was a good deal of restlessness, too, as some of the women followed the example of Doña Francisca Manuela, fanning themselves and flouncing their skirts as they rose from kneeling, at the Gospel. Behind them the Indians seemed somber in their rabbit-skin capes, or their blue-black blankets from Moqui, or just the bare brown skin above the loin-cloth of the men and the willow-bark skirts of the women. And they were curiously still, not moving again when they had risen or sunk to their knees.

As usual, when his eyes had been opened, the friar watched, and soon found fresh confirmation of his discovery. When the congregation pressed forward to receive the ashes on their foreheads at the conclusion of the Mass, the commander and his wife came first, and then the soldiers, and then the rest of the pueblo. At almost the end came Teresa, and to his astonishment, the friar saw that she was no longer wearing her bark skirt, but the long full skirt of the other soldiers' wives. She moved a little timidly, he thought. But now the Indians were coming up to the rail, and as they came up, the friar noticed with indignation how some of the settlers' wives pulled their children toward them so that the Indians would not brush against them as they passed.

It was then that the friar knew what his text would be for the first of the Lenten sermons. He always dreaded these formal sermons, for he had little eloquence or taste for eloquence. He liked to say what he had to say as simply and as concretely as possible. When he began to talk, he often found that he was deeply moved by the sight of all those eyes gazing so earnestly into his, and sometimes it seemed to him as if a flame ran from them through him, and he found himself saying things he had not thought of before. But he took no pleasure in them when people brought them to his mind afterward, for they were never more than a fragment of what should have been said on that theme.

But little as he liked the sermon, he always thought a good deal about the text on which he was going to preach. So he did this time. It was, "Have we not all one father? Hath not one God created us?" It seemed to Garcés that that text was the only possible charter for the pueblo. Somehow he must make his people understand.

They listened attentively. For he was speaking of the very simplest things. All children, even the children of the finest and the most distinguished of lineage, need help growing into the full stature of reasonable, Christian people. In the family the authority of the parents is the foundation of that growth. But the children need to help each other. In the pueblo every day one could see older children, particularly the girls, guiding and teaching the younger children. Or one would see a party of boys running down the road to see something exciting, perhaps the arrival of a courier, and as they ran, the small child at the end would stumble and fall and cry out. And then his older brother ahead would recognize his cry and would look back and see him. He might grumble at missing the fun ahead, he might even scold his small brother, but he would go back and help him to his feet. So it must be in any society, from the family in the pueblo to the empire of the King of Spain. Each member of the family must help the other, particularly the younger and the weaker members, those who had just come into the family of the faith, those who had just come out of the wilderness into the household of rational civilization.

They listened thoughtfully as he spoke, and afterwards when he came out into the plaza to greet them, a couple of the men murmured something about having liked the sermon. But it was not until later in the week that he received anything like a general reaction, and then it was from the women.

Barbara, darting out into the plaza to pull in two of her brood at the approach of some horses, said, "That was a fine sermon you gave us last Sunday, father." Rosalía, coming from the storehouse a bit further on, was less sure, "That was an interesting sermon, father, but I am not sure you can run a pueblo quite like a family. It's like so many things in the Bible—it would be nice, but it isn't so simple." But it was Doña Francisca Manuela who caught him as he was going into her husband's office, and came to the point, "Father Garcés, do you really think the Indians are as good as we are?"

It was that night that Barreneche asked him if he had noticed that the Indians were not coming to the church the way they had been.

Garcés hesitated. "Are you sure it is not that the Spaniards are coming more?"

But later in the week he missed Palma, and he went at once to his house to find out if he were ill, for he had heard nothing of his being away. Palma was at home, and he was quite well, he assured his visitor.

"I am glad," the friar said. "You see I missed you at church, for you are my most faithful assistant." He smiled as he said it so that Palma might not find any hint of reproach. But Palma did not smile.

"Old Man, the Spaniards do not believe you when you say that all the people in the pueblo are children of one father. They believe they have two fathers."

"The Church does not, Palma," said the friar gravely.

But Palma held his ground. "The church up there belongs to the Spanish father. The father of the Indians is not there."

Appalled, Fray Garcés took up the argument with Palma. When he left he thought he had convinced him that to the Church there was but one father for all men, and that to the Church all those children were equally dear. But Palma did not come to the church the next day nor the next. And when Sunday came, only Teresa was there with her husband.

Garcés went the next morning to Palma's house. And there he asked Palma if the Indians would come to church if they were assured that they would have half of the church to themselves.

But Palma did not answer. Instead, he asked a question of his own. "Would the God of the Spaniards come into an Indian house?"

Garcés was indignant. "You know, Palma, from the instruction Fray Juan Campa gave you that God is everywhere, in the humblest Indian hut as well as in the great cathedral where you were baptized."

But Palma did not seem to be paying any attention to what the friar was saying. Again, he asked his own question without regard to what had just been said, "If we build a house like this, will you say the long prayer in it?"

Garcés stared at him. Palma held out his hands, "The Spaniards do not want the Yumas in their house. The Yumas do not want to go there. Will not the Old Man come to the Yumas?"

The friar shook his head. "There are only two priests in the pueblo, Palma."

"It is only fair," said Palma, "one for them, one for us."

But when Garcés appealed to Commander Yslas, the latter declined to meddle in what was not his affair.

"But it is," the friar insisted. "For if we set up a separate church for the Indians, it will break the unity of the pueblo, and that is one of the essential features of these establishments."

The commander looked startled, but rallied quickly. "You are going too fast. It would be if it were a permanent arrangement we were contemplating. But it is just until the Yumas have been Christianized and civilized. After all, Father Garcés, the women do have something on their side. Those Indians are filthy, and they bring all kinds of vermin into the church. It doesn't much matter to them. Most of them don't wear enough clothes to cause them any discomfort. It's a different thing with all the clothes our women wear. And there is the smell, even if you don't notice it any more."

The next day Garcés rode over to San Pedro y San Pablo to see Díaz. The latter listened with sympathy to his colleague's story, but he was clearly not surprised. And when it came to Palma's suggestion, he nodded his approval. "I've been thinking of trying something like that here. The Indians are simply not coming in any numbers to justify any hope for the future. You are fortunate that Palma has suggested it."

"But it is a blow to the whole pueblo plan," protested Garcés. "After all, it is that which we are supposed to be trying to make work."

"It is only a means to our end," said Díaz firmly, "and not the means we chose, at that. If the commander sees no objection to it, I don't see how anyone can ever blame us. If we had time, I should consult Querétaro, of course, but I am afraid there is not time enough."

When the next day Garcés went back to Palma's house, he found a crowd of Indians in his path. At first he wondered if they had come to meet him. But in a moment he saw that they were completely absorbed in some business of their own. And as he came up to them, within a stone's throw of Palma's house, he saw that they were building a new house.

While Garcés stared at them, Palma stepped forward. "It is the house for the Father of the Yumas. Soon it will be ready for the Old Man to say the long prayer in."

By Sunday it was ready. Just after sunrise Garcés said the first Mass in the clean new chapel, stuffed to overflowing with the Yumas. And then he went back to the church at Concepción where his colleague was just finishing saying Mass for the pueblo. When the last prayers were said, Garcés stood in front of the altar rail and held up his hand for attention. He made no effort to preach a sermon that day, but very simply he told the people of Concepción about the new chapel and gave them a vivid picture of the bare Indian hut without any ornaments or equipment but the rough table on which he had set the altar stone. There was complete silence in the little church when he had finished.

That afternoon Rosalía came with a piece of linen she had just finished bleaching. And she was followed by Barbara who brought her greatest treasure, a very dusty and chipped statue of Our Lady of Guadalupe. The friar hesitated, and Barbara looked disappointed. So he hastened to thank her warmly. Then came Doña Francisca Manuela with her best dress, a golden brocade. "It is too fine to wear for a dress here, anyway," she said almost apologetically. He showed her Barbara's statue.

"I am going to call it the chapel of Our Lady of Guadalupe," he said.

To his surprise the commander's wife said nothing, and when he looked at her, he saw tears in her eyes. He thought of her that afternoon when he showed the statue to Palma and put it on the altar table. For his eyes were shining. "The beautiful lady has come to live with the Yumas, too," he said and fell on his knees.

8

HE had, Garcés knew, a little over a month now to the time when the Indians would begin to scatter for the main planting of the year. After that, it would be well into the fall before he could hope to gather any considerable number of them together again for instruction. This was, then, his great chance to win the Yumas. So every day at sunrise either Garcés or his assistant would walk over to the chapel of Our Lady of Guadalupe and say Mass. Sometimes the priest who came in the morning would spend the day in Palma's village, visiting the sick, instructing the children in the Spanish tongue, and talking with the older Indians in their language.

With all this and their work in the pueblo and occasional trips over to the other settlement down the river and into the villages farther away, the two friars had little time to worry about the future. The response to their efforts in both the pueblo and the Indian villages was good, indeed, far better than anything they had known since the arrival of the settlers.

The friars noticed, however, that the Indians no longer came much to the pueblo. They might be seen any day along the river, fishing, gathering driftwood that had been brought down from the mountains in the spring floods, or just watching the waters slowly recede from the higher reaches of the river valley. But they were careful to keep away from the settlement on the height. Sometimes the friar sent them on errands up to the pueblo or asked them to come up to the priests' house behind the church. But always he noticed, when their errand was done, they hurried away.

Now and then if something were going on like the making of a raft on the water's edge, or the construction of a weir to catch fish, or even a piece of building on the height, they would linger to watch, but always with a certain vigilance as if they expected to have to flee at any moment. This was in such contrast to their usual disposition to indulge the slightest pretext of curiosity to the full that the puzzled friar began to watch to see if he could discover for himself what the trouble was.

He got his first clue one day when he had been in to report to the commander that the Indians seemed to be responding very well indeed to the opportunities of their own chapel.

"I am glad to hear it," said the commander. "Of course, you can do more with them than anybody else. I have always heard that. But they are a lazy enough lot."

"Lazy?"

The surprise in the friar's voice was echoed in the commander's face. "I don't know what else you can call it. You certainly can't get them to do a single useful thing. I've tried, and the commissary has tried, and the settlers have tried. The women have tried, too, with their women, and it's the same story."

"What do you mean?" asked the friar.

"What I say," replied the commander with a tinge of impatience. "You catch one of these fellows poking around something that is being done. You ask him if he will help you, and he looks at you. Then you offer him some food, and you say you will give him food if he will get to work, and he works more or less for a day, and then he is off. Try to make him come back, and you have trouble on your hands. One of the settlers tried to get hold of a fellow who had promised to help him, and he was all but killed by some other Indians who were in the woods nearby."

"Have you talked to Palma?" asked the friar.

"Talked to Palma? Why should I talk to Palma? I have talked to Palma in times past, and all I have got has been some oration on his friendship with the Spaniards, and the great things the Yumas will do with the help of the power of the Spaniards."

The friar considered. He must make at least a beginning on bringing the Spanish authority to understand. "The Indians do not work quite the way we do. They decide in their councils that something will be done, and then they work together."

The commander shook his head with exasperation. "If the Indian is to be a member of this pueblo, he has to learn to work like a civilized man, steadily and regularly, and in the way the proper authority says."

Again, the friar tried to explain, but the commander apologized; he had work which he must do.

As the friar started back to the church, he happened to look down at the river. It was a pleasant sight, with a fringe of green all along the reddish-brown mud at the edge of the flood. Here and there in the green fringe, he could see little pools of lighter green where the Indians had made their February and March plantings. A couple of them were down there now, poking along, then straightening themselves up to talk to each other. They seemed to be going from patch to patch. The friar decided to go down and speak to them, for something in the way they talked together and gesticulated at each other suggested anxiety. But before he could speak, one of the Indians was clutching his sleeve and pulling him along to look at something. "See!" said the Indian angrily, pointing to the ground.

Then the friar saw. The ground was trampled with horses' hoofs, and the thin shafts of corn were all broken and ground into the brown earth.

"I planted that," cried the Indian, almost choking with anger.

"I am sorry," said the friar, "it is a mistake. Somebody let the horses come here, and did not notice the corn."

"A mistake!" cried the other Indian. "Old Man, the corn is broken in the patch I planted, and in all the patches, clear along the edge back to there." He pointed.

"I will see the man who has charge of the horses immediately," said the friar. The two Indians looked at him for a full minute.

Then one of them shrugged, "Will he listen to you?" There was no impertinence in the man's face. He was simply asking a question.

The soldier in charge of the horse herd was having his supper when Garcés found him. Quite cordially he invited the friar to sit down, and he called to his wife to bring another bowl for his Reverence. Hastily, the friar declined and asked him who had turned the horses loose in the Indians' corn and melon patches.

"Nobody has, father," said the man in obvious surprise. "The brush has come out green along the river so that there is something for the horses to eat. I remembered all that fuss about those weeds back in the paddock; so I thought this would be a good chance to let that place rest and grow in again. So I had the horses brought down along the river."

"Didn't you notice anything coming up there in those little patches?"

The Spaniard smiled, "Oh, those. Don't worry, father; there are no fields there. Just little patches of corn growing wild."

But there was worse to come. A couple of days later the friar was coming back from the early morning Mass in the Yuma chapel. He was anxious enough, for there had been very few Indians in attendance. He was trying to comfort himself with the thought that it was fine weather, and doubtless the Yumas had not been able to resist the temptation of getting the day's work under way as early as possible. Anyway, half the pueblo would be out in the fields in the river bottom. Even now, as he came along a ridge under the bank, he could see the figures of men ahead.

He looked again, and involuntarily his step quickened. For there were both Indians and Spaniards there, and from the way they faced each other in little clumps, it looked as if they were drawn up in opposing parties. Now, as he came closer, he could see that one of the Indians was gesticulating wildly while the other Indians stood stiffly behind him. In front he could see where some of the Spaniards shrank back. He began to run.

One of the Indians turned and, seeing him, uttered a glad cry, "It is the Old Man."

Then the Spaniards began to shout, "Father Garcés!" As he came up to them, both the Indians and the Spaniards crowded around him.

"Father!" shouted one of the Spaniards again, and the friar recognized Gabriel Tebaca, the settler whom the others had chosen for their quartermaster. As Garcés caught his breath, Tebaca rushed up to him. "Father, please tell these condemned fools of savages that we have already planted this piece of ground. We don't want them coming poking their sticks into it. They are so stupid they don't know a corn furrow when they see one, and they are breaking up the furrows with those sticks."

But one of the Indians caught the sleeve of his habit, and pointed to the man who was gesticulating. "Will the Old Man tell them that he has planted this ground since he was a man?"

"What is he saying, father?" The Spaniards gathered round.

"It is his field," said the friar sadly. "He has planted it ever since he was old enough to have a field."

"With those silly little sticks?" One of the Spaniards laughed as he pointed to the Indian's planting stick.

"That is not the point," said the friar sternly. "It is his field."

"I don't see any boundary marks," said the quartermaster truculently.

"You wouldn't, and I wouldn't," said the friar patiently. "But he can tell you where his land begins and ends without any difficulty. He knows by the landmarks of the place."

And he went up and took the gesticulating Indian by the hand, and held the hand until it lay tense but passive in his own firm grip. Then when he saw that the man recognized him, he asked him to point out the bounds of his fields.

At once, the Indian nodded, and, loping along eagerly, he went to an invisible corner of the field, and then walked, pointing, along a line to another corner where he stopped, and then started back toward still another corner, and then to a fourth, not far from where the crowd was waiting. When he reached that corner, he pointed again, and then came up triumphantly to the friar.

"Is that correct?" Garcés asked the other Yumas standing by.

Instantly, they all agreed.

"I don't believe it," said Gabriel Tebaca, but his puzzled eyes belied his words.

"It is his field all right," said the friar.

"You mean he owns it? Then ask him what he will take for it," said the quartermaster.

The friar shook his head. "He doesn't own it in that sense. The whole village owns it, but it is his to plant and to tend, and he takes the crop for the use of his family. He couldn't sell it if he wanted to, but no man can take it from him so long as he takes care of it."

A cunning look came into the face of Gabriel Tebaca. "Well, he doesn't plant it and take care of it this year, for I have done that already. So the crop goes to me according to his own law."

"No," said the friar. "Only the heads of his tribe can take the use of the land from him, and they haven't done it yet. Don't you see," the friar pleaded, "he has simply been robbed of his right."

But the Indians were calling out to the friar now in their tongue, and as he turned to face them, the friar saw that more of them were coming from the direction of the village. In alarm at their growing numbers, he called to the nearest Indian and in a low voice directed him to bring Palma at once. Then he turned to listen to the others. But even as he did so, he heard one of the Spaniards say, "We'd better get the soldiers here right away."

He looked around, and fixed the speaker with a dart of his arm and a shout. "Don't bring the soldiers into this. That will only make more trouble." Now thoroughly quelled by the alarm in the friar's voice, the man remained where he stood.

But the Indians in their turn were beginning to seize upon Garcés and to shout. Speaking rapidly in Yuma, the friar bade them take their hands away and speak one at a time. He had already guessed what they would say, namely, that since there was a dispute, they would settle it, as was their custom, by a tug of war between the Spaniards and themselves.

For a moment the friar hesitated. A tug of war would at once degenerate into a fight, and a fight now—quickly he made up his mind.

"This is nothing for us to settle. It is for the commander of the pueblo to settle with Palma." He said it first in Spanish, and then in Yuma. "This does not belong to us, but to his Majesty the King of Spain. It must be settled in his name, for we are all his subjects." Again he said the sentence first in Spanish, and then in Yuma. The Spaniards retreated a little, rebellious and yet clearly impressed by the appeal to the name of the king.

The Yumas looked bewildered and stood their ground uncertainly.

Then the friar appealed to Gabriel Tebaca, "Can't you put the men to working somewhere else for today? If you'll get your men away, I'll send the

Indians back to their village, and we'll have a chance to settle it without any fighting."

The quartermaster hesitated. He was a big man, and he scratched his head with a large gesture of bewilderment. "I don't know what to think, and that's a fact, father. But if you think I'm going to let any naked savage spoil my field—"

"I know; it's a beautiful job. But how much of it do you think will be left if it comes to a fight here? Look, man, I can appeal to your reason—"

He was, as the friar well knew, a good-natured fellow when his pride in his work was not touched. Now he laughed and threw up his hands, "I leave them to you, father. Apparently, you can make some sense out of that gibberish of theirs."

And with a large gesture he gathered up the crowd of Spaniards and sent them off up to the pueblo. Then the friar turned to the Indians. "You see that the Spaniards have left the field. If I see Palma just as soon as I can, will you go, too?"

"If the Old Man promises," said the leader of the Indians dubiously.

"I promise to see Palma," he agreed and waited for the Indians to go.

They went more slowly, some of them clearly not satisfied with the friar's promise, and yet not quite sure how far they might safely protest.

When the field was quite empty, Garcés drew a deep breath and started up the path to the top of the height. It had been a very close call, closer, he suspected, than either the Spaniards or the Yumas had quite known. But the respite was, he knew, but temporary.

As he drew near the commander's house, he saw that half the pueblo was in the plaza listening to the story of the men who had been in the field. Even as he looked for the quartermaster, the latter emerged from the door of the house. And when he saw the friar, he smiled at him and nodded as to a friend. Puzzled, Garcés hurried past him into the anteroom of the commander's office.

In a moment the commander was shaking his hand warmly and almost shouting in his excitement, "Thank God, father, you came along. If you hadn't stopped that fight, I don't know where we would be."

"It didn't quite come to a fight, commander. But the problem is a serious one."

Seemingly quite oblivious of past discussions on the subject, the commander agreed, "Land is always a problem. No matter what you do, somebody complains."

"But the Yumas know this land belongs to them. They cannot under-stand why it should be taken from them. It is what they depend upon for their staple crops. Without it they will starve."

The commander's cordiality melted in exasperation, "Father, do you think I have no conscience? They will not starve. The Yumas will eat like ev-eryone else in the pueblo if only I am allowed to carry out the arrangements which I have made."

"But they do not ask that you give them food, commander. All they ask is that they have their land to grow their food themselves. If they have their land, they will not trouble you."

"Must we go into all that again? This land is already planted. It is the land easiest for us to reach and to guard. We do not have enough men to do all the things that need to be done in this pueblo. If instead of fighting about land, the Indians would only get to work and help us, there would be plenty and more than plenty for all."

In vain, the friar told the commander that he had held the Indians off only by promising to see Palma. All he could get from Yslas was a repetition of the statement that the Indians would not want for food, that the friar could give that promise to Palma from him, from the king, if he wished to put it that way. And if he thought it would do any good, he would see Palma himself and tell it to him face to face. There was nothing more that the friar could do there. So he went straight to Palma's lodge.

The low, square house was full of men when Garcés entered. From their midst Palma rose and, coming up to the friar, saluted him gravely, then wait-ed for him to speak.

"Palma," said Garcés with equal gravity, "I have seen the commander, and I have told him what your men have said. The land has been already planted by his men, for he is charged by the king with the responsibility of feeding the pueblo. He tells me to tell you in the name of the king that the Yumas will not want, that the land which his men have planted will yield more corn than it has ever yielded before. He promises you in the name of the king that the Yumas will eat that corn even as the Spaniards will eat it, and none shall want."

A low, hostile murmur had risen as he talked. Now it died into a hushed expectancy as the whole house waited for Palma to speak. For a full minute he waited, and then in a low voice he asked, "Is this what it means to be a

Christian that a man should stand on the land of his fathers and beg for the corn that others have taken from it?"

Again, the whole house waited for the friar's reply to this, the first word of defiance which Palma had ever spoken to Garcés. As the Franciscan looked around the room, he felt the air tense with an hostility he had never met before save that last morning at Oraibe. He looked at Palma, and as he began to speak, he felt his voice steady, "Palma, this has nothing to do with my authority as a priest. It belongs to the authority which the king has given to the commander. God has given authority to the Church and to the king. Some things belong to one, some to the other. I have spoken to the commander, and he has promised to see you about this."

Again the Indian looked at the friar, and again the room waited.

"Is not the commander a Christian?" Palma asked slowly. "Does he not listen to what the Old Man says?"

Garcés had heard men speak of the age-old struggle between the two powers to whom in His wisdom God gave the authority in this world, but he had never really thought much about it, for he was not interested in power. Now, however, he knew he was face to face with something as basic, as ancient, and as inscrutable as what he had faced at Oraibe. And yet he knew he must make one more effort to avert the disaster closing in on Indians and Spaniards alike.

It was that urgency that filled his mind and made his voice ring out, clear and compelling in the hostile silence. "Palma, this is not within my power to settle but within the commander's. I have begged him to see you and to listen to what you have to say, for this is a matter that lies within your province as a chief of the Yumas. And the commander has listened to me to the extent that he has agreed to see you. So now I beg you to go to the commander."

Palma sighed, and then he spoke with great dignity, "I at least will listen to what the Old Man says, and I will go up and see the commander tomorrow."

The whole room seemed to relax, and the friar took his leave. Not until he was outside, making his way back to the height in the failing light of the dusk, did it occur to him that there were those in that room who at a word from Palma would have torn him to pieces. And when it did occur to him, he was too tired and too sick at heart to care. For he knew now that he was up against the wall of Oraibe again; only here there was no place to retreat to.

9

It was Barreneche's turn to go down to the Indian chapel to say Mass the next morning, but Garcés made an excuse of some necessary business in the Indian village and went down himself. As he had expected, there were even fewer of the Indians at Mass than before, but Palma was still there with a couple of the older men of his village standing behind him. When he read the Gospel, the friar glanced at the Yuma chief. It seemed to him that Palma was looking abstracted as if his mind were elsewhere, but he could not be sure.

He had hoped that Palma would wait after Mass to speak to him as he used to, but when the friar had finished his prayers of thanksgiving, the Indians had all gone.

José, who had taken to escorting the friar down to the chapel and serving his Mass, saw his face as he looked around the empty chapel.

"The wife of the Jamajab will give you breakfast, I know," he suggested.

But the friar shook his head. "It is no time to make it hard for our friends." The young man looked at him in astonishment, but Garcés put his finger to his lips and started at once for the pueblo.

As he went, he made up his mind to remain there until Palma should conclude his interview with the commander. But he had hardly sat down to his belated breakfast when Sebastián came in with a messenger from San Pedro y San Pablo. He brought a note from Díaz asking him to come at once.

For a moment Garcés hesitated. He wanted to be there when Palma came out of the commander's office, as he knew he would, disappointed and angry. Yet he knew, too, that Díaz would not have asked him to come at once if he had not thought it necessary. As he hesitated, he caught sight of Sebastián still lingering in the doorway, looking at him. The worried look on the Indian's face, echoing his own unacknowledged anxiety, irritated him, and he made up his mind.

"I am going over to see Father Díaz, Sebastián, but if anybody wants to see me, I shall be back tonight."

The Indian came toward him impulsively, "Let me go with the Old Man. It is better."

There was no mistaking the anxiety in his face now. The friar's unusual irritation intensified. "Nonsense, Sebastián. I know every inch of the way."

"But," Sebastián hesitated, "that Pablo is a bad one."

The friar was angry now. "You have Pablo on the brain! Don't let me hear of you saying a word of such nonsense to anybody in Palma's village. Everybody there is upset enough without your making any more trouble."

Sebastián looked surprised, obviously too surprised to say anything more.

But the friar thought of the look on his face as he rode down to the river bottom. It was like catching sight of your own frightened face in a mirror. It was an awkward time for Díaz to have sent for him, but now that he was on the road, it would do him good to get away from the pueblo for a few hours.

There was no release for him that beautiful June day, however. As he rode along the narrow trail through the heavy undergrowth of summer, he noticed that there were no Indians to be seen at work in the fields in the river bottom. A few of the Spanish settlers and laborers might be seen here and there, but for the most part the river bottom, which he had found teeming with life on previous visits, appeared almost deserted.

Once or twice he heard a rustling in the brush beside the trail, followed by a scurrying through the bushes. But he met no one until he had almost reached the new settlement. And then to his surprise he caught sight of Díaz sitting astride his horse, reading his breviary by the trail.

"Presently, we will go up and see Father Moreno and Sergeant Vega, but there is no need of alarming them just yet. I am sorry to have brought you here. But I don't like the way things are going, and I didn't think it wise to leave just now."

Garcés caught his breath. For a moment he was frightened, because he assumed that what must have happened here was even more alarming than what was worrying him. But in a moment he found his apprehensions absurd. For Díaz had sent for him to inquire what he knew about Indian magic. And then he went on to explain what had happened. He had become exasperated by Pablo's refusal to pay any attention to any of the messages he had sent him. So he had taken an Indian guide and gone himself to the chieftain's house. For a moment he did not think that Pablo's wife would let him enter, and then at a shout from the interior of the house, she had stepped aside, and the visitors had gone in. There they had found Pablo working over a man stretched out on the floor, rubbing him with sand, breathing into his ears, sucking at his breast—

"It was a typical wizard's healing of a sick man," said Garcés. "I have seen something like it before. And Father Eixarch saw Pablo himself going through that performance the winter he was here."

"Then Pablo is a wizard."

"Father Eixarch was sure of it," said Garcés cautiously.

"But the commander did not listen to his report?"

Garcés hesitated. "You remember the commander was not so much impressed by Palma as we were. He did not altogether like his oratory and his drama. The way in which Pablo hustled around to help him made more of an impression on his mind. And you remember that while Anza was here, Pablo showed himself almost as zealous as Palma in coming to church. And then when the commander went on to Monterey, and I went down the river, Pablo took to backsliding. And one day Father Eixarch heard that Pablo had gone back to his wizardry, and he went to see, and found pretty much what you found."

"Didn't he tell the commander when he came back?"

"I should imagine so. Remember I wasn't there. I was still on my way back from Upper California. I suppose he did tell the commander. But by that time Anza had heard so many rumors of what Pablo had done or was about to do that he had decided that it all was a little mischief-making from Palma's village. You see he has never altogether trusted Palma's love of striking an attitude. He is a soldier, and he cannot help thinking that Pablo is a simpler, more straightforward type of being, who would be better in the long run than he looked."

"I am afraid Palma is right on this," said Díaz stiffly.

Garcés hesitated. "I shouldn't say that the healing itself is definitive. It isn't always easy to be sure where medicine, true or false, ends, and witchcraft and magic begin. You know how it is with some of the more ignorant and superstitious of our own people."

Díaz's face stiffened.

"I should think anybody could tell the difference between heathen idolatry and superstition."

"There is no idolatry here," said Garcés firmly. "There is a lot of nonsense about dreams and some sort of power to cure one in dream journeys, and all that, but not idolatry."

"It is backsliding of a scandalous sort, anyway. I shall make another effort to see him, and then I shall denounce him and warn the other Christian Indians to beware of him."

Garcés shook his head.

"I should go carefully. He is less powerful than Palma, but he is as much the captain of his village as Palma is of his, and I have never been sure that he might not some day make real trouble for Palma."

But Díaz's mouth was a straight line, and Garcés knew that there was nothing he could say now. So he contented himself with giving his colleague a rapid survey of the latest developments in the land situation at Concepción. Díaz was instantly sympathetic. But now it was his turn to try to restrain his friend.

"Strictly speaking, it is not our affair at all. The commander is right there," he admonished his indignant colleague.

"That is true," said Garcés, "but we can lose the whole enterprise over this business. Palma was pretty close to saying last night that if this was what Christianity is, he would have none of it."

"Palma!"

Garcés nodded miserably, and then he told of the stormy interview in the Yuma captain's house.

"That is why I want to be back as soon as I can. If Palma does come to the prayers this evening, I want to be there to see him," he concluded, and Díaz was forced to agree. So Garcés rode back without even stopping for food.

But he was delayed on the return journey. Some Spanish boys from San Pablo were playing with an Indian bow and some arrows down in one of the fields by the river. The friar had nearly passed them when he remembered to wonder where they had got them. So he turned back and lost a good half hour while he extracted from them the story of how they had found them in the brush and convinced them that they were not treasure trove, but some Indian's property which he was counting on finding just where he had left them.

"War arrows, too, from the feathering," he thought as he hurried away, trying to make up for lost time. Resolutely he put the new worry from him as he coaxed his tired horse along the trail. But he knew even before he took the road down to the Indian village that he was too late. The light was failing already as he came in sight of the little chapel. How curiously deserted it looked there in its brush clearing! Beyond, he could see Palma's house, but there was no sign of any life there, either. And beyond was the house of the old Jamajab, and that, too, looked deserted. Then he noticed that the door of the little chapel was ajar. He pushed it open and scanned the interior. A shadow rose from in front of the altar and came toward him, and he heard his name whispered. It was Barreneche.

"What are you doing here at this hour?" asked Garcés.

The young man hesitated. "I came down for the evening prayers and instruction when I saw you had not come back. But very few came, just some children and women. None of the men came. I confess I did feel discouraged. And I remembered what they used to say in the novitiate, that a missionary cannot expect any more than he wins by his prayers. I have been busy lately."

The friar smiled, "So you thought you would put some prayers into our chapel? You are quite right. I have not been praying enough myself lately for thinking of too many other things. We'll do it together now."

But the young friar laid his hand on Garcés' arm, and his voice sank to a whisper, "The Jamajab is here. I was going to take him up to the house when it got dark. He very much wants to see you."

Then as the light of the candle burning in front of the statue of the Virgin flickered, the friar saw that there was another figure up close to the altar. As he looked, the man rose from the altar step where he must have been sitting. Garcés began to look for a candle, but the Jamajab put his hand on his arm.

"Better no light, Old Man. There is no need of letting them know I am here."

"What is it? Palma—" Garcés caught his breath.

"Palma?" The Jamajab was surprised. "No, it is Pablo who has been dreaming again and telling his dreams."

"Dreaming?" Garcés' voice rose in sheer incredulity. After the anxiety of the last two days it was simply preposterous.

The Jamajab clutched the friar's arm, hissing, "Lower, Old Man. They will hear you."

"Who will hear me?" but the friar's voice had sunk to a whisper.

"Pablo's men who have brought the arrows."

Then the friar remembered the bow and arrows with which the children had been playing. He sat down on the chest in which the few vestments and the utensils of the Mass for the chapel were kept locked in the absence of the friars, and he pulled the old man down beside him.

"Tell me from the beginning," he whispered.

"You know these dreams," Gerónimo began.

The friar nodded. He knew little enough, but with his own not yet entirely fluent Yuma and the Jamajab's accent he doubted if he would learn more just now.

"Pablo came over here night before last."

"Night before last. Then yesterday—"

"They were talking about it when you came in, Old Man, and when you went out."

Appalled, the friar waited.

"It was not a good time for the Old Man to come," said the Jamajab. "Pablo told them that he had dreamed and he had gone up to a high place. And he had come down, full of power. He had come down so full of power that he sent war arrows to all the villages of the Yuma people, and they came together and they made a great fire and they danced. And they said, 'The Yumas are not cowards any longer, for Pablo is full of power.' And Pablo gave to two of his chief warriors the feathered staves, and they took them out, and Pablo went ahead, and all the warriors of the Yumas followed them. And they fell upon the Jalchedunes in their villages up the river, and they burned their villages, and they killed their best warriors, and they took many prisoners. And they came back full of power, and they danced the scalp dance, and the Spaniards were afraid of the power that was in them, and they looked at them, and then they all fled away."

In spite of himself the Jamajab was carried away by the excitement of Pablo's speech. It must have been an astonishing thing to have heard all this from the usually taciturn Pablo.

"I never knew Pablo to say so much," said the friar aloud.

"That is like Pablo. Most of the time he says very little, and Palma says much. And then there comes a time when Pablo says much, very much, and then Palma says very little. When all the Spanish women and children and the men who do not fight came, then Pablo said much, and Palma said little."

"What did he say then?" asked the friar curiously. But he was not deceiving himself, for he knew he was but holding the horror of Pablo's dreams off a little until he should have the courage to look at it more steadily.

"What did he say?" repeated the Indian cautiously. "He taunted Palma as if he were a captive tied to the stake and he were going to burn him. He said, 'Where, oh great chief of the Yumas, are the guns and the horses of the Spaniards? Where is all the mighty magic and the power of the god of the Spaniards? Where is that power that will burn all the villages of the Jalchedunes and slay their strong men? Where is that power that will make the enemies of the Yumas flee before their faces like the dust of the desert trail?'"

Again, the friar saw that little sympathy as Gerónimo had for Pablo, he had been carried away by the force of Pablo's eloquence. He paused now as if lost in the recollection.

"Was that all?" asked the friar, still holding off the picture of those arrows which Pablo had that day sent up the river.

The Indian came back sharply to the present, and in a hurried whisper he went on, "Oh, he said it over and over again. And then he pointed his finger at Palma, and he almost screamed, 'And what has come? The hungry mouths of women and children for the Yumas to feed, for the Yumas to feed.' And that, too, he said over and over again."

"And did Palma say nothing at all to this talk of Pablo's?"

"He is a great man still, that Palma," said the Jamajab. "When Pablo had talked until he was tired and had lost his breath, then Palma rose, and he looked around until every man's eye was on him. And then he lifted his arms, and he said, 'This Pablo talks much, but where is the power in him? These are but women and children and men who do not fight who have come today, but the power of the Spaniards and the power of their god is in them, and you are fools who forget that. And behind them is more power, and that will come, too.'"

"And then?"

"They did not know what to think, and I think they were afraid. But Pablo said no more."

"But this is all in the past now," said the friar briskly, pulling himself together, for he saw through the door which he had left open that it was quite dark now. "Tell me about yesterday."

"I have told you," said Gerónimo. "Pablo said all those things. And Palma said, 'These are but dreams. No good will come of them, and no good will come of you, Pablo,' and Pablo rose and went toward the door, and at the door, he turned, and he said, 'Wait till you see my arrows.' And today the arrows have come."

"What will Palma do?"

"How should I know?" asked the Jamajab.

"What do you think he will do?"

The old man considered, and the friar heard his own breathing, hard and noisy in the dark.

Then Gerónimo answered with great deliberation apparent even in the whisper, "These arrows he will break. But—" he paused as if uncertain whether he should go any farther.

"But what?" urged the friar.

"You know as well as I, Old Man. There will come a day when he will not break the arrows."

IO

WHEN the next morning, just before dawn, Garcés opened the door of the priests' house, someone came out of the cooking shed behind, and came toward him. It was still too dark to see anything more than the moving darkness, but the friar waited.

"Old Man," said the soft voice of Sebastián, "are you going down there?" It was too dark to see, but the friar knew where he was pointing.

"Yes."

The Indian seized his arm. "Do not go. They will kill the Old Man."

"I know," said the friar quietly. "But not today."

By the time he reached the little chapel, the sun had just come over the rim of the mountains to the east.

The chapel looked quite normal except that there were perhaps more Indian women and children waiting around it than usual. At sight of him they all filed quietly in the door, and he saw that they had not been sure that he would come.

When he entered the chapel to begin Mass, he looked around. It was about the same assemblage as yesterday. The wife of the old Jamajab was there, and there were one or two old men, but no sign of Palma or any of the young man of his village. As he knelt down to begin the first prayers, the friar decided that he would try to see Palma when he had finished saying Mass.

But Palma was not to be found at his house, and his wife could or would give the friar no idea where he could be found.

Upon his return to the height Garcés went straight to the cooking shed behind the priest's house. He was hungry, and he wanted all his strength for what he must do this day. But he was surprised at the relief he saw on the face of Sebastián when he first caught sight of him.

As Garcés ate the hot gruel, he felt better. He could not afford to lose his head if he were to persuade the commander that his warning was to be taken seriously.

To his surprise Yslas seemed glad to see him. "I was just going to your house, myself, Father Garcés, to show you these." He took up a couple of three-vaned arrows from the table behind him and held them out to the friar.

After one look Garcés handed them back. "Yes, they are war arrows; hunting arrows have but two vanes."

The commander looked grave, as if he understood the seriousness of the situation, but he did not look in any way alarmed.

"In all the stories it is the friars who get the first warning of rebellion from the natives," said Yslas hopefully.

"Are they ever believed when they give the warning?" asked Gracés.

The commander had ceased to smile, "I am determined that this story is going to have a happy ending, as I am sure you are."

"Please God," said the friar simply.

"Who is making war against whom?" asked Yslas.

The friar clasped his hands tight, and then opened them, "You understand I know nothing myself except that there is trouble. The Yumas are restless—all that difficulty about the land, of which I have already told you."

"That is no excuse for rebellion." The line of the commander's mouth tightened. "I told Palma when he came the other day that I had my duty to do by the pueblo, and I meant to do it, for the sake of the Indians as well as the Spaniards. Did he not tell you that?"

"I have tried several times to see Palma since that interview, but I have not been able to find him."

"Where is he? Doesn't he know that no member of the pueblo is supposed to absent himself without my leave?"

"I don't know where Palma is. And I doubt if he would be able to understand that prohibition."

"For a supposedly remarkable savage and a baptized Christian there are too many things that Palma does not understand. I talked to him for half an hour, and I don't believe that he listened to any of it." A note of righteous indignation had come into the commander's voice.

"It is not easy for men of two races to understand each other when they know nothing of each other's ways of life and of thought," said the friar gently.

The commander frowned. "Come now, we are getting off the subject into a lot of theory that I haven't time for. What I want to know is what these arrows amount to. Can you tell me that?"

The friar shook his head. "That is hard for anyone to say. Probably Palma does not know himself. I have heard from one Indian I trust that Pablo is trying to rouse the Yumas to make war against some of their enemies."

"But that is forbidden. Surely, Palma knows that we will never stand for that. We couldn't if we wanted to. I have just had word of another party of settlers which Rivera is bringing through here for Los Angeles. We can't have silly Indian wars breaking out along their way."

The friar held up his hand. "So far as I have been able to find out, Palma's attitude has been quite correct so far. But these Yumas are warriors. When Palma refuses to make war against their enemies, it is easy for some would-be rival of his to say it is because Palma is afraid to fight, and it is easy to persuade young men that they should follow a bold leader rather than a cowardly one."

"But Palma is their legitimate ruler. You should tell Pablo, or since he is in his parish, have Father Díaz tell Pablo that the Spaniards have recognized Palma as their legitimate ruler."

Garcés smiled in spite of his perplexity. "Father Díaz tells me that Pablo is not coming to church any more, and he is doing healing in his house according to the old heathen rites. I am afraid Pablo will not listen to Father Díaz."

"But rebelling against his lawful pastor and witchcraft—those are charges that would eliminate any trouble-maker."

"Do you think we can disregard the opinion of the Indians when it comes to their own leaders?" The friar tried by the quietness of his voice to take out some of the sting of the challenge.

"But Palma is their leader, born that way, or however they get to be chief. Colonel Anza told me that he had expressly asked the Yumas if they recognized Palma for their ruler, and he said they did without opposition."

"That is the trouble," said the friar sadly. "That is always the trouble," he added. "When we talk, what we say means one thing to the Indians and another to us. Palma is the chief of the Yumas because he is the man among them who gives the rest of them the sense of having the most power in himself. I think it is partly religious. So long as the Yumas see in Palma the strongest and the most successful man in the tribe, they will accept his leadership. But if somebody else can persuade the Yumas that he is more powerful and more successful than Palma, then I am not at all sure that Palma will stay chief."

"But," interrupted the commander, "you forget the most important thing of all—I am not going to tolerate any frivolous putting-down and setting-up of leaders. Palma is wordy enough and dull enough and pig-headed enough, but I am not going to have the safety of everybody on the frontier put in jeopardy for any ugly little schemer like Pablo."

While Yslas waited with obvious impatience, Garcés considered. Finally, he made up his mind to face the issue squarely. "Suppose you tell Palma and Pablo this, that you will not have them disturbing the peace. It would strengthen Palma's hand."

"Against this Pablo? That would be fine. But I didn't like the tone Palma took the other day. No, I don't want to give him any idea that I'll support him no matter what he does. It would be better if you saw him and told him that so long as he behaves himself, he needn't worry about Pablo."

Again the friar hesitated, and again he made up his mind quickly, "You know, it is not just a matter of Pablo and the old enemies of the Yumas. If Pablo were successful against the Jalchedunes, say, then he might be able to turn the Yumas against the Spaniards."

"Against us? I'd like to see the rascal try. With our guns and horses, and—"

"How many are we?" asked the friar quietly. "Twenty fighting men and not many more settlers and laborers. There are three thousand Yumas, with perhaps five hundred fighting men."

The commander gazed thoughtfully at the friar. Then he spoke a little plaintively, "But that is your work to make them Christians so they will not fight. You should really talk to this Palma."

"I have tried to," said the friar. "He is moving rapidly to the point where he will not listen to me anymore."

The commander exploded in righteous indignation. "He is a baptized Christian, and he should know enough to know that he should listen to the admonitions of the Church."

"What he has told me on the land business indicates that he does not think the Christian always listens to the Church."

"That is a different matter. That is a secular matter. This is a matter of Christian order; it is a spiritual matter." He had begun to thump the table as he spoke.

In spite of himself Garcés' mouth must have twitched. For the face of the commander turned scarlet, "Come, we are just going round the old circle.

You see Palma and tell him that we must have no nonsense. The king expects him to do his duty, and you, too."

"I don't think Palma will listen to me," said the friar gravely. "I think it has gone too far. It is getting to the point where Palma will say that the king is far away, and Pablo is much too near for comfort."

The commander was shocked, "Are you suggesting that the Church could condone treason?"

Palma was right. Nothing which Garcés could say would make Yslas listen, let alone understand. So the friar promised that he would make one more effort to reach the Yuma captain.

It was again late before the friar could get away from the multitudinous calls of the pueblo. It was so late that he decided to eat some supper before he set out for the Yuma village. If he should reach there after dark, so much the better. Perhaps Palma would feel less constrained on a private visit than with the whole village standing round, watching.

When he went into the cooking shed, Sebastián looked up, and a rare smile appeared on his face. "Good, the Old Man is not going out tonight."

"But I am," said the friar, as he took the bowl of atole from the Indian's hands and sat down on a low bench to eat it.

But in a moment he was aware of the silence. He looked up and found the Indian standing with his back braced against one of the supporting posts and a look of sheer terror on his dark face.

"What is the matter, Sebastián?"

"I was down in the village today, and I heard men whispering."

The friar went on eating deliberately, "What nonsense were they whispering?"

"They were saying," and the Indian's voice sank even lower, "they were saying that last night Palma was talking to the scalps."

"Talking—" but before the friar could blurt out any more in the loud voice of outraged good sense, the Indian had caught his arm, and cried, "Hush!"

"Look here, Sebastián, what are you trying to say?"

"Do you not understand?" asked the Indian incredulously.

"I certainly do not. It sounded like"—at a frantic gesture from Sebastián he lowered his voice "talking to scalps!"

"Yes," said the Indian hurriedly, "when the Yumas are dreaming of war, the leader goes and speaks to the scalps. If he hears them laughing together, then he knows that the dead enemies are happy because soon the Yuma dead will be scalps in the jar of the Jalchedunes. But if they are weeping, then he knows that the scalps know that the Yumas will kill the Jalchedunes. And then the Yumas decide that the dreams of war are good dreams."

"Where are these scalps?" The friar hesitated. It sounded like another of Sebastián's stories, and yet—

"In a jar under the floor of Palma's house," said the Indian.

"But this is preposterous. This is a devilish heathen business, and to suppose that Palma, even after he has been baptized, would—"

Sebastián shook his head quietly in the light from the fire under the pot, "Palma is the chief of the Yumas, and the scalps are kept in his house."

"But I have been in that house so many times," protested the friar.

"Old Man, every house has its secrets."

Again, the Indian tried to dissuade Garcés from going down to the Indian village. But he soon perceived that the friar was resolved on going. Then he tried to persuade him to wait until morning. "See"—he pointed to heat lightning in the sky above the river—"it will thunder soon."

"I am less likely to be disturbed if it does storm," Garcés replied quietly, and went out into the night.

The air was heavy and hot, and there was a certain breathless suspension in the quiet of the night. He went along slowly, for he was tired. At first the stillness comforted him, and then it began to worry him.

Suddenly he heard a crackle at his back. He held his breath and waited, and there was another crackle nearer. In a low voice he called out, and Sebastián's voice answered.

"I come, too," he said briefly. The friar found and wrung his hand.

For some minutes the two made their way through the darkness without speaking. Then Sebastián put his hand on the friar's arm, "Wait here until I go ahead and see." Garcés was about to protest, and then he remembered that the almost naked Sebastián would move through the brush more quietly than he could in sandals and habit. They had reached the chapel now. So the friar sat down on the doorstep and waited. There was still no sign of life in the village, but in the distance across the river he could hear the thunder growling now and then. The air was heavy with the breathless expectancy of the storm.

Idly the friar thought that if Palma were not home, he could get back to the height in time to finish reading the day's office before midnight.

Yet he started when he heard the dry brush rustle behind the chapel. And he sprang to his feet. It was Sebastián.

At first the friar could see no sign of life about Palma's house, but Sebastián was groping his way along the laced sapling walls. Suddenly he stopped and pulled Garcés to him and motioned for him to stoop. Kneeling down, the friar caught sight of a chink of light. With a little maneuvering, he found he had a very effective peephole. For the little fire on the dirt floor of the house lighted up spasmodically but effectively a fair share of the interior.

Directly in front of the chink and to one side of the fire, Garcés caught sight of a kneeling figure scrabbling in the dirt of the floor. Then as the figure straightened himself up and came toward them to throw a stick of wood on the fire, the flame leaped up, and the Franciscan saw that it was Palma. For a moment, the Indian stood still there watching the fire, and then he turned back to whatever he had been doing. Garcés twisted and stooped, but he could not see around the bare flanks of Palma, crouched gleaming in the firelight. The Indian seemed to be talking to himself, but the words were quite unintelligible. The friar listened, but he could catch nothing but the rhythmic beat of the voice, as if the man were chanting.

A spell? The friar felt a chill of horror at the thought. And then Palma arose and brought something over to the fire and set it on the ground. It was something large, but not, to judge from the ease of the man's movement, heavy. Palma stepped back, and the now fairly steady glow of the fire fell on something black and shining. Garcés strained his eyes to make out its shape, and he saw that it was a large pottery jar of the same ware of which he had seen fragments in the ruins of the Casa Grande. It must be something very ancient, for the Yumas no longer made such ware, if they ever had. But now he could not see it clearly, for Palma had knelt down on the floor and had put his arms around the jar so that he seemed to be embracing it.

For some minutes Palma knelt there with his head against the jar, and the friar felt his own hair rise as he realized that the Indian chief was listening to whatever was inside it. He caught his breath, and he waited in that terrible stillness for some sound. Finally, he thought he heard a light rustle as if a rat were running through the brush. And at once Palma sprang to his feet, talking aloud as if he were addressing somebody. Now the friar had no difficulty in making out his words, for he was talking in Yuma, and he was all but shouting, "You lie, Pablo! They are laughing together at the Yumas who will die."

Horrified as he was, the friar yet sensed the relief in Palma's voice. He was saying it over and over again, "You lie, Pablo, you lie." Suddenly and astonishingly, he added in Spanish, "Thanks be to God." Then he took the jar in his arms, and he stooped down over the earthen floor beyond the fire. Garcés strained to find an angle from which he could see what he was doing, but in vain. In a few minutes, the Indian stood up and came back to the fire, rubbing his hands. Once he bent over the flame, but the friar could see nothing on the floor beyond. He must have put the jar back into its hole.

Garcés felt a tug at his sleeve and turned to find Sebastián pulling him away. For a moment he hesitated, and then he yielded. There was little light from the fire, and he doubted if he would see any more. With frantic gestures Sebastián was tugging him away. At that moment the first roar of the thunder broke over their heads.

Sebastián was running now, and the friar had all he could do to keep behind him. For a moment he thought of going back to Palma's house and seeking shelter, but he knew instinctively that whatever had been gained this night by the chance of the sound which Palma had heard would be lost if he discovered that his relapse was known.

Once they reached the river bottom below the height, Sebastián slackened a little, but he did not speak. When they were safe within the priests' house Garcés lighted a candle and held it up to see Sebastián face. Its usual sleek brown was a greenish-yellow, and stark terror looked out of the great eyes.

The friar caught his breath with a flash of pain in his side. "There is nothing to be afraid of in that mumbo-jumbo, Sebastián."

The flame of the candle raked the whitewashed timbers of the roof, and the friar putting out his hand to shield the flame, saw that it was shaking. Palma had returned to the rites of his fathers. And he remembered what Gerónimo had said, "Not today, but the day will come!"

$$* \quad VIII \quad *$$

THE RIVER OF THE MARTYRS

I

For the next week nothing happened. That June of 1781 was hot even for the land of the Yumas, and the pueblo on the height and the Indian village in the river bottom alike baked in seeming exhaustion. And then at the end of the week the scouts of the party for Upper California came into the plaza before dawn, and Garcés met them just as he was setting out for the Indian chapel.

For a moment, he thought of turning back to get the church ready for the welcome, for Barreneche had gone over to San Pablo and might not be back in time. But there was still that dismal remnant of his missionary hope, who would doubtless wait half the morning at the Indian chapel. They had their rights, too, for all his discouragement. So Garcés roused Sebastián, asked him to do what he could to make the church ready, and set forth again for the river bottom.

Great was the friar's surprise to find, when he reached the chapel a little late, quite the largest congregation he had seen there for weeks. For a moment—and then his heart stood still. There in the corner stood Palma with two of his younger warriors behind him. The astonished friar stared at the tall figure, but Palma seemed to be completely absorbed in the contemplation of the earthen floor.

Nor, so far as the friar could see when he turned around to face the congregation at various points in the Mass, did Palma ever raise his eyes to look at him. But there he was. The friar shuddered at the full implications of his presence. For in spite of what he had seen a week ago, he had not really accepted the fact of Palma's backsliding. He had hoped that it was a passing weakness, a momentary yielding to fear and old superstition, from which

Palma would slowly pull himself together. Now it was not possible to think that any longer.

As he knelt down at the foot of the altar for the Yuma prayers that usually closed the Mass, he reached a decision. He would make an excuse of the arrival of the party for Upper California and ask Palma to walk back to the height with him. That was the best he could do. But when he rose from his knees and turned around to speak to Palma, the Indian chieftain had already reached the door of the chapel and was leaving the building before the surprised friar could find voice to call to him.

But Garcés had little time to think of Palma that day. For he had hardly finished his breakfast when the first of the Upper California party began to trickle down the river from the ford where they had crossed. By noon all the party were in sight, and by early afternoon they had come up to the church to give thanks. Díaz and Moreno had accompanied Barreneche back to Concepción to greet the visitors, and now the four priests stood in their vestments ready to welcome the traveers to the first settlement they had seen for many a weary mile.

They looked tired, particularly the women and children, and travel-stained and disheveled, but their faces were shining as they came out into the plaza before the church. There were perhaps two dozen soldiers and some thirty-odd settlers with their wives and children. It would be a noble reinforcement for Los Angeles, but now they had forgotten their destination in the sheer relief of reaching civilization once more. There was something profoundly moving and gratifying in the awe with which the newcomers looked at the church and the pueblo behind it.

But even more touching to the friar was the pride of the people of the pueblo. It was their first chance to play host and to show what they had done, to sympathetic and admiring eyes. Both men and women had put on their Sunday best for the occasion, and though some of the older people had been left to guard the pots that were already sending an aroma of cooking meat through the warm air of the late June day, there was a large and excited crowd waiting for the priests to offer up the proper prayers of thanksgiving.

As Garcés listened to the responses of the congregation reverberating through the little church, he felt as if he were waking from a bad dream. There was something so sure, so confident, in the roll of those voices that he could hardly believe that he had been so worried only that morning. And as the company pressed up to kiss the crucifix in his hand, some of the women with tears of gratitude in their eyes, Palma standing there with downcast eyes in the Indian chapel seemed very dim and far-away, and his own shock incredible.

Another young friar had come with the party on his way to the Upper California missions, and now he went over the church with Garcés and afterward walked through the pueblo with him in a glow of admiration.

"It is a beautiful pueblo," he said again and again. "If only we can do half as well."

It was, the friar reflected, a fine sight. The thatched timber and mud buildings had stood the winter rains very well. And the whole little town was neat and clean, with something brisk and stirring about its very appearance. The fields below the height looked bright and neat, too, with countless shoots of glass-like green feathering their reddish brown furrows. Father Garcés turned away from the fields, for they reminded him of things he was glad to forget for a little while. Now the whole pueblo was coming out to the feast, the women of the visiting party almost as fresh and gay as their hostesses. Indeed, their clothes had a brighter color than that of the pueblo women, whose wardrobes were beginning to look a little worn.

But long before the feast was over, Yslas sent a soldier to look for Garcés and Díaz. He must have found the two friars sooner than the commander had anticipated, for when they arrived, Yslas was still talking loudly in his office to his visitors while the friars stood doubtfully in the doorway.

"Mind you, Rivera, they have never liked the arrangement from the start. So all this fuss may be just a scheme for getting their way in spite of everything."

"That's the devil of having to do with priests," said a heavy voice which Garcés at once recognized as that of the doughty captain. "I'm as good a Christian as anyone, but I'll be damned if I know where priests get the ideas they do. Serra—"

Díaz stiffened, and Garcés hastened to clear his throat as noisily as he could. Díaz's lips tightened as he looked at his colleague. But the voices in the next room fell.

They went on talking in low tones, however, while the two friars waited.

"Put a beggar on horseback," muttered Díaz.

"Palma came to church this morning," said Garcés, giving voice to the thought uppermost in his own mind in order to distract his outraged colleague.

"Palma! Well, doesn't he always?" Díaz at once saw through Garcés' clumsy ruse, as the latter knew he would. But for the moment, in his impatience at his colleague's temporizing Díaz forgot the insult of the delay.

"He's been staying away a good deal lately."

"Don't begin worrying about Palma. Pablo is enough to worry about."

"But didn't Father Barreneche tell you what has been happening?"

"Yes," said Díaz grudgingly. "All that trouble over the land is bad, but we must not lose our heads."

At that moment the door of the inner room opened, and Commander Yslas apologized profusely for the discourtesy of keeping them waiting. He and Captain Rivera had had so much business to settle. Father Garcés already knew Captain Rivera, did he not?

Rivera was polite enough but obviously on his guard.

"You have apparently had no trouble with your trip so far?" Garcés courteously opened the conversation.

"None whatever," said the commander confidently. He was wearing a fine new uniform, blue with yellow facings, almost as fine as the one which Bucareli had had made for Palma. In spite of a certain square-set portliness, he was an impressive figure in the military order, and he knew it, as he stood there beside the thinner, more indrawn-looking Yslas.

"Thank God," said Garcés.

"Oh," said the commander, "oh, yes, quite." And then as the little company waited, he stretched out his legs comfortably. "As I was just telling the commander here, what these savages need is a soldier's approach. Mind you, your Reverences, no one has a higher opinion than I of the Church in its own sphere, but here—well, they soon understand that a soldier means business."

Again, Díaz's mouth tightened into a line, but he said nothing. And again Garcés interposed hastily and awkwardly, "How did your animals stand the trip?"

Rivera shook his head approvingly, "You know what the problems of these desert expeditions are, by now, don't you, Father Garcés? I still insist that there would be no trouble if they would give you decent stock and decent horses in the beginning. But try and get anything decent out of these frontier presidios and pueblos!"

"I thought I saw most of your cattle train and horse herd across the river," said Garcés, paying no attention to the puzzled looks of Díaz.

"You did," said Rivera. "Most of the cattle are so worn-out that I don't dare to try to get them across the river. And half the horses are not much better. So I am going to let them feed and get in shape here for the next couple of months, and then I'll take them on to California myself. There is good pasturage over there across the river."

Garcés caught his breath.

"What is the matter?" asked Rivera. "It is the best-looking patch of mesquite that I have seen around here."

"That is it," said Garcés. "It is the best patch of mesquite for miles around since our horses and cattle cleared off the other side of the height."

A suspicious look had come into the face of Yslas, and a warning look into that of Díaz. Only the California commander seemed unaware of the growing tension in the little room.

"Good," he said. "It will last for six weeks at least, and by that time we can go on." And, then, as he saw the friar hesitate, he scowled, "What is the matter? What do you look so worried about?"

Garcés felt the anxious eyes of Díaz on his face, but he persisted. "Simply this, that since the patch in back of the height was destroyed, this is the only good patch of mesquite for quite a distance on the river. The Indians have always counted on the beans for their own food in the late summer."

Rivera stared incredulously at the friar. Commander Yslas flung up his arms, "What have I been telling you? This is what I am up against every time I try to do anything. It is the Indians this, and the Indians that. I do not care if I never hear of the Indians again."

But Rivera smiled, "That is the trouble with you friars. You think that nothing should be changed unless it is what you have planned. The Indians are used to eating this mesquite. If the Indians do not have this mesquite to eat, what will they do? I tell you, your Reverences, what they will do. They will cease their loafing around, and when the settlers offer them a chance to work in their fields and earn their bread in the sweat of their brow like reasonable beings, they will take it. And our settlements will be prosperous, and the king and the Church and honest citizens will get something out of them instead of always spending money on them."

"It will be hard to convince the Indians of that," said Garcés, obstinately, although he knew it was no use to say any more.

Rivera stared at him, "Who said anything about convincing them? Let them starve for once, and they'll learn fast enough."

But Garcés shook his head, "They will rebel first. They will attack the pueblo."

The warning look had vanished from the face of Díaz. He seemed to be completely absorbed in watching how far his colleague would go. A look of uncertainty had come into the face of Commander Yslas. Clearly, he had not yet forgotten the arrows. He was watching the face of the friar, too, as if he suspected that the latter knew more of this than he had told.

Only Rivera seemed completely undisturbed. He laughed, "You have been among the Indians too long, Father Garcés. You have forgotten the power of the King of Spain. What would the Indians fight with? Arrows against guns?" He laughed again at the absurdity of the picture.

"The Indians have fought arrows against guns, and Spaniards have died from those arrows," said the friar. It was warm in the room, but Yslas shivered.

Rivera was still scornful, however, "Oh, you've been reading some of those old martyrologies of yours. That was a long time ago. Our guns are better, for one thing "

"But the Yumas have something better than arrows," said Garcés.

"What?" asked both soldiers at once.

"War clubs!"

"Clubs? I haven't seen any clubs," said Yslas. "And I haven't heard of any."

"You have not seen the Yumas at war—yet," the friar added the last word after a pause.

Commander Yslas turned to Díaz. "Father Díaz, Father Garcés has been trying to scare me for days now with the notion that there is restlessness among the Yumas."

Díaz swallowed. He had been so absorbed in following the discussion that he had not thought of taking part in it himself. Now he broke in hastily, "Oh, there is restlessness among the Yumas all right. In fact, it is worse with us than at Concepción, I am sure. I have already told you about Pablo, and—"

For the first time Rivera looked as if he might be taking what was said seriously. He looked from Díaz to Yslas.

But the latter hastened to interrupt Díaz. "I know all that, your Reverence; I have seen the arrows, too. But what I mean is that all this is just among the Indians themselves; it doesn't touch us, does it?"

But once Díaz had joined in the argument, he was not the man to draw back. Now he shook his head positively. "We can't count on it. In fact, most men who have lived on the frontier, whether soldiers or missionaries, have held that any extended war between the tribes is bound to involve us, too.

When men are once on the warpath, they don't discriminate anymore."

Rivera looked soberly at Díaz. "He is talking sense, that one. I have always said that it was necessary to keep the Indians in their place, and keep them apart."

He was sober enough now, but still confident. A pleading note came into the voice of Commander Yslas, however, as he turned from Díaz to Garcés, "But, I am sure it has not gone anyway near that far yet, has it, Father Garcés?"

Garcés shook his head compassionately. "It has come very close to it."

Commander Yslas flushed, and a note of indignation came into his voice, "But I have counted on you to hold Palma to his duty."

Díaz caught his breath and waited. Garcés shrugged his shoulders miserably, "I am afraid Palma hasn't much faith in me anymore. He doesn't see why he should listen to me when he knows that no one else does." Curiously enough, there was no note of personal complaint in his voice, and the other men in the room unconsciously recognized it.

It was Rivera who broke the uncomfortable silence, "It looks as if I came along just in time. With a dozen of my men across the river there, you won't need to worry about Palma, whoever he is."

But Commander Yslas hesitated, "Father Garcés doesn't think that even with your men we'll have enough if the Yumas really take the warpath."

"Nonsense!" shouted Rivera. "It is time I came along, Yslas. You have been listening to the croakings of these friars too long. Of course, with all the attention they pay to the Indians, they're always hearing tales. But this is our business. We know what force is needed to hold a situation. It's a soldier's job. These good friars are in such a rush to get us to a better world that sometimes they hurry it a bit." And he laughed heartily, but he was the only one who saw anything funny in his jest. Both Commander Yslas and Díaz were looking at Garcés as if they thought he might tell them more than he had, and yet as if they dreaded to ask him.

So the interview ended. As they came out into the plaza of the pueblo, they saw that the sun was much lower in the sky now, and there was a soft glow on the raw surfaces of the settlement. Someone was playing a violin, and the younger people were dancing on the packed earth of the plaza. Nothing could be in sharper contrast to the conversation that had just ended.

Díaz put his hand on Garcés' arm, "So you think that trouble is at hand?"

Garcés nodded, a great pity filling his heart as he watched the bright colors of the girls' dresses whirling among the soberer figures of the men.

"I think you are right," said Díaz slowly.

2

A week later a great silence had settled over the hill of Concepción. Part of it was due to the weather, dead and unmoving July heat that baked the life out of everything that dared to thrust itself above the parched earth. But still more was due to the two moral crises through which the settlement had just passed.

The first came when Rivera decided to send back some of the settlers for California to Sonora. There were two of the families that had stood the trip so far but poorly. There were three of the single men who had given trouble, too, discontented at the slightest provocation, and apt to break ranks for a bit of hunting, or a petty raid on Indian fields or storage baskets. They were poor prospects for a remote colony like Los Angeles, and they embraced the chance to go back to the security of Sonora when Rivera offered it to them.

Some of the women at Concepción had stared wistfully after them as they rode away to the east. And Garcés had looked at some of the younger women, fresh and pretty in their now somewhat dingy everyday dresses, and he had thought of what their fate was likely to be when the Indian attack came. For a few minutes he had been tempted to ask the commander to send them back, too. But even to suggest that to Yslas would be sure to seem nothing better than desertion in the face of the enemy.

The second crisis came the next day when the rest of the party went on with about half the soldiers to Upper California. Strangely enough, this was harder on the women of the settlement than the departure for Sonora. After all, these women who went on to Los Angeles were comrades in the same sort of adventure. At any rate, the fiesta atmosphere went with them, in the cloud of dust that plunged into the jungle of the river bottom behind them.

Only a dozen of Rivera's soldiers, with half a dozen of the men who had come from the Upper California presidios to meet them, remained encamped on the eastern bank of the river with the cattle and horses. Their campfires seen in the morning and at night gave one a friendly sense of company of one's own kind within reach. But even so, they intensified the sense of isolation in a vast and alien world that seemed to close in upon the height those exhausting summer days.

Garcés suggested a novena for the safe arrival of the Upper California party, and he found that the idea was welcome to the women of the pueblo. This at least they could do to help these comrades of theirs who had gone out into the wilderness for their far-off new home. It was touching to see the eagerness with which these women, so lonely and so homesick themselves, reached out in prayer to help women who were even lonelier and farther from the homes they would never see again.

Garcés still went down to the Indian chapel, but here he found that he was only holding on to a faithful remnant of his original hope. Palma came no more, nor any of his young men. The friar made several attempts to see the chief at his house, but it was always the same story. Palma was away on business for the tribe. First, it was to find new places for the summer planting of peas and beans and corn. The friar winced at that excuse, and he thought he caught a look of satisfaction on the face of Palma's daughter, who was watching him closely. Another time, Palma was busy with a dispute which had arisen in another village. And on still another occasion, he had gone to visit some allies of the Yumas. Garcés suspected that the actual excuse did not much matter. Palma was keeping out of his reach.

Once Garcés sent a message to Palma by Gerónimo's wife. It was a simple one, that he felt sure would reach Palma without garbling from the various lips through which it must pass. It was that if Palma would send a guide to bring the friar to him, he would go anywhere Palma wished, to see him.

"You are a really brave man," said the old Jamajab, when the friar had made his wife repeat the message to make sure that there would be no mistake.

"What is there to fear?" asked the friar. And Gerónimo looked at him very thoughtfully.

The message did reach Palma, for the answer he sent was a repetition of what he had said the last time the friar talked with him. "Tell the Old Man that if the Spaniards will listen to him, then I will listen to him."

The friar winced when Gerónimo's wife repeated that message. He had said something like this himself to Díaz, but the latter had reminded him that it was the Indian missions to which he had devoted himself. And that had meant that in many ways he had cut himself off from his own people. But that suggestion did not bring much comfort to Garcés. For it had never seemed to him that the difference between civilized and uncivilized man was so important as most men made out. And if there had ever been a time when he felt more at home with a Spanish soldier than with an Indian, that time was long past.

But now the Indian was pretty much beyond his reach. True, there were the women and the children and the old men who still came to the little chapel; however, they were not only dwindling in numbers before his eyes, but there was little in their aspect to cheer him. Three of the boys were making progress in their Latin with Barreneche, who had the instincts of a teacher. But most of the little group came day after day with a docility and a stolid inertia that gave the anxious friar little encouragement. He felt that he must not fail them; so he went to them faithfully. But he had no illusion now that they were the seeds of any future.

On the other hand, he was becoming increasingly conscious of his duty to the people of the pueblo. He was their pastor, and he saw the day of judgment that was coming upon them as they could not. So he set himself to do all he could to make them ready for that day. It would not be an easy thing to manage. For whatever he was to do must be accomplished within the framework of the normal Christian approach to day-to-day life. If he began to tell his people that the pueblo was doomed, the commander would most certainly send him back to Sonora, and then there would be nothing he could do.

But there was more to it than that. For these simple men and women, the building of the pueblo, the maintenance of the health of the family, the day-by-day bringing up of the children, the knitting-up of the community life in the little charities and sociabilities of the daily routine, these were the instruments of their salvation. And these must be preserved with faith and devotion to the end. This was the saving grace of God's denial of foreknowledge to men, and Garcés saw that here he must not tamper with the safeguard of the divine mercy.

So he began to preach to his people at the Sunday Mass on the simplest of Christian themes: "For what is your life? It is a vapor which appeareth for a little while, and afterwards shall vanish away." He began with the concern which they had all felt for the safe journey of the Upper California party. He pointed out that in reality the party did not face any greater perils than people faced constantly in the older settlements. Death walked every day in Sonora. The perils of childbirth, a runaway horse, a fall from a roof, the slip of a knife, sickness—all of these inevitable accidents of normal life were there. No man when he came to think of it could be sure that he would be alive when the night fell, still less when the next Sunday came. When men faced a new and strange world, they became aware of the insecurity of life as if it were something new and strange. But, actually, there was nothing new or strange in it. Insecurity was the oldest and the most normal and the most fixed fact of human life. They should be grateful to the anxieties of pioneer existence, for they brought home to men the basic facts of all human life.

With a smile Garcés observed that all who were listening to him were looking unusually grave. If that meant that they were thinking seriously about what he was saying, that was good. If it meant that they were feeling depressed or frightened, then they were not facing these facts as a Christian should. For to the Christian there was no terror in the contemplation of the uncertainty of life. To the Christian the length of life was not the important thing but the kind of life. Anyone who had read the martyrology knew that there were men and women who had become converted to Christ in time of persecution and who had laid down their lives shortly afterward. And yet they had in those few days, sometimes not much more than hours, become saints. And everyone knew men and women who had had many years of life, and yet had done little to overcome their weaknesses and to do penance for their sins, so that length of days had been a loss to them rather than a gain. One day lived with the purpose to make it as perfect a day as possible might be worth more than fifty years lived blindly and indifferently.

But what day? There was but one answer to that for any rational man who remembered the insecurity of life. Today. This day, this hour, this moment. It might be all of life that God had given one, and yet it could be quite enough for a man to make up his mind that he would ask but one thing, that the will of God might be wholly fulfilled in him. If one did that, then he would cease to worry about the insecurity of life, for he would know that if it were the will of God that he should have but one day, that would be enough.

That did not mean that what he did with that day was not important. Quite the contrary. One day might be an infinitely precious thing. For in that one day one might lay hold upon God. And to lay hold upon God was to lay hold upon eternal life.

That meant that today one did those things that, if he died tonight, he would want to have done. Today one took stock of himself and asked if he were doing all that a Christian should; today one made the complete and absolute offering of himself to God that the will of God might be wholly fulfilled in him. Today, not tomorrow.

All this he said very simply and very directly, standing on the altar step in the little church, with the eyes of all his congregation upon him. The complete silence told him that they were listening attentively. So he forgot his usual diffidence, and it seemed to him that he was talking with each of those men and women in front of him, appealing to him or her individually. He was pleading with Rosalía that she who was so strong and decisive should be more patient with the slow and more humble with the weak. He was bidding Barbara not to worry so about her flock. He was entreating Doña Francisca Manuela to forget her disappointment and her discontent and to embrace the opportunity of usefulness that her husband's position in the pueblo and her own intelligence offered to her. He was asking Juan Miguel to be less anxious about everything, and Mateo, the blacksmith, to be a little more careful with his work, and José Barragan not to think so much about the aguardiente, and Gabriel Tebaca not to grab every patch of fertile ground he could find.

And they responded as he had never dreamed they would. For quite blindly and instinctively they recognized that he was speaking out of a surer knowledge than anything they possessed, that he had hold of something they would be needing. Of his inmost fears he said nothing. For they had ceased to be fears in the deep urgency that they had bred. There was little time now. That classic commonplace of all Christian preachers had become quite literally true. And he must wake the sleepers to use what little time yet remained for heart and will and mind. Those who listened to him that Sunday could not guess the springs of his certainty, but they caught the impact of the urgency.

They showed it in many ways. Some began to come to Mass every morning and to vespers in the afternoon. Others who had not been to the sacraments even for Easter came up to the priests' house to ask if they might make their confession. Rosalía astonished Juan Miguel when she told him not to worry when at sight of her coming across the plaza, he remembered an errand she had given him to do in the fields. And one day when Garcés arrived at the house of old Michaela, whose heart could not stand the hot weather, he was astonished to find Doña Francisca Manuela already there with some cooling herb drink which she had brought in a linen-swathed water bottle from her own house. On the hottest day of the summer, the friar met some of the laborers returning from the fields. He had alluded to the opportunities for charity in the day's work in his sermon the day before, and one at least of the settlers had remembered. So he found many little evidences that all sorts of men and women were taking to heart the things he was saying from the altar step. And that unexpected success whetted his yearning.

In the beginning he had prayed that whatever time he had might not be wasted. Now he asked that it might be enough to wake all his flock that they might be ready. And one thing more he prayed, that when the storm came, he might be spared long enough to seek out the laggards and the strays who had been slow in heeding his call. For now he felt perfectly sure that the end would come before he had time to round up all his flock.

He had been praying thus in the darkening church after vespers one hot night of that mid-July. Suddenly, it seemed to him that he was stifling, that he must have more air if he were to breathe any longer. So he went out into the little plaza in front of the church to see if he might catch a breath of the cool wind that came out of the desert at sunset. But it seemed that night as if there were not a leaf stirring in the cottonwoods down on the edge of the flood bottom of the river or in the ironwood and mesquite trees on the rim of the banks.

The whole river world seemed suspended in the quiet of that airless moment. He tried to think of all the Indian rancherías hidden among those trees and in the brush below. He tried to think of all those days of traveling he had spent down there. He tried to think of the bell that now would never break that stillness. But he could not. Those were things of which he had dreamed, in that past when he was always moving on from one village to another, from one dream to another. And this was the end of it all, here on this barren height, waiting for the storm to break.

This was the first time he had settled down where he was, to do what the Lord had given him to do, without any looking beyond the day's work. In the fullness of his time God would make manifest His presence on the river. That was no longer any affair of Francisco Garcés. His task was something much smaller, much simpler, here in this little space, in these few days, to lead his flock safely home through the storm he could not avert. If that were granted, he would ask nothing more for this world.

3

THE habit of silence about his deepest preoccupations had become so fixed in Garcés' consciousness these last weeks that it hardly occurred to him to wonder how all this sudden fever of activity must strike his young colleague. Once or twice Garcés thought he caught a curious, if not speculative look, in the tired eyes that confronted him at supper, but it seemed brutal to cast any of his burden upon those valiant young shoulders. So he would ask Barreneche how his Latin class in the chapel was coming on, or he would tell him some absurdity of the day in the pueblo, and they would smile together over the Indian boy's question or the Spanish boy's comment on human life.

Once when Garcés looked up from reading his breviary in the candle-light and surprised Barreneche's eyes upon him, he realized that the time would come when he must share his knowledge with him. But the young friar was so obviously tired and in need of his bed for the morning's early rising that he put it off for that night. And the next night they had company from the pueblo; so there was no chance then. And the next, Garcés was too tired himself to undertake the labor of explanation, to his temperament only less uncongenial than the labor of composition.

But he was hardly surprised when one morning in the middle of July Barreneche met him as he was coming from a sick-call, and asked if he might see him at once. There were a couple of other calls which Garcés had planned to get in before dinner that day, but at sight of the insistence in the young man's face, he hastily revised his plans. However, Barreneche did not speak until they reached the priests' house.

Then he came straight to the point, "Have you ever seen a red and black club among the Yumas?"

Garcés caught his breath. It had been Barreneche's turn to go down to the Indian chapel to say Mass.

"Yes," he said.

"Is it something they use in their ceremonials?" There was no mistaking the anxiety and the suspicion in the young friar's face.

Garcés hesitated, and then he decided that he had better be quite frank about this at least. "I should have said not. You see, I really know very little about the ceremonies of the Yumas because since I have known them they have been in the process of becoming Christians. I feel quite sure that there have been a good many of the old practices going on, but you can understand that they would be kept under cover, at least so far as I am concerned."

"Then you have never seen such a club?" The young man for all his habitual respect for his senior found it hard to conceal his disappointment.

"No, I wouldn't say that," Garcés hastened to correct the impression. "I was speaking only of the ceremonies. I have seen such a club in Palma's house and in other houses. It is a war club, the weapon upon which they rely in serious fighting."

Barreneche looked puzzled. "This didn't look strong enough for that."

Garcés smiled, "If it is the weapon I have had in my hands, it is, I assure you, quite strong enough to beat a man to death. It is of mesquite wood. But why do you ask?"

"You know that Nifora that we used to see with Palma sometimes? The one with the limp? They said he was taken as a child in one of their raids on the Jalchedunes and brought up as a slave?"

"Yes, he has always seemed a little cringing for an Indian, and the others do not attempt to hide their scorn of him. What about him?"

"He was painting the head of the club with red patterns on black, and doing a very careful job of it." Anxiety had made Barreneche very precise.

"Where did you see this?"

The young friar sat down. "You remember that little son of Palma's brother who has been in my Latin class? He hasn't come for several days now. So I went over to where their winter house was to see if I could find out whether he was ill or what the matter was. When I got there, there was nobody around but the Nifora. In fact, I should not have found him, but when no one answered my call, I went in. This fellow was quite alone, and he looked surprised. I suspect he had been so busy with what he was doing that he had not heard me."

"And he told you that he was getting the club ready for a dance?"

Barreneche smiled, "Yes, and he said that perhaps I had not better say anything to you, for you would not approve of the dance. He didn't seem worried about my approval."

"And no sign of the boy you had been looking for?"

"None. But what I want to know is, what is the significance of the club? And do the Indians usually go away this way in the summer? There was almost nobody at Mass, and only one of the boys came to class." The uneasiness of Barreneche had at last found expression, and his voice rose sharply with, the older friar now saw, all the unspoken questions of the last weeks.

That tone was not lost on Garcés' ear. He braced himself for the explanation ahead. "It is a war club which the Nifora was decorating. He may have been decorating it for a dance as he said." He hesitated. Now was no time to lose sight of the possibility that the less dramatic explanation might be the true one.

"But you don't think so?" The young man pounced at once on his hesitation.

Again, the older friar hesitated. "No, I don't think so," he answered at last.

"You mean he is getting that club ready to use seriously?"

Garcés nodded. He could see the next question in the large eyes of the young man. But before he could make up his mind how he should answer it, there came a knock at the door.

It was Díaz. His worried face broke into a slight smile at the warmth of Garcés' greeting. Then he looked at Barreneche. The young friar had got hold of himself now, and he came forward with his usual cordiality. Then Garcés went to the cooking shed to ask Sebastián to be sure of an extra portion for dinner. But he found Sebastián gazing thoughtfully at the door, and when Garcés appeared, he drew back as if he had been caught eavesdropping.

Garcés closed the door carefully behind him and turned to his guest. "It is good to see you." For a moment he wondered if he should tell him about the Nifora's war club. Perhaps he had better wait.

"Thank you," said Díaz. "But I need not tell you that I have not ridden over in this heat and at this time just for the pleasure of seeing you."

"What has happened?" Garcés could guess, but his heart beat quickly at the look on Díaz's face.

"Pablo has come back. You know he has been away for some weeks now, and no one has been able to give any real information as to where he has been, or, what I suspect is more like the truth, no one has been willing to say."

"Or perhaps dared to," Garcés added.

"Maybe," said Díaz indifferently. "At any rate he is back now. And a good many more Indians are to be seen down in the river bottom and in the woods along the banks. Not doing anything in particular, but there they are."

"Nothing to indicate plans for a dance or anything like that?"

Díaz shook his head, and then he added more cautiously, "Of course, there might be signs that you would recognize, but there is nothing that I can see."

Then Garcés nodded to his young colleague, and the latter told briefly the story of the Nifora and the war club. When he had finished, both of his companions looked at Garcés.

But he turned to Barreneche, "As you went through the village, did you form any impression that the people were coming back?"

"I am sure that they were not," said the young man positively.

"That may give us some time," said Díaz.

"I have tried to see Palma repeatedly. I can get no clue as to where he is. I'll ask Sebastián to help me."

"Perhaps," said Díaz thoughtfully, "we ought to tell the commander this."

"I don't think he will believe it," said Garcés, "but we ought to tell him nevertheless."

Garcés had foreseen, Yslas was incredulous. "But it is so hot that I cannot imagine anybody would start anything he didn't have to."

But Díaz presented his evidence patiently, and Garcés could see that the commander was impressed.

"What do you want me to do?" He looked from one friar to the other. Then he seemed to have an idea. "I am sending a courier to Arizpe with a report this afternoon. Do you think I should ask that those soldiers who are still owing to us for our guard should be sent at once?"

"It is too late," said Garcés quietly. "They will not get here in time." He had spoken on impulse, without reflection. His companions were staring at him in astonishment.

With an effort Yslas smiled, "Oh, come, Father Garcés, how can you say that? Surely, you don't think it is as bad as that, Father Díaz?"

"I am afraid I do," said Díaz.

For a minute no one spoke in the hot little room. Outside in the blazing sunshine they could hear the steady hum of gnats.

"Can't you do something with Palma, Father Garcés? He has always had such a respect for you—they all have."

Briefly the friar summed up the history of his efforts to appeal to Palma.

"Would it do any good to seize this rascal Pablo?"

"He would slip through your fingers," said Garcés.

"Can't you suggest anything?" asked the commander plaintively.

"I think that you might bring the people from our pueblo over here," said Díaz slowly.

The commander was delighted to be able to do anything. Tomorrow he would expect them. And tomorrow he would have Captain Rivera bring his men over too. If the Indians were planning mischief, they would be ready.

"Tomorrow?" Garcés repeated doubtfully.

"That is the earliest possible," said Díaz. "We shall have to work all tonight to be able to do it tomorrow."

Reluctantly, Garcés admitted it was true. The commander was inviting the friars to have dinner with him. But they declined. If things were to be set moving, Díaz must get away as soon as possible.

As he ate the stew Sebastián set before him, Díaz had a sudden idea, "I think we should send a report by that courier. You can do that this afternoon, Father Garcés."

"But what shall I say?" Garcés had been thinking that he would make one more effort to reach Palma that afternoon. "Haven't we said all that we could say? What else is there to say?"

Díaz's lips tightened in a straight line. "We can say that the things we have predicted have come to pass. And with your taste for giving the devil his due, you can add that for the first time the commander has listened to something that we have said."

The two friars of Concepción accompanied their guest to the church to ask for a blessing on his return journey. And when they had finished, he took leave of them at the doorway, "Look for us, then, before sunset tomorrow." Then Garcés became aware that his companion was staring at him with solemn eyes.

"Now we must do our part," said Garcés briskly. "And first of all, let's see Sebastián."

But Sebastián shrank away in fright when Garcés asked him to see if he could not find Palma and give him a message.

"He is not at home," he said firmly.

"I know he is not. But he is somewhere near, and there are people down there who know. There is the wife of the Jamajab, for instance. If you do not go, I shall have to go myself," said the friar firmly.

But at that Sebastián thrust out his hands in terrified pleading, "That will do no good."

"I do not think it will, either," said the friar. "That is why I am asking you to find Palma and tell him that I will meet him anywhere he suggests, only I must see him at once." At a sudden thought, he took the crucifix from his breast, "Here, he will know this. Show it to him that it may plead for me." But Sebastián would not take it.

"Let me go alone," he pleaded, and the friar put the crucifix back on his breast.

Then he took pen and ink and a sheet of paper and sat down at the table.

Yslas had said that he would send the courier in an hour, and half of that time had now gone. But what should he say? A sentence from a prayer of Saint Francis came into his mind, "My Lord, grant that I may not be anxious to be understood but only to understand." That was what he wanted to say. He wanted to get some word of this experience back to his brethren in Querétaro. So he began to write, "We have failed. It is not because we have not tried. It is because we have not understood." That was so clear that it seemed foolish to have written it. He considered beginning over again, but he knew that his time was running out. So he took a firm grip on his pen and began a new paragraph. "There is one thing that we ask now. It is this. There will be talk of punishing the guilty. It is very hard to find the guilty in such an affair as this. The innocent and the ignorant and the helpless will suffer, too, and that will breed hate and a desire for revenge, and the cycle will begin all over again. Only forgiveness will cut the evil round, and make it possible to begin again."

He looked over the badly scrawled sheet, but even as he looked, the courier was at the door. So he added, "Pray for us," and signed his name, and gave it to the soldier. And then he took up his breviary. Later, when Sebastián had returned, he might not have time to say the day's office.

He had finished it and was sitting there in the swiftly fading light of the desert world when he heard the hand on the door. Sebastián had come sooner than he could have hoped.

But it was not Sebastián. It was Gerónimo. It was a long time since he had come up into the pueblo, and the friar ran to the door to welcome him.

Then he motioned to him to sit down, but the Jamajab shook his head. "I have only a moment. They are busy talking over there in the woods, and I must be back in the village before they get there."

"Sebastián found you?"

"Yes."

"Where is he?"

Gerónimo looked at him. "You must not blame him. Palma told him that if he came back to the pueblo, he would kill him."

"Palma!"

The Jamajab smiled wryly. "The day has come."

"Where is Palma?"

Gerónimo shook his head. "He will not see you. He said that if any friend of the Old Man heard his voice, he should tell the Old Man to leave the pueblo at once. I think he guessed that I would try to see you."

"You know I cannot leave."

"Yes, I never thought you would. But I wanted to tell you one thing. My wife and I will give you shelter at any time."

"Thank you. You are running too great a risk," said the friar anxiously.

The old Jamajab smiled. "The living are here, and the dead are here." He lifted his hand above his head. "There is only a little dust between, and nothing of which a wise man need be afraid, as the Old Man knows."

"And Sebastián?"

"He has always been afraid of the dead, that one, of those who have died, and those who will die."

And without a word the old man vanished as swiftly as he had come. Garcés stood in the doorway, looking out into the dusk. He heard a quick step.

It was Barreneche.

He shut the door quietly and came up to Garcés. The latter took the young friar's hands and made him sit down.

"It will not be long now," said Garcés quietly.

"What shall we do?"

Garcés smiled. "The people will be here for vespers now. We shall go in and say vespers. And then we shall cook our supper."

"Supper?" The young man looked incredulous.

"Supper is an office that no good friar misses," Garcés replied lightly, and watched the strained face relax.

"You make it all seem very simple," said the young friar doubtfully as they entered the sacristy.

"It is simple," said Garcés. "Remember that if we could not do it, Our Lord would not have given it to us to do."

4

THE next morning, both friars went down to the chapel together at dawn. It was Barreneche's turn to go, and he refused to yield to Garcés' request that he let him go in his stead. So they had compromised by going together. But nothing happened. Except for the handful of women and children and a couple of old men who made up the little congregation, there was no sign of life in the Indian village. So Barreneche said Mass, and Garcés served. And if the congregation wondered at the two friars' coming together, they gave no sign but listened stolidly. Only when Mass was over, and the doctrine had been recited, a few of them still lingered in the doorway. And when Garcés looked back halfway down the path through the Indian village, they still stood there, gazing after the departing friars with the same stolid composure.

By the time the two friars came in sight of the height, the early morning coolness was wearing thin, and the sun was beating down on the river bottom. Already most of the settlers and the laborers were scattered through the fields.

Some of them raised their hoes and spades as the friars came to the path that went up to the height, and the friars waved in return. But for the heat that was settling like a blanket on the world, it was a beautiful day.

That morning almost all the women and children of the pueblo were in church, but as Garcés had expected, very few of the men. In the front of the church Commander Yslas stood quietly beside his wife, while in the back Corporal Baylon hovered on guard. While José swung the sacristy door open and folded his hands for the solemn entrance into the sanctuary, Garcés looked over the congregation and for the moment felt content. Then he noticed that Teresa was there in a corner close to the sanctuary, her large eyes fixed anxiously on José. That was curious. For some weeks now she had not been coming to the hill but going to the chapel in the village, for she was heavy with child.

And then Garcés forgot everything but the words of the Mass. "Kyrie eleison, kyrie eleison, kyrie eleison." José who had fumbled a little with the first responses was answering steadily now, and the mighty rhythm of the Mass was sweeping up both the celebrant and the server in one antiphonal unit. The rhythm broke a little when Garcés began to read the Epistle, for he had to pay more attention to these words which he did not say every day. But he finished the reading and closed the book, and waited for José to carry it from one side of the altar to the other.

There was a rustle as the women rose from their knees, and Garcés looked over the now standing congregation. Then as José laid the missal on the altar, Garcés turned back to read the Gospel. It was at that moment that he heard a yell outside, followed by a thud and a scream that soon choked off in a gurgle. With one hand outstretched to the book on the altar, Garcés stood frozen. Behind him he could hear the stillness in the church. Slowly he turned to face the congregation. There was that same frozen look on all the faces before him, that same look to all the standing bodies, as if they were poised on the empty air and might in a moment, when that support vanished, fall on their faces. It seemed to him that he must have stood for a full minute gazing on that breathless immobility. And then the whole air was shattered by a tremendous tumult.

The friar raised his still-outstretched hand, and he heard his own voice speaking as if from the other side of the church, "Just stay where you are." And then he was striding to the door. But Commander Yslas had reached it ahead of him, just behind Corporal Baylon, who had flung it open. There was a roar of sound from the blazing plaza outside, and then the roar seemed to burst through the open door. At his back the friar could hear a woman scream, but in front a wild fury had hurled itself upon Yslas.

The friar put out his hand to catch the bare brown body that had seized the commander, but Yslas broke from the Indian's grip, and running to the edge of the plaza, he shouted in a loud, clear voice to the fields below, "To arms, to arms!" Through the pueblo behind him the cry was taken up and echoed by the voices of a couple of the soldiers who had remained on duty in the guardhouse and by the laborers in charge of the horses and the cattle in the pastures behind the pueblo.

But a whirlwind of flailing arms and legs had seized on Yslas even as he was shouting, and now the astounded friar saw the flash of the red and black war clubs. He heard, too, a muffled gasp, and then he forgot everything but the effort to make his voice heard above the yelling of the Indians and the smashing thuds of the war clubs. He was tossed to one side, but as he fell, he saw José rush into the whirling tangle of brown bodies. A moment later, Garcés staggered to his feet, in time to see one of the dreaded clubs come crashing down on the young soldier's head.

Then the whirlpool of noise and thrashing limbs and bodies broke apart in front of the friar, and he saw one of the Indians pulling off Yslas' braided coat, while another tugged at his knee breeches. The commander's face had vanished in a pulp from which the bright blood was streaming over the dusty ground on which the body had been thrown. Again, the friar put out a futile hand, but before he could even find voice to protest, the blood-drenched clothes had been torn off, and the naked body flung out over the edge of the height. For an instant the white limbs flew out, sprawled against the brilliant blue of the sky, and then in a gush of blood from head and belly the mangled corpse plunged into the river far below.

Rooted with horror, the friar stood there and watched the reddish-brown river splash into foam as the body hit its sluggish surface. Then as if the far-away waters had found a voice, there came a muffled scream like the scream of an eagle on the rocky heights of the Gila Range. And looking over the edge of the bluff, the friar caught sight of some of the men who had been working in the fields running toward the height. Then in the silence he heard a light sigh behind him and turned just in time to see Doña Francisca Man-uela sink to the doorstep of the church.

But before he could reach her, he had to push a couple of half-fright-ened, half-inquisitive boys back into the church, and as he did so, he saw the body of José. He knelt down by his side. The young soldier's head was wet with blood, but he was still breathing.

The friar looked around. The tumult had swept away from the church, and he could hear the Indians yelling and thrashing their clubs around the corner of the pueblo. Perhaps they had gone to meet the men from the fields. He looked around the plaza. In the middle, in a pool of darkening blood, already buzzing with flies, lay doubled up a uniformed body with only bleed-ing pulp for a head. The friar looked at the uniform again—it was Corporal Baylon. Beyond, another soldier was lying doubled up in the same contorted fashion, but though his face was bleeding, he had apparently managed to dodge the worst force of the blow. As the friar stooped over him, he could hear the man's breathing, harsh and deep. So he knelt down and began the prayers for the dying. Before he had finished, the labored breathing rose al-most to a roar in the friar's ears, and then abruptly it ceased.

The friar finished the last blessing of the now dead body, and then bent over to close the horror-stricken eyes. As he did so the body relaxed and fell back so that he caught sight of the torn belly. Sick with horror, he turned away to find himself looking into the staring eyes of an Indian propped against the wall of the church. As he bent over him, Garcés recognized one of the men of the village whose wife and children used to come to Mass in the chapel, who had come sometimes himself. He had been thrust with a sword, probably Yslas' in his first rush from the door of the church. The sword had gone deep, and even as the friar stared at him, the man's eyes were glazing. Almost without thinking, Garcés dipped his fingers in the Indian's blood and signed his forehead with the cross, repeating the words of baptism. When he had finished, the eyes focused suddenly with a look of recognition, and then went blank.

There was no one else in the plaza now but the three dead men. Away in the distance the friar could hear the yelling and smashing of the war party. But the exercise of his functions in the last few minutes had freed him from the palsy of horror. With a clear head and steady nerves, he turned back to the church.

There he faced a scene of complete confusion. The women were clutching their children in tireir arms, and the children were crying as if they all expected to be massacred the next moment. Doña Francisca Manuela had come out of her faint and was sitting on the floor, sobbing and rocking herself back and forth on her haunches hysterically, while her mestizo maid tried noisily to comfort her. There was only one quiet place in the church, the sanctuary, and here Teresa, the Indian girl, sat very still with a bloody head in her lap while Barreneche worked over the blood-soaked body lying on the altar step.

"You are right; they are devilish things, the way they jab and smash," he said through tight lips as the older friar came up.

"Have you given him absolution?" Garcés asked in a whisper.

There was consternation on the white face of the young friar. "I have been so busy," he stammered, pointing to the blood-stained linen he was pushing into the broken body. Teresa was gently wiping the swollen face with a wet cloth; now she turned large eyes to Garcés.

But already he was kneeling by José and murmuring the now quite automatic words of the prayers for the dying. When he had finished, he rose and called his colleague's attention to José's face. It was purple from the blows and the bleeding, but even as they looked, the pallor of death was seeping through the bruises. Then Garcés took the head from between Teresa's hands and laid the body flat on the floor of the chancel. The clean towel which José had less than half an hour ago put on top of the little table to the side of the altar, for the ablutions of the Mass, Garcés laid gently over his still face. And then he took Teresa's hand and said, "There will be time enough to mourn the dead later. You must think of your child now." And he led her into the quiet of the sacristy and made her sit down while he went to the cupboard for the flask of wine.

Then he went into the priests' house and through that to the door that looked out into the main plaza of the pueblo. It was a scene of indescribable desolation, broken weapons, both Indian and Spanish, torn clothes, shattered furniture, dead bodies, but it was now quite deserted, unbelievably quiet in the heavy sunshine of that summer morning. From the rear of the pueblo he could hear the bellowing of a steer, the yells of the Indians, and one or two sharper cries that he hoped the women would be too busy to hear.

But here it was so quiet that Garcés started when he heard a step behind him. He turned quickly, and he was ashamed of his relief at beholding Barreneche. The young friar's face was white and sharp with horror, but there was in the bright eyes a light of excitement that made the older friar bless afresh the quick response of youth even to disaster.

A slight relaxation of relief came into Barreneche's face, too, and then a look of bewilderment.

"What I don't understand," he said, "is why none of the men have yet come up from the fields. Surely they heard Yslas' cry, and if they didn't, they must have seen his body."

"I doubt if they heard the cry, but they must have seen the body. I saw some of them running. They certainly heard the uproar."

"What do you think has happened, then?"

Garcés hesitated. There was no use now in trying to spare his young colleague. "It is hard to tell, but the most reasonable guess would be that they were cut off before they reached the path up the height. Some Indians could have come out of the village there without our knowing it."

Barreneche looked at his superior, "I want to go down there and see what has happened."

Garcés shook his head. "Don't forget that over there back of the pueblo there is another group of at least half a dozen men whom we do know something about. We heard the tumult over in the meadows where the cattle and horses are, and it's all quiet now. I think we had better take a look there even before we go down to the river."

"One of us could go one way, and the other the other?"

But Garcés shook his head. "No. If anybody is alive, we'll need help to get him up here. And if we run into an ambush, there is a chance that one of us might be able to break away and give a warning for whatever it would be worth."

"Do you think they will come back?" asked the young man, his white face stiffening.

"It depends on what this is. If it is just a raid, they may be satisfied. But—I don't know," he concluded lamely.

Barreneche looked at him for a moment, but before he could speak, Doña Francisca Manuela had come out of the church. Garcés turned toward her with alarm, but he saw to his surprise that she was quite cool and collected. The words of sympathy died on his lips, and in a low voice he explained what he and Barreneche were going to do.

"Let me go with you. I can help with the wounds." She was quite steady now, but the friar shook his head.

"We don't know what we will run into up there."

The proud white face smiled, "Do you think I am afraid now?"

"It isn't of you particularly that I am thinking," said Garcés. "You notice they have not attacked any women yet. I don't want them to begin. These are curious things, these Indian attacks, and I don't pretend to know much about them. But there are types of raids in which they do not kill the women or children. So I think we had better not take any chances. Besides, we need you here while we are gone."

She shrugged her shoulders. "It's the least I can do, father, after—everything." She hesitated a little before the last word, but the friar had no time to think of one woman then, and he saw she understood. For she went on briskly enough, "Better keep the children close to the church in case of any alarm?"

"Yes, it will be safer, and it will feel safer to be together. We'll be back as soon as we can."

But he had hardly moved from the door when Rosalía came up with fire in her eye, "Father, those rabbits are trying to stop me. Tell them to let me go."

"Where do you want to go, Rosalía?"

"Down to the fields to see what's keeping that fool Juan Miguel."

"Rosalía," said the friar wearily, "I can't stop to explain to you now. Doña Francisca Manuela will do that. You stay here. When we get back from the meadows, we'll go down ourselves."

And, followed by Barreneche, he turned back to the plaza. A couple of children had come running around the corner of the church, and he saw them stop curiously at the sight of the dead Indian. The face was almost hidden by the swarm of flies. Garcés looked around. Corporal Baylon's coat had fallen from his body and lay sprawled in the dust. The friar took it and threw it over the naked body, so that the face was covered. But the children had forgotten the dead Indian. For one of them, a little girl, was now over at the edge of the open space in front of the church, pointing out into space.

"See," she said with childish excitement, "they've built a big campfire over there to make their porridge."

"Look here," said the friar, "you go back to your mothers and do as they tell you." And then he stopped, for he saw what the little girl was pointing at. It was a column of thick gray smoke rising above the hill of San Pablo down the river. The air was so heavy and so still that it rose like a tower of darker cloud above the hill and hayed out in a fainter gray against the bright blue sky. ,

The children had run off, but Barreneche was at his colleague's shoulder.

"They've struck them, too," he whispered in horror.

<h1 style="text-align:center">5</h1>

"I suppose there's no use trying to send anyone over to San Pablo just now?" asked Barreneche as they went through the gate that led to the meadows behind the pueblo.

Garcés shook his head without slackening his pace to look at his colleague, "We've all we can take care of for now. If anybody's left, they'll come over here tonight."

Barreneche was about to speak again, but looking at the tight-clenched face of his companion, he thought better of it. They were going down the back of the height of Concepción into the meadows behind the pueblo now, and the little shack in which the cows were gathered for milking was in view. But there was no sign of life anywhere. For a moment Garcés stopped and listened. There was no sound but the whirring of some insects in the dry grass.

The first evidence of anything wrong was the couple of buzzards that rose from the grass in front of them. But it was only a dead cow, hideously red and black and sprawled open before them, but still a cow. With a grotesque impulse of relief Garcés laughed. Then, as if in rebuke, a groan came from over near the shed.

Now both friars ran to the shed.

It was Pedro Tapia, the chief herdsman, trying to sit up against the wall, and rubbing his face, and pawing with apparently uncontrolled movements at the air. Barreneche stooped over him, but he gave no sign of recognition.

The friar took hold of one of the groping hands, and the man collapsed in a heap on the ground.

Both friars knelt beside him. But in a moment Garcés rose.

"He's blind, I think, and quite out of his head. We can pick him up later."

"But can't we do something?" Barreneche's face was gray.

"There's a well beyond the shed. We could try to give him a drink, and throw some water over him. But that blow has mercifully taken away all sense of his pain. We had better get on, for there may be somebody around who needs our help at once."

But the next man was quite dead. The buzzards rising from the ground ahead gave notice of that as they had of the dead cow. There was nothing the friars could do but take the handkerchief from the dead man's pocket and put it over what once had been a face. For a second, Garcés thought he was going to be sick, but he heard his companion retching behind him. So he braced himself and went on.

Then in that silent place he heard a low cry, and he went over to find another man trying to sit up in the middle of a clump of mesquite bushes. Barreneche again reached him first and assisted him to sit up. He was quite conscious, and when he saw Garcés, he cried out with remarkable strength, "Thank God you got here, father." But the terrible stench, and the way he clutched his bleeding body left no doubt of his condition.

Barreneche ran back to the well for water while Garcés made the man repeat the act of contrition. Then he recited the words of absolution. The dying man said, "Amen," and slipped out of the friar's arms. Barreneche came back with a pail of water slopping on the dry bushes before him.

"He's gone. Keep it for the next." But this one was dead when they reached him. In spite of the crushed skull, Garcés recognized him as one of the herdsmen who had at last made his confession the night before.

They had reached the corral now, but it was quite empty. The Indians must have ridden all the horses off. For though there were several dead cows strewn around, there were no dead horses. Perhaps, the horses would content the raiders. But even as he reached for that shred of comfort, Garcés remembered that these were not Apaches.

The two friars were not sure how many men had been up with the horses and the stock that morning; so they decided to prowl cautiously around the corral. Just beyond, they caught sight of another figure. He was quite unconscious, but he was still alive, for he had been struck by the comparatively ineffectual arrows of the Yumas. Two Garcés pulled out as he stooped over the man, and then he bound up the wounds. But there was one in his chest still. So they lifted him up and started to carry him back.

"I doubt if there are any more," said Garcés. "Any way, there is a chance for this one. And he hasn't been near church for so long that he needs it."

The man they were carrying moaned a little, and the two friars hurried, but he was heavy. They had been gone well over an hour when they reached the pueblo. To their astonishment they found a crowd of women and children at the opposite end of the plaza, crying and calling. Under cover of their distraction they carried the wounded man into the priests' house and put him on a bed and drew a blanket over him. Then they hurried out into the plaza.

As they joined the crowd at the other end, they heard the women calling, "Where is Gabriel? Where is Pedro? Did you see my husband anywhere?"

Then a couple of them broke away, and plunged from sight. In a moment the friars had pushed to the front of the crowd, which began to shout at them that three of the men from the fields were coming up.

As Garcés started down the narrow path, he saw that a couple of the women had already reached the two men who were carrying a third up the steep way.

The man was quite conscious, but one of his legs was broken, and his uniform was blood-stained. The other two men stood looking at him. One, Garcés saw, had a torn cheek, and the other a badly bruised shoulder showing through his rent shirt. But they seemed quite oblivious of their own wounds as they looked at the friar.

"Get the aguardiente," said Garcés. "I can set the leg if that is all." It was not all, but the body wounds seemed trifling in comparison with what the friars had just seen.

The women were shrieking their questions now, and the men, seeing from the friar's manner that their patient had a chance, sat down on the ground, seemingly unconscious of the uproar about them.

"Stand back," said Garcés, and he rose as Barreneche took the bottle of aguardiente from Rosalía and held it to the wounded man's lips. "And keep still while the men tell us about it. Where are the others?" he asked gently. One of the men, now that his effort was over, seemed dazed. But the other snatched at the bottle which the friar held out to him. He drank greedily, and then he wiped his lips and brushed the back of his hand across his eyes as if to clear his vision.

Only then did he speak one word, "Dead."

There was a terrible silence in the little crowd behind him, a sudden vacuum of breath. And then a woman shrieked.

"Stop that," said the friar sharply, and then he saw it was Rosalía. He motioned to her, and one of the women put her arm around her. It was Doña Francisco Manuela. Another woman began to cry softly, and then another gulped with a horrible sucking sound.

"Where are Rivera's men?"

The man stared, and then he sighed, "Don't you know that little hill shuts them off from our view down by the river? And when I was over there yesterday, they said something about going out hunting this morning."

But Doña Francisca Manuela interrupted indignantly, "They wouldn't dare! I heard my husband tell Captain Rivera that he was to stay there within reach until things were better."

The friar shook his head. There was enough to do now. He told the women about the herdsman, and three of them volunteered to go with Barreneche. Then he despatched a couple of them to the priests' house to see what they could do for the wounded man there. And two more he set to work bathing and bandaging the wounds of the men who had escaped from the fields. He himself began to work on the broken leg. He was hardly a surgeon, but he had watched many a leg being set, and he had helped at various times. Now he was slow and awkward, but presently the bone snapped into place, and he fashioned a crude splint. All about him he could feel the bustle of the women, and he gave thanks that they had all these dungs to do for the living.

The terrible day was drawing to its close by the time he had seen the last of the injured into the church, where the women were trying to make them as comfortable as they could. He had promised that just as soon as possible he would give them all benediction, but, meanwhile, hadn't they better begin on some supper for the men who had not eaten since breakfast? It was only then that he remembered the column of smoke above San Pablo.

The sky was all aglow with the flaming sunset of a scorching day. But he thought he saw a brighter glow above the hill below. For a moment he watched, and then he heard a child's voice beside him, "It's been smoking all afternoon, father. I've been watching it."

The clouds over San Pablo were losing their color now, and he could see a thin trickle of smoke curling up.

"You know," he said to the little girl, "I don't think we had better say anything about that just now."

And he looked down at the child. She was Barbara's oldest, and doubtless she had learned early to take an adult's responsibility. Now she nodded with a look of sober intelligence that made the friar think of Teresa when he had first seen her. The memory shocked him, and he turned away that the little girl might not see his face.

While the women got supper in the open plaza, the two friars carried the bodies out of the sanctuary into the sacristy. They crowded the little room even when they were piled on each other. But the women and the children and the wounded must spend the night in the church.

When they had finished, they went back into the church to see how the wounded were coming on. They were already being fed from steaming bowls of porridge by a couple of the women. One of them, to Garcés' astonishment, Doña Francisca Manuela, looked up and nodded to him quietly and went on with her work.

The other, Garcés was not surprised to see, was Teresa. He waited until she had finished feeding a patient, and then he beckoned to her. As she came up to him at the altar rail, he pointed to the dead commander's wife. "Is she all right?"

"Yes," replied the Indian woman serenely. "When you left me, I ran back into the church, and I slapped her until she stopped crying and listened. And then I told her that you needed her help. She was going to begin crying again, but I told her that we knew the worst now. The others did not. Now, what is it you want me to do?"

"You have been through this thing before," said the friar gently. "Is it over? Or will they come back?"

She looked down for a moment as if thinking; then she faced the friar with those clear, steady eyes that always reminded him of the first time he had seen her, there in the field with the war party. "That depends. If this were just a raid, then I should say they had done all they meant to."

"You don't think it just a raid?"

She pushed her dark hair back from her forehead with a tired gesture. "I do not know."

On a sudden impulse he asked her the question that had come to his mind when he saw her in church that morning. "Was it because you thought something like this was going to happen that you came up here to Mass?"

She nodded, and then she hesitated, and the friar saw with compassion that the old Indian fear of naming the dead had come upon her. "He thought I was afraid to be left there; so he brought me. But I hoped I would be killed, too."

"And your child?" he asked gently.

There was a look of shock on her still face, "I thought only—"

He caught and held her eyes with his own, "Quite natural, my child. But do not forget José is all right now. Our Lady will take care of him. You are left here for something else."

"What can I do?" she said simply.

The friar's voice shook a little as he tried to put what he had been thinking about these last hours into words, "There are all these helpless ones. You can speak the language; they are your people"—he hesitated out of a sudden delicacy, but the steady eyes never flinched—"and perhaps you can help them when no one else could."

"What can I do?" she asked. For an instant he thought it was a cry of despair. And then he saw that she was simply waiting for directions.

"This," he said. "You can tell the Yumas what I say. I do not want the Spaniards to come and burn the Yuma villages and kill the Yumas. It will not bring José and the others back. Tell Palma and his men that if they keep the women and the children unharmed, and when the expedition comes, return them safely, I do not think the Spaniards will do anything more. Tell them that living or dead, I will pray God for that. But tell them that if they hurt the women and children, then I cannot answer for what will happen. Will you tell them that?"

She nodded, and then she turned and looked toward the sacristy.

"I will bury José myself tonight in the cemetery by the church," he promised. And she nodded again, still not able to find words.

"One thing more, Teresa"—he put his hand on her slim shoulder and looked down into the quiet face—"you will always know, wherever you are, that I am praying for you and for your child. You will not forget that?"

Only then did the composure of her face break, and she stooped and caught his hand and kissed it. Then still without a word she went back to the wounded.

6

DOUBTLESS, the night that followed seemed long enough to the wounded, who lay helpless in varying degrees of consciousness; and to the women, who wept for the dead or watched in an agony of uncertainty. But to the two friars it went swiftly enough. For the preparation of supper and the feeding of the wounded and the children took longer than they had expected. The swift dark of the desert had come before the church was quiet enough for benediction.

Even when the candles were lighted on the altar and the Host held aloft, the wounded tossed restlessly on their mattresses, and the children fidgeted curiously among the heaps of blankets. There was not enough light for Garcés to see much of his congregation, but he caught the whiteness of the upturned faces and the sharp glitter of the eyes which looked to the monstrance in his hands for an imploring moment, and then fell back into the shadow's. The shutters over the windows of the church were closed lest some raveling of light should recall the survivors to the festive minds of the raiders. But the chill of the desert evening had come into the church, and the response of the people, though muffled, was clear enough in its agony of intercession to come to the ear of the priest at the altar.

When the service was over, the friar led the congregation in the general confession, and then he gave them absolution. As he looked down on the bowed heads in the half-darkness, he could feel the kneeling figures brace themselves, and he was thankful that for some, at least, the bitterness of death was past. Then he led the congregation in the prayers for the dead. Only then did he say a few words to the waiting women.

It was not in any sense a sermon, but simply a brief instruction. They had made their peace with God, he told them, and they had asked His help for the living and His mercy on the dead. There was nothing more that they could do until the light came, and they could know where they were. The main thing now was to sleep, that they might renew strength of body and mind for whatever God would give them to do for the next day. Some of the women had begun to sob as he talked. He rebuked them gently, reminding them that there were the children who must not be frightened and the injured who must not be worried, to think of. Their task now was to bear with patience what could not be helped and to comfort the afflicted.

When he had finished, he went into the sacristy, and moving with care for the dead, he took off his vestments.

A couple of the older lads of the pueblo and the soldiers who had come up from the fields were waiting at the door. Quietly, they took up the spades they had brought and went to the little patch of bare ground in the angle formed by the walls of the sacristy and the church which had been decided on for a graveyard. Here they dug quickly a single but deep grave, digging until they struck the rock of the height.

Then still working in the dark, they went back and carried out the three bodies of the dead. The moon had come up now, and they could see its dim radiance on the water far below. But here on the height there was but a faint whiteness in the vast environing blackness. One of the lads held up a dark lantern and opened the shutter as Garcés began to read the burial prayers. He read quickly in a low voice, while the men and the boys stood round shielding the glow of the lantern from any wandering eye. When he had finished, the lantern was closed, and the whole company fell to shoveling back the earth.

It was then that Garcés remembered the body of the Indian. He had been baptized but the friar still did not feel sure but what the Indians might come to look for him. So he called to two of the lads, and between them they carried the body out to the gate to the west of the pueblo, and a little way out on the path to the old corral. There they laid the Indian down a little off the path and wrapped him in a blanket which the friar had thrown over him earlier in the day. It was too much of a risk to light any light here; so Garcés contented himself with blessing the body.

He thought of the dead lying out in the fields, and for a moment he hesitated. The Indians would almost certainly come back and scalp them; indeed, he could not understand why they had not already done so. But the boys who had come with him were turning back. He heard a rustling of sound in the stillness of the night air. The sound was not behind him; it was, he felt sure, coming from the other end of the pueblo. Once back to the cover of the storehouses at the end of the pueblo, his companions hesitated. The sound was quite clear now, a scraping and a sliding. Someone was coming up the path from the river bottom.

Whispering to his companions to wait, the friar left the shelter of the storehouses, but before he could start across the plaza, one of the lads was running lightly ahead of him, his bare feet making no sound on the dusty ground. And before he could catch up with the boy, he heard a cry of astonishment, followed by another cry, and then a sudden hush.

"Father, they have come from San Pablo."

"Good, but tell them to speak low. Who are they?"

"Two of the soldiers."

"Bring them to the priests' house and make no noise."

In silence the dark shadows crowded into the little house. When the door was closed, the friar went and fastened the shutters at the window. Only then did he take the flint and the tallow candle which Barreneche had found. Once the candle was lighted, he held it up so that they might see the newcomers. They were nearly exhausted, and their clothes were stained and torn. Garcés nodded to Barreneche, who in a minute returned with the aguardiente bottle and an earthen cup.

When the light first flickered at the candle tip, the men's eyes had shrunk from the light. Now that they had drunk the aguardiente, they began to look less like hunted animals. But before they could begin to speak, the friars brought out some food which the two men ate wolfishly.

"Well?" said Garcés. "We saw the smoke."

"Did they come here?" asked one of the men, shuddering.

The friar nodded somberly.

"We were down in the fields. That's how we escaped. When we saw them coming, we ran into the brush and hid. We could hear them, but we had no weapons with us."

"But what happened?" cried one of the soldiers sharply.

"I was telling you," said the man from San Pablo indignantly. "We could hear those clubs and the men screaming, and we couldn't do a thing."

He was little more than a boy, Garcés remembered now. He had looked so old and so tortured when he came in that the friar had not recognized him. He was one of the two unmarried youths who had been allowed to come with the party.

"Of course not. We are all glad you had sense enough to hide," said Garcés.

The young man looked at him, and his face cleared a little.

"You know, you think you ought to have been able to do something," he leaned forward a little, and one of the two Concepción soldiers who had climbed up from the fields groaned.

"We quite understand all that," said the friar gently. "Now tell us about it. Did they go up to the pueblo, too?"

Again, the youth shivered. "We heard the women screaming, and some firing. And then they took all the women away. We saw them on the path above, and we could not do anything."

"Did they hurt them?"

The whole room waited, breathless.

"No," said the youth doubtfully. "I mean"—as he caught the horrified suspense in the little room—"they didn't seem to have struck any of them, but they were making them go along with them."

"Where?" asked one of the younger boys.

The youth from San Pablo shook his head, "They were going in the direction of that devil Pablo's village, and there must have been fifty Indians driving them along."

A look of bafflement came into the horror on the youth's face. "I couldn't think of a thing to do."

But now his companion, an older man, obviously slower to find words, had recovered his wits, "I saw my wife with the youngest one. She was not crying or anything, but just going along with the two others hanging on to her skirts. She was a game one," he added with pride.

"I am sure she is all right," said Garcés. "The Indians will enslave them, but they will not hurt them."

He was himself surprised at the conviction with which he spoke.

The man looked at him, and a slow relief came into the anxious face. "If that's so, I don't mind the rest."

Then he looked embarrassed. "I am sorry, father; I really am sorry that the two fathers are dead."

"The fathers!" Barreneche and Garcés just looked at each other. It was the other men in the little room who spoke.

"Yes, they were dead all right."

"Then you went up to the pueblo?"

Garcés looked around. He thought it was one of the two men who had come up from the fields at Concepción who asked, but he could not be sure.

"Oh, yes," said the youth eagerly. "After they had all gone, we looked around the fields. We saw seven or eight of our men there. All but two of them were dead. One was dying; the other had a chance. I went down to the river and got water for them both, and then we started up to the pueblo to see if we could get some help. It was then that we saw the flames."

He waited, his face working pitifully at the remembrance of the terror. "But we went up just in case somebody were still alive. There were two men there, two of the herdsmen, who had heard the noise and come up from the fields on the other side. They had just come out of the church, and they were carrying one of the fathers. He still had the chalice in his hand, but he was quite dead. It was Father Díaz."

But now the older man was ready to resume, "The other friar was already lying on the ground in front of the church, but he was gone, too. He was simply drenched in blood."

For a moment nobody spoke. Then Garcés, making the sign of the cross, broke the silence, "May they both rest in peace. They were good friars, both, and they died at their post. Now tell us about the others."

"The others? It was just the same as in the fields. They brought one man who was still alive out of the church, and he just died when we got there. They had another one sitting up against the church. But the wall was getting hot; so they moved him away."

"They were the only survivors?"

"They said one of the other herdsmen had come down, too, but he had stopped for a horse. And when he saw what had happened, he rode off on the horse to get aid. But we haven't seen anything of him."

"But all the others were dead?"

"Yes," said the older man with a curious matter-of-factness. "Dead, all of them."

"We did find some aguardiente, and we gave it to the man up in the pueblo. But the fire was everywhere, then." Again, the youth paused. "So we carried the man who was still living down to the river bottom. And we put him there with the other man whom we had hidden in the brush, and we left them and came over here to see if we could get a horse or two. The savages took all ours but the one that herdsman got off."

"They took ours, too," said one of the boys.

And now it was the turn of Concepción to tell San Pablo of their disaster. Garcés caught the eye of Barreneche, and the two friars opened the door. It was a beautiful night, cool now, with the stars bright above the ghostly pueblo. The two friars moved away from the house they had just left.

"Do you think they will be back tomorrow?" asked the younger friar.

"They will be back to get their captives. They take a pride in them as evidence of their victory."

"And to kill us?"

"I suppose so," said Garcés absent-mindedly. He caught the sound of his companion's quickly-drawn breath, and he seized his arm, "There is one thing we have not done. The Indians may have caught Rivera and his men, too. But there is a chance there."

"I'll swim over," said the young friar eagerly.

Garcés shook his head. "I need you here. The women don't know what has happened over at San Pablo yet. They'll have to know tomorrow, and I'll need you. We'll ask one of the boys."

But when Garcés told the two boys what was in his mind, they both insisted that they were awake enough for anything, and that they had swum the river a dozen times. One of the men protested that he would find a reed bundle down on the river bank and take that, but the friar told him that that but increased the delay in getting across the stream, and the risk if dawn surprised him. And the two boys were emphatic that they were going to have the honor of saving Concepción.

To that the friar said nothing, but at once escorted the two lads to the edge of the pueblo to make sure that in their excitement they did not begin to whistle or sing, or make some other noise that would bring out a frantic mother. When they had been seen safely down the first turn of the path to the river, the two friars went back to the church.

It was astonishingly quiet as they shut the door behind them. The candles, guttering on the altar, were throwing fantastic shadows to the crossbeams of the ceiling. As they stood there listening by the shut door, a child stirred restlessly, a woman called a man's name, someone began to snore.

"What are you going to do now?" asked Barreneche as his companion noiselessly opened the gate in the rail.

"Sleep," and Garcés lay down with his head on the altar step. He heard Barreneche move past him, and in a moment the chill of the night vanished as he felt a cover fall on him, but he was too exhausted even to thank his colleague.

7

THE sleep into which he fell so heavily was an unquiet one. He was lost in the sand dunes beyond the meeting of the rivers, wave upon wave of that blinding sea, and he knew Captain Anza was waiting for him to find the way. He was talking to Palma, but Palma was not listening. He held a brown-ish-gray strip of skin in his hands with the black hair brushed shining from it, and he was turning it over and over. Garcés began to shout, but Palma paid no attention. And then Garcés found himself in the long corridor in the house at Querétaro, near the turn which led from the dormitory wing to the chapel. Someone was coming down that corridor, and he waited, suddenly terrified. But when the owner of those steps rounded the corner, it was Díaz, clutching a silver chalice to his breast. At sight of him all the terror vanished, for now Garcés knew that he, too, was dead.

And then he was listening for something, for some small sound that had stopped but would come again. He heard a child cry out for its mother, and a whispered hush. He heard the soft choking sound of a woman weeping, and then he raised himself on one elbow. He tried to make no noise, but he must have failed, for the faint choking sound stopped. Yet he felt sure it was not that that had awakened him. And then the sound came again, the sound of a body rubbing against the dry wall of the church. He looked up, and he saw that the little window in the right sanctuary wall was open, for through it he could see the whitening of the dawn. He got up as noiselessly as possible and moved into the sacristy, but not quickly enough. Someone was behind him.

"I saw the shutters open, father," said the voice of Doña Francisco Manuela.

Carefully, he closed the door behind him, and then they went through the priests' house out into the still dark plaza. There they stood and listened, but there was no stir of life anywhere. The sky was whitening above the black hulk of the pueblo, and the cool breeze of the dawn was gently swinging an open shutter in one of the deserted houses, but that was all.

Cautiously, they groped their way around the side of the church. But there was nobody there.

"It was probably only the wind," said Doña Francisca Manuela, calmly.

The friar agreed. It seemed quite unnecessary to point out to her that there was no need of saying anything about this. He was quite unprepared, therefore, when she started away from him to the other end of the pueblo. He caught her arm, "Where are you going?"

"To my own house."

"But it is too risky," he protested.

For the first time since yesterday morning he heard the low, clear laugh that, he realized now, was one of the things most characteristic of her.

"Father, if I am going to be killed today, I want at least to look decent. Really, I'll be right back."

He was so astonished that he made no further effort to stop her. In the last hours she had behaved superbly, taking the lead in seeing that the sensible thing was done, comforting others, doing everything she could to help the friars avert panic. And now this frivolity!

But it was not Garcés' habit to judge where he knew he did not understand; so he went back to the church. It was time to look to the wounded before the children should be stirring. And then he thought wistfully that it would not be long now that he could shield them from the horror of the world into which they had come.

The first man he touched was sleeping quietly with the light, even breathing of healthy sleep. The next made no sound whatever, and when the friar lifted his hand to feel the pulse, it was quite cold. He had received his release. The next was tossing and moaning under his breath, and the hand which the friar took was burning. So it went as he checked the wounded. He wished now that he had paid more attention to the medical studies in the Querétaro novitiate. They had not seemed entirely real to him at the time, and since then, he had been so busy. Now—it was growing lighter. He would still have a few minutes to make the wounded more comfortable before they faced the new day.

He went back to the priests' house to get the flask of wine in the cupboard there. He thought, then, of the fresh linen that would be needed to change the dressings, and he wondered if any of Doña Francisca Manuela's stores remained. Probably not, from what he had seen of the destruction on the way to the meadow. There was a strip of linen for the altar in the sacristy—but two of his guests were lying sleeping in front of the door. So he turned away and went out into the plaza. The dawn had come, whitening the emptiness of the pueblo. He heard a step behind him.

It was Doña Francisca Manuela. Again, he heard the light laugh, "They took all my clothes except a little linen and these earrings. But my face is clean, at least." And then, as he wondered whether he should rebuke the levity, she patted something over her arm, "But they left enough linen for the wounded, and my lavender water."

The friar made no reply, and they hurried together to the front of the church. As they came to the little cemetery, the friar glanced up to see if they had smoothed the ground enough in the dark. He heard Doña Francisca Manuela catch her breath, and then she clutched his arm. "A grave!"

For on top of the freshly-turned earth lay some yellow poppies.

Astonished, the friar bent over them. That must have been the sound that had awakened him, for over against the wall of the church under the window was a stool. He looked back at the flowers, and now more closely, for he had caught sight of something lying on top of them. It was a cross made of two sticks bound together by grass. He took up the rough cross, and he saw that it was made of broken arrows.

Doña Yslas pointed to it. "What does it mean? Does it mean some of the Indians are remaining Christian through it all?"

"It is Teresa, I am sure," he said sadly. "If I had only awakened a little sooner."

"Teresa? Oh, poor José's Indian wife! But how did she know?"

"I promised to bury her husband."

"And the cross?"

"I am not sure," said the friar, thoughtfully. "We'll leave the flowers there, but we'll take the cross."

When they returned to the church, Doña Yslas still looked puzzled, but she at once set about taking care of the wounded. And presently she was joined by another woman, Rosalía. In the wan light that now filled the church Rosalía looked pale and hollow-eyed, and then the friar remembered from what direction the muffled weeping had come. She looked bewildered, too, and suddenly weak and pitiful, but the lifelong habit of action carried her to Doña Francisca Manuela's side.

The friar went down to the sanctuary and woke up his colleague. For a moment Barreneche had forgotten where he was, for he answered the old monastic greeting with which Garcés had awakened him, with a smile. And the older friar, marvelling at the blessed resiliency of youth, smiled, too. And then the younger man sat up and glanced around, and his face shadowed. But he rose at once and followed his colleague out of the church and to the little cemetery.

There Garcés took the cross of arrows from his habit and showed it to him. Barreneche repeated Doña Francisca Manuela's question, "What does it mean?"

"I do not know," Garcés answered for the second time. But he was thinking of his last interview with Teresa.

Barreneche turned the cross over and over in his hands as if he could read its meaning from the broken arrows. "Does it mean that it is all over, that they will not come again?"

"No," said Garcés slowly. "If that were true, Teresa could have come openly."

"Then you think they will come again?"

"I have never doubted it," said Garcés. "Have you?"

"N-o," said Barreneche, but the hesitation in his usually sure and confident speech was eloquent. And the older friar thought with compassion how much harder it is to give up hope when one is young. And then, ashamed of the moment's patronage, he reminded himself how much more generous is the free sacrifice of youth.

"But why do they take so long about it? It was all over yesterday at San Pablo." For a moment Garcés wondered if Barreneche were weary of straining at the leash for the promised martyrdom. But he answered him soberly enough.

"I have been wondering about that, too. It may have been that Pablo was resolved on the complete destruction of the Spanish pueblo, and had persuaded his people to it. I feel sure that Palma has felt a good deal more hesitation, and I am sure that there have been some in his village who have not approved at all. That is one possibility. It is possible, too, that they have hesitated to set the pueblo ablaze for fear of alarming Rivera. And it is just possible that they are so pleased with their booty, the horses, and the clothes, and the food from the pueblo, that they have gone off to enjoy it, before doing anything more." Even as he spoke, Garcés suspected that this, the least dramatic of his suppositions, was the right one, but he doubted if the serious young man at his side would believe it.

"Can't we do anything?" asked the young friar. The sun was flooding the plaza, and the warmth of the new day coming into the chill of dawn brought new life into the anxious body.

"We can say a Mass for the souls of the dead. It will be a comfort for the women afterwards."

He hesitated on the last word, and the young friar looked at him sharply. "Afterwards? You think they will not kill the women?"

"I don't think so. I think that is the meaning of Teresa's cross."

"And?" There was a shadow of disappointment in the eyes of Barreneche.

Garcés smiled. "I have no doubt that we shall follow our brethren. But until then—" he started for the priests' house.

Garcés had been wondering whether he should break the news of San Pablo before they went back into the church or whether he should wait until he was ready to begin Mass. Turning this over in his mind, he went back to the church.

As he turned the corner into the plaza, Garcés saw that his problem was solved for him. The men had just come out, and at the sight of the two from San Pablo a scream of terror arose, as if every women knew at once what the presence of those two must mean. But when the extent of the disaster was known, there was silence in the plaza. And, presently, the women were gathering up their children and quietly coming back to the church to press as close as they could get to the altar with the statue of Our Lady still above it, and the light still burning in the small sanctuary.

There was absolute silence when Garcés, wearing the vestments of mourning, appeared and made his announcement, "We are now going to sing a Requiem Mass for all those who have died these last days." He had wanted to add, "Both those whose deaths we know of and those who may have died without our yet knowing," but looking into those white faces, he saw that it was not necessary.

He thought of Díaz with his chalice, and he wondered if he would be allowed to finish this Mass for the dead. But it proceeded without interruption. And when he had finished, he took his vestments off and laid them on the altar. He motioned for silence in the little church, and then he began to speak. He told them he knew their grief, and he would not have any of them think for a moment that he thought it a little thing. But he must remind them of what, as Christians, they already knew. This grief was the gate to a great joy.

Death had struck suddenly without warning and without the suffering and the discouragement of disease. It was a sharp but a very brief passage to rest and joy. For the dead the bitterness was past, and there was no sting in the glory into which they had come. Even for those in Purgatory, there was no fear, no bitterness in their purgation. They were safe in the arms of God's mercy. There was nothing to fear, and, here he looked to where Doña Francisca Manuela and Rosalía stood together, close to the wounded whom they had been nursing, there was nothing to regret. In the light of God's presence they might be sure that all the misunderstandings of life fell away, and love was free at last in its full perfection. That they should remember always.

But now he wanted to speak of the living. They knew what had happened at San Pablo, and that they might expect to have happen to them. He felt the horror of that sharply-drawn breath, but he went steadily on. They had nothing to fear there, either. The Indians were accustomed in their raids to take captives and to use them as slaves, but those slaves were not over-worked or ill-treated. They would have to obey the instructions of others, and they would have to be patient. He reminded them that there were a good many human beings who were slaves in this world, that slavery had been the lot of people more delicately nurtured than they, and the lot of great saints. In their thoughts and in their prayers they would be free. Their experience would be a great opportunity for their faith to show itself. What he had not been able to do by his preaching they might be able to accomplish by their example. For they would have an unrivalled opportunity to show the beauty of a Christian life.

That life would shine the more beautifully because it might be an un-comfortable life. But he wanted to remind them that comfort was no part of the calling of a Christian. They might have to go dirty and eat filthy food. Fastidiousness was the mark of a fine lady; it was not a Christian virtue. Great saints had been dirty in body but clean in spirit. No one but them-selves could stain their souls.

He had no doubt that they would be rescued. But till then they must be prepared to face great hardship and trial without the ordinary spiritual support of the Christian community, and without the sacraments. But they might be sure of the special intercession before the throne of God of their dead relatives and neighbors, and of that special grace which God gives to those who through no fault of their own are deprived of His ordinary aids. They might be sure of an especial tenderness from Our Lady who like any mother always yearns most over her sorest tried child.

And, finally, he would urge them never to forget that of all the forms of Christian worship none was more acceptable to God than the cheerful acceptance of His will because it was His will.

All weeping had ceased, and there was absolute stillness in the little church. It was his last sermon, and they had listened as no one had ever lis-tened before to his preaching. But he felt only a great yearning. For this was their Viaticum that he was giving them, something that would be strength and comfort to them when he could no longer speak. No, that was not it. He had never really thought to do that much for anybody. Rather he had tried to point out a way to them, a way along which they might go when he was no longer there to guide them. That was all he had ever thought to do, to open a way, a way to a help and a light beyond anything he had ever had in himself.

This was his final effort.

8

THE heat of the day deepened about them. The wounded were very thirsty and restless; some of the children were fretful; the faces of the mothers of the two boys who had crossed the river in the night were gray with worry. It seemed as if one had always been waiting for this storm to break. Only the women who knew that their husbands were dead were quiet, running their beads through their fingers. Every so often the others would wander out to the edge of the plaza in front of the church to look over into the fields below.

It was one of these who caught sight of one of the boys swimming back across the river. She let out a little scream of excitement, and as if in answer to that scream, an arrow whizzed out of the brush along the river bottom toward the swimmer, and then another, but still he kept on, until, presently, he was lost from view in the bushes along the water's edge. It seemed as if hours had passed, but it was less than a half hour later that the shining head of the boy appeared on the path.

He had been hit by one of the arrows, but he would not let anybody touch his shoulder until he had told his story. He and his comrade had had little trouble getting across the river in the dark, but once across, it had not been so easy to find the camp. Finally, they had decided to lie down in the brush and get some sleep until it would be light enough to see. They had been quite sure that the first ray of dawn would waken them, but they had not reckoned with the accumulated fatigue of the day and the sleepless night. It was so still there in the brush that they could not at first believe that what had happened the day before was anything but a nightmare. So they lay there for a moment watching a white butterfly flutter in and out of the dusty palo verde.

It was then that one of them noticed how high the sun was in the sky, and then they remembered. Now in the bright daylight they found the hill behind which Captain Rivera had encamped, without any difficulty, and they began to run, for they knew that it was later than it should have been. But before they had got very far, they caught sight of the bright flash of a uniform coming over the hill. So relieved were they at the appearance of one of Rivera's soldiers that they both shouted. And then, as the man turned, they saw at once that it was an Indian who was wearing the uniform.

Fortunately, they had presence of mind enough to drop to the ground and to hide in the brush. Presently, they heard somebody coming toward them, and they kept very still. In the silence they could hear him coming closer, they could even hear him thrashing a bit in the brush as if he were beating the bushes to see if anyone were in them. They realized now that he had a sword in his hand, Captain Rivera's sword it would be, and they lay as close to the ground as they could to escape that keen edge. He was talking now, and they were terrified at the thought that his comrades might have come up to help him in the search. But although they did not understand the words, it sounded from the steadiness of the rhythm and the fact that he was saying the same thing over and over again, as if he were chanting something to himself. And then they heard him go by quite close to them.

For a moment he had been clearly within their range of vision through the latticework of the bushes. And in that moment they say that the commander's suit was all stained with blood, but that the sword was bright and clean, flashing in the sun. For a long time they did not dare to move. But nobody else came in sight, and presently they sat up and began to whisper together. It was very still now, and they both agreed that all the company must be dead for the Indian to dare to take the commander's uniform. So they would go back, but separately so that there might be two chances of their getting the news to the pueblo.

The boy had told his story almost in a breath, for the dramatic character of his news and his sense of its importance had buoyed him up. But now his manliness seemed suddenly to collapse, and he turned to Garcés with a cry, "Oh, father, I am so sorry we slept!"

"That is all right, my son," the friar comforted him. "They attacked at dawn, and if you had not slept, we should have lost you, too."

And then they addressed themselves to the arrow. It was a shallow wound, and the friar reassured the mother that he had seen scores of such wounds among the Indians, and that he had never known them to do any harm. But now the other boy's mother, who from the edge of the height had been watching the stream, suddenly shouted, "There he is!"

But before anybody could reach her side, there was a yell from the fields to the back of the pueblo, followed by yells all around. The Indians had returned.

It was what they had been waiting for now these twenty-four hours and more, but for a moment everyone remained horror-stricken where he stood. Even the children stood poised in astonishment, staring at the Indians who came pouring in, apparently, from every side. Garcés had already started for the edge of the plaza, but now he stood halfway, slowly looking around, with a calmness that shocked him. The Indians were coming through the gate to the fields to the west of the pueblo, they were coming up the path from the river bottom, they were coming round the corner of the church from the steep slope to the south. They were coming yelling and swinging their red and black war clubs, and now some were bringing up flaming brands.

One of these latter with a whoop tossed his brand to the thatched roof of the church. The flame blazed through the air like a meteor and struck the tindery arrowweed. There was a crackle, and a little rill of pale light ran its fingers through the weather-gray thatch. Then a woman screamed and Garcés remembered the wounded lying on the floor of the church. As he shot to the door, the whole plaza behind him burst into screaming and running.

He had reached the church door when he was caught in a vise. He twisted, and from the other side, a second vise was clamped on. He looked around. Two Indians had seized him and held him. He begged them to let him get in to the wounded. But they seemed not to understand what he said, although he had spoken in Yuma. They were men he knew, too, men who had come to the chapel in the village. They were little more than youths, he knew, but they held him with a grip like iron. And when he pleaded with them, they listened with absolutely impassive faces.

"They will burn to death," he pleaded, but they did not seem to hear him.

But there was no time for him to attempt another plea, for they were dragging him down the steep slope to the south of the church with a speed that shook the breath out of his body. Once he nearly fell, but those strong arms jerked him to his feet; once he choked for want of breath, but the steel bands of those hands never relaxed their grip. Only when they had reached the bottom of the slope, did his captors pause in a clump of brush to sit down, one on each side of him.

Here it was incredibly quiet in the baking heat of midafternoon. He could hear the buzz of the insects in the dry clumps of sagebrush. He held his breath for a moment to listen. Yes, he could just catch a faint roar of indistinguishable sound, dull and heavy on the unmoving air. And then as he strained his eyes to hear more, he could not be sure. But his captors had leaped to their feet, and again they were half-dragging him along the rough ground. The spikes of underbrush caught at his habit and ripped it, scraped his bare ankles and tore at his face and hands as the Indians hurried on.

Now they must be passing under the height, for he could hear the tumult more distinctly, and presently he caught on the warm air the sharpening smell of burning wood. But he had no chance to linger. Several times they nearly ran into other Indians, but they all seemed to be fast in the grip of the intoxication of the raid, for they paid no attention to any of the uproar about them.

The friar and his captors were soon close to the path from the fields to the height. Garcés gave a cry, for there ahead was the boy who had gone across the river last night. He was starting quietly and unconcernedly up the path, with the sun shining in his dripping hair. He had not heard the friar's cry, but before Garcés could open his mouth again, the Indian behind him seized his jaw with a violence that made his teeth rattle in his head. For a few moments the friar struggled futilely, and then he looked to the path again. It was clear. He relaxed, and the Indians hurried on.

But they had only got a little beyond the path, when they stopped and listened. Unmistakably, the sound was coming toward them. For a moment they whispered together, speaking so quickly that he could catch only the words, "—right away. Better wait."

Then for the first time, one of the Indians addressed him, "Old Man, if you keep still and make no noise, we will not hurt you. If you do, we will knock the breath from your body."

Then they pushed him into the bushes and lay down on either side of him. After a moment he raised his head cautiously, and saw that the Indians had raised theirs and were watching something on the rising ground above. For a moment the friar groped in vain for the object of their interest, but he could see nothing stirring among the bushes. He was very tired, and his jaws were aching a little from the fierce clutch of the Indian's hand. He was about to put his head down on his arms, when he heard Indian voices coming toward him. Then he noticed the slight stiffening of his companions' bodies, and he followed their glance.

And now he saw where they were. They were just under a ridge along the side of the bank on which ran an old trail which led to an almost imperceptible crossroads not far from the chapel. He had taken it many a time. One well-worn trail led to Palma's village in the river bottom; the other went through a tangle of willow and cottonwood and ironwood up over the bank to a wood where the friar had for some time suspected Palma was gathering his people for secret meetings. A couple of Indians were coming along it now, and the friar in the bushes below could see them as if they were crossing a stage for his benefit. And then he nearly cried out in his anguish as he caught sight of the first of the women and the children of the pueblo coming along. They were a pitiful sight, tired and disheveled and frightened, with the children clinging to their skirts, and the Indians dancing all around them, still waving their war clubs, and yelling. Some of the children were crying, and their mothers were clutching them and trying their best to reassure them.

Then came Barbara. Her dress was half torn off, and her hair was flying, but there was something imperturbable in the way she carried her youngest on her shoulder and called out to the others not to lose hold of each other's hands.

"Don't be afraid," he heard her yell to one of the laggards, "Father Garcés, God rest his soul, said—" But an Indian came up, yelling and whooping, at that moment, and the friar could hear no more. Then he caught sight of Doña Francisca Manuela, slightly bent over—she was assisting one of the wounded men. So they had not killed them all. There was another woman, too, Rosalía. She looked very bedraggled, but she seemed to have eyes for nothing but the man whom she helped to hold up, bending over him and whispering encouragement. The friar looked back to Doña Francisca Manuela, and as he looked, she straightened up and swept her hair back from her face. For a moment he saw her face clearly, very calm and proud in its sooty pallor.

So they passed from view, that heartbreaking procession, and after them came a rout of Indians, cheering, and yelling, and whooping.

The friar buried his head in his arms, silently imploring the mercy of God upon the helpless captives. For some minutes he lay thus, struggling to keep the dry sobs from coming to the ears of his own captors. Then without warning he was jerked to his feet, and again the Indians were hurrying him on. They were scrambling up to the ridge now, pulling the weary friar stumbling after them. When they reached the ridge, the Indians paused for breath, and Garcés was able for the first time to look back in the direction of the height. A great cloud of smoke was billowing up into the bright blue sky. There was a red-streaked orange in the lower part of that cloud, and then it darkened, and then it seemed to lift and lighten again into the soft texture of a summer cloud. All up and down the rivers they must see that cloud, and he

sickened to think of the rejoicing and the fear that would come into countless bewildered hearts that beheld it.

9

BUT the Indians had jerked him back from the moment's contemplation of
that funeral pyre of all his hopes, and again they were hurrying. And now
for the first time it occurred to him to wonder where they were taking him.
Not after the captives, for they had been careful to wait until the last of
the jubilant Indians had disappeared from sight before they even ventured
up to the ridge trail. And, presently, when they reached the crossways, they
took the trail to the village, though the trampled condition of the other path
showed that the captives had been taken that way. But he did not have long
to wonder, for soon they were away from the trail and in the familiar clearing
in the brush, in front of the house of the Jamajab.

And then he knew what had happened. But when he tried to speak
to the Indians, they tightened their clutch on him and pushed him into
the darkness behind the willow-bark blanket that served as a door. At first,
he could not see anything, but he could hear a quick breath drawn in the
darkness.

"Is it you, my friend?" he asked quietly.

But the blanket behind was thrust aside, and a firm hand gripped his
arm, while a low voice hissed, "Fool, they will hear you." It was one of his
captors.

Garcés stood silent in the darkness. He thought he could hear a heart
beating, but it was probably his own. Then he heard a whisper. It was
Barreneche.

By now, his eyes had become accustomed to the darkness after the
glare of the day, and he could make out the thin spatterings of light that
fell through the chinks in the walls of the house where the dried mud had
dropped out. And he could see the darker shadow toward which he thrust
his hand, and then the two friars clung together. But neither spoke until they
had sat down under the low roof at the rear of the house. Here amid the
baskets of acorn meal and other stored provisions of the Indian household,
they leaned against each other.

"Have you seen anything of the others?" whispered Barreneche.

Briefly, Garcés told what he had seen.

"I think they are trying to save us," he added dryly. He tried to remember where the water was kept in this house. For he was parching from the heat and the running. He was sore from his bruises and the scratches, too, now that he had time to think of it.

"A funny way," said Barreneche. There was a little rustling under the thatch behind them. It might be a field mouse scuttering through the dry arrowweed. Neither friar stirred. Presently, Garcés heard the click of beads beside him in the darkness. His own rosary was broken, but his fingers found all but one of the beads. For some time there was no sound but the sound of their own breathing, and the steady click of the beads.

"I nearly fought them off," said Barreneche, "but I don't think it would have done any good."

"No," said Garcés.

After that, he must have fallen asleep. For when next he roused to consciousness, there was no chink of light to be seen in the great cave of darkness in which he lay. He had been dreaming, and for a moment he was still in his dreams. And then he heard a low voice almost at his ear, "Old Man, it is I."

He was awake now, and he knew the voice, the voice of Gerónimo.

Then Garcés felt something wet thrust against his hands, and he sat up and drank greedily from the water jar. He turned to Barreneche, but he was still breathing evenly. So he set the jar down carefully.

"Are the women all right?" he asked.

"They are all right. They are frightened at the preparations for the scalp dance, but once it is over, they will be all right."

"Thank God," said the friar.

But Gerónimo seemed not to have heard him, for he went on, "Listen to me, Old Man. Stay here and make no noise till Palma sends for you."

"Palma?" The friar made no effort to conceal his astonishment.

"Tonight," said the old Jamajab, "men are drunk with their victory. There is no sense talking to them. But tomorrow they will be tired, and the after-thoughts will come. Then Pablo's voice will not sound so loud."

Garcés started to speak, but before he could find a word, Gerónimo had slipped from the house. For a long time Garcés sat there in the dark listening. But he was too tired; so he lay down. He would say a rosary for tomorrow's appeal to Palma. But, presently, he was asleep, and he was dreaming, and this time he was on the road to Moqui to complete the bridge between the old mission frontier and the new.

But it was not that that was in his mind when he awoke to find the thin sunlight filtering through the latticework of the walls of the dried-out old house. It was rather the first crossing of the Colorado with Anza and his party. He had been watching the Indians swimming back and forth in the bright sunlight, churning the muddy waters to foam as they pushed over the supplies of the expedition on their traylike baskets. For a moment he could not remember where he was, and then as the breeze ran through the dry arrowweed heaped against the low roof overhead, he remembered. From the twittering of the birds all around, he knew it could not be long past dawn. He remembered what Gerónimo had said about talking to Palma today.

Then his heart leaped up, for outside he could hear two voices talking, and one was a voice he knew. It was the voice of Sebastián. He reached out his hand to waken Barreneche, and then he paused. For he had caught the tone of Sebastián's voice, half-indignant, half-persuasive.

"But I tell you it is not just the women's seeing ghosts. I saw them myself, and Palma saw them, and many others, too." It was Sebastián pleading for belief, and angry that his right was denied him.

"If you are trying to tell me that all those dead Spaniards got up out of the ashes and marched round that big house that isn't there anymore with burning brands in their hands, then I say you have been drinking, and it is past the season of the saguaro fruit when real Yumas get drunk," jeered another voice which might have belonged to one of the Indians of yesterday, but Garcés could not be sure.

Now he heard Barreneche stir at his side, and he laid a warning hand on his arm. And then Sebastián was speaking again. "But I tell you I saw it. They were all in white, and the church was there just as it used to be, and they walked around it, carrying lighted candles like the candles on the altar, and they went slowly as if there were music, and they were dancing to it."

They heard the other voice laugh, but it was, it seemed to Garcés, an uneasy laugh, and now another voice broke in, "It might be as Sebastián says. The Old Man had a strong magic."

"He's dead up there in the ashes," said still another voice, obviously fighting unwelcome belief.

"That would not stop him," said Sebastián, and now the listening friar recognized the familiar boasting note in his old servant's voice, and he shivered as he heard the voice rise triumphantly. "Even if he were dust, he would rise again."

Then he heard a more thoughtful voice, "It is a strong magic, the Old Man's prayers; it might make the dead rise again."

"You used to go to the chapel; you have heard what the Old Man said with the book about the dead rising again and living forever." It was Sebastián.

"You mean all the Spaniards came back on the height?" This was the voice that had jeered at Sebastián, not nearly so certain now.

"Yes," said Sebastián, positively.

But the Indian who had captured them yesterday, seemed less sure, for he answered more doubtfully, "If what the Old Man said is true."

"It is lies, all of it," said a contemptuous voice that had not spoken before, and this voice Garcés recognized at once. It was the voice of the Nifora, and now the friar remembered that it was he whom Barreneche had surprised painting the war club. Now there was no mistaking his scorn as he went on. "Pablo says they make foolish men believe their lies so that they may work their magic on them. And then they lose all their strength for fighting, and they are no better than men who have put on women's clothes."

"That Pablo says many foolish things," said the captor, who, Garcés now realized, had been left on guard by Gerónimo. It was said with surprising mildness, but the taunt was unmistakable. There was a little scuffle. Sebastián cried out, and a new voice a slight distance off, rang out sharply, "Put those clubs down. Don't you know the fighting is over?"

There was silence for a minute as if the antagonists were measuring each other.

Then the Nifora spoke contemptuously, "There never would have been any fighting at all if we had listened to Palma."

No one took up the challenge. But Garcés could feel the tension beyond that willow-bark curtain.

Then he heard a confident step approaching, and in a moment a firm voice was saying authoritatively, "Put those clubs where they belong. It is all over."

"Pablo says—"

The authoritative voice lashed the whining protest, "I have heard all I want to hear of what Pablo says. If we listen any more to what Pablo says, there will be no end to the troubles we will bring on ourselves. Only Pablo would think of giving arms to slaves."

And then the blanket covering the door was brushed aside, and the morning sun streamed into the dark house. Someone was coming in with a quick step, and the voice of Palma's favorite nephew rang through the house, "Come, Old Man. Palma has sent for both of you."

"Thank God," said Barreneche, embracing his colleague. Brushing aside the latter's whispered blessing, he strode up to the Indian and out through the door. Garcés heard the gasp that went round the company outside, and then he himself went out more slowly into the radiant sunlight of the early morning. After the darkness of the hut, his eyes dazzled in the brilliance of the morning light, but his lungs drew in hungrily the freshness of the morning air, soft with the distilled fragrance of the sundrenched mesquite and sage.

He looked around for Sebastián and found his brown face gray with horror, and his eyes staring as if they had veritably seen a ghost. He muttered, "He has come out of the ashes," and he tore into the brush and vanished.

"Sebastián," the friar called, "I am a living man like yourself." But he was gone. And now Garcés was aware of the other Indians who stood round the door of the house, waiting with a kind of suspended animation that must for half of them at least have been sheer astonishment. He looked at Palma's nephew, who stood there with so much of his uncle's easy dignity, and yet with a kind of youthful arrogance of his own added to it. He seemed completely confident of his hold on the situation.

Beside him the one of yesterday's captors who had stayed on guard looked uncertain and even, it seemed to the friar, anxious. Neither of them, he observed had any arms. Opposite them stood three Indians, the Nifora, with a companion scowling at his side, and another Yuma, who seemed to have just come up, and was now standing behind them, in the process of setting his war club on the ground. The Nifora and his companion had their clubs firmly gripped in their hands.

"You had better get out of the way," said Palma's nephew contemptuously.

"Where are you taking them?"

"What business is it of yours?" The contempt in the young man's voice would have withered any normal conceit. But the friar saw the look in the Nifora's eyes, and knew that he was fast reaching the point where he would be past reasoning.

"Don't you think we had better go?" he asked the young man in an undertone, but the latter seemed not to have heard.

"Are you going to let them live?"

The young man looked startled at the challenge. "Why not? Palma has said to my father that they are good men, who have done no harm to anyone. Why, then, should they die?"

"Proud fool!" cried the Nifora, his thin face taut with rage. "What is the use of having killed the rest, if you let them live? They have the magic of the crossed sticks, and if they live, it is as if the others had never died. And where then is our victory?"

IO

IN a flash Garcés' eyes swept the scene. He saw the anger flame in the young man's face, he saw the fear in the eyes of the Indian who had been left to guard them, and he saw the madness of the Nifora seize upon his two companions like the flaming brand which had been hurled into the thatch of the church roof on the height.

But he did not see Barreneche until he stepped forward and lifted his hand to ask for attention. Instantly, he saw that the gesture had been misunderstood, and he leaped to his colleague's side, but before he could reach him, the war clubs had flashed, and the young friar had fallen under their blows. One Garcés caught with his right arm, and the arm fell to his side, but he felt no consciousness of pain as he knelt down by his fellow friar. The young man's head was crushed, and his chest, too, and his breath was coming in deep gasps.

He opened his eyes, and he smiled at Garcés, and there was a triumph in the smile. Garcés tried to lift his right arm, for the last blessing, and he found he could not move it. Slowly he rose to his feet, staggering a little for want of balance. As he did so, he felt the first surge of burning pain in the crushed arm. But he regained his feet, and he faced the Indians. The Yuma who had been left to guard them shrank back in terror; Palma's nephew stood rooted in sheer astonishment, which, even as the friar looked at him, blazed into anger.

Garcés turned to the Nifora, but before the friar could speak, another blow caught him, and he staggered to recover his footing. And now something seemed to have happened to his sense of time. For he saw the war clubs poised over his head, and he knew that he was moving slowly, for it seemed as if every nerve and muscle in his body were crying to his consciousness.

But yet he stood on his feet. And though he could not see anything but the gleaming clubs distinctly, his head was perfectly clear. Only he was having difficulty remembering something. He was in the middle of a very important rite, and he could not remember the proper words. "Father, forgive them," no, that was what Christ had said on the cross. That was nothing for a sinner to say of his fellow sinners. "Lord, forgive us, for we know not what we do." That was better, but it still did not sound as if he had the words right.

Again, he heard the clubs whistle through the air, and, again, the sea of flame burst over his body and rose above his head. And in a mighty agony the spirit thrashed that it might not be completely engulfed in the body's foundering. And then above the pain there shot up like a hand above a sinking head, a sharp spear of consciousness, and he cried out, "My Lord!" and then he knew with a great clarity that this time the words did not matter. For He would understand.

Again, the clubs swung and fell, but this time Garcés made no effort to get up. For he did not hear their gleaming hiss, and the heavy crash of their fall. He was listening to a bell ringing out from a great height, ringing up and down the rivers, ringing the joyous words of the *Magnificat*, "My soul doth magnify the Lord." And high above the dusty brush of the river bottom, he saw the shining highway stretch, and he saw a host of men, women, and children down the broad way, white and brown, Indian and Spanish, the living and the dead alike, and they were singing the triumphant words to the measured sweetness of the bell.

But of this Gerónimo could know nothing when he came down the path to his house an hour later to find out why the friars had not been brought into the presence of Palma. For all he could see was the two bodies lying in the bloodstained dust. The face of Barreneche was still smiling, but nothing recognizable was left of the body of Garcés except the torn and blood-soaked robe, the broken rosary, and the crucifix that seemed to be bleeding with his blood.

When the old Jamajab saw this unmistakable evidence of the failure of his intercession with Palma, he fell to his knees and wept. There Palma's nephew, when he returned from chasing out of the village the Nifora and his companions, found him. The young man was ashamed to face Gerónimo, but the latter bade him not to grieve. For he was quite sure that the Old Man had dreamed that this would be the end. Indeed, it was he who should be ashamed of weeping, for was not this the ancient way of things, that the innocent should pay the debt of the guilty?

The word spread fast. The guard who had been too surprised to intervene in the play of the clubs carried the story. And before the day was out, many of the neophytes came to look at the mangled bodies and to weep. Word came to Palma, too, and it was he who gave order that the bodies should be buried where they fell. And so it was done. There was no one to perform the burial rites, but the Indians recited all the prayers they knew by the two graves. And then the next morning some of the Indian women came at dawn and planted the grave of Garcés with flowers.

They were blooming when the expedition which Croix sent to find the bodies of the dead friars reached the river nearly five months later, and it seemed to the members of the expedition that this was a miracle. For nowhere on all that dusty winter journey had they seen such splendor of color or such sweetness of fragrance as burgeoned out of this blood-stained earth. But there was a greater miracle in store for them when they went over into the meadows and woods back of the height and recovered the captives whom Palma had released to their ransom. For they found to their astonishment that none of the women had been harmed, and this they all attributed to the intercession of Father Garcés.

Father Font spoke of these things eloquently and well when he preached at the funeral rites of the four friars in the church at Tubutama. It was a sunny day in late winter when the immortality of the things that are finished comes like the first breath of spring to the withered hopes of men. And the door of the lovely church stood open so that the sunlight streamed in and mingled with the cloud of incense that rose from the chest in which they had carried the broken bodies. And when the last strains of the *Dies Irae* had died away, and the last blessing had been given, and all things had been done with that perfection that was the particular gift of Father Font, they laid the chest under the pavement of the church on the Epistle side of the high altar.

But the story of these things flew far and wide, and it was heard with horror and grief and fear and wonder and pride and awe, according to the disposition of the hearer. It flew up and down the lonely trails of the frontier from campfire to campfire, from ranchería to ranchería, from mission to mission, from presidio to presidio. It was carried officially to Croix at Arizpe, and the viceroy in Mexico City, and the father guardian and the brethren at Querétaro, and Father Lasuén at San Juan Capistrano and Father Serra at Monterey, and Governor Anza at Santa Fé, and across the seas to the King in Madrid, and the Pope in Rome.

And in all these places, men spoke much of the faith and the endurance of the martyrs, and of the travels of Francisco Garcés, and of the procession of the dead with their lighted candles around the ashes of the burned church, and of the graves that flowered, and of the captives who for once had suffered no outrage. But there was one miracle of which they never spoke in any of these places. And yet this was the miracle of which the Indians spoke most often in the flood bottoms and on the high banks of the great rivers. The Spaniards sent expeditions to ransom the women and children and the few men who remained alive in captivity, and then later to recover the bodies of the friars, and, finally, for one brief skirmish in which some of the Yumas were slain, but even that one turned back without reaching the great body of the Yumas. And that was all. They never came back to the Yuma lands, to burn their houses and shoot their warriors and carry off their women and children into slavery. All the Indians to the south and to the east who heard the Yumas tell of what they had done assured them that this would be the end. In vain the Yumas tried to tell them that the Old Man had promised them that if they spared the women and children they would not be punished by the Spaniards. Friend and foe alike, their hearers laughed and asked them if they had ever heard of a promise which white men had made to Indians and kept. But the Spaniards did not come.

In Arizpe, Croix, and his successors after him, cursed the lack of sufficient forces to pacify the frontier. But the Yumas said to each other, "The Old Man did not forget his promise." And the men and women and children who used to come to the chapel in the river bottom kept it clean and put flowers on the altar, and kneeling there said the prayers which Garcés hack taught them. And they piled fresh arrowweed on the roof when the rains came, and they banked the sides as they did with their own houses. And this they continued to do until at last after many rains, one came with a wind that swept off the roof, and toppled the altar from its place. This was beyond their understanding how to repair; so it fell into the rich earth of the river bottom, even as the body of its founder crumbled into dust in the chest at Tubutama. But the Indians still spoke of the Old Man who had remembered them even in Heaven, and there were not wanting those who in their dreams saw him again coming down the path from the height to Palma's village. And now no one scoffed when that dream was told.